DATE DUE

APR 13 2005		
MAY 11 2005		

GAYLORD   PRINTED IN U.S.A.

Also by Frank O'Connor

A SET OF
VARIATIONS

A SET OF
VARIATIONS

*TWENTY-
SEVEN
STORIES* BY

FRANK
O'CONNOR

Alfred A. Knopf   New York   1969

This is a Borzoi Book
Published by Alfred A. Knopf, Inc.

 *Introduction*

FOR FRANK O'CONNOR the most important single element in any story was its design. It might be years between the moment of recognizing a theme and finding the one right shape for it—this was the hard, painful work—the writing he did in his head. But once he had the essential bony structure firmly in place he could begin to enjoy the story and to start "tinkering" with the details. It was this "tinkering" which produced dozens of versions of the same story. The basic design never changed, but in each new version light would be thrown in a different way on a different place. Frank O'Connor did this kind of rewriting endlessly—he frequently continued it even after a story had been published. Though this confused and sometimes annoyed editors, reviewers, and bibliographers, the multiplicity of versions was never a problem to him. When there were enough stories to form a new collection he didn't try to choose between the many extant versions of them—he simply sat down and prepared to rewrite every story he wanted in the book.

That particular rewriting was directed toward a definite aim, which was to give the book of stories a feeling of being a unity rather than a grab bag of miscellany. He believed that stories, if arranged in an "ideal ambiance," could strengthen and illuminate each other. This unity was only partly preconceived; he continued to create it as he went along. He never wrote a story specifically to fit into a gap in a book, nor did he change names or locations to give superficial unity. Rather it was as though the stories were bits of a mosaic which could be arranged harmoniously so that the pattern they made together reflected the light each cast separately. Ultimately this unity probably sprang from his basic conviction that the writer was not simply an observer: "I can't write about something I don't

admire. It goes back to the old concept of the celebration: you cele-
brate the hero, an idea."

This means, of course, that Frank O'Connor had very definite
ideas about the contents and arrangement of each new book of
stories. If he had lived, this might have been a different book. As it
is, I have had to choose, not only which and how many stories to
include, but also which of the many versions of each story to
print. There was also the problem of that "ideal ambiance" and the
comfort of the knowledge that even his own "ideal ambiance
would be shattered by the time the book appears."

I do not doubt that I shall have to answer to the author for each
of these decisions. But for the stories themselves no one need answer.
They are pure Frank O'Connor.

—*Harriet O'Donovan (Mrs. Frank O'Connor)*

CONTENTS

A SET OF VARIATIONS

A Set of Variations on a Borrowed Theme

KATE MAHONEY was sixty when her husband died and, like many another widow, she had to face the loss of her little home.

Her two daughters, Nora and Molly, were married, and even if either of them had been in a position to offer her a home, she would have hesitated over it. As she said in her patient, long-suffering way to her old crony Hanna Dinan, they shouted too much. Hanna raised her head in mock surprise and exclaimed, "You don't say so, Ma'am!" Kate looked at her reproachfully for a moment and then murmured with almost sensual bliss, "Oh, you cheeky thing." The truth was, as Hanna implied, that Kate shouted enough for a regimental sergeant major, and the girls, both gentle and timid, had learned early in life that the only way of making themselves heard was to shout back. Kate didn't mind that; in fact, she rather enjoyed it. Nor did she shout all the time. She had another tone, which was low-pitched and monotonous, and in which she tended to break off a sentence as though she had forgotten what she was saying. But low-pitched or loud, her talk was monumental, like headstones. Her hands and legs were knotted with rheumatics, and she had a battered, inexpressive countrywoman's face, like a butcher's block, in which the only good feature was the eyes, which looked astonishingly girlish and merry. Maybe it would be only later that you would remember the hands—which were rarely still—fastening or unfastening a button on her blouse.

Her cottage was in a lane outside Cork. There was high rocky ground behind it that could never be built on, and though as a result it got little or no sunlight and another row of cottages between her and the roadway shut off the view, it was quiet and free of traffic. She wanted to die there, in the bed her husband had died in, but with the rheumatics she couldn't go out and do a day's work, as other widows did. It was this that made her think of taking in a foster child. It was a terrible comedown—more particularly for her, a respectable woman who had brought up two honest transactions of her own, but at her age what else could she do? So she took her problem to Miss Hegarty, the nurse.

Miss Hegarty was a fine-looking woman of good family, but so distracted with having to deal with the endless goings on of male and female that there were times when she didn't seem right in the head. "Ahadie!" she would cry gaily to a woman in labor. "Fun enough you got out of starting it. Laugh now, why don't you?"

But Kate found her a good friend. She advised Kate against taking foster children from the local authorities, because they paid so badly that it was no better than slavery. The thing to do was to take the child of a girl of good family who could afford to maintain it.

"Ah, where would I meet a girl like that?" Kate asked humbly, and Miss Hegarty gave a loud, bitter laugh and stood up to lean against the mantelpiece with her arms folded.

" 'Tis easy seen you don't know much about it, Mrs. Mahoney," she said. "What chance, indeed, and the whole country crawling with them!"

"Oh, my!" said Kate.

"But I warn you, Ma'am, that you can't rely on any of them," said Miss Hegarty. "They're so mad for men they'll go anywhere for them. And for all you know, a girl like that would be off next month to London and you might never hear of her again. The stick, Ma'am, the stick is what the whole lot of them want."

Kate, however, decided to take the risk; there was something that appealed to her in the idea of a child of good family, and Miss Hegarty knew the very girl. She was the manageress of a store in Waterford, who had got entangled with a scoundrel whose name nobody even knew, but indeed he couldn't be much good to leave her that way. When Kate told her daughters, Nora, the flighty one, didn't seem to mind, but Molly, who was more sensitive, wept and begged her mother to come and live with them instead. "Oh yes, what a thing I'd do," said Kate, whose mind was made up. From Nora, who now had children of her own, she borrowed back the old family perambulator, and one spring morning it appeared again outside the door in the lane, with a baby boy asleep in it. "My first!" Kate shouted jocosely when any of the neighbors commented on it, and then she went on to explain, in the monotonous voice she used for solemn occasions, that this was no ordinary baby such as you'd get from the workhouse, without knowing who it was or where it came from, but the child of a beautiful educated girl from one of the best families in Waterford. She went on to tell how the poor child had been taken advantage of, and the neighbors tch-tch'd and agreed that it was a sad, sad story and didn't believe a word of it. The young married women didn't even pretend to believe in Kate's rigmarole. They muttered fiercely among themselves that you couldn't let decent children grow up alongside the likes of that, and that the priest or the landlord should put a stop to it. But they didn't say it too loud, for however embarrassed Kate might be by her situation she was a very obstinate old woman, and she had a dirty tongue when she was roused.

So Jimmy Mahoney was allowed to grow up in the lane along with the honest transactions, and turned into a fat, good-looking, moody boy, who seemed to see nothing peculiar in his mother's being a cranky old woman with a scolding tongue. On the contrary, he seemed to depend on her more than the other kids did on their mothers, and sometimes when she left him with Hanna Dinan and went off to see one of her daughters, he sat and sulked on the doorstep till she got home. One day when Hanna's back was turned, he went after Kate, right across the city to Molly's house on the Douglas Road. Kate, talking to Molly, glanced up and saw him glaring at her from the doorway and started, thinking that something must have happened to him and this was his ghost. "Oh, you pest!" she shouted when she saw that it wasn't. Then she gave him a grin. "I suppose it was the way you couldn't get on without me?"

Molly, a beautiful, haggard woman, gave him a smile of Christian charity and said quietly, "Come in, Jimmy." It was a thing she would not have wished for a pound, for it would have to be explained to her neighbors, and she felt it degraded them all. But after that, whatever she or Nora might think, Kate had to bring Jimmy with her by the hand. It didn't look right—their old mother in her black hat and coat hobbling up to the door with a child younger than their own by the hand.

Even then Jimmy wasn't satisfied. He wanted a brother or sister as well—preferably a brother. He had a great weakness for babies and was mad jealous of other boys who had babies to look after. "Every bloomin' fella in the road have a brudder or sister except me," he said to Kate. But she told him roughly that they couldn't afford it.

All the same, he got his wish. One evening Miss Hegarty came to her and asked if she would take in the child of a well-to-do girl in Bantry. The mother was engaged to marry a rich Englishman, but at the last moment she had thrown herself into a wild affair with a married man who had courted her when she was only seventeen. "Oh, my, my, the things that go on," sighed Kate.

"Mrs. Mahoney," Miss Hegarty cried, "don't talk to me about it! If you knew the half of it, it would make you lose your faith in religion."

Then and there Kate accepted. Later she felt she had been hasty. She needed the money, but not as badly as all that. When Nora came to see her and Kate told her what she had done, there was a terrible scene.

"Ah, Mammy, you're making a holy show of us!" Nora cried.

"*I'm* making a show of ye?" Kate pointed at her bosom with the mock-innocent air that had so often maddened her daughters. "I do my business, and I don't cost ye a penny. Is that what ye call making a show of ye?"

"Ah, you'd think we were something out of a circus, instead of an old respectable family," Nora said. "That I can hardly face the neighbors when I come up the lane! Ahadie, 'tis well my poor daddy can't see what you're making of his house! He's the one that would deal with you. A woman of sixty-five! I suppose you think you're going to live forever."

"God is good," Kate muttered stiffly. "I might have a couple of years in me yet."

"You might," Nora said ironically. "And I suppose you imagine that if anything happens you, Molly and I will carry on the good work."

"Ye mightn't be asked," said Kate. "Their people have plenty—more than you'll ever be able to say." This was a dirty thrust at Nora, whose poor husband was not bright. "And how sure you are of yourself! My goodness, that we'd never do anything if we were to be always thinking of what might happen us. And what about my rent? Are you going to pay it?"

"Ah, 'tisn't the rent with you at all," Nora said. "Nor it never was. You only do it because you like it."

"I like it? An old woman like me that's crippled with the rheumatics? Oh, my, that 'tis in a home I ought to be if I had my rights. In a home!"

"Ah, I'd like to see the home that would keep you," Nora replied contemptuously. "Don't be making any more excuses. You love it, woman. And you care more about that little bastard than you ever did about Molly or me."

"How dare you?" Kate cried, rising with as much dignity as the rheumatics permitted. "What way is that to speak to your own mother? And to talk about a poor innocent child in my house like that, you dirty, jealous thing! Yes, jealous," she added in a wondering whisper as though the truth had only dawned on her in that moment. "Oh, my! Ye that had everything!"

The scene upset her, but not because of the row with Nora; the Mahoneys always quarreled like that, at the top of their lungs, as though they all suffered from congenital deafness, and they got the same pleasure out of it that a baby gets out of hammering a tin can. What really mortified her was that she had given herself away in front of Nora, whose intelligence she had no respect for. It was true that she had taken Jimmy in for perfectly good mercenary reasons; and it was very wrong of Nora to impute sentimental considerations to her—a determined, managing woman, who had lived that long with no thanks to anybody. But all the same, Nora wasn't altogether wrong. Motherhood was the only trade Kate knew, and though her rheumatics were bad and her sight wasn't what it used to be and she had to get Jimmy to thread her needles for her, she felt the older she got the better she practiced it. It was even true to say that she enjoyed Jimmy more than she had enjoyed her own children, but this was natural enough, because she hadn't the same anxieties about him. If you had pressed her hard enough, she would have said that if there was a better boy on the road she didn't know him. And was there anything wrong with that? You could say what you liked, but there was something in good blood.

She might have got angry if you had accused her of being an old dreamer who was really attracted by the romance and mystery of Jimmy's birth—something she had missed in her own sober and industrious life—but that was what she and Hanna enjoyed speculating about over a little glass when Jimmy was in bed. And later, when she had covered him for the night and lay awake in the next room saying her rosary, she would often forget her prayers and imagine how she would feel if one stormy night—one of those nights when the whole harbor seemed to move in on the town and try to push it down—there came a knock to the door and she saw Jimmy's father standing outside in the lane, tall and handsome, with a small black mustache and the tears in his eyes. "Mr. Mulvany," she would say to the teacher (she was always making up ideal names and occupations for Jimmy's father), "your son wants nothing from you." Or, if she was in a generous mood, "Senator MacDunphy, come in. Jimmy was beginning to think you'd never come."

Nora was right. Stupid or not, Nora had seen through her. She was an old fool. And when Miss Hegarty had dangled the extra money in front of her, it wasn't the money that appealed to her so much as the girl who had been ready to throw away her chances with the rich Englishman for the sake of one wild fling with an old sweetheart. "An old fool," Kate said to herself. She didn't feel repentant, though.

But dreamers are forever running into degrading practical realities, and there was one thing about her extraordinary family that Kate could do nothing about. Before she even laid eyes on him, the second boy was also christened James, and, so that Jimmy shouldn't be too upset and that she herself should do nothing against the law, she called him James—an unnatural name for any child, as she well knew. James was a baby with a big head, a gaping mouth, and a sickly countenance, and even from the first day he seemed to realize that he was in the world only on sufferance, and resigned himself to it. But Jimmy could see nothing wrong with him. He explored the neighborhood to study all the other babies, and told Kate that James was brighter than the whole lot of them. He adopted a possessive attitude, and wheeled the perambulator up and down the main road so that people could see for themselves the sort James was. When he came back, he reported with great satisfaction that three people, two men and a woman, had stopped him to admire his baby brother.

II

A couple of times a year, Jimmy's real mother, whom he knew as Aunt Nance, came to stay with the friends in Cork who had arranged with Miss Hegarty for his being boarded out, and then Jimmy visited there and played with the two children, Rory and Mary. They were altogether too polite for Jimmy, but he liked his Aunt Nance a lot. She was tall and plump and good-looking, with a swarthy complexion and dark, dark hair. She talked in a crisp, nervous, almost common way, and was always forgetting herself and saying dirty words, like "Cripes!" and "Damn!," that only men were supposed to know. Kate liked him to go there, and when he got home, she asked him all sorts of questions about his visit, like how many rooms there were in the house, what he ate, what sort of furniture there was and the size of the garden—things that never interested Jimmy in the least.

When James began to grow up, he too asked questions. He wanted to know what school Rory and Mary went to, what they learned there, and whether or not Mary played the piano. These too were questions that did not interest Jimmy, but it dawned on him that James was lonely when he was left behind and wanted to see the Martins' place for himself. This seemed an excellent idea to Jimmy, because James was a steady quiet kid who would get on much better with Rory and Mary than he did, but when he suggested it Kate only said James was too young and Aunt Nance said she'd see.

It ended by his suspecting that there was something fishy about James. There always had been something unusual about him—as though he weren't a member of the family at all. He didn't like rough games and he preferred little girls to little boys. Jimmy didn't know how you did become a member of the family, but from what he could see your mother had either to go to the hospital or lie up in the house, and he couldn't remember that Kate had done either. James had just been there one morning when he woke. The more he thought of it, the surer he became that James was adopted. He didn't know what "adopted" meant, except that kids it happened to lived with people who weren't really related to them, and he found the idea of this very stimulating.

One evening, when Kate was complaining of her rheumatics, he asked her if she hadn't gone to hospital with it.

"Oye, why would I go to hospital?" she asked sourly. "I was never in one in my life and I hope I'll never have to go there."

James was sitting by the window, scribbling, and Jimmy didn't say anything more. But later, when James was in bed, he asked her casually, "You're not James's mother, are you, Mammy?"

He was surprised at the way she turned on him. "What's that you say?"

"Nothing, only that you're not James's mother."

"Who told you that?" she asked angrily.

"Nobody told me," he said, becoming defensive, "but you never went to hospital, like Mrs. Casey. You told me yourself."

"Don't let the child hear you saying things like that, you caffler!" she hissed.

"I never told him anything," he said sullenly. "But it's true, isn't it? That's the reason you get the money."

"Mind your own business!" she retorted.

Still, she was frightened. "Oh, my! The cunning of him!" she said next day to her old crony. "The way he cross-examined me—that poor Jack Mahoney never did the like! And what am I to say to him? Who will I get to advise me?"

Hanna, who had an answer for everything, was all for telling Jimmy the whole truth at once, but what did Hanna know about it and she an old maid? The other neighbors were inclined to think it was a judgment on Kate for her foolishness. And all the while, Jimmy's behavior got worse. At the best of times it wasn't very good. Though sometimes he was in high spirits and entertained herself and James telling funny stories, more often he was low-spirited and lay on his bed sulking over a comic. After that, he would go out with other boys and return with a guilty air she could spot from the end of the lane, and she would know he had been up to mischief and broken a window or stolen from a shop. At times like that, she was never free of anxiety for him, because apart from the fact that she had a holy terror of the law, she knew his naughtiness threatened the sufferance the neighbors extended to him on her account, and that they would be only too ready to say that it was all you could expect of a boy like that.

Finally, she decided to take Hanna Dinan's advice. But when James was asleep and she and Jimmy were sitting together in the darkness over the fire, she lost courage. She had no notion of how he would take it, and if he took it badly, she'd get the blame. She told him, instead, about James and his mother. She told him how some people, like herself, were lucky, because their fancy never strayed from the one person, while others, like James's mother, had the misfortune to love someone they couldn't marry. She was pleased by Jimmy's silent attention. She thought she had impressed him. But his first words startled her. "All the same, Mammy," he said, "James should be with his own mother."

She was astonished at the maturity in his tone. This was no longer any of the Jimmys she had known, but one who spoke with the sort of authority poor Jack had exercised on the rare occasions when he had called his family to order.

"Ah, how could he be with her?"

"Then she ought to tell him who he is and why she can't have him."

"Is it to be upsetting the child?" she asked complainingly.

"If she doesn't upset him, somebody else will," he said with his brooding, old-mannish air.

"They will, they will, God help us!" she sighed. "People are bad enough for anything. But the poor child may as well be happy while he can."

But it wasn't of James that she was thinking. James might get by, a colorless, studious, well-behaved boy who never gave offense to anybody, but one day Jimmy would beat up another boy or steal from a shop, and some woman would spite him by using the word Kate now dreaded—the word she had so often used lightly herself when she had no one to protect from it. Again she was tempted to tell him the whole truth, and again she was too afraid.

Meanwhile, for a short time at least, she had given Jimmy a purpose in life. Jimmy was always like that, either up or down, either full of purpose or shiftless and despondent. Now he took James over personally. He said it was bad for James to be so much alone, and took him along with him when he went down the Glen with the bigger boys. James didn't like being with the bigger boys. He liked to go at his own slow pace, gaping at everything, and he didn't in the least mind being left alone, but he was flattered by Jimmy's attention. When he came home he repeated his adventures to Kate in the manner of a policeman making a report. "Jimmy showed me a blackbird's nest. You can't touch a bird's nest, because the bird would know and leave the little eggs to die. I think it is wrong to rob a bird's nest, don't you, Mammy?" James collected bits of information, right and wrong, apparently thinking that they would all come in handy someday, and to each he managed to attach a useful moral lesson. No wonder he made Jimmy laugh.

But Jimmy still continued to worry about James's future. He waited till Aunt Nance came to Cork, and when he got her to himself he poured it all out to her in his enthusiastic way. He had managed to persuade himself that Kate didn't understand the seriousness of the situation but that Aunt Nance would. Before he had even finished, Aunt Nance gave him a queer look and cut him off. "You're too young to understand these things, Jimmy," she said.

"But don't *you* think he should be with his mother?" he asked indignantly.

"I don't know a thing about it, and if I did I wouldn't be able to do anything."

Jimmy left her in one of his mutinous, incoherent fits of rage. Instead of taking the bus, he walked, and when he reached the river he stood on the bank in the darkness throwing stones. It was late when he got home, but Kate was waiting up for him. He tossed his cap on the chair and went upstairs.

"What kept you?" she asked after him.

"Nothing."

"Don't you want a cup of tea?"

"I don't."

"He knows about it," Kate muttered to herself. "She must have told him. Now what'll I do?"

After a time she went upstairs to bed, but she heard him from the little attic room next door, where he and James slept, tossing and muttering to himself. She lit the candle and went in. He sat up in bed and looked at her with mad eyes.

"Go away!" he said. "You're not my mother."

"Oye!" she whimpered, sleepy and scared. "You and your goings on."

"You're not, you're not, you're not," he muttered. "I'm like James, only you wouldn't tell me. You tell me nothing but lies."

"Whisht, whisht, and don't wake the child!" she whispered impatiently. "You ought to be ashamed, a big boy like you. Come into the other room."

He stumbled out ahead of her, and she sat on the edge of her bed and put her arm round him. He was shivering. She no longer felt capable of handling him. She was old and tired and bothered in her head.

"What made you think of that, child?"

"Aunt Nance," he said with a sob.

"What did she tell you?"

"She wouldn't tell me anything, only I saw she was afraid."

"What was she afraid of?"

"I asked her to get James's mother to bring him home and she got frightened."

"Oh, oh, oh, you poor misfortunate child!" she said with a wail. "And you only did it for the best."

"I want to know who my mother is," he cried despairingly. "Is it Aunt Kitty or Aunt Nance?"

"Look, child, lie down here and you can sleep with Mammy."

"How can I sleep?" he asked frantically. "I only want to know who my mother is, and ye all tell me lies." Then, turning suddenly into a baby again, he put his head in her lap and bawled. She put her hand under his nightshirt and patted his fat bottom.

"Oh, you poor putog, you're perished," she sighed. Then she raised him onto the bed and pulled the covers about his shoulders.

"Will I get you a cup of tea?" she asked in a loud voice, and as he shook his head she muttered, "I will, I will."

She threw an old coat round her and went downstairs to the kitchen, where the oil lamp was turned low. There was still red ash in the grate, and she blew on it and boiled the kettle. Then her troubles seemed to get the better of her, and she spoke to herself in a loud, angry, complaining tone, " 'Twas the price of me for having anything to do with them—me that was never used to anything but decent people." When she heard herself she was ashamed. And then she shrugged, and whined, "I'm too old." As she climbed awkwardly back up the stairs with the two big mugs of tea, she heard him still sobbing, and stopped, turning her eyes to the ceiling. "God direct me!" she said aloud.

She sat on the edge of the bed and shook him. "Drink this!" she said roughly.

"I don't want it," said Jimmy. "I want to know who my mother is."

"Drink it, you dirty little caffler!" she said angrily. "Drink it or I won't tell you at all."

He raised himself in the big bed and she held the mug to his lips, though he could not keep himself from shivering and the tea spilled over his shirt and the bedclothes. "My good sheet," she muttered, and then took up her own cup and looked away into a corner of the room as if to avoid his eyes. "She is your mother, your Aunt Nance," she said in a harsh, expressionless voice, "and a good mother she is, and a good woman as well, and it will be a bad day for you when you talk against her or let anyone else do it. She had the misfortune to meet a man that was beneath her. She was innocent. He took advantage of her. She wasn't the first and she won't be the last."

He said nothing for a while, then he asked in a low voice, "And who was my daddy?"

"How would I know who he was? Whoever he was, he wasn't much."

"When I find out I'm going to kill him."

"Indeed you'll do nothing of the sort," she said sharply. "What ever he did, he is your father and you wouldn't be here without him. He's there inside you, and the thing you will slight in yourself will be the rock you will perish on."

"And why did Aunt Nance like him if he was what you said?"

"Because she had no sense," said Kate. "What sense have any young girl? 'Tis unknown what they expect. If they had more sense they would be said by their fathers and mothers, that know what life is like, but they won't be said nor led by anyone. And the better they are the more they expect. That was all that was wrong with your mother, child. She was too innocent and too hopeful."

The dawn came in the window, and still she rambled on, half dead with sleep. Later, when she reported it to Hanna, she said that it was nothing but lies from beginning to end, and what other way could it be when she hadn't a notion how a girl like that would feel, but at the time it did not seem to be lies. It seemed rather as though she were reporting a complete truth that was known only to herself and God. And in a queer way it steadied Jimmy and brought out the little man in him.

"Mammy, does this mean that there's something wrong with James and me?" he asked at last, and she knew that this was the question that preoccupied him above all others.

"Indeed, it means nothing of the sort," she cried, and for the first time it seemed to herself that she was answering in her own person. "It is nothing. Only bad, jealous people would say the likes of that. Oh, you'll meet them, never fear," she said, joining her hands, "the scum of the earth with their marriage lines and their baptismal lines, looking down on their betters. But mark what I say, child, don't let any of them try and persuade you that you're not as good as them. And better! A thousand times better."

Strange notions from a respectable old woman who had never even believed in love!

III

What it all meant was brought home to her when Jimmy was fourteen and James between eight and nine. Jimmy's mother married a commercial traveler from Dublin who accepted Jimmy as a normal event that might happen to any decent girl, and he had persuaded her they should have Jimmy to live with them. It came as a great shock to Kate, though why it should have done so she couldn't say, because for years it was she who had argued with Hanna Dinan that the time had come for Jimmy to get a proper education and mix with what she called his equals. Now she realized that she was as jealous and possessive as if she were his real mother. She had never slighted Jimmy's mother, or allowed anyone else to do so, but she did it now. "She neglected him when it suited her, and now when it suits her she wants him back," she said to Hanna, and when Hanna replied that Kate wasn't being fair, she snapped, "Let them that have it be fair. Them that haven't are entitled to their say."

Besides, Jimmy provoked her. He had no power of concealing his emotions, and she could see that he had thoughts only for the marvelous new world that was opening up before him. He returned in high spirits from an evening with his mother and his new stepfather, and told Kate and James all about his stepfather's car, and his house outside Rathfarnham, at the foot of the Dublin Mountains. He told Kate blithely that he would always come back for the holidays, and comforted James by saying that his turn would come next. When Kate burst out suddenly, "Yourself is all you think about—no thought for me or the child," he got frantic and shouted, "All right, I won't go if you don't want me to!"

"Who said I didn't want you to go?" she shouted. "How could I keep you and me with nothing? Go to the well-heeled ones! Go to the ones that can look after you!"

By the time he left, she had regained control of herself, and she and James went with him to the station. They were stopped several times by old neighbors, who congratulated Jimmy. At the station he broke down, but she suspected that his grief wouldn't last long. And she had the impression that James felt the parting more deeply, though he was a child who didn't show much what he felt. He seemed to have come into the world expecting this sort of thing.

And yet, curiously, next day, when she woke and remembered Jimmy was gone, she had a feeling of relief. She realized that she wasn't the one to look after him. He was too big and noisy and exacting; he needed a man to keep him in his place. And besides, now that she had become old and stiff and half blind, the house-keeping was more of a trial. She would decide to give the boys a treat, and go to town to get the stewing beef, and suddenly realize when she got back to the kitchen that she didn't remember how to make stew. Then she would close her eyes and pray that God would direct her how to make stew as she made it when she was a young married woman—"delicious" poor Jack used to say it was. James was an easier proposition altogether, a boy who would live forever on tea and sweet cakes, so long as he got the penny exercise books for his writings and drawings.

The loss of Jimmy showed her how precarious was her hold on James, and in the evenings, when they were alone, she sat with him before the kitchen fire and let him hold forth to her on what he was going to be when he grew up. It seemed, according to himself, he was going to be a statue, and sometimes Kate suspected that the child wouldn't notice much difference, because he was a bit that way already. Jimmy had been a great boy to raise a laugh, particularly against himself, and James seemed to think it was his duty to do the same, but if she was to be killed for it she couldn't laugh at James's jokes. And yet she knew that James was gentler, steadier, and more considerate. When you asked him to do anything you had to explain to him why, but you never had to explain it twice. "Jimmy have the fire, but James have the character" was how she put it to Hanna.

And yet she fretted over Jimmy as she wouldn't have fretted over James. From Dublin he had sent her one postcard, that was all, and he hadn't replied to either of the letters James wrote to him. "As true as God, that fellow is in trouble," she said.

"It's not that, Mammy," said James, "it's just that he doesn't like writing."

"Who wants him to write? All I want is to know how he is. If he was dying that vagabond wouldn't tell me!"

It was a queer way for a woman to feel who had been congratulating herself on having got rid of him.

Then, one morning, she heard a hammering at the front door and knew that the thing she had been dreading had happened. Without even asking who it was, she stumbled down the stairs in the darkness. When she opened the door and saw Jimmy, she threw her arms about his neck. "Oh, child, child!" she whimpered. "Sure, I thought you'd never come home! How did you get here?"

"I came on the bike," he said with a swagger.

"You did, you did, you divil you, you did," she muttered, seeing the bicycle against the wall. And then, her voice rising to a squeal of anguish, "Are them your good trousers?"

"Who is it, Mammy?" James shouted from upstairs.

"Come down yourself," she said, and went to lay the fire. James came down the stairs sedately in his nightshirt. Jimmy went up to him with a grin, and it startled her to see how big and solid he looked beside the frail, spectacled boy.

"Hallo, James," Jimmy said, shaking hands. "I suppose you're sorry I'm back?"

"No, Jimmy," James said in a small voice, "I'm glad you're back. The house isn't the same without you."

"Put on your topcoat, you little divil!" cried Kate. "How often have I to be telling you not to go round like that? That fellow," she said to Jimmy, "he have the heart scalded in me. I'd want ten eyes and hands, picking things up after him. . . . Go on, you little gligeen!"

It was a joyous reunion in the little kitchen when the sun was just beginning to pick out the high ground behind the house. Kate marveled how she had managed to listen to James all that time and the way Jimmy could tell a story. Whatever James told you, the point of it always seemed to be how clever he was. Jimmy's stories always showed him up as a fool, and somehow it never crossed your mind that he was a fool at all. And yet there was something about him this morning that didn't seem right.

"Never mind about that!" Kate cried at last. "Tell us what your mother said."

"How do you mean?" asked Jimmy, turning red.

"What did she say when you told her you were coming back?"

"She didn't say anything," Jimmy replied with a brassy air. "She doesn't mind what I do."

"She doesn't, I hear," Kate retorted mockingly. "I suppose 'twas jealous you were?"

"What would I be jealous of?" Jimmy asked defiantly.

"Your stepfather, who else?" she said, screwing up her eyes in mockery at him. "You wanted all the attention. And now she'll be blaming it all on me. She'll be saying I have you spoiled. And she'll be right. I have you ruined, you little caffler! Ruined!" she repeated meditatively as she went and opened the back door. The whole hill behind was reflecting the morning light in a great rosy glow. "Oh, my!" she said as though to herself. "There's a beautiful morning, glory be to God!"

Just then she heard the unfamiliar sound of a car in the lane, and it stopped outside the front door. She knew then what it was that had seemed wrong in Jimmy's story, and turned on him. "You ran away from home," she said. "Is that the police?"

Jimmy didn't seem to be listening to her. "If that's my stepfather, I'm not going back with him," he said.

Kate went to the front door and saw a good-looking young man with large ears and the pink-and-white complexion she called "delicate." She knew at once it was Jimmy's stepfather.

"Mrs. Mahoney?" he asked.

"Come in, sir, come in," she said obsequiously, and now she was no longer the proud, possessive mother whose boy had come back to her but the old hireling who had been caught with property that wasn't hers.

The young man strode into the kitchen with a confident air and stopped dead when he saw Jimmy.

"Now, what made me think of coming here first?" he shouted good-humoredly. "Mrs. Mahoney, I have the makings of a first-class detective, only I never got a chance."

When Jimmy said nothing, he tossed his head and went on in the same tone, "Want a lift, Jimmy?"

Jimmy glared at him. "I'm not going back with you, Uncle Tim," he said.

"Oh, begod, that's exactly what you *are* going to do, Jimmy," his stepfather said. "If you think I'm going to spend the rest of my days chasing you round Ireland, you're wrong." He dropped into a chair and rubbed his hands, as though to restore the circulation. "Mrs. Mahoney," he asked, "what do we have them for?"

Kate liked his way of including her in the conversation. She knew, too, he was only talking like that to make things easier for Jimmy.

"I don't want to go back, Uncle Tim," Jimmy said furiously. "I want to stop here."

"Listen to that, Mrs. Mahoney," his stepfather said, cocking his head at Kate. "Insulting Dublin to a Dublin man! And in Cork, of all places!"

"I'm not saying anything against Dublin!" Jimmy cried, and again he was a child and defenseless against the dialectic of adults. "I want to stay here."

Kate immediately came to his defense. "Wisha, 'tis only the way he got a bit homesick, sir. He thought he'd like to come back for a couple of days."

"I don't want to come back for a couple of days!" Jimmy shouted. "This is my home. I told Aunt Nance so."

"And wasn't that a very hard thing to say to your mother, Jimmy?" his stepfather asked. He said it gently, and Kate knew he liked the boy.

"It's true," Jimmy said. "I knew I wasn't wanted."

"You really think that, Jimmy?" his stepfather asked reproach-fully, and Jimmy burst into wild tears.

"I didn't say *you* didn't want me. I know you did want me, and I wanted you. But my mammy didn't want me."

"Jimmy!"

"She didn't, she didn't."

"What made you think she didn't?"

"She thought I was too like my father."

"She said you were too like your father?" his stepfather asked incredulously.

"She didn't have to say it," sobbed Jimmy. "I knew it, every time she looked at me when I done something wrong. I reminded her of him, and she doesn't want to think of him. She only wants to think of you. And it's not my fault if I'm like my father, but if she didn't want me to be that way she should have took me sooner. She shouldn't have left it so late, Uncle Tim."

His stepfather said nothing for a moment and then rose in a jerky movement and walked to the back door. "You might be right there, son," he said with a shrug. "But you're not going the right way about it, either."

"All right, Uncle Tim," Jimmy cried. "What is the right way? I'll do whatever you tell me."

"Talk it over properly with your mother, and then come back here after the holdiays," his stepfather said. "You see, old man, you don't seem to realize what it cost your mother to bring you to live with her at all. Now, you don't want her explaining why you ran away after a couple of weeks, do you?"

"He's right, Jimmy boy, he's right," Kate pleaded. "You could never go back there again, with all the old talk there'd be."

"Oh, all right, all right," Jimmy said despairingly, and went to get his cap.

"Sit down, the pair of ye, till I make a cup of tea!" cried Kate. But Jimmy shook his head.

"I'd sooner go now," he said.

And it was real despair, as she well knew, not sham. Of course, he showed off a bit, the way he always did, and didn't kiss her when he was getting into the car. And when James in his gentle way said, "You'll be back soon," Jimmy only drew a deep breath and looked up at the sky.

But she knew he really meant it, and that day she had great boasting over it among the neighbors. "A boy of fourteen, Ma'am, that was never away from home all the days of his life, coming back like that, on an old bicycle, without food or sleep. Oh, my! Where would you find the likes of him?"

The neighbors, too, were impressed. "Well, Jimmy," they said, when he came back at the end of the holidays, to go to school. "You couldn't do without us, I see."

There was only one change in the relationship between Kate, James, and Jimmy. The day after his return, Jimmy said, "I'm not going to call you Mammy any more."

"Oye, and what are you going to call me?" she asked with sour humor.

"I'm going to call you Granny," he said. "The other sounds too silly."

After a few weeks James said "Granny," too. Though she didn't complain, she resented it. Stumbling about the house, talking to herself, she would suddenly say, "Glad enough they were of someone to call Mammy."

IV

After Jimmy had been back for a year or so, Kate's health began to break up. She had to go to hospital, and Nora and Molly offered to take one of the boys each. But neither Jimmy nor James would agree to this. They didn't want to leave the house and they didn't want to be separated, so they stayed on, and each week one of the girls came to clear up after them. They reported to Kate that the mess was frightful. But it wasn't this that really worried her, it was the wild streak in Jimmy. In the evenings, instead of doing his lessons like James, he was tramping the city with wild young fellows. He had no sense of the value of money, and when he wanted it thought nothing of stealing from herself or James.

She came home before she should have, but even then she was too late to prevent mischief. While she was away, Jimmy had left school and got himself a job in a packing store.

"Oh, you blackguard, you!" she said. "I knew well you'd be up to something when my back was turned. But to school you go tomorrow, my fine gentleman, if I have to drag you there myself."

"I can't go back to school," Jimmy said indignantly. "They could have the law on me if I didn't give a month's notice." He knew she was very timid of policemen, lawyers, and officials and even at her age was in great dread of being dragged off to jail for some crime she didn't even know she had committed.

"Who's the manager?" she said. "I'll see him myself."

"You can't," said Jimmy. "He's on holidays."

"Oh, you liar," she muttered. "The truth isn't in you. Who is it?"

"Anyway, I have to have a job," said Jimmy. "If anything happened you while you were in hospital, who was going to look after James?"

She was taken aback, because that was something that had been all the time on her own mind. She knew her James, and knew that if she died and he was sent to live with some foster mother who didn't understand him, he would break his heart. In every way he was steadier than Jimmy, and yet he was far more defenseless. If you took Jimmy's home away from him, he would fight, steal, or run away, but James would only lie down and die. Still, though she was impressed by Jimmy's manliness, she wasn't taken in by it. She knew that in an emotional fit he was capable of these big gestures, but he could never live up to them, and in no time he would be thinking how he could turn them to his own advantage.

" 'Tisn't James at all with you," she said. " 'Tis more money you want for yourself. Did you tell your mother first?"

"I'm working till after six every night!" he cried, confounded by her injustice. "What time have I to write to my mother?"

"Plenty of time you have to write to her when 'tis something you want," she said. "Sit down and write to her now, you scamp! I'm not going to be taking the blame for your blackguarding."

Jimmy, with a martyred air, sat at the table and agonized over a note to his mother. "How do you spell 'employment'?" he asked James.

"Listen to him!" Kate said, invoking Heaven. "He wants to give up school and he don't know how to spell a simple word."

"All right, spell it you, so," he said.

"In my time, for poor people, the education was not going," she replied with great dignity. "Poor people hadn't the chances they have now, and what chances they had, they respected, not like the ones that are going today. Go on with your letter, you thing!"

Again his Uncle Tim came and argued with him. He explained patiently that without an education Jimmy would get nowhere. Unless he finished his schooling, he couldn't go to the University. Jimmy, who couldn't stand gentleness in an argument, broke down and said he didn't want to go to the University, he only wanted to be independent. Kate didn't understand what Jimmy's stepfather meant, but she felt that it was probably only the old conflict in a new form; Jimmy's stepfather wanted him to be one of his own class, and Jimmy didn't. Leaving school at that age was what a working-class boy would do. Except for the occasional brilliant boy who was kept on at the monks' expense, there was no education beyond sixth book.

His stepfather seemed to realize it, too, for he gave in with a suddenness that surprised her. "Oh, all right," he said. "But you'd better let me try and find you something better than the job you have. And for God's sake go to night school and learn office work."

When he left, Jimmy accompanied him to the car, and they had a conversation that made Kate suspicious.

"What were you talking to your stepfather about?" she asked.

"Nothing," said Jimmy. "Only asking him who my father was."

"And did he tell you?"

"He said he didn't know."

"How inquisitive we're getting!" said Kate.

"He said I was entitled to know," Jimmy said defensively. "He told me to ask Nance the next time I go up to them." She noticed that sometimes he said "Mother" and sometimes "Nance," and both sounded awkward.

When next he came back from a holiday in Dublin he had discovered what he wished to know. As he described the scene with his mother, Kate was again overcome by a feeling of the strangeness of it all. At first his mother had refused point-blank to tell him anything. She had been quite cool and friendly about it, and explained that she had been only a girl when it all happened and when she had been deserted had cut Jimmy's father out of her life. She hadn't spoken his name since and never proposed to speak it. When Jimmy persisted, arguing and pleading with her, she had grown furious. "Christ, boy," she said, "it's my life as well as yours!" Then she had wept and said she never wanted him in the house again. At this moment, her husband had walked into the room, looking like murder, Jimmy said, and snapped, "All right, Jimmy. Beat it!" He had closed the door after Jimmy, and Jimmy heard the pair of them arguing from the kitchen. Finally, his stepfather had come out and shouted, "Your mother wants to see you, Jimmy," and rushed upstairs. When Jimmy went into the living room, she was standing by the fireplace, pale and dry-eyed. "Your father's name is Tom

Creedon," she said coolly. "He had a business in Tramore, but he's left it for years. The last I heard of him he was in London. If you want any more information, you'll have to ask one of his friends. A man called Michael Taylor in Dungarvan is your best chance." And then she, too, had gone out and followed her husband upstairs, and Jimmy had sat by the fire and sobbed to himself till it was nearly out and the whole house was silent. He felt he had outraged two people who cared for him for the sake of someone who had never inquired whether he was alive or dead.

When he had finished his story, Kate felt the same. "And what use is it to you, now you know it?" she asked maliciously.

"I had to know it," Jimmy said with easy self-confidence. "Now I can go and see him."

"You can what?" she asked wearily.

"I can go and see him. Why wouldn't I?"

"Why wouldn't you, indeed, and all the attention he paid to you," she said sourly. "You're never right."

There were times when she almost thought he wasn't right in the head. For months on end he never seemed to think at all of his parentage, and then he would begin to daydream till he worked himself up into a fever of emotion. In a fit like that she never knew what he might do. He was capable of anything—of anything, that is, except writing a letter. One weekend he set off on his bicycle for County Waterford and came back with his father's address. After· that it was only a question of getting a friend on the cross-Channel boat to fix him a passage for nothing.

All the time he was away Kate fretted, and, being Jimmy, he didn't even send her as much as a picture postcard. She had the vague hope that he wouldn't be able to locate his father. She thought of it all as if it were something she'd read in a newspaper—how in a terrible fit of anger Jimmy struck and killed his father and then turned himself in to the police. She could even see his picture in the paper with handcuffs on his wrists. "Ah," Hanna Dinan said, "God is good!" But this didn't comfort Kate at all.

And then, one autumn morning after James had left for school,

Jimmy walked in. He had had no breakfast, and she fumbled blindly about the little kitchen getting it ready for him, and cursing old age that made it seem such a labor. But all the same, her heart was light. She knew now that she had only been deceiving herself, pretending to think that Jimmy and his father might disagree, when all she dreaded was that they would agree too well.

"Well," she said fondly, leaning on the kitchen table and grinning into his face. "Now you seen him, how do you like him?"

"Oh, he's all right," Jimmy said casually—too casually, for her taste. "He's drinking himself to death, that's all." And instantly she was ashamed of her own pettiness, and tears came into her eyes.

"Wisha, child, child, why do you be upsetting yourself about them?" she cried. "They're not worth it. There's no one worth it."

She sat in the kitchen with him while he unburdened himself about it all. It was just as when he had described to her how he had asked his mother for his father's name, as though he were saving up every detail—the walk across England, the people who had given him lifts, the truck driver who had given him a dinner and five bob after Jimmy confided in him, till the moment he knocked at the door of the shabby lodging house near Victoria Station and an unshaven man with sad red eyes looked out and asked timidly, "Yes, boy, what is it?" As though nobody ever called on him now with anything but bad news.

"And what did you say?" Kate asked.

"I said, 'Don't you know me?' and he said, 'You have the advantage of me.' So I said, 'I'm your son.'"

"Oh, my!" exclaimed Kate, profoundly impressed, though she had resolved to hate everything she heard about Jimmy's father. "And what did he say to that?"

"He didn't say anything. He only started to cry."

"'Twas a bit late in the day for him," said Kate. "And what did he say about your mother?"

"Only that she didn't miss much when she missed him."

"That was one true word he said, anyway," said Kate.

"He paid for it," said Jimmy.

"He deserved it all," said Kate.

"You wouldn't say that if you saw him now," said Jimmy, and he went on to describe the squalid back room where he had stayed for a week with his father, sleeping in the same dirty bed, going out with him to the pub. And yet through Jimmy's disillusionment Kate felt a touch of pride in the way he described the sudden outbursts of extravagant humor that lit up his father's maudlin self-pity. He described everything, down to the last evening, when his father had brought him to Paddington Station, forced him to take the last five shillings he had in the world, tearfully kissed him, and begged him to come again.

She knew from Jimmy's tone that it was unlikely that he would go again. His father was only another ghost that he had laid.

V

When he was eighteen, Jimmy took up with a girl of his own, and at first Kate paid no attention, but when it went on for more than six months and Jimmy took the girl out every Friday night, she began to grow nervous. Steady courting of one girl was something she had never thought him capable of. When she learned who the girl was, she understood. Tessie Flynn was an orphan who had been brought up by a staid old couple on the road as their own daughter. They had brought her up so well that every other young fellow on the road was in dread to go near her, and when the old couple discovered that she was actually walking out with Jimmy they didn't talk to her for days. She wasn't allowed to bring Jimmy to the house, and Kate, for the sake of her own self-respect, was forced to invite her instead.

Not that this made her like Tessie any the more. She dreaded Friday evenings, when Jimmy would come in from work, and shave, and strip to wash under the tap in the back yard, and then change into his best blue suit and put cream on his hair.

"You won't be late tonight?" she would ask.

"Why wouldn't I be late?" Jimmy would ask cheerfully.

"You know I can't sleep while you do be out."

It was true. Any other night of the week she could sleep comfortably at her proper time, but when she knew he was out with "that vagabond," as she called poor Tessie, she would lie awake worrying and saying her rosary. Even James reproved her. One Friday evening, he closed his book carefully, raised his big glasses on his forehead, and said, "Granny, you worry too much about Jimmy and his girl friend. Jimmy is much steadier than you think."

But James didn't realize, as she did, that even in his choice of a girl Jimmy was only reliving the pattern of his own life. To anyone else he might seem the most ordinary of young fellows, but she could watch the fever mount in him, and always she was taken aback at the form it took. Once, he lit out on his bicycle to a little town eighty miles away, where his father's brother had a grocery shop. Another time, with the help of his sailor friend, he crossed again to Fishguard and cycled through southern England to the little seaside town in Dorset where he had been born. And she knew that whatever she might say he would go on like that to the end of his days, pursued by the dream of a normal life that he might have lived and of a normal family in which he might have grown up.

James observed it, too, but with a deep disapproval. He thought Jimmy cheapened himself.

"Ah, that's only because you can get away from them, boy," Jimmy said with his toughest air. "Boy, if my family was living in England, *I* wouldn't worry about them, either."

"Well, your father *is* living in England, and you went to see him," said James. "I daresay I'll see my family, too, one day, but I don't want to see them now, thank you."

"If you have any sense you'll have nothing to do with them," said Jimmy. "They'll only look down on you."

"I don't think so," said James. "At the moment they might, but if they meet me when I'm a professor at the University, or a senior civil servant, they'll behave differently. You see, Jimmy," he went on in the tone he would use when he was a professor at the University, "people like that pay far too much attention to public opinion, and they won't neglect anyone who can be useful to them."

Kate felt that there was a sad wisdom in what James said. While Jimmy, who had something of his father's weakness and charm, might prove a liability to those who didn't understand him, James would work and save, and only when he was established and independent would he satisfy his curiosity about those who had abandoned him. And, though she mightn't live to see it, James would make quite certain that nobody patronized him. She would have given a great deal to see how James dealt with his family.

But she knew that she wouldn't see it. She fell ill again, and this time Molly came to the house to nurse her, while Nora, who looked after Molly's children, came in the evenings, and sometimes one of the husbands. Molly made an immediate change in the house. She was swift and efficient; she fed the boys and made conversation with callers, leaning against the doorpost with folded arms as though she had no thought in the world but of them, though occasionally she would slip away into the front room and weep savagely to herself for a few minutes before returning to her tasks.

The priest came, and Molly invited him into the front room and chatted with him about the affairs of the parish. After he had left, Kate asked to see Jimmy and James. They went up the stairs quietly and stood at either side of the bed. Her eyes were closed and her hands outstretched on the bed. Jimmy took one, and after a moment James took the other. James was never a boy for a deathbed.

"Don't upset yeerselves too much over me," she said. "I know ye'll miss me, but ye have nothing to regret. Ye were the two best boys a mother ever reared, and I'm proud of ye." She thought hard for a moment and then added something that shocked them all. "And yeer father is proud of ye, I'm sure."

Molly, who was standing with Nora behind James, leaned forward and said urgently, "Mammy, 'tisn't who you think. 'Tis Jimmy and James."

Kate opened her eyes for a moment and looked straight at her, and her eyes were no colder than the words she spoke. "Excuse me, child, I know perfectly well who I have." Her eyes closed again, and she breathed noisily for what seemed a long, long time, as though she were vainly trying to recollect herself. "Don't either of ye do anything yeer father would be ashamed of. He was a good man, and a kind man, and a clean-living man, and he never robbed anyone of a ha'penny. . . . Jimmy," she added in a voice of unexpected strength, "look after your little brother for me."

"I will, Mammy," Jimmy said through his tears.

Something in that sudden reversion to the language of childhood made Molly break down. She left the room and took refuge in the parlor downstairs. Nora, realizing that something had upset her sister, followed and shouted at her as all the Mahoneys had always shouted at one another. "Wisha, Molly, will you have a bit of sense? Sure you know poor Mammy's mind was wandering."

"It was *not* wandering, Nora," Molly said hysterically. "She knew perfectly well what she was saying, and Jimmy knew it, too. They were her real children all the time, and we were only outsiders. Oh, Nora, Nora, how could she do *that* to us?"

That night, when Kate was quiet at last in her brown shroud, with her hands clutching the rosary beads on her breast, and the neighbors were coming from all parts into the little front room to say a prayer for her, people in every little house around were asking the same question that Molly had been asking herself, though they asked it with a touch of envy. How could a woman who was already old take the things the world had thrown away and out of them fashion a new family, dearer to her than the old and finer than any she had known? Hanna Dinan had the last word. Having sat there for an hour, she took a last look at her old crony on the bed, then pulled her coat about her and said casually, "Wisha, wasn't she a great little woman! She had them all against her and she bested them. They had everything, and she had nothing, and she bested them all in the end."

The American Wife

ELSIE COLLEARY, who was on a visit to her cousins in Cork, was a mystery even to them. Her father, Jack Colleary's brother, had emigrated when he was a kid and done well for himself; he had made his money in the liquor business, and left it to go into wholesale produce when Elsie was growing up, because he didn't think it was the right background for a girl. He had given her the best of educations, and all he had got out of it was to have Elsie telling him that Irishmen were more manly, and that even Irish-Americans let their wives boss them too much. What she meant was that *he* let her mother boss him, and she had learned from other Irish people that this was not the custom at home. Maybe Mike Colleary, like a lot of other Americans, did give the impression of yielding too much to his wife, but that was because she thought she knew more about things than he did, and he was too softhearted to disillusion her. No doubt the Americans, experienced in nostalgia, took Elsie's glorification of Irishmen good-humoredly, but it did not go down too well in Cork, where the men stood in perpetual contemplation of the dangers of marriage, like cranes standing on one leg at the edge of the windy water.

She stood out at the Collearys' quiet little parties, with her high waist and wide skirts, taking the men out to sit on the stairs while she argued with them about religion and politics. Women having occasion to go upstairs thought this very forward, but some of the men found it a pleasant relief. Besides, like all Americans, she was probably a millionaire, and the most unworldly of men can get a kick out of flirting with a real millionaire.

The man she finally fell in love with did not sit on the stairs with her at all, though, like her, he was interested in religion and politics. This was a chap called Tom Barry. Tom was thirty-five, tall and thin and good-looking, and he lived with his mother and two good-looking sisters in a tiny house near the Barrack, and he couldn't even go for a walk in the evening without the three of them lining up in the hallway to present him with his hat, his gloves, and his clean handkerchief. He had a small job in the courthouse, and was not without ambition; he had engaged in several small business enterprises with his friend Jerry Coakley, but all they had ever got out of these was some good stories. Jerry was forty, and *he* had an old mother who insisted on putting his socks on for him.

Elsie's cousins warned her against setting her cap at Tom, but this only seemed to make her worse. "I guess I'll have to seduce him," she replied airily, and her cousins, who had never known a well-bred Catholic girl to talk like that, were shocked. She shocked them even more before she was done. She called at his house when she knew he wasn't there and deluded his innocent mother and sisters into believing that she didn't have designs on him; she badgered Tom to death at the office, gave him presents, and even hired a car to take him for drives.

They weren't the only ones who were shocked. Tom was shocked himself when she asked him point-blank how much he earned. However, he put that down to unworldliness and told her.

"But that's not even a street cleaner's wages at home," she said indignantly.

"I'm sure, Elsie," he said sadly. "But then, of course, money isn't everything."

"No, and Ireland isn't everything," she replied. It was peculiar, but from their first evening together she had never ceased talking about America to him—the summer heat, and the crickets chattering, and the leaves alive with fireflies. During her discussions on the stairs, she had apparently discovered a great many things wrong with Ireland, and Tom, with a sort of mournful pleasure, kept adding to them.

"Oh, I know, I know," he said regretfully.

"Then if you know, why don't you do something about it?"

"Ah, well, I suppose it's habit, Elsie," he said, as though he weren't quite sure. "I suppose I'm too old to learn new tricks."

But Elsie doubted if it was really habit, and it perplexed her that a man so clever and conscientious could at the same time be so lacking in initiative. She explained it finally to herself in terms of an attachment to his mother that was neither natural nor healthy. Elsie was a girl who loved explanations.

On their third outing she had proposed to him, and he was so astonished that he burst out laughing, and continued to laugh whenever he thought of it again. Elsie herself couldn't see anything to laugh at in it. Having been proposed to by men who were younger and better-looking and better off than he was, she felt she had been conferring an honor on him. But he was a curious man, for when she repeated the proposal, he said, with a cold fury that hurt her, "Sometimes I wish you'd think before you talk, Elsie. You know what I earn, and you know it isn't enough to keep a family on. Besides, in case you haven't noticed it, I have a mother and two sisters to support."

"You could earn enough to support them in America," she protested.

"And I told you already that I had no intention of going to America."

"I have some money of my own," she said. "It's not much, but it could mean I'd be no burden to you."

"Listen, Elsie," he said, "a man who can't support a wife and children has no business marrying at all. I have no business marrying anyway. I'm not a very cheerful man, and I have a rotten temper."

Elsie went home in tears, and told her astonished uncle that all Irishmen were pansies, and, as he had no notion what pansies were, he shook his head and admitted that it was a terrible country. Then she wrote to Tom and told him that what he needed was not a wife but a psychiatrist. The writing of this gave her great satisfaction, but next morning she realized that her mother would only say she had been silly. Her mother believed that men needed careful handling. The day after, she waited for Tom outside the courthouse, and when he came out she summoned him with two angry blasts on the horn. A rainy sunset was flooding the Western Road with yellow light that made her look old and grim.

"Well," she said bitterly, "I'd hoped I'd never see your miserable face again."

But that extraordinary man only smiled gently and rested his elbows on the window of the car.

"I'm delighted you came," he said. "I was all last night trying to write to you, but I'm not very good at it."

"Oh, so you got my letter?"

"I did, and I'm ashamed to have upset you so much. All I wanted to say was that if you're serious—I mean really serious—about this, I'd be honored."

At first she thought he was mocking her. Then she realized that he wasn't, and she was in such an evil humor that she was tempted to tell him she had changed her mind. Then common sense told her the man would be fool enough to believe her, and after that his pride wouldn't let him propose to her again. It was the price you had to pay for dealing with men who had such a high notion of their own dignity.

"I suppose it depends on whether you love me or not," she replied. "It's a little matter you forgot to mention."

He raised himself from the car window, and in the evening light she saw a look of positive pain on his lean, sad, gentle face. "Ah, I do, but—" he was beginning when she cut him off and told him to get in the car. Whatever he was about to say, she didn't want to hear it.

They settled down in a modern bungalow outside the town, on the edge of the harbor. Elsie's mother, who flew over for the wedding, said dryly that she hoped Elsie would be able to make up to Tom for the loss of his mother's services. In fact, it wasn't long before the Barrys were saying she wasn't, and making remarks about her cooking and her lack of tidiness. But if Tom noticed there was anything wrong, which is improbable, he didn't mention it. Whatever his faults as a sweetheart, he made a good husband. It may have been the affection of a sensitive man for someone he saw as frightened, fluttering, and insecure. It could have been the longing of a frustrated one for someone that seemed to him remote, romantic, and mysterious. But whatever it was, Tom, who had always been God Almighty to his mother and sisters, was extraordinarily patient and understanding with Elsie, and she needed it, because she was often homesick and scared.

Jerry Coakley was a great comfort to her in these fits, for Jerry had a warmth of manner that Tom lacked. He was an insignificant-looking man with a ravaged dyspeptic face and a tubercular complexion, a thin, bitter month with bad teeth, and long lank hair; but he was so sympathetic and insinuating that at times he even gave you the impression that he was changing his shape to suit your mood. Elsie had the feeling that the sense of failure had eaten deeper into him than into Tom.

At once she started to arrange a match between him and Tom's elder sister, Annie, in spite of Tom's warnings that Jerry would never marry till his mother died. When she realized that Tom was right, she said it was probably as well, because Annie wouldn't put his socks on him. Later she admitted that this was unfair, and that it would probably be a great relief to poor Jerry to be allowed to put on his socks himself. Between Tom and him there was one of those passionate relationships that spring up in small towns where society narrows itself down to a handful of erratic and explosive friendships. There were always people who weren't talking to other people, and friends had all to be dragged into the disagreement, no matter how trifling it might be, and often it happened that the principals had already become fast friends again when *their* friends were still ignoring one another in the street. But Jerry and Tom refused to disagree. Jerry would drop in for a bottle of stout, and

Tom and he would denounce the country, while Elsie wondered why they could never find anything more interesting to talk about than stupid priests and crooked politicians.

Elsie's causes were of a different kind. The charwoman, Mrs. Dorgan, had six children and a husband who didn't earn enough to keep them. Elsie concealed from Tom how much she really paid Mrs. Dorgan, but she couldn't conceal that Mrs. Dorgan wore her clothes, or that she took the Dorgan family to the seaside in the summer. When Jerry suggested to Tom that the Dorgans might be doing too well out of Elsie, Tom replied, "Even if they were, Jerry, I wouldn't interfere. If 'tis people's nature to be generous, you must let them be generous."

For Tom's causes she had less patience. "Oh, why don't you people do something about it, instead of talking?" she cried.

"What could you do, Elsie?" asked Jerry.

"At least you could show them up," said Elsie.

"Why, Elsie?" he asked with his mournful smile. "Were you thinking of starting a paper?"

"Then, if you can't do anything about it, shut up!" she said. "You and Tom seem to get some queer masochistic pleasure out of these people."

"Begor, Elsie, you might have something there," Jerry said, nodding ruefully.

"Oh, we adore them," Tom said mockingly.

"You do," she said. "I've seen you. You sit here night after night denouncing them, and then when one of them gets sick you're round to the house to see if there's anything you can do for him, and when he dies you start a collection for his wife and family. You make me sick." Then she stamped out to the kitchen.

Jerry hunched his shoulders and exploded in splutters and giggles. He reached out a big paw for a bottle of stout, with the air of someone snaring a rabbit.

"I declare to God, Tom, she has us taped," he said.

"She has you taped anyway," said Tom.

"How's that?"

"She thinks you need an American wife as well."

"Well, now, she mightn't be too far out in that, either," said Jerry with a crooked grin. "I often thought it would take something like that."

"She thinks you have *problems*," said Tom with a snort. Elsie's favorite word gave him the creeps.

"She wouldn't be referring to the mother, by any chance?"

For a whole year Elsie had fits of depression because she thought she wasn't going to have a baby, and she saw several doctors, whose advice she repeated in mixed company, to the great embarrassment of everybody except Jerry. After that, for the best part of another year, she had fits of depression because she was going to have a baby, and she informed everybody about that as well, including the occasion of its conception and the probable date of its arrival, and again they were all embarrassed only Jerry. Having reached the age of eighteen before learning that there was any real difference between the sexes, Jerry found all her talk fascinating, and also he realized that Elsie saw nothing immodest in it. It was just that she had an experimental interest in her body and mind. When she gave him bourbon he studied its taste, but when he gave her Irish she studied its effect—it was as simple as that. Jerry, too, liked explanations, but he liked them for their own sake, and not with the intention of doing anything with them. At the same time, Elsie was scared by what she thought was a lack of curiosity on the part of the Cork doctors, and when her mother learned this she began to press Elsie to have the baby in America, where she would feel secure.

"You don't think I should go back, Tom?" she asked guiltily. "Daddy says he'll pay my fare."

It came as a shock to Tom, though the idea had crossed his mind that something of the kind might happen. "If that's the way you feel about it, I suppose you'd better, Elsie," he replied.

"But you wouldn't come with me."

"How can I come with you? You know I can't just walk out of the office for a couple of months."

"But you could get a job at home."

"And I told you a dozen times I don't want a job in America," he said angrily. Then, seeing the way it upset her, he changed his tone. "Look, if you stay here, feeling the way you do, you'll work yourself into a real illness. Anyway, sometime you'll have to go back on a visit, and this is as good an occasion as any."

"But how can I, without you?" she asked. "You'd only neglect yourself."

"I would not neglect myself."

"Would you stay at your mother's?"

"I would not stay at my mother's. This is my house, and I'm going to stop here."

Tom worried less about the effect Elsie's leaving would have on him than about what his family would say, particularly Annie, who never lost the chance of a crack at Elsie. "You let that girl walk on you, Tom Barry," she said. "One of these days she'll walk too hard." Then, of course, Tom walked on *her,* in the way that only a devoted brother can, but that was no relief to the feeling that something had come between Elsie and him and that he could do nothing about it. When he was driving Elsie to the liner, he knew that she felt the same, for she didn't break down until they came to a long gray bridge over an inlet of water, guarded by a lonely gray stone tower. She had once pointed it out to him as the first thing she had seen that represented Ireland to her, and now he had the feeling that this was how she saw him—a battered old tower by a river mouth that was no longer of any importance to anyone but the sea gulls.

She was away longer than she or anyone else had expected. First there was the wedding of an old school friend; then her mother's birthday; then the baby got ill. It was clear that she was enjoying herself immensely, but she wrote long and frequent letters, sent snapshots of herself and the baby, and—most important of all—had named the baby for Jerry Coakley. Clearly Elsie hadn't forgotten them. The Dorgan kids appeared on the road in clothes that had obviously been made in America, and whenever Tom met them he stopped to speak to them and give them the pennies he thought Elsie would have given them.

Occasionally Tom went to his mother's for supper, but otherwise he looked after himself. Nothing could persuade him that he was not a natural housekeeper, or that whatever his sisters could do he could not do just as well himself. Sometimes Jerry came and the two men took off their coats and tried to prepare a meal out of one of Elsie's cookbooks. "Steady, squad!" Tom would murmur as he wiped his hands before taking another peep at the book. "You never know when this might come in handy." But whether it was the result of Tom's supervision or Jerry's helplessness, the meal usually ended in a big burnup, or a tasteless mess from which some essential ingredient seemed to be missing, and they laughed over it as they consoled themselves with bread and cheese and stout. "Elsie is right," Jerry would say, shaking his head regretfully. "We have problems, boy! We have problems!"

Elsie returned at last with trunks full of new clothes, a box of up-to-date kitchen stuff, and a new gaiety and energy. Every ten minutes Tom would make an excuse to tiptoe upstairs and take another look at his son. Then the Barrys arrived, and Elsie gave immediate offense by quoting Gesell and Spock. But Mrs. Barry didn't seem to mind as much as her daughters. By some extraordinary process of association, she had discovered a great similarity between Elsie and herself in the fact that she had married from the south side of the city into the north and had never got used to it. This delighted Elsie, who went about proclaiming that her mother-in-law and herself were both displaced persons.

The next year was a very happy one, and less trying on Elsie, because she had another woman to talk to, even if most of the time she didn't understand what her mother-in-law was telling her, and had the suspicion that her mother-in-law didn't understand her either. But then she got pregnant for the second time, and became restless and dissatisfied once more, though now it wasn't only with hospitals and doctors but with schools and schoolteachers as well. Tom and Jerry had impressed on her that the children were being turned into idiots, learning through the medium of a language they didn't understand—indeed, according to Tom, it was a language that nobody understood. What chance would the children have?

"Ah, I suppose the same chance as the rest of us, Elsie," said Jerry in his sly, mournful way.

"But you and Tom don't want chances, Jerry," she replied earnestly. "Neither of you has any ambition."

"Ah, you should look on the bright side of things. Maybe with God's help they won't have any ambition either."

But this time it had gone beyond a joke. For days on end, Tom was in a rage with her, and when he was angry he seemed to withdraw into himself like a snail into a shell.

Unable to get at him, Elsie grew hysterical. "It's all your damned obstinacy," she sobbed. "You don't do anything in this rotten hole, but you're too conceited to get out of it. Your family treat you as if you were God, and then you behave to me as if you were. God! God! God!" she screamed, and each time she punched him viciously with her fist, till suddenly the humor of their situation struck him and he went off into laughter.

After that, he could only make his peace with her and make excuses for her leaving him again, but he knew that the excuses wouldn't impress his sisters. One evening when he went to see them, Annie caught him, as she usually did, when he was going out the front door, and he stood looking sidewise down the avenue.

"Are you letting Elsie go off to America again, Tom?" she asked.

"I don't know," Tom said, pulling his long nose with an air of affected indifference. "I can't very well stop her, can I?"

"Damn soon she'd be stopped if she hadn't the money," said Annie. "And you're going to let her take young Jerry?"

"Ah, how could I look after Jerry? Talk sense, can't you!"

"And I suppose we couldn't look after him either? We're not sufficiently well read."

"Ah, the child should be with his own mother, Annie," Tom said impatiently.

"And where should his mother be? Ah, Tom Barry," she added bitterly, "I told you what that one was, and she's not done with you yet. Are you sure she's going to bring him back?"

Then Tom exploded on her in his cold, savage way. "If you want to know, I am not," he said, and strode down the avenue with his head slightly bowed.

Something about the cut of him as he passed under a street lamp almost broke Annie's heart. "The curse of God on that bitch!" she said when she returned to her mother in the kitchen.

"Is it Elsie?" her mother cried angrily. "How dare you talk of her like that!"

"He's letting her go to America again," said Annie.

"He's a good boy, and he's right to consider her feelings," said her mother anxiously. "I often thought myself I'd go back to the south side and not be ending my days in this misfortunate hole."

The months after Elsie's second departure were bitter ones for Tom. A house from which a woman is gone is bad enough, but one from which a child is gone is a deadhouse. Tom would wake in the middle of the night thinking he heard Jerry crying, and be half out of bed before he realized that Jerry was thousands of miles away. He did not continue his experiments with cooking and housekeeping. He ate at his mother's, spent most of his time at the Coakleys, and drank far too much. Like all inward-looking men he had a heavy hand on the bottle. Meanwhile Elsie wavered and procrastinated worse than before, setting dates, canceling her passage, sometimes changing her mind within twenty-four hours. In his despondency Tom resigned himself to the idea that she wouldn't return at all, or at least persuaded himself that he had.

"Oh, she'll come back all right," Jerry said with a worried air. "The question is, will she stay back. . . . You don't mind me talking about it?" he asked.

"Indeed no. Why would I?"

"You know, Tom, I'd say ye had family enough to last ye another few years."

Tom didn't look up for a few moments, and when he did he smiled faintly. "You think it's that?"

"I'm not saying she knows it," Jerry added hastily. "There's nothing calculating about her, and she's crazy about you."

"I thought it was something that went with having the baby," Tom said thoughtfully. "Some sort of homing instinct."

"I wouldn't say so," said Jerry. "Not altogether. I think she feels that eventually she'll get you through the kids."

"She won't," Tom said bitterly.

"I know, sure, I know. But Elsie can't get used to the—the irremediable." The last word was so unlike Jerry that Tom felt he must have looked it up in a dictionary, and the absurdity of this made him feel very close to his old crony. "Tell me, Tom," Jerry added gently, "wouldn't you do it? I know it wouldn't be easy, but wouldn't you try it, even for a while, for Elsie's sake? 'Twould mean a hell of a lot to her."

"I'm too old, Jerry," Tom said so deliberately that Jerry knew it had been in his mind as well.

"Oh, I know, I know," Jerry repeated. "Even ten years ago I might have done it myself. It's like jail. The time comes when you're happier in than out. And that's not the worst of it," he added bitterly. "The worst is when you pretend you like it."

It was a strange evening that neither of them ever forgot, sitting in that little house to which Elsie's absence seemed a rebuke, and listening to the wind from the harbor that touched the foot of the garden. They knew they belonged to a country whose youth was always escaping from it, out beyond that harbor, and that was middle-aged in all its attitudes and institutions. Of those that remained, a little handful lived with defeat and learned fortitude and humor and sweetness, and these were the things that Elsie, with her generous idealism, loved in them. But she couldn't pay the price. She wanted them where she belonged herself, among the victors.

A few weeks later, Elsie was back; the house was full of life again, and that evening seemed only a bad dream. It was almost impossible to keep Jerry Og, as they called the elder child, away from Tom. He was still only a baby, and a spoiled one at that, but when Tom took him to the village Jerry Og thrust out his chest and took strides that were too big for him like any small boy with a father he admired. Each day, he lay in wait for the postman and then took the post away to sort it for himself. He sorted it by the pictures on the stamps, and Elsie noted gleefully that he reserved all the pretty pictures for his father.

Nobody had remembered Jerry's good advice, even Jerry himself, and eighteen months later Elsie was pregnant again. Again their lives took the same pattern of unrest. But this time Elsie was even more distressed than Tom.

"I'm a curse to you," she said. "There's something wrong with me. I can't be natural."

"Oh, you're natural enough," Tom replied bitterly. "You married the wrong man, that's all."

"I didn't, I didn't!" she protested despairingly. "You can say anything else but that. If I believed that, I'd have nothing left, because I never cared for anyone but you. And in spite of what you think, I'm coming back," she went on, in tears. "I'm coming back if it kills me. God, I hate this country; I hate every God damn thing about it; I hate what it's done to you and Jerry. But I'm not going to let you go."

"You have no choice," Tom said patiently. "Jerry Og will have to go to school, and you can't be bringing him hither and over, even if you could afford it."

"Then, if that's what you feel, why don't you keep him?" she cried. "You know perfectly well you could stop me taking him with me if you wanted to. You wouldn't even have to bring me into court. I'll give him to you now. Isn't that proof enough that I'm coming back?"

"No, Elsie, it is not," Tom replied, measuring every word. "And I'm not going to bring you into court, either. I'm not going to take hostages to make sure my wife comes back to me."

And though Elsie continued to delude herself with the belief that she would return, she knew Tom was right. It would all appear different when she got home. The first return to Ireland had been hard, the second had seemed impossible. Yet, even in the black hours when she really considered the situation, she felt she could never resign herself to something that had been determined before she was born, and she deceived herself with the hope that Tom would change his mind and follow her. He must follow her. Even if he was prepared to abandon her, he would never abandon Jerry Og.

And this, as Big Jerry could have told her, was where she made her biggest mistake, because if Tom had done it at all it would have been for her. But Big Jerry had decided that the whole thing had gone beyond his power to help. He recognized the irremediable, all right, sometimes perhaps even before it became irremediable. But that, as he would have said himself, is where the ferryboat had left him.

Thanks to Elsie, the eldest of the Dorgans now has a job in Boston and in the course of years the rest of them will probably go there as well. Tom continues to live in his little bungalow beside the harbor. Annie is keeping house for him, which suits her fine, because Big Jerry's old mother continued to put his socks on for him a few years too long, and now Annie has only her brother to worship. To all appearances they are happy enough, as happiness goes in Cork. Jerry still calls, and the two men discuss the terrible state of the country. But in Tom's bedroom there are pictures of Elsie and the children, the third of whom he knows only through photographs, and apart from that, nothing has changed since Elsie left it five years ago. It is a strange room, for one glance is enough to show that the man who sleeps there is still in love, and that everything that matters to him in the world is reflected there. And one day, if he comes by the dollars, he will probably go out and visit them all, but it is here he will return and here, no doubt, he will die.

The Impossible Marriage

IT WASN'T TILL he was nearly thirty that Jim Grahame realized the trick that life had played on him. Up to that time he had lived very much like any other young man, with no great notion that he was being imposed upon. His father had died ten years before. Jim, an accountant in a provision store, had continued to accept his father's responsibilities, and his mother, a lively, sweet-natured little woman, had kept house for him in the way that only mothers can. They lived on in the house into which she had married; a big, roomy, awkward house on the edge of the country where the rent they paid was barely enough to keep the building in repair. Jim had never been very shy with girls, but none of them he had met seemed to him to be half the woman his mother was, and, unknown to himself, he was turning into a typical comfortable old bachelor who might or might not at the age of forty-five decide to establish a family of his own. His mother spoiled him, of course, and, in the way of only children, he had a troubled conscience because of the way he took advantage of it. But spoiling is a burden that the majority of men can carry a great deal of without undue hardship.

Then, by the seaside in Crosshaven, one Sunday, he went for a walk with a girl called Eileen Clery who lived in the same quarter of Cork as himself, though he had never noticed her before. She wasn't the sort of girl who thrusts herself on people's attention, though she was good-looking enough, with a thin face that lit up beautifully when she smiled, and pale hair with gold lights in it. He tried to flirt with her, and was surprised and a little offended by her quick, almost violent, withdrawal. He had not mistaken her for a flighty type, but neither had he expected to meet an untouchable.

The curious thing was that she seemed to like him, and even arranged to meet him again. This time they sat in a nook on the cliffs, and Jim became more pressing. To his astonishment, she began to cry. He was exasperated, but he pretended a solicitude he did not altogether feel, and when she saw him apparently distressed, she sat up and smiled, though her tears still continued to flow freely. "It's not that I wouldn't like it, Jim," she said, drying her eyes and blowing her nose into a ridiculous little scrap of a handkerchief, "only I don't like thinking about it."

"Why on earth not, Eileen?" he asked with some amusement.

"Well, you see, I'm an only child, and I have my mother to look after," she said, still sniffing.

"And I'm an only child, and I have a mother to look after," Jim replied triumphantly, and then laughed outright at the absurdity of the coincidence. "We're a pair," he added with a rueful chuckle.

"Yes, aren't we?" Eileen said, laughing and sobbing at once, and then she rested her head on his chest, and made no further difficulties about his love-making.

Now, all books on the subject describe attraction in similar terms; tanned chests and voluptuous contours which really have very little to do with the matter. But what they rarely mention, the most powerful of all, is human loneliness. This is something that women face earlier than men, and Eileen had already faced it. Jim, though he had not faced it in the same way, was perceptive enough to see it reaching out before him, and up there on the cliffs overlooking Cork Harbour, watching a score of little sailing boats headed for Currabinny, they realized that they were in love, and all the more in love because their position was so obviously hopeless.

After that, they met regularly every week in Cork, to walk, or go to the pictures when it rained. They did it in the way of only children, taking precautions that became something of a joke to those who knew them. One evening, a girl crossing the New Bridge saw Jim Grahame standing there, and when she came to the second bridge was amused to see Eileen. "Excuse my interfering, Miss Clery," she said, "but if it's Mr. Grahame you're waiting for, he's waiting for you at the other bridge." Eileen didn't know where to look; she blushed, she laughed, and finally joined her hands and said, "Oh, thank you, thank you," and ran like the wind.

It was like them to meet that way, miles from home, because they were pursued by the sense of guilt. They felt more pity for their mothers than for themselves and did their best to hide their dreadful secret out of some instinctive understanding of the fear of loneliness and old age that besets women whose families have grown and whose husbands are dead. Perhaps they even understood it too well, and apprehended more of it than was really there.

Mrs. Grahame, whose intelligence service was better than Mrs. Clery's, was the first to speak of the matter to them.

"I hear you're great friends with a girl called Clery from the Cross," she said one evening in a tone of modest complaint. Jim was shaving by the back door. He started and turned to her with a look of amusement, but she was absorbed in her knitting, as always when she did not wish to look him in the face.

"Go on!" he said. "Who told you that?"

"Why wouldn't I hear it when the whole road knows it?" she replied, avoiding his question. She liked her little mysteries. "Wouldn't you bring her up some night?"

"You wouldn't mind?"

"Why would I mind, child? Little enough company we see."

This was another of her favorite myths; that she never saw or spoke to anyone, though Jim could do little or nothing that she didn't hear about sooner or later.

One evening he brought Eileen home for tea, and though she was nervous and giggly, he could see that his mother took to her at once. Mrs. Grahame worshipped her son, but she had always wished for a daughter, someone she could talk to as she could not talk to a man. Later in the evening, Eileen, realizing that she really was welcome, began to relax, and she and his mother exchanged the sort of gossip they both loved.

"Ah, Dinny Murphy was a bad head to her," his mother would say darkly, referring to some object of charity in the neighborhood.

"No, no, no, Mrs. Grahame," Eileen would say hastily, in her eagerness laying her hand on Mrs. Grahame's arm. "Poor Dinny wasn't the worst."

"Look at that now!" Mrs. Grahame would cry, putting down her knitting to fix Eileen with eyes that were bleak with tragedy. "And the things they said about him! Eileen, haven't people *bad* tongues?"

"No, he wasn't, he wasn't," Eileen would repeat, shaking her head. "He took a drop, of course, but which of them doesn't, would you tell me?"

And Jim, who said nothing, smiled as he noticed how the voice of Eileen, young, eager, and intelligent, blended with his mother's in a perfect harmony of gossip. Mrs. Grahame did not let her go without hinting delicately at her lost and lonely condition that made it impossible for her to know the truth about anything, and made her promise to come again. She became accustomed to Eileen's visits, and was quite hurt if a week went by without one. She even said with great resignation that of course she was no company for a lively young girl like that.

Then it was Mrs. Clery's turn. She might hear of Eileen's visits to the Grahames, and be upset, but, on the other hand, she might be equally upset by an unexpected visit. So Eileen had to prepare her by telling her first how Jim was situated with regard to his own mother so that she wouldn't think he came to the house with any designs on Eileen. All they had to live on was Eileen's earnings and a few shillings' pension which her mother drew.

They lived in a tiny cottage in a terrace off the road, with a parlor, a kitchen that they used as a living room, and two attic bedrooms upstairs. Mrs. Clery was a shrewd old lady with a battered humorous face. She suffered from a variety of ailments, and, being slightly deaf, complained of them at great length in a loud, hectoring tone. She would put a firm hand on her interlocutor's knee while she talked, to make sure he didn't escape, and then stare blankly at the fireplace in concentration.

"So then, Jim, I had this second pain I was telling you about, and I had Doctor O'Mahoney to the house, and he said—what did Doctor O'Mahoney say about the second pain, Eileen?"

"He said you were an old humbug," bawled Eileen.

"Dr. O'Mahoney?" her mother said in wonderment. "He did not. Ah, you divil you!"

At home, Eileen talked nervously, at the top of her voice, interrupting, contradicting, and bantering her mother till the old woman's face wrinkled up with glee and she blinked at Jim and groaned: "Didn't I say she was a divil, Jim? Did you ever hear a girl talk to her mother that way? I'll engage you don't talk like that to your own poor mother."

"His mother isn't always grousing," Eileen yelled blithely from the back yard.

"Grousing? Who's grousing?" asked Mrs. Clery, her eyes half-closing with pleasure, like a cat's when you stroke it. "Oh, my, I live in terror of her. Jim, boy, you never heard such a tongue! And the lies she tells! Me grousing!"

All the same it was pleasant for Jim and Eileen to have a place to turn to on a wet night when they didn't want to go to the pictures. Mostly, they went to Jim's. Mrs. Grahame was more jealous than Eileen's mother. Even a hint of slight on the part of either of them would reduce her to mutinous tears, but if they sat with her for half an hour, she would get up and tiptoe gently out of the room as though she thought they were asleep. Her jealousy was only the measure of her generosity.

"Wisha, Jim," she said roguishly one evening, putting down her knitting, "wouldn't you and Eileen make a match of it?"

"A match?" Jim repeated mockingly, looking up from his book. "I suppose you want to get rid of me?"

His mother could usually be diverted from any subject by teasing because she took everything literally even if she rarely took it far.

"Indeed, what a thing I'd do!" she said in a huff and went on with her knitting, full of childish rage at his reception of her generous proposal. But, of course, it didn't last. Ten minutes later, having forgotten her huff, she added, this time as though speaking to herself: "Why, then, you wouldn't find many like her."

"And where would we live?" he asked with gentle irony.

"My goodness, haven't ye the house?" she said, looking at him severely over her glasses. "You don't think I'd stop to be in your way?"

"Oh, so you'd go to the workhouse and let Mrs. Clery come here?"

"Wisha, aren't things very peculiar?" she said vaguely, and he knew that she was brooding on the coincidence by which he and Eileen had been drawn together. His mother and he were both familiar with the situation in its simple form, common as it is in Ireland, and could have listed a score of families where a young man or woman "walked out" for years before he or she was in a position to marry, too often only to find themselves too old or tired for it.

"We're not thinking in that direction at all, Mrs. Grahame, thank you all the same," he said, giving her a sweet smile. "It's got to be a double murder or nothing at all."

He knew that in spite of her jealousy, Mrs. Grahame resented this fate for them, but Mrs. Clery jovially pretended that they should be grateful for their good fortune.

"Ye don't know how well off ye are," she said. "Ye're young and healthy; a lot ye have to complain of. The way they rush into marriage you'd think they were robbing a bank. Soon enough they get tired of it, and then, oh, my! Nothing is bad enough for them to say about one another."

"So you don't approve of marriage, Mammy?" Eileen would ask demurely.

"Who said I don't approve of marriage?" her mother asked suspiciously, certain that the "divils" were trapping her again. "What matter whether you approve of it or not? That doesn't make it any better. Let ye be young while ye can, Jim," she counseled, laying a rocky hand on Jim's knee. "Ye'll be married long enough."

But, of course, Eileen and himself did not share her views. On their evening walks they usually passed through one of the new developments, glanced into half-built houses with the enthusiasm of the children who played cowboys and Indians in them; chatted with young husbands digging in little patches of garden that were mainly builders' rubble, and let themselves be invited in for cups of tea by young couples in all the pride and joy of recent possession. They saw nothing of the ugliness of it. They saw only the newness of everything as though it were life itself renewed; the way the evening sunlight brought up the freshness of the paint, the whiteness of the curtains, the tender green of the new grass. Later in the evening Eileen would say, shaking her head: "I didn't think the curtains were right in the big corner windows, Jim, did you?" and Jim would know she had furnished the house in her own mind.

That year Jim suggested that he and Eileen should take their holidays together. This didn't suit Mrs. Clery at all. She was sure it would give Eileen a bad name. Mrs. Clery was all for their being young while they could, but only as long as they were being young under her eye. Jim knew it wasn't Eileen's good name that her mother worried about at all, but the possibility that their holiday might start something she could not control. He had his way; they went to a seaside place north of Dublin, and walked and swam and sun-bathed to their hearts' content for a fortnight, going into the city when it rained.

On their way home, looking out at the Galtee Mountains from

the window of their carriage, he said: "Next time we go on holidays like that, we should be married. It's not the same thing."

"No, Jim, it isn't," she agreed. "But what can we do?"

"What's to stop us getting married?" he asked with a smile.

"Now?" she asked in alarm. "But what would we do with our mothers?"

"What we do with them now," he said with a shrug.

"You mean get married and go on the way we're going?"

"Why not? Of course, it's not what we want, but it's better than nothing."

"But suppose—well, Jim, you know yourself there might be children."

"I should hope so," he replied. "We can cross that bridge when we come to it. But anyhow, there's no particular reason we should have kids yet."

"But Jim," she asked timidly, "wouldn't people talk?"

"Do you think they don't talk now?"

Jim was like that, and what Jim thought his mother would think, regardless of public opinion. She, of course, had seen nothing wrong with their going on holidays together, and Eileen, who had felt rather doubtful of it herself, now knew that she was right. She felt he was probably right now too, but she wasn't sure.

The more she thought of it, the more she felt he was, though her reasons were of a different kind. Jim didn't want to wait; he didn't want to grow old and sour in expectation of the day when they could get married; he wanted something, however little it might be, of the pleasure of marriage while they were still young enough to enjoy it. Eileen thought of it in a more mystical way, as a sort of betrothal which would bind them to one another, whatever life might have in store for them. She knew it was too much to hope that she and Jim would both be set free at the same time; one would be bound to be free long before the other, and then the real temptation would begin.

But she knew that even this she would not get without a fight with her mother. Mrs. Clery was conventional to the heart, and besides she knew what happened in marriage. Eileen was very sweet and gentle now, but Eileen as wife or mother would be an altogether different proposition and one an old lady might be unable to handle at all.

"What a thing you'd do!" Mrs. Clery gasped with one hand on her hip. "What sort of marriage would that be? Him living there and you living here! You'd have the whole town laughing at you."

"I don't really see what they'd have to laugh at, Mammy," Eileen said earnestly. "Any more than they have now."

"Go off with him!" her mother said brokenly. "Go on off with him! I'd sooner go to the workhouse than be disgraced by ye."

"But, Mammy," persisted Eileen, laughing in spite of herself, "we won't do anything to disgrace you, and you won't have to go to the workhouse or anywhere else."

Mrs. Grahame was upset too, but it was her pride that was hurt. What the neighbors would say did not worry her at all, but it seemed to her that it was her dependence on Jim that forced him into this caricature of a marriage. If by getting out of his way she could have made it easier for him, she would cheerfully have gone into the workhouse. But when Jim explained that even if he agreed to her doing so, it would change nothing regarding Eileen and her mother, she saw that he was right. When next Eileen called, Mrs. Grahame embraced her and muttered: "Ye poor children! Ye poor, distracted children!"

"You don't think we're doing wrong, Mrs. Grahame?" Eileen asked, beginning to be tearful herself.

"Sure, how could you be doing wrong, child?" Mrs. Grahame exclaimed angrily. "Why would ye care what anybody thinks? People who never sacrificed a thing in their lives!"

Then Mrs. Clery threw a fit of the sulks, would not speak to Jim when he called, and finally refused to attend what she called "the mock wedding." Mrs. Clery had little experience of that sort of thing but she did know when she had been tricked, and she had been tricked by Jim. He had come to the house as a friend and stolen her only daughter from under her eyes. As for all this talk of putting her first, she didn't believe a word of it. A man who would do what he had done would think nothing of putting arsenic in her cup of tea.

Before she left for the church that morning, Eileen went in to her mother and asked gently: "Mammy, won't you even wish me luck?" But all her mother said was "Go away, you bold thing!"

"I'll be back tomorrow night in time to get your supper, Mammy," Eileen said meekly.

"You needn't come back at all," said her mother.

Eileen was very upset, but Mrs. Grahame only scoffed at it when they said goodbye outside the church.

"Ah, she'll get over it, child," she said. "Old people are all lick alike. I'm the same myself, if the truth was known. I'll see her on the way home and give her a bit of my mind."

"And, Mrs. Grahame, if you wouldn't mind making her an egg flip, she'd be easier to talk to," Eileen said earnestly. "She's very fond of egg flips, and she likes a lot of whiskey in them."

"I'll give her an egg flip," said Mrs. Grahame, suddenly light-hearted because her own savage jealousy melted in the thought of comforting another old woman in her tantrums. She had a job on her hands, even with the egg flip.

"Don't talk to me, Ma'am!" cried Mrs. Clery. "Young people today are all the same; all selfish, all for pleasure."

"How can you say it, Mrs. Clery?" Mrs. Grahame asked indignantly. "There isn't a better daughter in Ireland. I'd be the last to criticize Jim, but I only wish I had one like her."

"And when the children start coming?" asked Mrs. Clery, looking at her as if she were out of her mind.

"You reared one yourself."

" 'Tisn't alike, Ma'am," said Mrs. Clery and refused to be comforted. She was intelligent enough to realize that the presence of another baby in the house might rob her of some of the attention to which she felt entitled, and might even result in her being totally deprived of her privileges. Young people today were so selfish!

After their one-day honeymoon, Jim and Eileen obediently returned to their duties as though they had never been married at all. Yet Eileen, when you met her on the road, was exceedingly lighthearted and lightheaded, sporting her ring like any young bride. She needed all the joy her new position gave her because her mother had been shrewd enough in her summing up of what the neighbors' attitude would be. The marriage had become a matter of scandalous jokes, and remained so as long as it lasted. Even from intimate friends, Eileen got little jabs that reminded her of her anomalous wifehood. It wasn't that the neighbors were uncharitable, but their feelings about marriage, like their feelings about death, had a certain fierceness that was obvious even in their dislike of second marriages. This marriage that seemed to end at the church door was a mockery of all they believed in, so they took their revenge as people will whose dearest beliefs have been slighted.

Jim affected not to notice the scandal: he had his mother's curious imperviousness to public opinion, and he dropped in on Eileen as though nothing in particular could be said against him. Eileen dropped in rather more frequently on him and his mother, and Jim and she went off for a fortnight in the summer to Kerry or Connemara. It took Mrs. Clery a full year to get used to it, and all that time she watched Eileen closely, expecting her each week to show signs of pregnancy. Perhaps it was fortunate that there were none. Heaven alone knows what she might have done.

Then Mrs. Grahame fell ill, and Jim nursed her by day while Eileen took over from him at night. She was dying, and in the intervals of consciousness, she molded Eileen's hands with her own and said: "I always wanted a daughter, and I had my wish. I had my wish. Ye'll be happy now that ye have the house to yerselves. You'll look after Jim for me?"

"I'll look after him for you," Eileen said, and on the night when his mother died, she let him sleep on.

"I thought I'd better not wake you, Jim," she said when she roused him next morning. "You were so tired and Mammy went so peacefully. . . . That's the way she'd have wished it, Jim," she added gravely when she saw his look of surprise.

"I dare say you're right, Eileen," he agreed.

But their troubles were far from being at an end. When they proposed to shift into Jim's house, Mrs. Clery raised more of a hullabaloo than she had raised over the marriage.

"Is it up among strangers?" she cried aghast.

"Strangers half a mile away, Mammy?" Eileen exclaimed, still unable to conceal a laugh at her mother's extraordinary reception of every new proposal.

"Half a mile?" her mother echoed dully. " 'Tis a mile."

"And you think your old friends would desert you?" asked Eileen.

"I wouldn't ask them," her mother replied with dignity. "I couldn't sleep in a place where I wouldn't hear the sound of the trams. Jim's mother died in her own house. Oh, my, isn't it a queer thing he wouldn't let me die in mine!"

And once more Jim and Eileen had to resign themselves to frustration. They could offer no adequate substitute for the soothing squeak of the trams climbing Summerhill from the city, and as Eileen saw, it would be folly for them to give up Jim's excellent house, which they would need later on, and come to share her own tiny cottage with a cranky mother-in-law.

Instead, they played at being married. On a couple of evenings each week, Eileen would give her mother supper early, and then come to Jim's house and have supper ready for him when he got in from the shop. When she heard his key in the lock, she ran to the front door to meet him in her white housecoat, and he would let on to be suitably astonished at seeing her. As they went in, she would point silently to the big fire she had lit in the living room, and they would have supper together and read or talk till he saw her home coming on to midnight. Yet, even with the extra work, it gave them both a deep pleasure to make the big bed that Eileen never slept in except as a visitor, to wash up together, or best of all, to entertain some friends, just as though Eileen did not, like Cinderella, have to fly back at midnight to her old part as daughter and nurse. Someday, they felt, the house would really be theirs, and she would open the door in the morning to milkman and breadman.

But this was not how things happened. Instead, Jim fell seriously ill, and rather than consent to the conflict which he knew this would set up in Eileen's mind between her duty to him and her duty to her mother, he chose to go to hospital. Two years after his mother's death, he died there.

Something seemed to happen to Eileen at this point that made even her mother afraid. There was no argument between them as to what she should do. She shut up her own cottage, and her mother joined her in Jim's house, where she received his relatives. The body had been taken to the church, and when Jim's family came, Eileen had lunch ready for them, and chatted as she served, as though the trouble had been theirs rather than hers. It was a cold lunch, and she was full of apologies. At the graveside while they wept, she showed no sign of tears. When the grave had been covered over Jim and his mother, she stood there silently, her head bowed, and Jim's aunt, an enormous woman, came up and took her two hands.

"You're a great little girl," she whispered huskily. " 'Twon't be forgotten for you."

"But, Auntie," Eileen replied, "that's the way Jim would have liked it. It makes me feel close to him, and it won't be too long till we're together again. Once Mammy goes, there'll be nothing to keep me."

There was something about her words, and her dry-eyed air and her still youthful face, that the other woman found disconcerting.

"Ah, nonsense, child!" she said lightly. "We all feel that way.

You'll be happy yet, and you'll deserve it. One of these days you'll have a houseful of your own."

"Oh, no, Auntie," Eileen replied with a sweet smile that was curiously knowledgeable and even condescending, as though Jim's aunt were too much of a child to understand. "You know yourself I could never find another husband like Jim. People can't be as happy as that a second time, you know. That would be too much to ask."

And relatives and even neighbors began to realize that Eileen was only telling the truth; that in spite of everything she had been intensely happy, happy in some way they could not understand, and that what had seemed to them a mockery of marriage had indeed been one so complete and satisfying that beside it, even by their standards, a woman might think everything else in the world a mere shadow.

The Cheat

THE ONLY THING that distinguished Dick Gordon from the other young men of my time in Cork was his attitude to religion. As an engineer he seemed to feel that he could not afford to believe in anything but the second law of thermodynamics: according to him, this contained everything a man required to know.

For years he courted a girl called Joan Twomey, and everyone expected he would marry her and settle down as most men of his kind do. Usually, they are of a serious disposition and settle down more easily than the rest of humanity. You often see them in their later years, carrying round the collecting bag at twelve-o'clock Mass, and wonder what has happened all their wild dreams of free thought and social justice. Marriage is the great leveler.

But Joan's mother died, and she had to do the housekeeping for a father and two younger sisters, so she became serious too, and there was no more reckless behavior in the little seaside house they rented in summer. She was afraid of marrying a man who did not believe in anything and would probably bring up his children the same way. She was wrong in this, because Dick was much too tolerant a man to deprive his worst enemy of the pleasure of believing in eternal damnation, much less his wife, but Joan's seriousness had developed to the dimensions of spiritual pride and she gave him up as she might have given up some pleasure for Lent.

Dick was mystified and hurt: it was the first shock to his feeling of the basic reasonableness of life; but he did not allow it to change him. After all, his brother Tom was an ex-cleric and he had been worked on by experts. Some time later he met a girl called Barbara Hough who was a teacher in a Protestant school and started to walk out with her. On the surface Barbara was much more his style. She was good-looking and urbane, vaguely atheistic and left-wing in her views, and she thought that all Irish people, Catholic and Protestant, were quite insane on the subject of religion. All the same, for a young fellow of good Catholic family to take up with a Protestant at all was a challenge, and Barbara, who was a high-spirited girl, enjoyed it and made the most of it. His friends were amused and his family alarmed. Of course, Dick could get a dispensation if Barbara signed the paper guaranteeing that their children would be brought up as Catholics, but would Barbara, who was a rector's daughter, agree to it? Characteristically, when his brother Tom asked him this, Dick only smiled and said, "Funny, isn't it? I never asked her." He would probably have been quite safe in doing so, for though Barbara herself did not recognize it, she had all the loneliness of one brought up in a minority religion, always feeling that she was missing something, and much of Dick's appeal for her was that he was a Prince Charming who had broken the magic circle in which she felt she would be trapped until the day she died. But Dick did not ask her. Instead he proposed a quiet register-office marriage in London, and she was so moved by his consideration for her that she did not even anticipate what the consequences might be.

You see, it was part of Dick's simplicity of mind that he could not realize that there were certain perfectly simple things you couldn't do without involving yourself in more trouble than they were worth, or if he did see it, he underrated its importance. A few of his old friends stood by him, but even they had to admit that there was an impossible streak in him. When Barbara was having a baby the family deputed his brother Tom to warn him of what he was doing. Tom was tall, good-looking, dreamy, and morbidly sensitive. He did not want to approach Dick at all, but seeing that he was the nearest thing to a priest in the family, he felt that it might be his duty.

"You know what people are going to think, Dick," he said with a stammer.

"The same as they think now, I suppose," Dick replied with his gentle smile.

"This is different, Dick."

"How, Tom?"

"This concerns a third party, you see," said Tom, too embarrassed even to mention such things as babies to his brother.

"And a fourth and fifth, I hope," Dick said cheerfully. "It's a natural result of marriage, you know. And children do take after their parents, for the first few years anyway."

"Not in this country, they don't," Tom said ruefully. "I suppose there are historical reasons for it," he added, being a great student of history.

"There are historical reasons for everything in this country, Tom," said Dick with a jolly laugh. "But because some old fool believes in the fairies for good historical reasons is no excuse for bringing up my kids the same way."

"Ah, well, it's not as foolish as all that, Dick," said Tom, looking more miserable than ever. "It's poetic, or fanciful, or whatever you like, but it's what we were brought up to believe, and our fathers and grandfathers before us."

"And the monks told us that Ireland was such a holy country that we'd have the end of the world eight years before anywhere else. . . . I'm not sure what the advantage was supposed to be. . . . I don't suppose you still believe that?"

"Why would I?" asked Tom. "It's not an article of faith."

"It was an article of faith to you and me, and I wouldn't have liked to be the fellow that disbelieved it," said Dick with a sniff. "Anyway, it's no worse than the rest of the nonsense we listen to. That sort of thing is looked on as childishness everywhere else today, and it'll be looked on as childishness here, too, in your lifetime and mine. In fifteen years' time people will only laugh at it."

That was Dick all out, entirely reasonable and tolerant, and yet as big a misfit as if he had two heads. How could any responsible superior recommend a man as pig-headed as that for promotion? The sensible thing for Dick would have been to emigrate and start all over again in England or America where apparitions were not so highly regarded, but there was a dogged, cynical streak in him that derived a sort of morose pleasure from seeing some devotee of apparitions promoted over his head and making a mess of some perfectly simple job.

He had a number of friends who sympathized with his views and who met at his little house in the College Road on Sundays to discuss the latest piece of jobbery in the university. They grew mad about it, but Dick's attitude of amused tolerance rarely varied. At most he sighed: it was as though he saw things that they could not see. One old schoolteacher called Murphy used to grow furious with him over this. He was a gloomy-looking, handsome man who was at the same time very pious and very anticlerical. Passion made him break out in angles, as when he called his old friends "Mister."

"Mister Gordon," he shouted one night, "you're out of your mind. A hundred years from now the descendants of those hobblers will still be seeing apparitions behind every bush."

"They won't, Ned," Dick said with a smile. He was particularly fond of Murphy and enjoyed seeing him in a rage.

"What'll stop them, Mister Gordon?"

"Facts, Ned!"

"Facts!"

"Facts impose their own logic, Ned. They're imposing it now, at this very minute, here and elsewhere, even though we may not see it. It's only an elaboration of skills. Skills here are still too rudimentary. But women are beginning to do men's work, and they'll have to think men's thoughts. You can't control that, you know. The world you're talking about is finished. In ten or fifteen years' time it'll be a joke. Simple facts will destroy it."

II

That was all very well. Dick might have a good eye for what was going on in the outside world, but he had no eye at all for what was going on in his own very house. One evening, after they had been married for ten years, Dick was at home and Barbara out with their son, Tom, when there was a knock at the door. Outside was a young priest; a tall, thin, good-looking young man with a devil-may-care eye.

"Can I come in?" he asked, as though he had no doubt whatever of his welcome.

"Oh, come in, come in!" said Dick with a thin smile. He hated those embarrassing occasions when people with more self-confidence than manners enquired how his soul was doing. He was a friendly man and did not like to have to appear rude or ungrateful.

"Mrs. G. out?" the priest asked cheerfully.

"Yes, gone into town for some messages," Dick said resignedly. "She won't be long."

"Ah, it gives us the chance of a little chat," said the priest, pulling at the legs of his trousers.

"Look, father, I don't want a little chat, as you call it," Dick said appealingly. "This town is full of people who want little chats with me, and they can't understand that I don't appreciate them. I gave up religion when I was eighteen, and I have no intention in the world of going back to it."

"Did I ask you to go back to it?" the priest asked with an air of consternation. "I wasn't expecting to see you at all, man! I came here to talk to your wife. You are Mrs. Gordon's husband, aren't you?"

"Yes," Dick replied, somewhat surprised by the priest's tone.

"Well, she's been receiving instruction. Didn't you know that?"

Dick was a hard man to catch off balance, and when he replied he did not even sound surprised.

"Instruction? No. I didn't."

"Crumbs, I'm after saying the wrong thing again!" the priest said angrily. "I shouldn't be left out without a male nurse. Look, I'm terribly sorry. I'll come back another time."

"Oh, as you're here, you may as well stay," Dick said amiably. It was partly pride, partly pity. He could see that the priest was genuinely distressed.

"Another time! Another time!"

"Who will I say called?" Dick asked as he saw him to the door.

"The name is Hogan. Mr. Gordon, I wouldn't have wished it for a hundred pounds."

"It was hardly your fault," Dick said with a friendly smile.

But as he closed the door the smile faded and he found himself cold and shaking. He poured himself a drink but it only made him feel sick. Nothing that could have happened him would have been quite so bad as this. He had been betrayed shamelessly and treacherously and he could already see himself as the laughingstock of the city. A man's loneliness is his strength and only a wife can really destroy him because only she can understand his loneliness.

He heard her key in the lock and wished he had left before her return. He liked to be master of himself and now he feared he had no control over what he did or said.

"Dick!" she called in her clear ringing voice and opened the living-room door. "Is something wrong?" she asked as he did not turn round. "One moment, Tom!" she said to the child in the hall. "Run upstairs and take your things off. I'll call you when tea is ready. Don't argue now, sweetheart. Mummy is busy." She closed the door behind her and approached him. "I suppose Father Hogan called," she added in her weary well-bred voice. "Was that it? You should know I intended to tell you. I wanted to make up my own mind first." Still he did not reply and she burst out into a wail. "Oh, Dick, I've tried to tell you so often and I didn't have the courage."

She knew the moment he looked at her that she had fooled herself; persuaded herself that he was dull and tolerant and gentle and that nothing she did to him would affect their relationship. It is the weak spot in the cheat, man and woman.

"You hadn't the courage," he repeated dully. "But you had the courage to make a fool of me before your clerical friends."

"I didn't, Dick," she said hotly. "But you know yourself it's something I can't discuss with you. It's a subject you can't be reasonable about."

The word "reasonable" stung him.

"Is that what you call being reasonable?" he asked bitterly. "I should have been reasonable and made you conform before I married you. I should have been reasonable and brought Tom up as my family wanted him brought up. Every day of my life I had to accept humiliation on your account when I could have been reasonable about it all. And then you don't even have the courage to discuss with me what you're going to do or what the consequences will be for Tom. You prefer to bring him up believing that his father is damned! There's reasonableness for you!"

"But I'd discuss it with you now, Dick, if only you'd listen to me patiently." She began to wring her hands. "It's not my fault if I can't live without believing in something."

"In Heaven," he said cynically.

"In Heaven, if you like. Anyway, in something for you and me and Tom. I was brought up to believe in it, and I threw it away because I didn't value it, and now I need it—maybe because I haven't anything else. If only you wouldn't tell me it's all just nonsense!"

"Why should I tell you anything?" he asked. "You have better advisers now."

In fact, he never did discuss it with her. He even allowed Tom to go to Mass with her and attend the local monks' school without protest. The older Tom was Barbara's biggest surprise. She knew that in arguments with Dick he had taken her side, but when they discussed it together he seemed to judge her far more severely than Dick. It was curious, because the diffidence, the slight stammer, the charming smile did not change.

"Of course, Barbara, as a Catholic I am naturally pleased, for your sake and the kid's, but as Dick's brother I can't help feeling that it's unfortunate."

"But don't you think it may help Dick to see things a bit differently in the course of time?"

"No, Barbara, I don't," he said with a gentle, almost pitying smile.

"But, Tom, I don't see that it should make any more difference than it does between you and Dick."

"Marriage is different, Barbara," he said, and she didn't even see anything peculiar about being told of marriage by a man who had almost been given up by his own family as unmarriageable. "People don't know it, but they marry for protection as much as anything else, and sometimes they have to be protected at the cost of other people's principles."

"And you think Dick needs protection?" she asked wonderingly.

"I think Dick needs a great deal of protection, Barbara," he said with an accusing look.

There was a good deal of talk in the city, much of it ill-natured, though on the whole it did Dick less harm than good. He had ceased to be an active force for evil and become a mere figure of fun, as vulnerable to ridicule as any University intriguer. It had even become safe to promote him.

But it was old Ned Murphy who said the thing that stuck. He and two of Dick's other friends were drinking in a public house one night, and the others—Cashman and Enright, who was a bit of a smart aleck—were making good-humored fun of Dick. Murphy alone did not laugh at all. He scowled and rubbed his forehead with his first till it grew inflamed.

"It's like your wife having an affair with another man," he said sourly, and because he was unmarried, Cashman and Enright laughed louder. Still there was something uncomfortably apt about the analogy; both were married men and there had been a small scandal about Enright's wife, who had had an affair with a commercial traveler. They knew there was always another man, a shadowy figure, not real as they were, and they dreaded his presence in the background.

"Still, you'd think he'd have given her some cause," said Cashman.

"He gave her plenty of cause," said Murphy.

"But they always got on well together."

"They got on all right," Murphy admitted. "But she must have had a terrible life with him. She's a religious girl."

"Lots of religious girls marry men like that, though," said Enright, as though he were following the conversation, which he wasn't.

"Not men like Dick Gordon," Murphy said broodingly. "He's an optimist, and optimism is the plague of a religious mind. Dick has no notion how intolerable life can be. A man like that doesn't even believe in evil."

III

Dick's optimism was tested severely enough a few years later. He was ill, and word was going round that he would never be well again.

This put half Cork in a flutter, because everyone who had ever had a conversation with him seemed to feel a personal responsibility for seeing that he was converted, and those who might see him were warmly advised of what they should do and say. His boss put a car at the disposal of his friends so that they could rush a priest to his bedside at any hour of the day or night. "Vultures are a breed of bird that has always fascinated me, though I thought they were supposed to be extinct," said Ned Murphy.

Barbara was exasperated by all the hysteria, more particularly because it put her in such a false position, and her replies became shorter. "I'm afraid it is a matter I never discuss with my husband," she said. "There are certain things that are too personal even for a wife." Even that did not put people off the subject. They said that converts were never really like their own people.

One rainy evening Dick was alone in the house, trying to read, when a strange priest called. He was tall and fat and very grave.

"Mr. Gordon?" he said.

"Yes," said Dick.

"Can I come in for a moment?"

"Oh, certainly. Sit down."

"You don't know who I am, Mr. Gordon," the priest said jovially as he took a chair. "I know quite a lot about you, though. I'm the parish priest, Father Ryan."

Dick nodded.

"Mr. Gordon, I want to talk to you about your soul," he said with a change of tone.

Dick smiled and lit a cigarette. He had been through it all so often.

"Surely, among your congregation you could find plenty of others," he suggested mildly.

"Not many in such danger, shall we say," the priest replied with a smile. Something about the smile shook Dick. It seemed to radiate a sort of cold malice which was new to him.

"Considering that we've only just met, you seem to know a lot about the state of my soul," Dick said with the same weary sarcasm.

"Mr. Gordon," the priest said, raising his hand, "I wasn't speaking only of your spiritual danger. Mr. Gordon, you're a very sick man."

Dick rose and opened the door for him.

"Father Ryan, you're concerning yourself with things that have nothing to do with you," he said icily. "Now, do you mind getting out of my house?"

"Your arrogance won't last long, Mr. Gordon," the priest said. "You're dying of cancer."

"You heard me," Dick said menacingly.

"You have less than three months to live."

"All the more reason I shouldn't be persecuted by busybodies like you," Dick said with sudden anger. "Now get out before I throw you out."

He scarcely raised his voice, but anger was so rare with him that it had a sinister quality that overawed the priest.

"You'll regret this," he said.

"Probably," Dick said between his teeth. "I'll regret that I didn't treat you as you deserve."

Afterward he went back to his book, but he was even more incapable of reading or of understanding what he read. Something about the priest's tone had upset him. He was himself almost devoid of malice and had shrugged off the opposition to himself as mere foolishness, but this was something more and worse than foolishness. This was foolishness going bad, foolishness turning into naked evil. And Dick, as Ned Murphy had said, did not really believe in evil.

When Barbara came in he was still sitting in darkness before the fire, brooding.

"Hello, dear," she said with false brightness. "All alone?"

"Except for a clerical gentleman who just called," he said with an air of amusement.

"Oh, dear!" she said in distress. "Who was it?"

"His name is Ryan. A rather unusual character."

"What did he want?"

"Oh, just to tell me I had cancer and had less than three months to live," Dick said bitterly.

"Oh, God, no, Dick! He didn't say that?" she cried, and began to weep.

He looked at her in surprise and concern and then got up.

"Oh, don't worry about that, Babs!" he said with a shrug. "It's only their stock in trade, you know. You should have heard the pleasure with which he said it! Where would they be without their skeleton to brandish?"

It was only the sort of thing he had said to her in the early days of their marriage and had not said since her conversion. She did not know whether he really meant it or said it just to comfort her. After their years of married life he was still gentle and considerate. His brother Tom was little help to her.

"I'll only have to try and be at the house more," he said gloomily. "This thing could happen again."

"But can't we complain to the bishop about it?" she said angrily.

"I'm afraid that wouldn't do much good, Barbara. The bishop would be more likely to take Father Ryan's side. By the way, have you confidence in that doctor of yours?"

"Dr. Cullen? Oh, I suppose he did what he could."

"I don't mean that," Tom said patiently. "Are you sure he didn't go to Father Ryan himself?"

"Oh, God, Tom!" she said. "What sort of people are they?"

"Much like people anywhere else, I suppose," he said despondently.

After this, she dreaded leaving Dick alone. She knew now the hysteria that surrounded them and knew that those who indulged in it were ruthless in a way that Dick would never understand.

One day she was upstairs chatting with him when the doorbell rang. She answered it and saw Father Hogan outside. He was now parish priest in a village ten miles outside the town, and they saw less of him. He was one of the few friends she had whom Dick seemed to like.

"Come in here, please, Father," she said, and led him into the little front room. She closed the door and spoke in a low voice. "Father, I can't have Dick persecuted now."

"Persecuted?" he asked in surprise. "Who's persecuting him?"

"You know what he believes," she said. "I daresay he's wrong, and if you catch him in a moment of weakness he may say he's wrong, but it will be his weakness, not him."

"What the hell are you talking about?" he asked angrily. "Are you out of your mind? I rang him up when I heard he was sick, and he asked me to call for a drink. I'm not going to do anything to him —except maybe give him conditional absolution when it's all over, and that won't be on his account. There are people in this town who'd try to refuse him Christian burial. You don't know it, but you wouldn't like it. No more would his family."

"You had nothing to do with the man who told him he was dying?"

"Why?" he asked quietly. "Did someone do that?"

"The parish priest did it."

"And am I to be held responsible for every fool and lout who happens to wear a soutane?" he asked bitterly. "He asked me in for a drink, Barbara, and I'm going to have it with him, whatever you may think. . . ." Then with one of his quick changes of mood he asked, "Did it upset him?"

"Fortunately, he didn't believe it."

"Didn't believe it, or pretended not to believe it?" he asked shrewdly and then threw the question away. "Ah, how would you know? I won't disturb him, Barbara," he added gently. "I wish I was as sure of my own salvation as I am of his."

"So do I—now," she said, and he knew as though he were inside her that she was regretting the weakness of years before and wishing that she could go into the dark with her husband as they had both imagined it when they were young and in love. It was the only way that would have meant anything to Dick now. But he was a good priest and he could not afford to brood on what it all meant. He still had a duty to the living as well as to the friend who was about to die.

The Weeping Children

JOE SAUNDERS AND HIS WIFE, Brigid, had been married a year when they had their first baby—a little girl they called Nance, after Brigid's mother. Brigid was Irish, and Joe had always had a feeling that there must be some Irish blood in himself. She was a Catholic, and, though Joe was an unbeliever, he liked it in her, and encouraged her to put up holy pictures and statues all over the house. He even went to Mass with her occasionally, but she said he put her off her prayers with his air of devotion, which made him laugh. She often made him laugh, and he liked it, because he had a natural gravity that turned easily to melancholy and even tears. She had good breeding as well, and he liked that too, though she sometimes upset him by the way she unconsciously patronized his mother and sisters. They were common, and he knew they were common, but he didn't like it to be rubbed in. Brigid had kept her girlish gaiety and her delight in flirting shamelessly with any man who fancied her. It amused Joe, because for all her charm, he knew the wild, chaste, innocent streak in her, and realized that the smart operators would get absolutely nowhere with her.

After Nance's birth Joe felt that life had done him proud. There were times when he saw everything with a sort of double vision, as though he were not only doing whatever he was doing—like pushing the pram round the estate, or creeping into the back room at night to see that the baby was covered—but watching himself do it, as though he were someone in a film or a book, and the conjunction of the two visions gave the thing itself an intense stereoscopic quality. He was sure that this must be what people meant when they talked of happiness.

But he realized that it was different for Brigid. Though at times she could forget herself and play with the baby like a girl with a doll, she was often gloomy, tearful, and irritable. This was not like her. Joe's great friend, Jerry Cross, called it something like postpartum psychosis, and though Joe had no great faith in the long names Jerry liked to give things, he accepted his advice and took Brigid for a week to Brighton. It did her good but only for a short while. Joe—a sensitive man—sometimes thought he knew exactly how she felt—a wild girl with a vivacious temperament, who loved outings and parties, trapped by a morsel of humanity who took everything and gave nothing.

Joe was attentive to the point of officiousness, seeing that she went to the cinema and visited friends. But even to old friends she had changed, and had taken a positive dislike to Jerry Cross. Though Jerry was great at giving women little presents, he didn't seem to like them much, and now Brigid chose to interpret this as dislike of herself. With a sort of schoolgirl pertness that drove Joe to despair she mocked Cross about his overheated bachelor flat, his expensive gramophone and collection of records, and his liqueur cabinet that always seemed to contain some new exotic drink that Jerry would press on his visitors, rubbing his hands and saying in his anxious way, "It's not bad, is it? I mean, it really is not bad. You think that, too, Joe." Twice, to protect Cross, Joe had to reprove her, and though he did it gently, it cut him to the heart to have to do it at all.

"Why can't you be nicer to Jerry?" he asked as they were going home one night. "He hasn't so many friends."

"He has no friends at all, if you ask me," Brigid said coldly. "He's too bloody selfish to afford them."

"Selfish?" Joe exclaimed, stopping dead. "A man who put a check for two hundred quid on my mantelpiece while I was out of the room!"

"We know all that," Brigid said contemptuously. "Damn well he knew you wouldn't take it."

"He knew more than I did," Joe said, resuming his walk. "Anyway, it wasn't the money that mattered at the time. It was his confidence in me. It gave me confidence in myself. I tell you, Brigid, there are things between men that you'll never understand, not till the day you die."

But argument had no effect on Brigid except perhaps to give her fresh grounds for spite. One evening at Joe's house, Cross was boasting innocently of some shady deal he had refused to be connected with, and Brigid, with mock admiration, drew him skillfully out. It was one of Cross's little weaknesses that he liked to think himself a really shrewd businessman—"a bloody dreamer" was how an uncle had described him to Joe.

"You always play it safe, Jerry, don't you?" she asked at last.

"What's that, Brigid?" Cross asked eagerly, too pleased with himself to be aware of her malice.

"Brigid!" Joe said warningly.

"Anyone who had anything to do with you would want to watch out," she said.

Cross got up and clutched the lapels of his coat as though he were about to make a speech. It suddenly struck Joe that he was a little man who lived in expectation of having to make speeches—unpleasant ones, in his own defense.

"I assure you, Brigid, that nobody who had anything to do with me ever had to watch out, as you put it," he said overloudly, speaking as it were to a faraway audience. "I do play it safe, though. You're right there, I do. And I'll play it safer for the future by not calling here, as I have been doing."

Then he made for the door, and Joe, holding his coat for him, realized that he was shivering violently. Joe opened the door, put his arm round Cross's shoulder, and walked slowly to the gate with him. Cross walked close to him, so as not to break the embrace, and yet Joe knew he did not feel it in a homosexual way. The estate road went uphill to the bus stop on the tree-shaded suburban road, and the two men walked together like sweethearts till they reached it. Then Joe took Cross's hand in his own two.

"Try not to think of it, Jerry," he said in a low voice. "She doesn't even know what she's saying. The girl is sick in her mind."

"She is, Joe, she is, she is," Cross said with pathetic eagerness. "I thought it from the first, but now I'm sure. I'm sorry I was so sharp with her."

"You weren't, Jerry; not so sharp as I'd have been."

It was only when he had waved goodbye to Cross from the pavement that Joe gave way to tears. He walked slowly up and down the road till the fit had passed. As he entered the house, Brigid was waiting for him in the sitting room, sitting exactly as when he had left.

"Come in, Joe," she said quietly. "We have to talk."

"I'm sorry, Brigid, but I don't want to talk," he said, feeling sure that if he did he would break down again.

"I want to talk," she said in a flat tone. "It may be the last chance we'll get. I'll have to clear out."

"What's that?" he asked incredulously.

"I have to clear out," she said again, and he knew that she meant it.

It was at moments like these that all the wise passivity in Joe came on top. In his time he had been humiliated, hurt so that the pain had never left him, but he knew you had to give in to it, let the pain wash over you, if you didn't want it to destroy you.

"Why do you think you have to clear out, dear?" he asked mildly, taking a chair inside the door and joining his hands before him.

"Because I don't want to destroy your life the way I destroyed my own," she said.

"Well, I should have something to say to that," he said. "So should the baby, of course. Unless you're proposing to take her with you."

"I'm not," she said with artificial casualness. "I daresay your mother can look after her."

"I daresay she could," he said calmly. "But it's not my idea of what a child needs."

"At least your mother won't insult your friends," Brigid said bitterly. He knew then that she had no illusions about her behavior to Cross, and his heart softened.

"You mean more to me than any of my friends, dear," he said. "Even Jerry—and Heaven knows, he means quite a lot. But why do you have to do things like that? They hurt you as much as they hurt other people. What is it, Brigid? Why don't you trust me? Is it another man?"

For a moment Joe thought she really was going to strike him. Then the humor of it seemed to dawn on her, and she gave a weak grin.

"You have a very poor opinion of yourself, haven't you?" she asked pertly. "Even that jenny-ass Cross wouldn't think of a silly thing like that. I never looked at the side of the road a man walked at since I married you."

There was no mistaking the absolute truthfulness of that, and again he felt the sense of relief, and with it the old tenderness and admiration.

"Naturally, that's what I hoped, dear," he said. "And damn it all, nothing else matters."

"Not even the ones I met before I met you?" she asked mockingly, and her tone struck him cold again.

"I see," he said. "You mean there was someone else?"

"Naturally," she said angrily. And then, as though reading his thoughts, she reverted to her tone of exasperated amusement. "Now, I suppose you think I'm breaking my heart over him? I am, like hell! I hope to God I never lay eyes on him again. I wish I could say the same thing about his child."

"His child?" Joe repeated stupidly. Now he felt that the world really was collapsing about him. "You mean you had a child already?"

"What do you think brought me over to London in the first place?" she asked reasonably.

"I don't know," Joe said with simple dignity. "I just thought you might have been telling me the truth when you said you came over for a job. I suppose you're right to think I'm a bit simpleminded."

"I never thought you were simpleminded," she retorted with the fury of a hellcat. "I thought you were too good to be true, if you want to know what I thought."

"And you have this child where? With your people?"

"No, outside Cork," she said shortly. "I suppose I wanted her as far away as possible. And, as I'm about it, there's another thing. I pinched some of the housekeeping money to support her. After I left the job I had nothing of my own."

"You could scarcely have left the child to starve," he said lightly. "That doesn't count beside the other things."

"What other things?"

"All the lies you've told me," he said bitterly. "I didn't deserve that from you. Look, Brigid, it's no use pretending I'm not hurt—not by what you've just told me. That was your business. But you might have told me before you married me."

"So that you needn't have married me?" she asked bitterly.

"I mean nothing of the sort," said Joe. "I don't know what I should have done, but I don't think it would have come between you and me. You were unfair to me and unfair to the child. You might have trusted me as I trusted you."

"As if the two things were alike!" she retorted. "I told you I thought you were too good to be true. You weren't, but to get to know you that way I had to marry you first, and to marry you I had to tell you lies. At least, that's how it seemed to me. And a hell of a lot of good it did me!"

Joe sighed.

"Anyway, we have to think what we're to do about this child, and that's something we can't decide tonight."

"There's only one thing to do, Joe," she said. "I'll have to go back to London and get a job." She said it manfully enough, but he knew she didn't mean it. She was begging him to find some way out for her.

"We don't have to break up this house," he said with determination. "Damn it, it's our own. We can still bring her to live with us."

"But I don't want her to live with us," she said angrily. "Can't you understand? It was all a miserable bloody mistake, and I don't want to have to live with it for the rest of my life. And I don't want you to have to live with it either. It's just that I feel such a bitch, having everything in the world I want while she has nothing."

"I see that," Joe said gently. "I see it's not an easy question. We'll have to think of something, that's all."

He thought a lot about it that night, though less of what they were to do with Brigid's child than of the disaster that had over-taken his beautiful world. Again he could see himself acting, doing whatever he felt he had to do, but beyond that he could see it all as though it were happening to someone in a book or a movie. He could almost hear his own voice as if it were in the third person. " 'We'll have to think of something, that's all,' he said." And he supposed that this must be what people meant when they talked of grief.

Yet when Brigid waked him, bringing him a cup of tea in bed, it seemed to have taken nothing out of her. Unburdening herself of her secret seemed to have restored all her native liveliness, in fact.

When he got home that evening, he was astonished to see Cross waiting for him in the front room, and he knew from Cross's manner that Brigid had made her peace with him. At any other time this would have made him happy, but now it merely seemed an irrelevance. As he saw Cross off, Cross said urgently, "You won't think me interfering, Joe, but Brigid came to the office and told me about your little trouble. I guessed there was something upsetting her. I only wanted to say how sorry I am." Joe was amused at Cross's delicacy, and touched that Brigid, for all her fierce pride, had humiliated herself so abjectly before him, but this didn't seem to matter either.

"I know, Jerry, I know," he said, squeezing Cross's arm, but Cross was full of the subject.

"It's going to be terrible, however you arrange things," he said, "and I only want you to know that I'll be delighted to do anything.

Delighted! Because I have a great admiration for Brigid, Joe. You know that." Joe realized that by ways that could have been no great pleasure to her, Brigid had at last managed to pierce Cross's defenses. Being Cross, he was doing more than interceding for her. He was hiding the check on the mantelpiece.

After supper Joe said to Brigid:

"I've been thinking this thing over, dear, and I see only one way out. We have to bring the child here."

"I've been thinking it over too, and I don't see the necessity for that at all," she said hastily. "Cross thinks the same. To tell you the truth, I think 'twould be impossible for everybody."

Joe could see exactly what she was thinking about. Now that the burden of secrecy had been lifted, she had fled to the opposite extreme of self-confidence. Only a wild outburst of self-confidence could have given her the courage to go to Cross at all. But with self-confidence she had regained all her old devious personality, and was plotting like mad to retrieve as much as possible from the wreck and avoid humiliating herself before the neighbors and before Joe's decent, common working-class family.

"Not impossible," he said. "Difficult, I grant you. We've made a good many friends on the estate, and it's not going to make our position here any better. But others have had to do the same and worse."

"It's easier for a man than for a woman," Brigid said ruefully.

"It's harder for a woman because she does more to make the position she finds herself in," said Joe sternly. "It's not easy for anybody. All the same, it doesn't count compared with a child's life."

"And there's your mother to be considered," she said.

"Exactly. There's Mother, and there's Barbara and Coralie, and we know what they'll think and say. They'll make you pay, Brigid, and I'll suffer for it. But that's not the worst. The worst is that we may get the kid too late for her to be able to fit in. Still, bad as that is, it will be easier now than it would be in ten or fifteen years' time."

"I don't know, Joe," Brigid said earnestly. "I cracked up on you before because I was trying to handle it on my own. I won't crack up on you again, and I think there are a lot of things I can do without making ourselves miserable into the bargain."

"Such as?"

"Well, it was really Jerry who suggested it—getting her over here to a decent home where we can keep an eye on her, taking her on holidays with Nance, and seeing that she goes to a good school when she's old enough."

"And I suppose Jerry offered to help?"

"He did," she admitted. "He's damn decent."

"He is decent," said Joe. "All the same, he's wrong. Dead wrong." Like many gentle souls, Joe had a streak of iron in him, and when he made up his mind about something he could be very obstinate. "Jerry is a bachelor. He doesn't even know what he's talking about. You can cut off a man or woman as a loss, and feel that maybe they'll keep afloat, but you can't do that to a child. A child is too helpless. And this time, it isn't only you who have to live with the consequences. I have to live with them as well, and if anything happened that child, I'd be a murderer as well. I've got my faults, Brigid, but I'm not a murderer."

A fortnight later they were flying in from the sea over Dublin, and Joe knew that Brigid was losing her nerve. Every moment seemed to leave her more panic-stricken. When they traveled into the city on the tall, bumpy, swaying bus, she kept silent, but in the hotel room she broke down.

"Look, Joe, I can't face it," she said.

"Now, Brigid, you've done things a great deal more difficult than this," he said comfortingly.

"I haven't, Joe," she said. "You don't understand, I tell you. I can't go down to Cork tomorrow and meet people I used to know, and start inventing excuses for coming back."

"You don't have to invent excuses," he said patiently. "You're just here with your husband on a holiday—what's wrong with that?"

"And with a two-year-old baby in my arms?" she said bitterly. "I tell you, Joe, I don't give a damn what happens the child. I'm not going down."

She frightened Joe. It was as though behind this façade of a capital with its Georgian squares and flashy hotels and expensive restaurants there was a jungle of secrecy and panic. But he did not want Brigid to see how he felt about it.

"Very well, dear," he said patiently. "I'll go. I daresay your family can direct me."

"I suppose they could," she said doubtfully. "But if you have any consideration for them, you'll keep as far away from them as you can."

He knew it was unsafe to argue with her. She was close to hysteria or he would have said it was rather peculiar to have a foreigner searching in unfamiliar country for a child of his family who had already been neglected for two years.

"Very well, dear," he said. "If you say so, I shall."

The trip on the train to Cork was pleasant, and his only regret was that Brigid wasn't there to share it with him and point out the places of interest: it seemed like the waste of a good excursion. The city itself seemed pleasant enough too, and he had a good view of the river and quays from his bedroom window. Downstairs, he talked to the hotel manager, who was big-boned, deep-voiced, and amiable and threw himself into the business of getting Joe to his destination as though he had no other aim in life. "Throw" seemed the word that suited him, for he literally heaved himself across the desk, looking at a map and studying a timetable, bellowed softly to members of the staff who might help, and even called in casual passers-by. This scared Joe, who did not want his business made public too soon. It would be time enough for explanations when he returned to the hotel with a baby—a difficult moment enough, as even he realized.

But the last ten miles of his journey seemed the most difficult of all.

"It's all right, Mr. Coleman," said Joe. "I'll hire a car."

The hotel manager glanced at the clock in the hall and said in his deep voice:

"You won't hire any car. I'll take an hour off after dinner and drive you."

"That's very kind of you," whispered Joe, "but it might be better if I did take a car. You see, it's rather a delicate matter."

"Oh, sorry, I didn't mean to be inquisitive," Coleman said with a touch of resentment.

"Don't be silly!" Joe said with a laugh. "You're not being inquisitive. I haven't anything to hide, and anyhow I'd have had to tell you sooner or later. Sit down for a moment and let me explain."

The two men sat in a corner of the lounge and Joe explained. The hotel manager listened with a vague smile.

"So far as I'm concerned, I can keep my mouth shut," he said. "But don't be surprised if a lot of the staff know who you are already. If they don't know tonight they'll know tomorrow. They'll also know who your wife is. This may seem a big city to you, but it's not big enough for those who have to live in it. Mind," he added with a smile, "I wouldn't let that disturb me too much either. Will I get a cot into your room?"

"Not tonight," said Joe. "I've tried to sort this thing out. It isn't easy for a man, you know, but I don't think it would be fair to the kid to bring her back tonight, particularly with no woman around. Even if Brigid was here it would be a shock. No, I thought I'd go to this house first, and let the kid get to know me before I bring her back."

"Tomorrow I have the whole morning clear," said Coleman.

"No, I didn't mean it that way either," said Joe. "I can afford to hire a car. Damn it, having come all this way, I can't be stopped by the hire of a car."

"No reason you should unless you want to," Coleman said gruffly. "I think you're wise not to bring her back tonight, though. I'll see you in the lounge after dinner. I'd stick to the roast beef, if I were you."

After dinner the two men set off in Coleman's old car. After a few minutes Coleman spoke.

"This isn't an aspect of life you get much advice on when you go into the hotel business," he said in his good-humored way. "But, if you'll excuse my being personal, Mr. Saunders, you seem to me a rather unusual sort of man."

"Do I?" Joe asked in genuine surprise. "I should have said in my circumstances most men would have felt the same."

"Felt the same, I've no doubt," said Coleman. "I'm not so sure they'd have acted the same, though. Naturally, the first thing I did when you told me your story was to ask myself what I'd have done in your place."

"Yes?" Joe said eagerly.

"And I decided—don't think me impertinent now!—that I'd think twice about it."

"Don't worry, old man," Joe said with a loud laugh. "I did. I thought three times about it, as a matter of fact."

But those few words seemed to have cleared the air between them. They had passed the city boundaries and were driving along a riverbank with a tree-lined walk at the other side of the water. The main road led along a smaller river wooded to its bank. Finally they reached a little village with a church and public house where they went off on a byroad up the hill. They came out of it above the river and harbor, stopped to inquire their way, and drove slowly for some miles along a deserted upland road. It was darkening, and Coleman drove more carefully. There was a cottage on their right and two small children with bare feet were playing in the roadway outside. He stopped the car suddenly.

"I have a feeling this is it," he said, and bellowed to the children: "Is this Mrs. Ryan's?"

"What's that, sir?" asked a little boy.

"Mrs. Ryan's, I said."

" 'Tis, sir."

"And is this Marie?" Coleman asked, pointing to the little girl who accompanied him.

"No, sir, 'tis Martha," said the child.

"Then where is Marie?" Coleman asked, and suddenly a tall, rough-looking woman with rosy cheeks appeared by the white gatepost. Afterward Joe thought he would never forget that first impression of her with the white gatepost and dark fuchsia bushes, cut out against the sky.

"Is this the gentleman from England I have?" she called. "Marie is inside, gentlemen. Won't ye come in?"

Joe got out first and held out his hand.

"I'm Joe Saunders, Brigid Healy's husband," he said. "And this is Mr. Coleman, the hotel manager from Cork. He was kind enough to give me a lift."

"I was after giving up expecting ye," she said, showing her big teeth in a smile. "Come in, let ye! I'm afraid the house is in a mess, but 'tis only the children."

"You don't have to apologize, Mrs. Ryan," Joe said. "I come of a large family myself."

But even Joe's large London family had not prepared him for the little cottage, even if the shadows inside gave little opportunity for deciding whether or not it was in a mess. An open door into the bedroom suggested a big bed that had not been made, and the walls of the kitchen were bare but for a grocer's calendar inside the door. Sitting round the open fire were three other children whose faces he could scarcely see, but it was clear that the bare-legged two-year-old who toasted her feet before it was Brigid's child. Suddenly he wondered what he was doing there.

"This is Miss Healy's little girl, gentlemen," said Mrs. Ryan. "She's the spit of her mother, but ye can't see. I'll light the lamp. I suppose ye'd like a cup of tea after yeer journey?"

"No, thanks, Mrs. Ryan," said Joe. "We've only just had dinner. Besides, we won't stay long. We thought we'd come back tomorrow morning for Marie, just to give you time to get her ready. . . . Hello, Marie," he said, taking the child's hand. "I bet you don't know who I am."

"Hullo, Marie," Coleman said with casual amiability and took her hand as well. She looked up at them without expression and Joe suddenly recognized her resemblance to Brigid. That gave him a turn too.

"Run out and play with Martha and Michael," Mrs. Ryan shouted to the other boy in the room. "And bring Kitty along with you." Silently the two children got up and went out, closing the half door behind them. It was not as though they were frightened but as though they saw no reason for disobeying, and for some reason this struck Joe as even worse. He felt that a natural child should be curious. Mrs. Ryan lit the lamp, squinting up at it.

"Wisha, sit down, let ye," she said, pulling up two chairs and wiping the seats vaguely with her apron. "And how is Miss Healy? You'll have to forgive me. I forget her married name."

"Saunders," said Joe, sitting down and opening the little case he had brought with him. "She's fine, Mrs. Ryan. She probably told you we have a little girl of our own now. She wasn't well or she'd have been here herself. I don't want to rush you. These are a few clothes I brought, and perhaps you can tell me if they'll fit."

He passed the frock, overcoat, and hat to her and she held them to the light with a vague smile. Then she peered at the shoes.

"Wisha, aren't they lovely?" she said. "Aren't you the lucky girl, Marie? Ye're sure ye won't have the tea? 'Twouldn't take me a minute to boil the kettle."

"Certain, thanks," said Joe, who only wanted to get out of the house quick. He crossed to the half door, and again he caught an image he felt he would never forget of the lamplight on the hedge and whitewashed gatepost where four children were crowded together, talking in whispers. "Better come in now," he said with a laugh. "I bet you heard every word we said. Are they all yours, Mrs. Ryan?"

"Ah, no, sir," she replied almost reproachfully. "We had no children of our own. 'Tis on account of my husband's death I had to take them."

The four children came in and stood fidgeting by the dresser, two little boys and two little girls, apparently well fed if not well dressed or clean, but somehow lacking all the spontaneity of other children. Joe took out a fistful of coins and distributed them. The children took the money meekly, without gratitude.

"Well, Marie," he asked, stooping over the child on the stool, "how do you think you're going to like me for a daddy?"

"She's strange," Mrs. Ryan said apologetically. "Most of the time she have plenty to say for herself."

"I'll bet she has," said Joe. "And in a couple of days she'll be giving me cheek as well. Won't you, old lady?"

They sat and talked for a few minutes longer. Then Joe said good night, kissed Marie, and patted the other children on the head. It was already dark on the road, and he was glad of the headlights that made the green banks seem theatrical but concealed his face.

"Well, I don't know how you feel, but I'm ready for a drink," said Coleman. "A large one, at that."

"What I should like is to buy a few toys for the other kids," said Joe.

"Too late for that, I'm afraid," said Coleman. "The shops are shut until Monday. You might be able to pick up a few cheap toys in a sweetshop, and a couple of bags of sweets. If you mean they won't have the money long I'm inclined to agree with you."

As they entered the hotel the tall night porter looked up from his evening paper and said, "Night, sir. Night, Mr. Saunders," and already Joe knew that his business was being discussed. The waiter who brought them their drinks in the lounge seemed to know as well, but Joe had the idea that he approved. He might have been a father himself. He might even have known Brigid and Marie's father. The pair of them might have sat drinking in this very lounge like any of the couples who sat there now. It was only the other side of the picture that he had been looking at that evening in a lonesome cottage on the hills. He felt very depressed.

Next morning he was more cheerful. He woke to the sound of bells. He had never heard so many bells, or else they sounded louder in the hollow of the city. A pious people all right, he thought. On their way out of town he saw the well-dressed crowds on their way to Mass. In the first village they came to there was a large group outside the church and a smaller one outside the public house.

The four elder children were waiting for them in the roadway, and as they approached, two of these rushed in to give warning. They had all been washed and two of them even wore boots. When they went into the cottage Marie was sitting stiffly on a low chair by the door, as though she had been glued there to keep her from soiling her new dress, and she looked up at them blankly and pointed to her shoes. "Look! Shoes!" she said shrilly, and Joe, stooping to admire them, saw that they were too big.

"We'll get you properly fitted tomorrow, old lady," he said.

He distributed the few presents he had managed to buy, shook hands with Mrs. Ryan, and carried Marie to the car. The other children followed, and he shook hands with each in turn, and then laid his hand gently on each one's head. Over the low wooden gate he could see the tall figure of Mrs. Ryan, holding the doorpost and gazing up and down the deserted road.

As the car started he turned to wave to the little group of children. They stood in the roadway, their presents clutched in their hands, and he saw that they were all weeping quietly. It seemed to him that they were not weeping as real children weep, with abandonment and delight, but hopelessly, as old people weep whom the world has passed by. He was the world and he had passed them by. He knew now why he had not dared to kiss any of them. If he had kissed them he could not have left them there. His first thought was to prevent Marie's seeing them, but he realized that he needn't have worried. She was leaning forward, enchanted, trying to touch her beautiful new shoes. Coleman drove with his eyes fixed on the winding roadway over the hills, and his fat sulky face was expressionless.

"I wonder if you saw what I did?" Joe said at last to break the silence, and Coleman stared at him despairingly.

"I'm in dread I'll never forget it," he said.

The Saint

AS A KID I HAD great devotion to the Blessed Virgin. I found it difficult to pray to the Sacred Heart because I was always rather intimidated by men with beards. At that time I was going through a real religious phase, collecting new prayers to say, and going through agonies of scruples trying to say them in a recollected way while my mind went off at a thousand tangents about football, air rifles, mountain climbing, and birds' nests. Sometimes I began a prayer twenty times and each time got lost in the relative clauses till my head sagged onto the bed and I was barely able to climb in between the sheets, exhausted. To help me to concentrate I had made an ingenious shrine out of a wooden packing case, stuffed with brown paper that I had sized to make it look like rocks, and with a hole cut in the back where I could mount a small statue or a picture, lit by a hidden candle. It really was quite smashing.

For a time I felt that Our Lady thought a lot of me, too. It was just little things she did for me without any of the usual fuss I had with favors I asked of the saints. I even had the notion that she liked me so much that one day she'd appear to me and give me messages for the Bishop and the Government about the way she wanted things done, as she had in France. If this happened, I felt pretty certain it would be either in the quarry or down the Glen, so I took to rambling there in the dusk by myself. I thought it would be the Glen, more likely, because though the quarry had lots of suitable grottoes, it was too close to the public road, and you couldn't appear there without drawing a crowd. I had it all worked out pretty carefully, how I'd go up to Farranferris to the Bishop's Palace, and he wouldn't believe me—bishops never do in the lives of the saints—and then I'd have to produce a sign, like a flower out of season, and he'd send me off on the train to Dublin to see the Government.

For months I went into the church every day on my way home from school to say a prayer. It was always nice then, deserted and dark and silent after the street outside, with only the small red lamp burning before the sanctuary, and one great grove of candlelight in the corner on your left with the statue of Our Lady rising out of it, framed in dark rocks. There was rarely a sound, except the screech of a tram passing outside, the slow solemn tick-tock of the clock like silence breathing, or the padding of Mickie Mac's felt slippers and the swish of his soutane as he genuflected before the high altar. Mickie Mac was the sacristan; a man with a bald brow, a shrill voice, and a most edifying presence, who I always felt was probably more than halfway to being a saint too.

I always had some new favor—intention, we called it—to ask about long division or an air gun, and it really was remarkable the number of them I was granted. Normally, I couldn't get my compositions put on display because, however I managed it, they were always full of blots, but when I made it an intention I had two put up in quick succession, blots and all.

But what I really loved was when I had a penny to buy a candle from the box beside the shrine and could light one myself. Then I could stay there any length of time, and when I left, I felt that Our Lady had something to remember me by until Mickie Mac came round with the snuffers and there was nothing left alight but the one red sanctuary lamp. I often thought of her, alone there with the little lamp and nothing but the sound of the clock. Anyhow, it was natural for me to buy her candles. I always liked giving things to people I was fond of, and felt there was something mean about asking the Blessed Virgin to do this, that and the other thing for

me and never giving her anything back. My poor mother was persecuted for pennies.

"Another penny?" she'd say with a harassed air.

"I know, Mummy," I replied meekly, "but I have another
intention. I have, really."

"Ah, you can't be lighting candles all the time, child. Besides,
Our Lady doesn't expect it from poor people like us."

I did my best to keep my patience the way the saints always did
and only said, "Very well, Mummy," but I couldn't help feeling it
was easy for her to talk. A lot she knew about what Our Lady
expected!

Then one evening I made the mistake of asking for the penny
when my father was in. Now, Father wasn't an irreligious man, far
from it, but he was full of worldly wisdom and suspicious of all
the channels down which his good money might disappear. I was
one, religion was another, and the conjunction probably evoked
visions of destitution in the poor man's mind.

"A penny for a candle?" he exclaimed, walking across the
kitchen in a state of acute irritation. "What do you want a penny for
a candle for? That's no way to go wasting money."

My mother, who secretly cherished hopes that I might become a
bishop, didn't at all like this loose, worldly talk before me.

"There are worse ways of spending money," she replied with
heat.

"But do you know how much these candles cost?" he asked
indignantly.

"What matter what they cost?" she snapped. "I suppose they
have to be special candles."

"They do not have to be special candles," my father shouted
angrily. "Eight a penny is the price they pay for those candles, and
then they sell them at a penny apiece. Sure, the thing is daylight
robbery."

My mother gave me the penny then, just to undo whatever
harm my father might have done me, but it was too late; the harm
was already done. Next day it was with real resentment that I put

a penny in the offertory box when I took my candle—half a far-thing's worth. I felt that I was being exploited; still worse, I felt that Our Lady was being exploited. In a properly organized society, for that penny I could be burning candles to her every day of the week, instead of coming in day after day with the poor mouth on me.

And from then on, the poor mouth was a genuine grievance to me. It wasn't any longer my personal loss but the whole world's loss. My devotion to Our Lady became all mixed up in my mind with my devotion to social reform, and one day, when the saint wasn't feeling up to scratch, the social reformer took charge.

My plan didn't involve any difficulties. At that hour of day there was rarely anyone in the church, only Mickie Mac, padding and swishing his surplice about the high altar. If there did happen to be anyone at the shrine I could wait. Then a glance to make sure I wasn't observed, and I picked up a candle, lit it, and stuck it in one of the empty holders. I can't say I was ever very easy in my mind about it; not that I thought it wrong, but it always had so much the air of an adventure that I found it hard to be recollected in my prayers.

This went on for weeks during the summer. Then one day when I went into the church there was another small boy, about the same age as myself, there. He was a fellow you wouldn't pay much attention to. I went in briskly, genuflected, and went to the shrine to light my candle and then knelt and covered my face with my hands. I really had developed something of a professional clerical manner. Soon after, the small boy got up and went out creakily on tiptoe.

Outside the church door I was suddenly pounced upon. It was Mickie Mac, not looking in the least saintly or even half saintly. He looked more like an enraged old market woman, and swore in a shrill voice harmless oaths he had made up out of hymns and prayers.

"God of Mercy and Compassion!" he hissed, dragging me after him with one hand while he held the other raised, ready to knock me flat. "So you're the dirty little thief I'm watching these months? Oh, you savage, stealing from the House of God!"

"I didn't, I didn't, Mr. Mac," I screamed, trying to break free.

"Sweet Spirit, will you listen to him!" chanted Mickie Mac, almost turning purple. "In front of the House of God, telling damn lies!"

"I'm not telling lies," I screamed. "I'm not. I'm not. I paid—ah, please, Mr. Mac, let me go!"

Instead, I was dragged triumphantly toward the presbytery, where the curate on duty was saying his office in the sunlight outside, his biretta down over his eyes.

"There he is, Father!" Mickie Mac squeaked scornfully, almost hurling me at the priest. "There's the little caffler I'm watching for night and day these three weeks past. Would you look at the size of him and he ready for all that wickedness?"

"Did you steal candles from the church, boy?" the priest asked.

"I didn't, Father," I protested. "I paid for them. I swear I did."

"False oaths to the priest of God!" moaned Mickie, clapping his hands in despair. "First he steals from Our Blessed Lady, and then he swears false oaths to the priest. Didn't Charlie Donnellan see you, you Turk?" he added, chokingly.

"What were you doing with those candles?" asked the priest.

"Lighting them, Father," I said.

"Where were you lighting them?"

"To Our Lady, Father."

"Oh," he said with a change of tone, "you weren't taking them away with you?"

"Oh, no, Father," I sobbed, horrified at the suggestion.

"I see," he said. "Well, why couldn't you pay for them like anyone else?"

"But I did, Father," I said. "Last Friday, really I did."

"Last Friday?" he repeated in a puzzled tone. "What did you pay for last Friday?"

"The candles, Father."

"How much money did you put in the box last Friday?"

"A penny, Father."

"Very well. And how many candles did you light since then?"

"Three, Father."

"And you never paid for them?"

And suddenly all my father's worldly wisdom dropped away from me. I knew now that my mother was right and that it didn't matter what the candles cost to buy.

"No, Father," I said, and this time I began to cry with real bitterness because I knew I had no defense.

"Do you come into the church every day?" he asked.

"Yes, Father."

"Well, now, don't you think it would hurt Our Blessed Lady to see you taking candles from her shrine and not paying for them?"

It hadn't occurred to me that she would take that point of view at all, but when he put it up to me it struck me as a likely enough thing from a woman.

"Yes, Father."

"Tell me, how many did you take in all, do you remember?"

"I don't, Father," I said. "About twelve, I think."

"Very well so," he said smoothly. "We'll call it twelve. Now, don't forget that you owe Our Lady twelve pennies, and that you must put them in her box as you get them, and not be lighting any more candles till you have it all paid. Do you understand that?"

"Yes, Father."

"All right so," he said with a smile.

He was a nice priest, and he didn't make it seem so bad, but one look at the faces of Mickie Mac and the altar boy, who both seemed to think penal servitude for life was the least I ought to expect, and I burst into a fresh flood of tears and ran all the way home, sobbing.

Every week for twelve solid weeks I took in my penny and put it in the box. I did it coldly and resentfully. I never waited to say a prayer. Instead, I went up to the shrine of St. Francis and prayed to him. My devotion to the Blessed Virgin waned, and not only to her but to the saints as well, even the little St. Thérèse. They were all very well when they were in good humor, but like all other women, you could never rely on them.

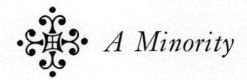 *A Minority*

Denis Halligan noticed Willy Stein for the first time one Sunday when the other fellows were at Mass. As Denis was a Protestant, he didn't go to Mass. Instead, he sat on the steps outside the chapel with Willy. Willy was a thin, seedy little chap with long, wild hair. It was an autumn morning; there was mist on the trees, and you could scarcely see the great ring of mountains that cut them off there in the middle of Ireland, miles from anywhere.

"Why did they send you here if you're a Proddy?" asked Willy.

"I don't know," said Denis, who felt his background was so queer that he didn't want to explain it to anybody. "I suppose because it was cheap."

"Is your old fellow a Catholic?" asked Willy.

"No," replied Denis. "Is yours?"

"No," Willy said contemptuously. "He was a Proddy. My old one was a Proddy, too."

"Where do they live?" asked Denis.

"They're dead," Willy said, making the motion of spitting. "The bloody Germans killed them."

"Oh, cripes!" Denis said regretfully. Denis had a great admiration for everything German, particularly tank generals, and when he grew up he wanted to be a tank general himself, but it seemed a pity that they had to kill Willy's father and mother. Bad as it was to have your parents separated, as his own were, it was worse having them dead. "Was it a bomb?" he asked.

"No," Willy replied without undue emotion. "They were killed in a camp. They sent me over to the Cumminses in Dublin or I'd have been killed, too. The Cumminses are Catholics. That's why I was sent here."

"Do you like it here?" asked Denis.

"I do not," Willy said scornfully in his slummy Dublin accent, and then took out a slingshot and fitted a stone in it. "I'd sooner Vienna. Vienna was gas. When I grow up I'm going to get out of this blooming place."

"But what will you do?"

"Aw, go to sea, or something. I don't care."

Denis was interested in Willy. Apart from the fact that they were the only Proddies in the school, Willy struck him as being really tough, and Denis admired toughness. He was always trying to be tough himself, but there was a soft streak in him that kept breaking out. It was breaking out now, and he knew it. Though he saw that Willy didn't give a rap about his parents, Denis couldn't help being sorry for him, alone in the middle of Ireland with his father and mother dead half a world away. He said as much to his friend Nigel Healy, from Cork, that afternoon, but Nigel only gave a superior sniff.

"But that fellow is mad," he said, in his reasonable way.

"How is he mad?" asked Denis.

"He's not even left go home on holidays," explained Nigel. "He has to stay here all during the summer. Those people were nice to him, and what does he do? Breaks every window in the place. They had the police to the house twice. He's mad on slingshots."

"He had one this morning," said Denis.

"Last time he was caught with one he got flogged," said Nigel. "You see, the fellow has no sense. I even saw him putting sugar on his meat."

"But why did he do that?" asked Denis.

"Said he liked it," replied Nigel with a smile and a shrug. "He's bound to get expelled one of these days. You'd want to mind yourself with him."

But for some reason that only made Denis more interested in Willy Stein, and he looked forward to meeting him again by himself the following Sunday. He was curious to know why the Germans would want to kill Stein's father and mother. That seemed to him a funny thing to do—unless, of course, they were spies for the English.

Again they sat on the steps, but this morning the sun was warm and bright, and the mountains all round them were a brilliant blue. If Stein's parents were really spies, the idea of it did not seem to have occurred to him. According to him, his father had been a lawyer and his mother something on a newspaper, and he didn't seem to remember much about them except that they were both "gas." Everything with Stein was "gas." His mother was gentle and timid, and let him have everything he wanted, so she was "great gas." His father was sure she was ruining him, and was always on to him to study and be better than other kids, and when his father got like that he used to weep and shout and wave his hands, but that was only now and then. He was gas, too, though not, Denis gathered, great gas. Willy suddenly waved his hands and shouted something in a foreign language.

"What's that?" asked Denis with the deepest admiration.

"German," Stein replied, in his graceless way.

"What does it mean?" asked Denis.

"I dunno," Stein said lightly.

Denis was disappointed. For a fellow like himself, who was interested in tanks, a spatter of German might one day be useful. He had the impression that Stein was only letting on to remember parents he had lost before he was really old enough to remember them.

Their talk was interrupted by Father Houlihan, a tall, morose-looking priest. He had a bad belly and a worse temper, but Denis knew Father Houlihan liked him, and he admired Father Houlihan. He was violent, but he wasn't a stinker.

"Hah!" he said, in his mocking way. "And what do you two cock sparrows think you're doing out here?"

"We're excused, Father," Denis said brightly, leaping to his feet.

"No one is excused anything in this place till I excuse him," snarled Father Houlihan cheerfully, "and I don't excuse much. Run into Mass now, ye pair of heathens!"

"But we're Protestants, Father!" Stein cried, and Denis was half afraid of seeing the red flush on Father Houlihan's forehead that showed he was out for blood.

"Aha, what fine Protestants we have in ye!" he snorted good-humoredly. "I suppose you have a Protestant slingshot in your pocket at this very minute, you scoundrel, you!"

"I have not!" Stein shouted. "You know Murphy took it off me."

"Mr. Murphy to you, Willy Stein," said the priest, pinching his ear playfully and pushing him toward the chapel. "And next time I catch you with a slingshot I'll give you a Catholic cane on your fat Protestant backside."

The two boys went into chapel and sat together on a bench at the back. Willy was muttering indignantly to himself, but he waited until everyone was kneeling with bowed head. Then, to Denis's horror, he took out a slingshot and a bit of paper, which he chewed up into a wet ball. There was nothing hasty or spontaneous about this. Stein went about it with a concentration that was almost pious. As the bell rang for the Consecration, there was a ping, and a seminarist kneeling at the side of the chapel put his hand to his ear and looked angrily round. But by this time Stein had thrown himself on his knees, and his eyes were shut in a look of rapt devotion. It gave Denis quite a turn. Even if he wasn't a Catholic, he had been brought up to respect every form of religion.

The business of going to Mass and feeling out of it made Denis Halligan completely fed up with being a Proddy. He had never liked it anyway, even at home, as a kid. He was gregarious, and a born gang leader, a promoter of organization, and it cut him to the heart to feel that at any moment he might be deserted by his gang because, through no fault of his own, he was not a Catholic and might accidentally say or do the wrong thing. He even resented the quiet persuasion that the school authorities exercised on him. A senior called Hanley, whom Nigel described sarcastically as "Halligan's angel," was attached to Denis—not to proselytize but to give him an intelligent understanding of the religious life of the group. Hanley had previously been attached to Stein, but that had proved hopeless, because Stein seemed to take Hanley's company as a guarantee of immunity from punishment, so he merely involved Hanley in every form of forbidden activity, from smoking to stealing. One day when Stein stole a gold tiepin from a master's room, Hanley had to report him. On Hanley's account, he was not flogged but told to put the tiepin back in the place from which he had taken it. Stein did so, and seized the opportunity to pinch five shillings instead, and this theft was discovered only when someone saw Stein fast asleep in bed with his mouth open and the two half crowns in his jaw. As Hanley, a sweet and saintly boy, said to Denis, it wasn't Stein's fault. He was just unbalanced.

In any other circumstances Denis would have enjoyed Hanley's attention, but it made him mad to be singled out like this and looked after like some kid who couldn't undo his own buttons.

"Listen, Hanley," he said angrily one day when he and Nigel were discussing football and Hanley had slipped a little homily into the conversation. "It's no good preaching at me. It's not my fault that I'm a Proddy."

"Well, you don't have to be a Proddy if you don't want to be," Hanley said with a smile. "Do you?"

"How can I help it?" asked Denis.

"Well, who'd stop you?"

"My mother would, for one."

"Did you try?"

"What do you mean, Hanley?"

"I mean, why don't you ask her?" Hanley went on, in the same bland way. "I wouldn't be too sure she wants you to be a Proddy."

"How could I ask her?"

"You could write. Or phone," Hanley added hastily, seeing the look on Denis's face at the notion of writing an extra letter. "Father Houlihan would let you use the telephone, if you asked him. Or I'll ask him, if you like."

"Do if you want to," said Denis. "I don't care."

He didn't really believe his mother would agree to something he wanted, just like that, but he had no objection to a free telephone call that would enable him to hear her voice again. To his astonishment, she made no difficulty about it.

"Why, of course, darling," she said sweetly. "If that's how you feel and Father Houlihan has no objection, I don't mind. You know I only want you to be happy at school."

It was a colossal relief. Overnight, his whole position in the school changed. He had ceased to be an outsider. He was one of the gang. He might even be Chief Gang Leader in the course of time. He was a warmhearted boy, and he had the feeling that by a simple gesture he had conferred an immense benefit on everybody. The only person who didn't seem too enthusaistic was Father Houlihan, but then he was not much of an enthusiast anyway. "My bold young convert," he said, pulling Denis's ear, "I suppose any day now you'll start paying attention to your lessons."

Yet the moment he had made his decision, he began to feel guilty about young Stein. As has been said, he was not only gregarious, but he was also a born gang leader, and had the feeling that someone might think he had deserted an ally to secure his own advantage. He was suddenly filled with a wild desire to convert Willy as well so that the pair of them could be received as a group. He saw it as even more of a duty of Willy's than of his own. Willy had been saved from his parents' fate by a good kind Catholic family, and it was the least they could expect that Willy should show his gratitude to them, to the school, and to Ireland.

But Willy seemed to have a deplorable head for theology. All the time they talked Denis had the impression that Willy was only planning some fresh mischief.

"Ah, come on, Willy," he said authoritatively, "you don't want to be a blooming old Proddy."

"I don't want to be a Cat either," said Willy with a shrug.

"Don't you want to be like the other fellows in the school?"

"Why don't they want to be like me?" asked Stein.

"Because there's only two of us, and there's hundreds of them. And they're right."

"And if there were hundreds of us and two of them, we'd be right, I suppose?" Stein said with a sneer. "You want to be like the rest of them. All right, be like the rest of them, but let me alone."

"I'm only speaking for your own good," Denis said, getting mad. What really made him mad was the feeling that somehow Stein wasn't speaking to him at all; that inside, he was as lonely and lost as Denis would have been in similar circumstances, and he wouldn't admit to it, wouldn't break down as Denis would have done. What he really wanted to do was to give Stein a sock in the gob, but he knew that even this was no good. Stein was always being beaten, and he always yelled bloody murder, and next day he came back and did the same thing again. Everyone was thinking exclusively of Stein's good, and it always ended up by their beating him, and it never did him any good at all.

Denis confided his difficulties to Hanley, who was also full of concern for Stein's good, but Hanley only smiled sadly and shook his head.

"I know more about that than you do, Denis," he said, in his fatherly way. "I'll tell you if you promise not to repeat it to a living soul."

"What is it?" asked Denis eagerly.

"Promise! Mind, this is serious!"

"Oh, I promise."

"The fact is that Stein isn't a Proddy at all," Hanley said sadly.

"But what is he?"

"Stein is a Jew," Hanley said in a low voice. "That's why his father and mother were killed. Nobody knows that, though."

"But does Stein know he's a Jew?" Denis asked excitedly.

"No. And mind, we're not supposed to know it, either. Nobody knows it, except the priests and ourselves."

"But why doesn't somebody tell him?"

"Because if they did, he might blab about it—you know, he's not very smart—and then all the fellows would be jeering at him. Remember, Denis, if you ever mentioned it, Father Houlihan would skin you alive. He says Stein is after suffering enough. He's sorry for Stein. Mind, I'm only warning you."

"But won't it be awful for him when he finds out?"

"When he's older and has a job, he won't mind it so much," said Hanley.

But Denis wasn't sure. Somehow, he had an idea that Stein wanted to stay a Proddy simply because that was what his father and mother had been and it was now the only link he had with them, and if someone would just tell him, he wouldn't care so much and would probably become a Catholic, like Denis. Afterward, when he did find out that everything he had done was mistaken, it might be too late. And this—and the fact that Father Houlihan, whom Denis admired, was also sorry for Willy Stein—increased his feeling of guilt, and he almost wished he hadn't been in such a hurry himself about being converted. Denis wasn't a bright student, but he was a born officer and he would never have deserted his men.

The excitement of his own reception into the Church almost banished the thought of Stein from his mind. On the Sunday he was received, he was allowed to sleep late, and Murphy, the seminarist, even brought him comics to read in bed. This was real style! Then he dressed in his best suit and went down to meet his mother, who arrived, with his sister Martha, in a hired car. For once, Martha was deferential. She was impressed, and the sight of the chapel impressed her even more. In front of the high altar there was an isolated prie-dieu for Denis himself, and behind him a special pew was reserved for her and his mother.

Denis knew afterward that he hadn't made a single false move.

Only once was his exaltation disturbed, and that was when he heard the *ping* of a slingshot and realized that Stein, sitting by himself in the back row, was whiling away the time by getting into fresh mischief. The rage rose up in Denis, in spite of all his holy thoughts, and for a moment he resolved that when it was all over he would find Willy Stein and beat him to a jelly.

Instead, when it was over he suddenly felt weary. Martha had ceased to be impressed by him. Now she was just a sister a bare year younger who was mad with him for having stolen the attention of everybody. She knew only too well what a figure she would have cut as a convert, and was crazy with jealousy.

"I won't stand it," she said. "I'm going to be a Catholic, too."

"Well, who's stopping you?" Denis asked.

"Nobody's going to stop me," said Martha. "Just because Daddy is fond of you doesn't mean that I can't be a Catholic."

"What has Daddy to do with it?" asked Denis with a feeling of alarm.

"Because now that you're a Catholic, the courts wouldn't let him have you," Martha said excitedly. "Because Daddy is an atheist, or something, and he wanted to get hold of you. He tried to get you away from Mummy. I don't care about Daddy. I'm going to be converted, too."

"Go on!" growled Denis, feeling sadly how his mood of exaltation was fading. "You're only an old copycat."

"I am not a copycat, Denis Halligan," she said bitterly. "It's only that you always sucked up to Daddy and I didn't, and he doesn't care about me. I don't care about him, either, so there!"

Denis felt a sudden pang of terror at her words. In a dim sort of way he realized that what he had done might have consequences he had never contemplated. He had no wish to live with his father, but his father came to the school to see him sometimes, and he had always had the feeling that if he ever got fed up with living at home with his mother and Martha, his father would always have him. Nobody had told him that by becoming a Catholic he had made it impossible for his father to have him. He glanced round and saw

Stein, thin and pale and furtive, slouching away from the chapel with his hand in his pocket clutching his slingshot. He gave Denis a grin in which there was no malice, but Denis scowled and looked away.

"Who's that?" asked Martha inquisitively.

"Oh, him!" Denis said contemptuously. "That's only a dirty Jew-boy."

Yet even as he spoke the words he knew they were false. What he really felt toward Willy Stein was an aching envy. Nobody had told him that by changing his faith he might be unfaithful to his father, but nobody had told Stein, either, and, alone and despairing, he still clung to a faith that was not his own for the sake of a father and mother he had already almost forgotten, who had been murdered half a world away and whom he would never see again. For a single moment Denis saw the dirty little delinquent whom everyone pitied and despised transfigured by a glory that he himself would never know.

An Out-and-Out Free Gift

WHEN JIMMY BEGAN to get out of hand, his father was both disturbed and bewildered. Anybody else, yes, but not Jimmy! They had always been so close! Closer, indeed, than Ned ever realized, for the perfectly correct picture he had drawn of himself as a thoughtful, considerate father who treated his son as though he were a younger brother could have been considerably expanded by his wife. Indeed, to realize how close they had been you needed to hear Celia on it, because only she knew how much of the small boy there still was in her husband.

Who, for instance, would have thought that the head of a successful business had such a passion for sugar? Yet during the war, when sugar was rationed in Ireland, Celia, who was a bit of a Jansenist, had felt herself bound to give up sugar and divide her ration between Ned and Jimmy, then quite a small boy. And, even at that, Ned continued to suffer. He did admire her self-denial, but he couldn't help feeling that so grandiose a gesture deserved a better object than Jimmy. It was a matter of scientific fact that sugar was bad for Jimmy's teeth, and anything that went wrong with Jimmy's teeth was going to cost his father money. Ned felt it unfair that in the middle of a war, with his salary frozen, Celia should inflict additional burdens on him.

Most of the time he managed to keep his dignity, though he could rarely sit down to a meal without an angry glance at Jimmy's sugar bowl. To make things harder for him, Jimmy rationed himself so that toward the end of the week he still had some sugar left, while Ned had none. As a philosopher, Ned wondered that he should resent this so deeply, but resent it he did. A couple of times, he deliberately stole a spoonful while Celia's back was turned, and the absurdity of this put him in such a frivolous frame of mind for the rest of the evening that she eventually said resignedly, "I suppose you've been at the child's sugar again? Really, Ned, you are hopeless!" On other occasions, Ned summoned up all his paternal authority and with a polite "You don't mind, old man?" took a spoonful from under Jimmy's nose. But that took nerve, and a delicate appreciation of the precise moment when Jimmy could be relied on not to cry.

Toward the end of the war, it became a matter of brute economic strength. If Jimmy wanted a bicycle lamp, he could earn it or pay up in good sugar. As Ned said, quoting from a business manual he had studied in his own youth, "There is no such thing in business as an out-and-out free gift." Jimmy made good use of the lesson. "Bicycle lamp, old man?" Ned would ask casually, poising his spoon over Jimmy's sugar bowl. "Bicycle lamp *and* three-speed gear," Jimmy would reply firmly. "For a couple of spoons of sugar?" his father would cry in mock indignation. "Are you mad, boy?" They both enjoyed the game.

They could scarcely have been other than friends. There was so much of the small boy in Ned that he was sensitive to the least thing affecting Jimmy, and Jimmy would consult him about things that most small boys keep to themselves. When he was in trouble, Ned never dismissed it lightly, no matter how unimportant it seemed. He asked a great many questions and frequently reserved his decisions. He had chosen Jimmy's school himself; it was a good one for Cork, and sometimes, without informing Jimmy, he went off to the school himself and had a chat with one of the teachers. Nearly always he managed to arrange things without embarrassment or pain, and Jimmy took it for granted that his decisions were usually right. It is a wise father who can persuade his son of anything of the sort.

But now, at sixteen, Jimmy was completely out of control, and his mother had handed him over to the secular arm, and the secular arm, for all its weight, made no impression on his sullen indifference. The first sign of the change in him was the disintegration of his normally perfect manners; now he seemed to have no deference toward or consideration for anyone. Ned caught him out in one or two minor falsehoods and quoted to him a remark of his own father's that "a lie humiliates the man who tells it, but it humiliates the one it's told to even more." What puzzled Ned was that, at the same time, the outbreak was linked in some ways to qualities he had always liked in the boy. Jimmy was strong, and showed his strength in protecting things younger and weaker than himself. The cat regarded him as a personal enemy because he hurled himself on her the moment he saw her with a bird. At one time, there had been a notice on his door that read, "Wounded Bird. Please Keep Out." At school, his juniors worshipped him because he would stand up for them against bullies, and though Ned, in a fatherly way, advised him not to get mixed up in other people's quarrels, he was secretly flattered. He felt Jimmy was taking after him.

But the same thing that attracted Jimmy to younger and weaker boys seemed now to attract him to wasters. Outside of school, he never associated with lads he might have to look up to but only with those his father felt a normal boy should despise. All this was summed up in his friendship with a youngster called Hogan, who was a strange mixture of spoiling and neglect, a boy who had never been young and would never be old. He openly smoked a pipe, and let on to be an authority on brands of tobacco. Ned winced when Hogan addressed him as a contemporary and tried to discuss business with him. He replied with heavy irony—something he did only when he was at a complete loss. What went on in Hogan's house when Jimmy went there he could only guess at. He suspected that the parents went out and stayed out, leaving the boys to their own devices.

At first, Ned treated Jimmy's insubordination as he had treated other outbreaks, by talking to him as an equal. He even offered him a cigarette—Jimmy had stolen money to buy cigarettes. He told him how people grew up through admiration of others' virtues, rather than through tolerance of their weaknesses. He talked to him about sex, which he suspected was at the bottom of Jimmy's trouble, and Jimmy listened politely and said he understood. Whether he did or not, Ned decided that if Hogan talked sex to Jimmy, it was a very different kind of sex.

Finally, he forbade Hogan the house and warned Jimmy against going to Hogan's. He made no great matter of it, contenting himself with describing the scrapes he had got into himself at Jimmy's age, and Jimmy smiled, apparently pleased with this unfamiliar picture of his grave and rather stately father, but he continued to steal and lie, to get bad marks and remain out late at night. Ned was fairly satisfied that he went to Hogan's, and sat there smoking, playing cards, and talking filth. He bawled Jimmy out and called him a dirty little thief and liar, and Jimmy raised his brows and looked away with a pained air, as though asking himself how long he must endure such ill breeding. At this, Ned gave him a cuff on the ear that brought a look of hatred into Jimmy's face and caused Celia not to talk to Ned for two days. But even she gave in at last.

"Last night was the third time he's been out late this week," she said one afternoon in her apparently unemotional way. "You'll really have to do something drastic with him."

These were hard words from a soft woman, but though Ned felt sorry for her, he felt even sorrier for himself. He hated himself in the part of a sergeant major, and he blamed her for having let things go so far.

"Any notion where he has been?" he asked stiffly.

"Oh, you can't get a word out of him," she said with a shrug. "Judging by his tone, I'd say Hogan's. I don't know what attraction that fellow has for him."

"Very well," Ned said portentously. "I'll deal with him. But, mind, I'll deal with him in my own way."

"Oh, I won't interfere," she said wearily. "I know when I'm licked."

"I can promise you Master Jimmy will know it, too," Ned added grimly.

At supper he said in an even tone, "Young man, for the future you're going to be home every night at ten o'clock. This is the last time I'm going to speak to you about it."

Jimmy, apparently under the impression that his father was talking to himself, reached for a slice of bread. Then Ned let fly with a shout that made Celia jump and paralyzed the boy's hand, still clutching the bread.

"Did you hear me?"

"What's that?" gasped Jimmy.

"I said you were to be in at ten o'clock."

"Oh, all right, all right," said Jimmy, with a look that said he did not think any reasonable person would require him to share the house any longer with one so uncivilized. Though this look was intended to madden Ned, it failed to do so, because he knew that, for all her sentimentality and high liberal principles, Celia was a woman of her word and would not interfere whenever he decided to knock that particular look off Master Jimmy's face. He knew, too, that the time was not far off; that Jimmy had not the faintest intention of obeying, and that he would be able to deal with it.

"Because I warn you, the first night you're late again I'm going to skin you alive," he added. He was trying it out, of course. He knew that Celia hated expressions of fatherly affection like "skin you alive," "tan you within an inch of your life," and "knock your head off," which, to her, were relics of a barbarous age. To his great satisfaction, she neither shuddered nor frowned. Her principles were liberal, but they were principles.

Two nights after, Jimmy was late again. Celia, while pretending to read, was watching the clock despairingly. "Of course, he may have been delayed," she said smoothly, but there was no conviction in her tone. It was nearly eleven when they heard Jimmy's key in the door.

"I think perhaps I'd better go to bed," she said.

"It might be as well," he replied pityingly. "Send that fellow in on your way."

He heard her in the hallway, talking with Jimmy in a level, friendly voice, not allowing her consternation to appear, and he smiled. He liked that touch of the Roman matron in her. Then there was a knock, and Jimmy came in. He was a big lad for sixteen' but he still had traces of baby fat about the rosy cheeks he occasionally scraped with Ned's razor, to Ned's annoyance. Now Ned would cheerfully have given him a whole shaving kit if it would have avoided the necessity for dealing with him firmly.

"You wanted to talk to me, Dad?" he asked, as though he could just spare a moment.

"Yes, Jimmy, I did. Shut that door."

Jimmy gave a resigned shrug at his father's mania for privacy but did as he was told, and stood against the door, his hands joined and his chin in the air.

"When did I say you were to be in?" Ned said, looking at the clock.

"When?"

"Yes. When? At what time, if you find it so hard to understand."

"Oh, ten," Jimmy replied wearily.

"Ten? And what time do you make that?"

"Oh, I didn't know it was so late!" Jimmy exclaimed with an astonished look at the clock. "I'm sorry. I didn't notice the time."

"Really?" Ned said ironically. "Enjoyed yourself that much?"

"Not too bad," Jimmy replied vaguely. He was always uncomfortable with his father's irony.

"Company good?"

"Oh, all right," Jimmy replied with another shrug.

"Where was this?"

"At a house."

"Poor people?" his father asked in mock surprise.

"What?" exclaimed Jimmy.

"Poor people who couldn't afford a clock?"

Jimmy's indignation overflowed in stammering protest. "I never said they hadn't a clock. None of the other fellows had to be in by ten. I didn't like saying I had to be. I didn't want them to think I was a blooming . . ." The protest expired in a heavy sigh, and Ned's heart contracted with pity and shame.

"Juvenile delinquent," he added patiently. "I know. Neither your mother nor I want you to make a show of yourself. But you didn't answer my question. Where was this party? And don't tell me any lies, because I'm going to find out."

Jimmy grew red and angry. "Why would I tell you lies?"

"For the same reason you've told so many already—whatever that may be. You see, Jimmy, the trouble with people who tell lies is that you have to check everything they say. Not on your account but on theirs; otherwise, you may be unfair to them. People soon get tired of being fair, though. Now, where were you? At Hogan's?"

"You said I wasn't to go to Hogan's."

"You see, you're still not answering my questions. Were you at Hogan's?"

"No," Jimmy replied in a whisper.

"Word of honor?"

"Word of honor." But the tone was not the tone of honor but of shame.

"Where were you, then?"

"Ryans'."

The name was unfamiliar to Ned, and he wondered if Jimmy had not just invented it to frustrate any attempt at checking on his statements. He was quite prepared to hear that Jimmy didn't know where the house was. It was as bad as that.

"Ryans'," he repeated evenly. "Do I know them?"

"You might. I don't know."

"Where do they live?"

"Gardiner's Hill."

"Whereabouts?"

"Near the top. Where the road comes up from Dillon's Cross, four doors down. It has a tree in the garden." It came so pat that

Ned felt sure there was such a house. He felt sure of nothing else.

"And you spent the evening there? I'm warning you for your own good. Because I'm going to find out." There was a rasp in his voice.

"I told you I did."

"I know," Ned said between his teeth. "Now you're going to come along with me and prove it."

He rose and in silence took his hat from the hall stand and went out. Jimmy followed him silently, a pace behind. It was a moonlit night, and as they turned up the steep hill, the trees overhung a high wall on one side of the street. On the other side, there were steep gardens filled with shadows.

"Where did you say this house was?"

"At the top," Jimmy replied sullenly.

The hill stopped, the road became level, and at either side were little new suburban houses, with tiny front gardens. Near the corner, Ned saw one with a tree in front of it and stopped. There was still light in the front room. The family kept late hours for Cork. Suddenly he felt absurdly sorry for the boy.

"You don't want to change your mind?" he asked gently. "You're sure this is where you were?"

"I told you so," Jimmy replied almost in exasperation.

"Very well," Ned said savagely. "You needn't come in."

"All right," Jimmy said, and braced himself against the concrete gatepost, looking over the moonlit roofs at the clear sky. In the moonlight he looked very pale; his hands were drawn back from his sides, his lips drawn back from his teeth, and for some reason his white anguished face made Ned think of a crucifixion.

Anger had taken the place of pity in him. He felt the boy was being unjust toward him. He wouldn't have minded the injustice if he'd ever been unjust to Jimmy, but two minutes before he had again shown his fairness and given Jimmy another chance. Besides, he didn't want to make a fool of himself.

He walked up the little path to the door, whose colored-glass panels glowed in light that seemed to leak from the sitting-room door. When he rang, a pretty girl of fifteen or sixteen came out and screwed up her eyes at him.

"I hope you'll excuse my calling at this unnatural hour," Ned said in a bantering tone. "It's only a question I want to ask. Do you think I could talk to your father or your mother for a moment?"

"You can, to be sure," the girl replied in a flutter of curiosity. "Come in, can't you? We're all in the front room."

Ned, nerving himself for an ordeal, went in. It was a tiny front room with a fire burning in a tiled fireplace. There was a mahogany table at which a boy of twelve seemed to be doing his lessons. Round the fire sat an older girl, a small woman, and a tubby little man with a graying mustache. Ned smiled, and his tone became even more jocular.

"I hope you'll forgive my making a nuisance of myself," he said. "My name is Callanan. I live at St. Luke's. I wonder if you've ever met my son Jimmy?"

"Jimmy?" the mother echoed, her hand to her cheek. "I don't know that I did."

"I know him," said the girl who had let him in, in a voice that squeaked with pride.

"Fine!" Ned said. "At least, you know what I'm talking about. I wonder if you saw him this evening?"

"Jimmy?" the girl replied, taking fright. "No. Sure, I hardly know him only to salute him. Why? Is anything wrong?"

"Nothing serious, at any rate," said Ned with a comforting smile. "It's just that he said he spent the evening here with you. I daresay that's an excuse for being somewhere he shouldn't have been."

"Well, well, well!" Mrs. Ryan said anxiously, joining her hands. "Imagine saying he was here! Wisha, Mr. Callanan, aren't they a caution?"

"A caution against what, though?" Ned asked cheerfully. "That's what I'd like to know. I'm only sorry he wasn't telling the truth. I'm afraid he wasn't in such charming company. Good night, everybody, and thank you."

"Good night, Mr. Callanan," said Mrs. Ryan, laying a hand gently on his sleeve. "And don't be too hard on him! Sure, we were wild ourselves once."

"Once?" he exclaimed with a laugh. "I hope we still are. We're not dead yet, Mrs. Ryan."

The same girl showed him out. She had recovered from her fright and looked as though she would almost have liked him to stay.

"Good night, Mr. Callanan," she called blithely from the door, and when he turned, she was silhouetted against the lighted doorway, bent halfway over, and waving. He waved back, touched by this glimpse of an interior not so unlike his own but seen from outside, in all its innocence. It was a shock to emerge on the roadway and see Jimmy still standing where he had left him, though he no longer looked crucified. Instead, with his head down and his hands by his sides, he looked terribly weary. They walked in silence for a few minutes, till they saw the valley of the city and the lamps cascading down the hillsides and breaking below into a foaming lake of light.

"Well," Ned said gloomily, "the Ryans seem to be under the impression that you weren't there tonight."

"I know," Jimmy replied, as though this were all that might be expected from him.

Something in his tone startled Ned. It no longer seemed to breathe defiance. Instead, it hinted at something very like despair. But why, he thought in exasperation. Why the blazes did he tell me all those lies? Why didn't he tell me even outside the door? Damn it, I gave him every chance.

"Don't you think this is a nice place to live, Dad?" asked Jimmy.

"Is it?" Ned asked sternly.

"Ah, well, the air is better," said Jimmy with a sigh. They said no more till they reached home.

"Now, go to bed," Ned said in the hallway. "I'll consider what to do with you tomorrow."

Which, as he well knew, was bluff, because he had already decided to do nothing to Jimmy. Somehow he felt that, whatever the boy had done to himself, punishment would be merely an anticlimax, and perhaps a relief. Punishment, he thought, might be exactly what Jimmy would have welcomed at that moment. He went into the sitting room and poured himself a drink, feeling that if anyone deserved it, he did. He had a curious impression of having been involved in some sort of struggle and escaped some danger to which he could not even give a name.

When he went upstairs, Celia was in bed with a book, and looked up at him with a wide-eyed stare. She proved to be no help to him. "Jimmy usen't to be like that," she said wistfully, and he knew she had been lying there regretting the little boy who had come to her with all his troubles.

"But why, why, why, in God's name, did he tell me all those lies?" Ned asked angrily.

"Oh, why do people ever tell lies?" she asked with a shrug.

"Because they hope they won't be found out," Ned replied. "Don't you see that's what's so queer about it?"

She didn't, and for hours Ned lay awake, turning it over and over in his mind. It was easy enough to see it as the story of a common falsehood persisted in through some mood of bravado, and each time he thought of it that way he grew angry again. Then, all at once, he would remember the face of Jimmy against the pillar in the moonlight, as though he were being crucified, and give a frustrated sigh.

"Go to sleep!" Celia said once, giving him a vicious nudge.

"I can't, damn it, I can't," he said, and began all over again.

Why had the kid chosen Ryans' as an excuse? Was that merely to put him further astray, or did it really represent some dream of happiness and fulfillment? The latter explanation he rejected as too simple and sentimental, yet he knew quite well that Ryans' house *had* meant something to the boy, even if it was only an alternative to whatever house he had been in and the company he had met there. Ned could remember himself at that age, and how, when he had abandoned himself to something or somebody, an alternative image would appear. The image that had flashed up in Jimmy's mind, the image that was not one of Hogan's house, was Ryans'. But it needed more than that to explain his own feeling of danger. It was as though Jimmy had deliberately challenged him, if he were the man he appeared to be, to struggle with the demon of fantasy in him and destroy it. It was as though not he but Jimmy had been forcing the pace. At the same time, he realized that this was something he would never know. All he ever would know was that somewhere behind it all were despair and loneliness and terror, under the magic of an autumn night. And yet there were sentimental fools who told you that they would wish to be young again.

Next morning at breakfast, he was cold and aloof, more from embarrassment than hostility. Jimmy, on the other hand, seemed to be in the highest spirits, helping Celia with the breakfast things, saying "Excuse me, Daddy" as he changed Ned's plate. He pushed the sugar bowl toward Ned and said with a grin, "Daddy likes sugar."

Ned just restrained himself from flinging the bowl at him. "As a matter of fact, I do," he said coldly.

He had done the same sort of thing too often himself. He knew that, with the threat of punishment over his head, Jimmy was scared, as well he might be. It is one thing to be defiant at eleven o'clock at night, another thing altogether to be defiant at eight in the morning.

All day, at intervals, he found himself brooding over it. At lunch he talked to his chief clerk about it, but MacIntyre couldn't advise him. "God, Ned," he said impatiently, "every kid is different. There's no laying down rules. My one told the nuns that her mother was a religious maniac and kicked the statue of the Blessed Virgin around the floor. For God's sake, Ned, imagine Kate kicking a statue around the floor!"

"Difficult, isn't it?" replied Ned with a grin, though to himself he thought complacently that that sort of fantasy was what he would expect from Kate's daughter. Parents so rarely sympathize with one another.

That evening, when he came in, Celia said coolly, "I don't know what you said to Jimmy, but it seems to have worked."

Relief came over Ned like a cold shower. He longed to be able to say something calm like "Oh, good!" or "Glad I could help" or "Any time I can advise you again, just let me know." But he was too honest. He shook his head, still the schoolboy that Celia had loved such a long time ago, and his forehead wrinkled up.

"That's the awful part of it," he said. "I said nothing at all to him. For the first time in my life I didn't know what to say. What the hell could I say?"

"Oh, no doubt you said something and didn't notice it," Celia said confidently. "There's no such thing in business as an out-and-out free gift."

 *Anchors*

MY PAL MICK DOWLING started losing his faith very early, when he wasn't more than eighteen. I was sixteen at the time, and my feeling for him was one of complete devotion. It wasn't only that he was two years older than I; in character he was ten years older, mature, sedate, thoughtful, and full of principle; while even when I reached his age I was still a creature of emotion, swayed by every fancy.

I had realized from the first that religion meant more to him than it did to any of his acquaintances, but it was only in easy stages (for he didn't like disturbing what he thought the convictions of a kid like myself) that he told me why. It came as a complete surprise to me. Never having seen him anything but thoughtful and industrious, it had never struck me that he was really a fellow of violent appetites and that but for the safeguards of religion he would turn into a monster. Naturally, I accepted these revelations as gospel; on consideration they made him even more interesting. Babiche Regan, the girl he walked out with, tended to make light of them, but that, Mick said, was only because she was so innocent and pure. I thought it was because she was really such a damn fool, though I didn't tell Mick that. Naturally, I didn't intend to let her rob Mick of his fascination for me, and continued to admire him as a marvel of self-control, being devoured from within by passions, though, as to myself, I didn't feel the conflict at all.

Now, of course, I realize that a lot of Mick's trouble was his mother. His father, except for a tendency to quarrel violently about politics, was a man of high character, and Mick worshipped him, but his mother was a constant irritation. She was a tall, thin, mournful-looking woman; still, because of her blue eyes and clear complexion, good-looking and attractive, but harried to death by work and piety. She had lost Mick's younger brother in childbirth, and, being incapable of having any more, brooded over it. She had no method, and was always losing or mislaying money, borrowing to make it up so that her husband wouldn't know, backing horses to repay the borrowings and taking sips of whiskey on the side to nerve her for the final ordeal of "telling Dowling." No wonder the poor woman was in and out of churches all day, and trying to pump the sly ones with friends in the priesthood to tell her who were the best saints for a poor lone woman that was never out of trouble. If she worried about the souls of her husband and son, that was pure good nature on her part, because she had enough to worry about on her own account. All the same it riled Mick, particularly when she made novenas for him to pass his exams. It's not a nice thing at that age, when you work like the devil and everyone in the University recognizes your brilliance, to have all the credit go to the Infant Jesus of Prague or St. Rose of Lima.

"If I get plowed," Mick told her angrily, "it'll be my fault, not St. Rose of Lima's."

"How sure you are of yourself!" she wailed with a smile like an April shower. "There's many would be glad of her help."

"Too many," Mick said. "If all the other mothers in Ireland are going on like you, she'll have a job to get all the candidates through."

Mrs. Dowling couldn't understand this intellectual sort of argument at all. She was a plain woman, who looked on Heaven as a glorified extension of the County Council, and the saints as councilors, going from department to department, looking after the interests of their relatives and friends. Some had more influence than others, of course. You could open the daily paper and there would be a list as long as your arm of acknowledgments of favors granted "on promise of publication," and by a simple process of counting on your fingers, you could see which of the saints had the most influence at the moment. If Mrs. Dowling ever dreamed of the saints, it must have been with horses' faces.

"Musha, if they were all praying together, 'twouldn't mean they'd all have their prayers answered," she said with a pitying smile.

"No," growled Mick, " 'twould mean there was favoritism in Heaven. But if you think the examiners are going to change their markings on account of St. Rose of Lima, you're much mistaken."

"Ah, we're all smart when we're your age," she said, driving Mick mad entirely.

Mick's father never interfered in these discussions, and for all the apparent interest he took in them, might just as well not have been listening. Mick told me he must have lost his mental edge very early in life. The only comment Mick could get out of him about religion was some blasting snarl at Father Dempsey, the P. P. whom he disliked as much as his wife liked him. Though Mick and his father always went to Mass together, they never went to the parish church for fear Mr. Dowling would be subjected to the ordeal of listening to Father Dempsey; they went to the Franciscan church in Sheares Street instead. The Franciscans had hidden Mr. Dowling during the Civil War, and he was a man who never forgot a kindness. After Mass they usually took a walk up the tree-lined Mardyke, over the bridge and back through the swanky suburb of Sunday's Well. Mick enjoyed these walks enormously, because they were the only occasions when he really had his father to himself and could tap the old man's fund of reminiscence and humor.

One Sunday Mick broke the news to him.

"There's something I want to say to you, Dad," he said gravely.

His father started. He didn't like the serious approach to anything. With his wife it always meant fresh losses, and his secret panic was that Mick might take after her.

"What is it?" he asked suspiciously.

"I don't think I can come to Mass with you any more."

"Why can't you?" his father asked in the same tone.

"Because I don't know that I believe in God any longer."

"You what?" snapped his father, stopping dead in his tracks.

This was what Mick had feared. He knew that when you touched the quick of his father's principle he reacted violently.

"I'm sorry," Mick said, growing red. "I was afraid it might upset you, but I can't help it. I have to try and hold on to what I think is the truth."

His father drew a deep breath through his nose, gave Mick a sharp look and then reached for his pipe. He went behind a tree to light it, and went on again, taking a couple of pulls as though to steady himself.

"I was afraid you were going to tell me something serious," he said with complete gravity.

Mick was surprised. He knew his father wasn't pietistic, but he had never seen him bend on a matter of principle. It made Mick suspicious.

"It's serious enough for me," he said.

"You're sure 'tis God and not Father Dempsey you don't believe in?" asked his father with a sideways look.

"What's the difference?" asked Mick.

"Oh, now, there's a big difference," replied his father warmly. "One is anticlericalism, a view taken only by the most religious people—myself for instance; the other is atheism—another view held by a lot of religious people."

Mr. Dowling had the same sort of poker-faced humor as Mick himself, though in him it was more sardonic, and Mick knew better than to take liberties with it. He knew he must draw his father out without making him blow up.

"Which is the best side for a religious chap to take?" he asked.

"Well," his father said slyly, "that would depend on how much you had to do with Dempsey."

"Oh, Dempsey," said Mick gloomily, "Dempsey is everywhere."

"Exactly!" said his father enthusiastically. "Dempsey is only an ignorant poor devil among people more ignorant than himself. That's why you mustn't mix up religious people and religion. You imagine 'tis religion you're up against when 'tis nothing only a lot of craw-thumping old women in a blooming provincial town."

"And where do you leave Mother?" Mick asked with a grin.

"Where the betting left her," said his father. "With the also-rans. Your poor mother, you must be very patient with her. . . . But religion!" he went on with growing enthusiasm. "Religion is something bigger than all of them."

"I'm not sure that I know what you mean by religion," said Mick.

"What *I* mean by it?" his father said testily. " 'Tisn't what I mean by it at all. Damn it, boy, the best brains of the world have been hammering away at it for thousands of years, and you talk of what *I* mean by it."

"Well, I've only been hammering for six months so I have a lot of way to make up," Mick said good-humoredly. "What do you think I ought to do?"

"I think you ought to make sure what you're giving up before you do it," said his father hotly, "and not be coming to me in a couple of months' time and telling me you've made some astounding discovery that you could have found in a penny catechism. Then, if you want to quit, I won't try to stop you. You ought to know that."

"I know that," Mick said solemnly, "and that's the very reason I don't want to do anything without getting your advice."

"Oh, advice!" said his father. "I'm not a proper person to advise you. I'm out of touch. You ought to get hold of some intelligent priest, some young fellow with a bit of imagination, and talk to him. There's little Father Felim in the Franciscans, for instance; he has his head screwed on. There ought to be a couple of books at home too."

This was the first Mick had ever heard of religious books in the home, apart from some detestable tracts. His father searched for them among a pile of old papers and pamphlets in the attic, secret newspapers from the days of the fighting, election handbills, broadsheet ballads—his father's wild oats. Mr. Dowling lost himself among them. "There's the account of poor Mick Tracy's trial," he said. "You ought to read that. Mick Tracy was a great man, God rest him." He had lost interest in the books by the time he found them. They must have been secondhand even when he got them first; a handbook of dogmatic theology, a couple of volumes of Newman and a study of St. Thomas Aquinas. The very look of them gave Mick a shock, for they revealed a side of his father that he had never known. One was heavily underlined, and the underlinings alone would have fascinated Mick. His father grinned when he saw them and started flicking over the pages. "That's well written," he said. "You ought to like that. Pretty tough going, though. Ah, Pascal is the fellow you'll have to get hold of. Pascal was the boy for them." He read a couple of the passages he had underlined, and his face took on an air of reverent wonder. He nodded once or twice but the nod was more by way of salute to his past than anything else. However strange Joe Dowling of twenty years before might be to Mick, he was just as strange to himself, and it made him uneasy. It was now clear that he felt he had discharged his responsibilities as a father, and didn't propose to do anything more.

So far as Mick was concerned, he had. He started learning whole pages by heart, and then read outward through religious journalism like Chesterton's to the Modernists, whose brilliance delighted him though he approved their condemnation. He lent the books to me in the spirit of a confirmed gambler who lends money to his opponent in order to play with him. Though I shirked the more exacting of the religious exercises that Mick indulged in, I was intellectually game.

But as always between Mick and me, it went far deeper than that in him. He had thought he was all alone in his doubts and difficulties, and the discovery that he shared them with great thinkers of all ages calmed the tumult in his mind, and brought out a new and happier side of him. He had always been naturally kind, but, because he was rather ashamed of it, he had made a convention of strength of mind. Now that he had found another source of strength, a real one this time, the convention was superseded. He was no longer ashamed of being seen coming up the road with one ragged child riding on his neck and another swinging from his arm.

Just because his mother had always been such a trial to him he felt it his duty to be particularly kind to her, and even to take her part when she disagreed with his father. On his way to early Mass, he lit the fire for her and made her a cup of tea. She replied by doing everything to make his kindnesses even more meritorious by her suspicion of them. It was a most extraordinary thing, but the one person you would have expected to be pleased at Mick's conversion was the one who wasn't pleased at all. I could see that for myself. When she answered the door for me one evening I called for Mick, she gave me a smile like a bog at evening and said, "He's gone out to Benediction."

"Is it at the Augustinians?" I asked, determined on finding him.

"I daresay," she said, giving her upper lip a mournful hitch. "He's getting so religious you wouldn't know where he'd be."

"Well," I said encouragingly, "you know wherever he is, he'll be all right."

"I hope so, indeed," she said despairingly.

She left me under a strong impression that she did not approve of men saving their own souls, and that, like cooking, this was something that should be done for them by their womenfolk. He didn't, fortunately, take his finals into his own hands, and contented himself with suggesting gently that she should give the favorites a rest and try an outsider.

"Why don't you try someone who might be interested in education?" he asked with a smile. "St. Thomas Aquinas, for instance."

"Who was he?" his mother asked wearily (by this time she had convinced herself that Mick was making up saints just to annoy her).

"He happened to be the greatest intellect of the Church," said Mick.

"Was it he wrote that old book you were reading?" she asked.

"It was not," said Mick.

"Wouldn't you think if he was so great that someone would find it out before this?" she asked.

Mick gave up telling her about the lives of his favorite saints. He realized that his father was right, and that his mother's brand of Catholicism was not of a strictly orthodox kind. But he couldn't take it philosophically as his father did. He worried over it. She gave him even greater cause for worry. She had never really been able to get over the loss of Mick's brother. She had, in fact, created a sort of fantasy life for him into which she retreated in fits of depression. She had nursed him through serious illnesses, sent him to school, comforted him in various troubles. He had no clear outline in her mind except that he didn't in any way resemble Mick. Naturally, he had shown a vocation from the earliest age, become a priest, and was expected to be a bishop. He would close her eyes in death, and afterward, by his prayers, give her soul a clear lead on those of the sly ones with inside knowledge who had begrudged a poor lone woman a tip about the saints.

"Ah, he's better off among the holy angels in Heaven," she said one day when again she was resigning herself to the hard blows of the world.

Mick gave her a sharp look. He had often heard the words before but had never attached any significance to them.

"How could he be in Heaven?" he asked mildly enough.

"Ah, what are you saying?" she asked, half in amusement, half in alarm. "Is it an innocent child?"

"Aren't you forgetting original sin?" Mick asked.

"Ah, for all the sin my poor child had on him!" she wailed. "Where else would he be but in Heaven, the little angel?"

"There's only one place he could be," said Mick. "Limbo."

"Limbo! What would he be doing in Limbo?"

"That's the teaching of the Church."

"Whoever teaches it, they're wrong," she said.

"What you mean is that you believe whatever suits you," Mick said sharply.

His father gave a loud sniff and went out to the garden.

"Will you listen to him?" Mrs. Dowling moaned to the blessed angels. "I believe what suits me!"

"Well, it's true," Mick said, forgetting his intention of being gentle with her. "You believe things no one asks you to believe, and don't believe things you're required to believe. What sort of religion is that?"

"Ah," she said, "I was practicing my religion before you were born. And my mother before me."

There was no logic in her. Mick went out to his father who was prying viciously at a bit of garden wall with a chisel. He was still riled. He knew he had upset his mother, and that, instead of going to someone in authority and finding out that he was right, she would only redouble her prayers and penances.

"Will you look at that for masonry?" his father said with a malice which was half triumph.

"Wouldn't you think they'd try to knock some of that superstition out of people?" Mick asked gloomily.

"Did you ever know a woman that wasn't superstitious?" retorted his father.

Mick had a date with Babiche, and the pair of them went up the woods over the river. They sat there, looking at the serpentining brightness behind the tree trunks, and Mick went over the scene with his mother. He was still angry and argumentative, and to his astonishment Babiche became argumentative too. It wasn't like Babiche, who never made an attempt to follow up an idea, but caught up some name or phrase that amused her and repeated it for months in contexts with which it had nothing on earth to do. But she seemed to resent Limbo almost as a personal affront.

"That was a very silly thing to say," she pouted.

"What's silly about it?" Mick asked angrily. "It's dogma."

"That has nothing to do with it. She was his mother after all."

"And what the blazes has that to do with it?" asked Mick. "I was his brother."

"Oh," she said with a shrug, "you don't care."

"I don't care about what?"

"You don't care about the unfortunate kid. If you had another brother you could say was in Hell you'd be made for life. You don't care for him any more than you care for me."

"I don't care for you?" he repeated, his face darkening.

"Well, isn't it true? I'm only in your way. You want to put on a Roman collar and go hunting down unfortunate old women to know do they believe in Limbo. I'm not going to stand in your way."

Mick was flabbergasted. He realized as she spoke that though he had had no such conscious desire, in fantasy he had been bringing light to a darkened world, and been slightly envious of those who, being able to get on without Babiches, could do it in reality. And his heart was touched at the idea that she had been aware of it, and hurt and lonely.

"I don't want to put on a Roman collar at all," he said flatly.

"Then what do you want?"

"What I've always wanted: get a job and marry you."

She shrugged her shoulders again and did something in a hurry with her shoe.

"Well, there's nothing very difficult about that," she grumbled, and at the same moment a grin came over her face. "But if I have a kid like that and you start telling me he's in Limbo, you won't find me as easygoing as your mother."

Mick set out to make up to her for the past misunderstandings, and Babiche let herself be persuaded. She was not a profound thinker. After that he went home in blind panic. The wild beast was in danger of breaking out again. It was horrible. You swung from instinct to judgment and from judgment back to instinct, and it never got any better and nothing seemed able to arrest the pendulum.

But next morning when he woke the sun was shining through the attic window, and he lay watching it, feeling that something very peculiar had happened to him. He didn't know what it was, but it was something very pleasant. It took him five minutes to realize what it was. The pendulum had stopped. He had lost faith. It was all like a dream, the previous months of exaltation and anxiety, and yet he wasn't in the least unhappy. He wasn't even afraid of the wild beast in himself. He knew the wild beast would never break loose because he was far too fond of human beings to let it.

The following Sunday he went out to Mass as usual with his father, and when they reached the church door he stopped.

"I'll see you after, Dad," he said.

His father showed no sign of surprise, but there was a pause before he said on an even tone:

"I think we might go down the Marina Walk for a change, don't you?"

Mick was heartsick at his father's disappointment and the noble way in which he tried to keep his word.

"You know the way I feel," he said miserably.

"What?" his father asked sharply. "Oh, yes. We all go through it. You have plenty of time. . . . Tell me," he went on inquisitively, "who's that little black-haired girl you're knocking round with?"

"Babiche Regan," said Mick, surprised that his father knew he was knocking round with anyone at all.

"Is she one of the Regans of Ballintemple?"

"That's right," said Mick, mystified by the turn the conversation had taken.

"I knew her father in the County Council," said his father approvingly. "A good family. Is she a fancy or a regular?" he added, as though he didn't know that Mick with his monumental gravity would have let a fancy die on his hands.

"I'm hoping to marry her when I can get a job, if you call that a fancy," growled Mick.

"You might do worse," said his father. "Ah, well, by the time you're settled down you'll be able to make up your mind. . . . Don't be late for that walk," he added warningly, and went in.

Mick strode up the Mardyke by himself, a free man for the first time but slightly anxious. It had sounded almost as though his father had expected Babiche to turn out like his mother, and Mick like himself. At the same time, he could scarcely mean that he expected Babiche to be so irrational or himself so weak.

Of course, it couldn't be; yet there was quiet triumph about his father's surrender that made Mick uneasy, as though it weren't all over yet.

 *Sue*

GOD FORGIVE ME, I could never stand my sister's young men. Even if she had had taste, I should still have resented them. Our house on the outskirts of Cork was small, and there simply wasn't room in it for me and a courting couple. After a day's work in the office, I would get settled with a book by the fire in the front room, and then I would hear the creak of the gate, the steps on the path, the knock, the boisterous voice in the hall—my hall! Sometimes I continued to read, and dared the fellow to come in and interrupt me, but there was never any false modesty about Sue's young men. They always had a warm corner in their hearts for themselves. Occasionally I went off to read in the kitchen, but there, apart from Mother's solicitude about whether I was warm enough and whether I could see with "the old gas"—meaning the gaslight fixture that I was reading by—I was almost certain to be interrupted again by the arrival of one of her old cronies, come to sit and gossip with her in the kitchen. So, most often, when I heard Sue's young man, I went off, cursing, to my own bedroom, where there was no heat and "the old gas" was worse even than in the kitchen. There, lying on my bed with a blanket over my feet, I listened to the cheerful voices of Sue and her young man sitting in comfort downstairs before the fire— my fire! Is it any wonder I grew lepping mad? Sue, of course, said I was sulky and unsociable, and Mother, who had an excuse for everybody, said the Horgans were all like that. I grew up with a considerable respect for the sensitiveness and intelligence of the Horgans.

Sue never had any taste in young men. There was a long string of them, only one of whom I ever liked and she dropped him inside a fortnight. She said he was dull! Mind, I had no very exaggerated notion of *her* charms. I knew she wasn't steady and was always excited or depressed about something, and when she had nothing to be excited or depressed about, she came up with the most extraordinary old pisherogues and superstitions that were supposed to be lucky or unlucky, according to the mood she was in. But she was warmhearted and generous, and she had a very good intelligence whenever the fancy took her to be intelligent. At any rate, she was a cut above the fellows she walked out with, though it wasn't until Harry Ridgeway came on the scene that I began to appreciate what an interesting girl she was.

I had also better be fair and admit that Ridgeway had his points, even though I didn't like him. I always thought him a bit too much of a dandy. He had a pink-and-white complexion like a girl's, and he dressed as carefully as any girl. Usually he wore a well-cut, tight-fitting suit that never had a trace of beer or tobacco ash on it, and a pale, correct-looking tie. And he had the impudence to jeer at my tweeds and my battered old tie and about how I needed a haircut. At a party, he was always in charge of entertaining the dolls, while I sat with a couple of friends, and a half dozen of stout hidden behind the sofa, and hoped to God the dolls would let us alone to talk politics or religion. Ridgeway had no politics, and his religion was like his ties—pale and correct. What I really mean is that he was a lightweight, a lady's man, though with occasional flashes of wit and intelligence, but definitely not the sort with whom you'd like to go to a bar and spend the evening discussing what was wrong with the country.

Still, I was rather puzzled by Sue's behavior, because, though she went out quite a lot with Ridgeway, she continued to go out as well with Sidney Healy, who had now been the resident pest for close on six months. I saw no reason for having two of them about the house, disturbing me.

"Are you going steady with that masher?" I asked her one evening while she was ironing and Mother washing up.

"What masher?" she asked, growing nervous and defensive, though I hadn't even raised my voice.

"How do you expect me to remember all their names? The sickly fellow with the queer ties."

"Harry Ridgeway?" she said in the same tone. "Why would I go steady with him? Sure, he's mad on Judy Holmes."

"Then why the hell doesn't he go to Judy Holmes's house instead of coming here?" I asked. "Who is this Holmes one, anyway?"

"She's the bank manager's daughter from Montenotte."

"Old Holmes's daughter?" I asked in surprise. "But aren't they Protestants?"

"I suppose they are. What about it?"

"Nothing, only he's not going to find it very easy to marry her, is he?"

"I don't know. I suppose he can get a dispensation. They have money enough, anyway. I advised him to propose to her months ago."

"Very handsome of you, I'm sure," I said with a sniff.

"There's nothing handsome about it. She's the right sort of girl for him, and she has a bit of money. The poor devil is crazy to get out of that house of his. His old fellow drinks, and his poor mother is in and out of hospital the whole time."

"I see," I said. "And because Mr. Ridgeway isn't happy at home, he thinks he's entitled to come and make sure that I'm not happy here."

That evening, I didn't move when Ridgeway came in. It's bad enough getting out of a comfortable room for another man, but at least you have the feeling that one of these days things are going to even out. But to let him have it as a free gift—chair, fire, gaslight, and all—was more than anyone could expect. Ridgeway didn't seem to resent my staying, and except for that silly-looking tie of his and his mincing way of balancing a teacup on his knee, I had nothing to complain of. The man had plenty of conversation, of a kind. Later in the evening, Sue asked him about Judy Holmes, and he didn't seem to resent that, either.

"Oh, Judy's playing at the School of Music concert next week," he said excitedly.

"Go on!" said Sue. "What's she playing?"

"The Mozart E-Flat, with Humphreys doing the violin part."

"Cripes, I'd love to hear her," said Sue.

"We can go together, if you like. What about you, Jack?"

"No, thanks," I said with a smile. I was fond of music, all right, but I avoided the local amateurs.

However, when Sue returned from the concert, she was full of Judy Holmes, and I knew there must have been something to her playing, for Sue in one of her intelligent phases was quite a good critic. She could have been a good pianist as well, but, being Sue, she never took the trouble to practice. She sat at the piano to illustrate what she was saying, and I filled in the violin part with three fingers while she showed how Judy did it, and when she played a wrong chord she used a dirty word. I laughed. I was always amused at the contrast between Sue's character and the language she used.

In a funny way, hearing about the concert gave me a sort of personal interest in the Holmes girl, and next time I met her in town I raised my cap to her. She smiled back rather coolly, and I wondered if she even knew who I was. She was a tall, thin girl with a long, pale face, and a good figure concealed in a wide coat like a tent. Her hat was a plain felt one, like a schoolgirl's. She was dressed expensively but plainly. After that, whenever I found myself daydreaming, I would think of her as the sort of girl you could take up as you took up politics or religion—a girl of natural seriousness, who could play

Mozart as he should be played, and with no nonsense about her. Now when Ridgeway talked about her to Mother and Sue, I found myself listening to him. They were fascinated by everything he told them about the Holmeses, and it wasn't only the money and the bit of style that interested them, though clearly, for them as for Ridgeway, it had the appeal of a fairy tale. But besides this they both had a genuine admiration for the qualities of character the Holmeses displayed: Judy's daily two hours of piano practice, her dutifulness in answering letters and remembering birthdays, her mother's social work, and the strict and narrow piety of an Irish Protestant family. How narrow that could be I was reminded one night when Ridgeway reported that one of Judy's girl friends had used a Biblical phrase by way of a joke and Mrs. Holmes had pointed out that it was blasphemy.

"Sure, when the girl didn't mean it!" protested Mother, who never really minded what people said so long as they smiled at her while they were saying it.

"Ah, they don't look at it that way at all, Mrs. Horgan," Ridgeway said with a frown. "Of course the girl didn't mean it, but still they don't think you should say such things. And I can't help admiring them for it."

I could see that Ridgeway had Mother and Sue admiring them for it as well.

But then an extraordinary thing happened. Ridgeway proposed, but he proposed not to Judy but to Sue. I couldn't understand it. I knew that he wanted to make a home of his own, and it wasn't only that his father drank and his mother was so sickly that she could not keep abreast of the housekeeping. He wanted a background to go with the ties and suits, and he must have been miserably self-conscious about any friends that called to his house. You could see the sort of place he would try and make for himself—a small house in a modern terrace, with a neatly covered suite of furniture, bought on time, a few water colors, and a vase of flowers; and there he would give little musical parties, and tea would be served in rather dainty cups. But Sue's background was just the same as his own, and imagine Sue keeping a house like that for him. She would wreck the damn place in a week.

I could see that the proposal had come as a real shock to Sue. She couldn't understand it, either, and as a result she couldn't stop talking of it.

"But you like him," I said. "Why shouldn't you marry him if you want to?"

"Ah, how could I?" she asked doubtfully. "He's not in love with me. Isn't that enough?"

"How sure you are of it!" I said. I wasn't really any fonder of Ridgeway than I had been, but I realized that he would make somone an excellent husband and that Sue was the sort of girl who might very easily marry the wrong man—or no man at all. "Isn't that for him to say?"

"Ah, it's not that," she said, and she still sounded doubtful. "I suppose he felt he had to ask me."

"He needn't have felt that at all," Mother said earnestly, "but it showed very nice feeling. I was always very fond of Harry, and I only wish you could marry him."

"Oh, for God's sake, hold on!" I said, getting angry with them again. "I don't think Sue even knows what she's doing. Nobody ever proposes to a girl just out of nice feeling."

"Harry would," Sue said flatly. "He's too soft for his own good. I daresay he thought people were talking about us."

"Nonsense!" I said shortly. "He knows more about girls than that. Probably he proposed to Judy Holmes and got the cold shoulder."

"I wouldn't say so," Sue said thoughtfully. "I think he'd have told me."

"For a man you won't marry you seem to have a remarkably high opinion of him," I said sarcastically. "I'd wait and see about that."

"Ah, I don't think so," Sue said complacently. "Even if he did propose to her, she'd hardly talk about it."

"She'd be the first woman in history that didn't," said I.

"I wouldn't be too sure about that, either," said Sue. "Harry probably has his own reasons for not proposing to her. I daresay his family wouldn't like his marrying a Protestant."

And suddenly she rang a bell in my head. You see, there were certain things that I seemed always to have known about myself. One was that if I fell in love there would be no walking out with other girls. Another was that if I did fall in love with someone I knew my family and friends would disapprove of—a Jew or a Protestant—I would not allow myself to be influenced by them. Whatever other faults I might have, I knew myself to be a man of seriousness and strength of character. And these, I knew, were precisely the qualities that Ridgeway hadn't got.

"Ah, so that's the reason!" I said, and I daresay triumph showed in my voice, for Sue turned on me.

"And what's wrong with it?" she asked.

"Nothing," I said. "Except that now you're talking sense."

I liked that explanation because it enabled me to go on looking down on Ridgeway. But I still couldn't understand why Sue didn't want to marry him when, quite clearly, she liked him so much. I knew that she wasn't acting like the heroine of a sentimental novel and refusing him for fear of injuring his career. Apart from anything else, Sue had never read enough novels to know that a heroine might be expected to act in this peculiar way, and if you had explained it to her, she would merely have gaped and asked in her commonest tone, "What sort of bloody idiot do you think I am?" No, the girl had got it firmly fixed in her head that Ridgeway didn't care for her, and for that reason would not marry him.

Yet they continued to go out together. After his proposal, I felt that Ridgeway was entitled to whatever facilities the house offered, and I left the parlor to them. One night, I was sitting with Mother in the kitchen. Sue and Ridgeway were supposed to be courting in the front room. All at once a most unholy row began. We couldn't hear what they said, but he was talking in a low, bitter voice and Sue was yelling her head off at him. Mother clasped her hands in prayer and made to get up, but I signaled to her to stay where she was.

"The poor child!" Mother moaned. "God direct me!" she added, meaning that she distrusted my direction. The sitting-room door opened and I distinctly hear Ridgeway use a dirty word. Two dirty words! Fortunately, Mother either didn't hear or didn't understand. Then the front door slammed behind him, and Mother, with another glance at the ceiling, from which God could be supposed to be directing her, muttered, "And without even saying good night to me!" It was a real tragedy for Mother, because she loved Harry Ridgeway's little airs of politeness, so different from the roughness of Sue and me. Then Sue came into the kitchen, bawling, and for five minutes it was impossible to get a stim of sense out of her.

"Child!" Mother cried with what she clearly believed to be sternness. "You must tell your brother and me what he said to you." When she referred to me as Sue's brother, she promoted me to a position of authority.

"He asked me to marry him again," sobbed Sue.

Mother, being one of the sympathetic souls of the world, was just on the point of saying "The blackguard! He should be ashamed of himself!" when she realized that it wouldn't be altogether appropriate, so she just wrung her hands and said, "Well! Well! Well!"

"After all, that's nothing to snivel about," I said coldly.

"Who's sniveling?" Sue asked, flaring up, as I had expected her to do. "He said things were desperate in his house. It's not the only bloody house things are desperate in, if you ask me."

"Oh, Sue—" Mother was beginning when I broke in.

"And what did you tell him?"

"The same thing I told him before, of course. So he said he was going straight off to ask Judy Holmes."

"All right," I said. "And isn't that what you wanted?"

"Whether I wanted it or not has nothing to do with it," she said. "How the hell could I marry a fellow like that, that would hate the very sight of me before the honeymoon was over?"

"Oh, Sue, how can you say things like that?" Mother exclaimed indignantly.

"Because it's true, woman. I know Jack thinks he is a bit of a snob. What's wrong with that? Ye're all terrified out of your lives of trying to make yourself out a bit better than ye are. I'd be a snob, too, if only I had something to be a snob about. He hates a girl even to use a dirty word."

"And perfectly right he is!" Mother cried. "What right has any decent girl to use language like that, picked up at street corners?"

"Then what does he want with me? He heard me use it. He told me if I ever used a word like that again he'd slap my face."

"And what did you do?" I asked, knowing perfectly well what Sue would do if I told her that.

"I said it, of course."

"Sue, you didn't!" exclaimed Mother.

"I did," said Sue, and then began to giggle faintly.

"And what did he do?" I asked.

"Oh, he slapped my face, all right," said Sue, her face lighting up. Obviously, the incident had made a favorable impression. "What should he do?"

"He should talk to you seriously, Sue," Mother said passionately. "He should not do a thing like that. I'm surprised at him—such a nice boy! Eleven years I lived with your poor father, God rest him, and never once did he lift a hand to me."

"A pity he didn't lift it to us a bit oftener," said Sue.

"The dear knows, it's hard to know what to do," Mother said, turning away and shaking her head despondently.

"Anyway," I said, realizing what was in Sue's mind, "you know he's not going to ask Judy."

"That's all you know about him," Sue replied, beginning to sob again. "He's probably asking her now. And she's the right girl for him, whatever his family or anyone else thinks."

Then she went up to her room to live it all through again, and bawl a bit more, while Mother sat by the fire and sighed over the contrariness of everything. Of course, she knew that Sue was doing the right thing, but she couldn't help wishing she weren't. As for me, I was beginning to make discoveries about my extraordinary sister. I knew now that she had refused to marry Harry Ridgeway because she genuinely believed he didn't care for her. The poor fool had so often expressed his admiration for Judy and her family that he had even persuaded those two romantic women to admire them as well, and Sue could only think of love in terms of admiration. Admiration, that is, of positive virtues she recognized and respected. She was quite certain that she had none of those particular virtues herself, and yet she would keep on hoping that someday some man would discover something positive to admire in her. Perhaps, after all, she wasn't even so extraordinary; perhaps a lot of other women confuse love and admiration in the same way, and never realize that a man may love them as much for their faults as their virtues, and may think with delight of the way they begin to sparkle when everyone else is going home, or forget themselves and swear. At the same time, I knew it was something I should never be able to explain to Sue, and for some reason this made me feel unusually tender to her in the weeks that followed. I even took her to the pictures a couple of times, when she and everyone else knew I hated the pictures.

But she had been right about Harry Ridgeway. That night or next day, he had gone straight to Judy Holmes and proposed to her and been accepted. He'd even induced herself and her family to sign along the dotted line in connection with the religion of the children. I had to admit that when it came to the point, Ridgeway, ties and all, was masculine enough.

It might have been better for him if he hadn't been. I met the pair of them one night on Patrick's Bridge. She was, as usual, plainly dressed, while Ridgeway was even more the dandy than before. Between them they made me feel very awkward, with my long hair, my cap, and my rough tweeds, but Ridgeway seemed very pleased to meet me.

"You've heard of Sue's brother Jack," he said to Judy.

"Almost as much as I've heard of Sue," she said with a thin smile. "I suppose he's another charmer?"

"Oh, begod, he is not," Ridgeway said with a loud laugh. "Sourest blackguard you'll find about this town."

"Ah, he probably only needs a girl to make a lot of him, as you do of Sue," she said archly.

"Come on, Holmes!" he cried. "You never heard the half of Sue."

"No, you didn't get much chance of talking about her, did you, poor fellow?" she said in a mocking drawl. "But you do get these dreadful obsessions with people."

We said good night, and I went on through town. It was only when I was halfway down Patrick Street that it dawned on me that Judy hadn't been exactly pleasant to me. For some reason, I always approach people on the assumption that they intend to be nice to me, and it usually takes time before I realize that they haven't been. I had gone the full length of the street before I thought, My God, that girl is a devil!

As I strolled home that night, I could see as clearly as if I were living through it how dearly Ridgeway was going to pay for his harmless snobbery. I could also see why he might have been afraid of bringing a girl like that into his own family. People of our class are plain and rough, but nobody is so plain and rough that they wouldn't resent her tone, and from this time on Ridgeway would have to depend for his friendships on his wife's family and their friends.

I was so full of my own discovery that while I was telling Mother and Sue, it never once struck me that they might feel differently about it. They listened in silence, and then Sue lit a cigarette and said, "God damn her!" and Mother didn't even protest. She was too shaken. "The poor, deluded boy!" she said softly, clasping and unclasping her hands.

Then I saw that both had tears in their eyes, not only for Harry Ridgeway and his aspirations but for their own. It was as if life had betrayed them by being less generous than they themselves were. I kissed them before I went to bed. It was not a custom of mine, but I felt extraordinarily proud of them both.

Music When Soft Voices Die

DURING THE LUNCH HOUR the male clerks usually went out, leaving myself and the three girls behind. While they ate their sandwiches and drank their tea, they chattered away, thirteen to the dozen. Half their converastion I didn't understand at all, and the other half bored me to tears. I usually drifted into the hallway with a Western. As a boy, I acted out whatever I was reading—taking steady aim, drawing rein, spurring to the rescue, and clutching at my shoulder where an Indian arrow had lodged—and the girls interrupted me with their comments.

They were nice girls, though. Joan, who was nineteen, was my favorite. She was masterful and warmhearted; she would take my part when I got in trouble, and whenever she saw me with the sign of tears, she would put her arm round me and say, "Look, Larry— *you* tell Mr. Scally if he says *another* word to you, I'll tear his *eyes* out." She talked like that, all in italics. I liked Nora, too, but not so much. Sometimes she was very sweet and sometimes she didn't see you, and you never knew which it would be. Marie I didn't really like at all in those days. She was the prettiest of the three—thin, tall, and nunlike, with a queer stiff way of holding herself and an ironic intonation in her beautiful voice. Marie usually just didn't see you. I thought she was an old snob.

The three girls had fellows, and I knew these, too, mostly from seeing them hang about the office in the evening. Joan was going with a long-haired medical student called Mick Shea, with no hat and no religion, and she was always making novenas for his conversion. Nora went with a dressy fellow in Montenotte, the classy quarter of Cork, but she had a sort of underground understanding with a good-looking postman called Paddy Lacy, who used to stop me in the street and give me gallant messages for her. She never walked out with him that I knew of, but he was certain she loved him, and it shocked me that a superior fellow like a postman would not have more sense. Marie was going strong with a chap called Jim Holbrook, a rather snobbish intellectual type, who lived up my way.

Thirty years has turned the girls and myself into old friends. Only Nora is still at the office. Joan owns a private hotel, and Marie is the harassed mother of two wild children. She is still beautiful, sedate, and caustic. Not one word of their conversation ever seemed to register in my memory, which was full of valuable information about American states and Indian nations, wigwams, colts, derringers, and coyotes; yet now that I cannot remember anything of what I read, it seems to me that I can hear the girls as though they were in the same room with me, like the voices of Shelley's poem, trembling on the edge of pure music.

"Do you know, I have a *great* admiration for that girl?" Joan begins in her eager italics.

"Go on!" Nora says lightly. "What did she do?"

"I admire her pluck, Nora," Joan says, emphasizing three syllables out of seven. "When I *think* what she went through!"

"Ah, for God's sake, what did she go through?" Nora asks skeptically.

"That's all you know, Nora," Joan says in a bloodcurdling voice. "You never had an illegitimate kid to support, as Susie had."

"Good job, too," Nora says. "I can't support myself."

"What did you say she had, Joan?" Marie asks incredulously.

"A kid."

"Well!" Marie exclaims, looking brightly from one to the other. "The friends some people have!"

"Oh, it's true, Marie."

"That's what makes it so peculiar, Joan," Marie says with a shrug.

"What did she do with it?" Nora asks inquisitively.

"I suppose I really shouldn't say it, Nora, but of course it's really no secret. With the way the police watch girls like that, everything leaks out eventually. She had to farm him out in Rochestown. He must be about twelve now."

"And does he know who his mother is?" asks Nora.

"Not at all, girl," says Joan. "How could she tell him? I suppose she's never even seen him. Gosh, I'm sorry for that girl!"

"I'd be sorrier for the kid," Nora says.

"Oh, I know, Nora, I know," Joan says earnestly. "But what could the poor girl do? I mean, what would *we* do if we were in her place?"

And now that the voices grow clearer in my mind, I realize that Joan is the leader of the trio. It is she who sets the tempo, and it is her violin that holds it all together. Marie, with her deep beautiful voice, is the viola; Nora, for all that her voice sounds thin and squeaky is the cello.

"Honestly, Joan, the things you say!" Marie cries, but without indignation. Marie sometimes behaves as though Joan is not really right in the head, and manages to suggest that she herself alone, with her nunlike air and caustic tongue, represents normality.

But Joan, who believes that Marie cultivates a blind spot for anything it doesn't suit her to see, only smiles knowingly. "Well, we're all human, girl," she says.

"Ah, nonsense, Joan!" says Marie. "There must be something wrong with a girl like that."

"There's something wrong with every girl or else she'd be a man," says Nora.

"Ah, with the best will in the world, girl, I couldn't imagine myself going on like that," says Marie. "I suppose I mustn't be human," she adds with a shrug, meaning that if this is what it's like to be human, so much the worse for humanity. "Of course," she ends, to show she has feelings, like anyone else, "we all like a bit of sport, but that's different."

"Oh, but it's not different, Marie," Joan says warmly, and again the fiddle proclaims the theme. "That's where you make your big mistake. What you call 'a bit of sport' is only a matter of degree. God knows, I'm not what you'd call a public menace, but if I didn't watch my step, I could very easily see it happening to me."

"So could I," Nora says, and then begins to blush. "And I don't know what I'd do about it, either."

"Well, what could you do?" asks Marie. "Assuming that such a thing could happen, which is assuming quite a lot."

"I suppose I'd have to go to England and have it there," says Nora gloomily.

"England?" says Marie.

"That would be all right if you knew someone in England, Nora," says Joan. "I mean, someone you could rely on."

" 'All right'?" echoes Marie. "I should think starting life again in a foreign country with a baby, like that, would hardly be described as 'all right.' Or maybe I'm lacking in initiative?"

"Well, it would either be that or make him marry you," says Nora.

"I was wondering when you'd think of marriage," says Marie.

"That mightn't be as easy as it sounds, either, Marie," says Joan. "I think Nora means the fellow wouldn't want to marry you."

"Yes, and I think it's rotten!" says Nora. "A fellow pretending to a girl that she's the only thing in the world he cares for, till she makes a fool of herself for him, and then he cuts his hook."

"Well," Joan says practically, "I suppose we're all the same when we get what we want."

"If that's all a man wants, couldn't somebody give it to him on a spoon?" says Nora.

"I'd simply say in a case like that that the man began to see what sort the girl was," Marie says, having completely misunderstood Nora's remark.

"And what sort would you say *he* was?" Nora asks.

"Ah, well," Marie replies comfortably, "that's different, Nora. Considering the sort of sheltered lives women lead, it's up to them to set a standard. You can't expect the same sort of thing from men. Of course, I think he should be made to marry her."

"But who'd make him, Marie?" asks Joan.

"Well, I suppose his family would, if it was for nothing but to avoid a scandal."

"Ask any mother in Cork would she sooner a scandal or a daughter-in-law," Nora says cynically.

"Then of course the priest would have to make him," says Marie, still unperturbed.

"That's what I find so hard to imagine, though," Joan says, and then her tone changes, and she becomes brilliant and mocking. "I mean, it's all very well talking about it like this in the peace and quiet of the office, but imagine if I had to go up tonight after dark to the presbytery and talk to old Canon Cremin about it. 'Excuse me, Canon, but I've been keeping company with a boy called Mick Shea, and it just so happens that he made a bit too free with me, and I was wondering would you ever mind running down and telling him to marry me.' Cripes, if I was the Canon, I'd take my stick to a one like that!"

"Lovely marriage 'twould be anyway," says Nora.

"Exactly, Nora," Joan says, in her dramatic way, laying her hand on Nora's arm. "That's just what I mean. How on earth could you spend the rest of your life with a man after having to do that to get him to marry you?"

"How he could spend the rest of his life with me is what I'd be worrying about," says Nora. "After all, I'd be the one that was to blame."

"Never mind about him at all, now, girl," Joan says with a jolly laugh. "It's my own troubles that I'm thinking about. Honestly, do you know, I don't think I could face it!"

"I'm full sure I couldn't," says Nora, lighting a cigarette.

"But what else could you do?" Marie asks. She obviously thinks they are two very peculiar girls, and no wonder. They were peculiar, like all delightful girls.

"Do you know, Marie," says Joan, "I think I'd sooner marry the first poor devil that came the way."

"Aren't you lucky, being able to pick them up like that?" Marie asks dryly.

"Ah, well, Marie," says Joan, "a girl would be in a bad way entirely if there wasn't one man that would take her on."

"Like Paddy Lacy," says Nora, with a giggle. "He stopped me on the road the other day while he was delivering the letters, and I declare to God I didn't know which way to look."

"I see," says Marie. "So that's why you keep Paddy Lacy on. I was wondering about that."

"You needn't," Nora says with sudden temper. "I'm pretty sure Paddy Lacy would be just as tough as the rest of them if I went along and told him a thing like that."

"But why would you have to tell him, Nora?" Joan asks anxiously. "Wouldn't you let him find out for himself?"

"And a nice situation I'd be in when he did!"

"Oh, I wouldn't be too sure," Joan says with another laugh. "Before a man made up his mind about a thing like that, I'd like him to have a chance of seeing the full beauty of my character. Like the boatman in Glengarriffe, I'm at my best on a long stretch."

"I think I'd as soon live with a man I forced to marry me as one I tricked into marrying me," Nora says. "And I'd sooner do either than what your pal did—farm out a child. I don't think I'd ever have a day's luck after."

"Now, you're misjudging the girl there, Nora," Joan says earnestly. "You are, really! It's not the same thing when you never have the chance of getting attached to a child. And when there isn't a blessed thing you can do about it, I don't honestly believe that there's any moral responsibility."

"Responsibility?" Nora says, getting up. "Who's talking about responsibility? I'd live in dread of my own shadow for the rest of my days. I wouldn't be able to see a barefooted kid in the street without getting sick. Every knock that came to the door, I'd be in dread to open it. Every body that was picked out of the river, I'd feel it was my kid, and I was the one to blame. For God's sake, don't talk to me!"

"There's another cup of tea left, Nora," Joan says, a little too brightly. "Would you like it?"

"In a minute, Joan," says Nora, and goes out to the Ladies'. When she returns a few minutes later, she looks as though she had been crying. To me it is a great mystery, because no one speaks crossly to her. I assume that, like myself, she has a father who drinks.

"Cripes, I'm sorry for poor May Jenkins," Joan begins on another day, after Nora has poured out the tea. That is her time for a new theme, when there is no serious danger of interruption.

"Who's *she* when she's at home?" Nora asks lightly.

"May Jenkins? You'd hardly know her, Nora. She's from the South Side."

"And what ails her now didn't ail her before?" asks Nora, who is full of local quips and phrases.

"Oh, the usual thing," says Joan with a shrug. "Phil Macken, her husband, is knocking round with the Archer girl, on the Wellington Road—the Yellow Peril."

"Really, Joan," Marie says, "I don't know where you come across all those extraordinary people."

"I don't see what's so extraordinary about that at all," Nora says. "People are always doing it."

"And people are always getting terrible diseases, only we don't go out of our way to inquire," says Marie primly. "Really, there must be something wrong with a woman like that."

"Like May, Marie?" Joan asks in mock surprise.

"No, like that other creature—whatever you said her name was."

"Oh, I wouldn't say that at all, Marie," says Joan. "Some very respectable people live on the Wellington Road. And a lot of men find her attractive."

"Then there must be something wrong with the men."

"Or the wife, why don't you say?" cries Nora.

"Or the wife," Marie agrees with perfect placidity. "She should be able to mind her own husband."

"She'd want roller skates," says Joan, and again I hear the high note of the violin, driving the trio onward. "No, Marie, girl," she says, resting her chin on her hands, "you have to face the facts. A lot of women do get unattractive after marriage. Of course, I'm not blaming them. We'd be the same ourselves, with kids to mind and jobs to do. They can't waste time dancing and dolling themselves up like Maeve Archer, and if they did, their houses would soon show it. You see, it's something we all have to be prepared for."

"If I felt that way, Joan, I'd go into a convent," Marie says severely.

"But after all, Marie," says Joan, "what could you do? Suppose you were married to Jim and a thing like that happened?"

"What could I do?" Marie echoes, smiling at the thought of anything of the sort happening with Jim. "Well, I suppose I could walk out of the house."

"Ah, come now, Marie," Joan says. "It's not as easy as all that. Where would you walk to, in the first place?"

"What's wrong with going home?"

"With a houseful of kids?" says Joan. "Of course, I know your father is very fond of you and all the rest of it, but all the same, we have to be reasonable."

"I could go somewhere else," says Marie. "After all, Jim would have to support me—and the kids, as you say."

"Of course he would. That's if you didn't mind spending the rest of your days as a grass widow. You know, Marie, I saw one or two women who did that, and it didn't look too promising to me. No, in the way of husbands and fathers and so on, I don't think you can beat men. A dog won't do."

"But do you mean you'd let him go on seeing a filthy creature like that?" asks Marie. "Really, Joan, I don't think you can be serious."

"Oh, I never said that," Joan says hastily. "I'm sure I'd make it pretty uncomfortable for him."

"Which mightn't be such a bad way of making the other woman more attractive," Nora says dryly.

"Oh, we all know what Nora would do," Joan retorts with affectionate mockery. "She'd sit down and have a good cry. Wouldn't you, love?"

"I might," Nora replies doubtfully. "I'd sooner that than calling in the neighbors."

"Oh, I admit you'd have to keep your dignity, Nora," Marie says, being particularly susceptible to any appeal to her ladyhood. "But surely someone would have to interfere."

"I saw too much interference, Marie," Nora says grimly. "It's mad enough thinking you can spend your whole life with a man and still be in love with him, but 'tis dotty entirely if you imagine you can do it with half Cork acting as referee."

"All the same, Nora," Joan says, in her practical way, "before I saw a woman like that making off with a husband of mine, I'd get a fistful of her hair, and I wouldn't mind who knew it, either. I'd read and spell her, I give you my word."

"I certainly wouldn't degrade myself by quarreling with a creature like that," says Marie.

"I wouldn't have the nerve," says Nora, lighting a cigarette. "Look, it's all very well to talk about it like that, but suppose it was the other way around? Suppose you were making a fool of yourself over another man, and your husband disgraced you all over Cork by fighting him?"

"Really, Nora," says Marie, with her Mona Lisa smile, "you have a remarkably vivid imagination."

"Oh, I don't know that that's all imagination, either, Marie," says Joan, who enjoys nothing better than imagining things. "That could happen, too, mind you!"

"But that would make you no better than the woman you're just talking about," says Marie.

"Who said we were any better?" asks Nora. "I might be worse, for all anyone knows."

"But do you know, Nora," Joan says, "I'm not at all sure but I'd like Mick to do it."

"To shame you all over Cork?" Nora asks.

"Oh, no. Just to stand up for his rights. Nobody wants a doormat."

"Give me doormats every time," says Nora, with a sinister pull at her cigarette.

"But, Nora," Marie asks in horror, "you don't mean you'd just sit at home and do nothing?"

"I don't know, girl. What could you do?"

"And wait till he changed his mind and came back to you?"

"Maybe," says Nora, with a shrug. "I mightn't be there when he got back. I might have a fellow, too."

"Really," Marie says, scratching her long neck. "I'm beginning to see a number of uses for this Paddy Lacy of yours."

"That's where women have the worst of it," Joan says quickly, to head off a reply from Nora about Paddy Lacy. "It's not as easy for a married woman with a couple of kids to find someone to go off with. It's too chancy giving children a stepfather, no matter how fond you might be of him. No, what I can't imagine," she adds earnestly, "is what you'd do when he did change his mind. I often wonder could you ever behave in the same way to him."

"Of course not, Joan," Marie says. "Naturally, if there were children, I could understand remaining in the same house with him, just for their sake, but living with him as husband and wife is a thing I could never imagine doing."

"Ah, now, Marie, you're a girl of great character," Joan says. "But that sounds to me too much like giving up sweets in a sweetshop. Of course, I know people do it when they get tired of one another, but it never seems natural to me. I wouldn't do it just for fun," she adds gravely. "I'd want to be pretty sure that he was still fond of me."

"I'm afraid I wouldn't have much faith in the affections of a man like that," Marie says.

"What about you, Nora?" Joan asks.

"Me?" Nora says, blushing. "Oh, I suppose 'twould depend."

"You mean, depend on how he behaved to you?"

"Yes," Nora replies with a frightened air. "And how he behaved to the other one."

"Well, really, Nora, this is going beyond the beyonds!" Marie exclaims, putting down her cup with a ladylike air of finality. "Are we supposed to take *her* feelings into consideration as well?"

"I suppose she might have feelings, too?" Nora replies gloomily.

"I know what Nora would do!" Joan says triumphantly, bringing her hand down flat on the table. "I know it just as if I was there. She'd tell her husband to go to blazes, and skelp off to the other woman's house to console her."

"By the way she's talking, it sounds as if she'd leave her husband and live with the other one," Marie says.

"I might even do that," says Nora, moving toward the door.

"Ah, go on, girl!" Joan says boisterously. "Don't you know we're only making fun of you? I know what's going to happen to you," she adds comfortingly. "You'll marry a fine steady slob of a man that'll stick his two heels on the mantelpiece and never look at the side of the road another woman is walking at. Look, there's a cup of tea in the pot still!"

"I don't want it, Joanie, thanks," says Nora, and goes off to the Ladies'.

Marie gives a shrug. "For an intelligent girl, Nora does talk the most extraordinary nonsense," she says with finality.

"Oh, I wouldn't be too sure it was nonsense, Marie," Joan says, in her loyal way. "I think Nora might surprise us all."

But Nora, worse luck, has never had the opportunity of surprising anyone; nor has Joan—two fine women who have never met with men astute enough to grab them. As for Marie, she rules her husband gently but firmly, like a Reverend Mother dealing with a rather dull undergardener. Of the three, she is now the one I am most intimate with. Sometimes I even think that if I were ever to forget myself and make advances to her, instead of slapping my face indignantly she would only laugh and say, "Ah, Larry, will you have a bit of sense?"—which from Marie would be almost like a declaration of love. And I think the reason is that, like me, she hears those voices "vibrate in the memory" and wonders over them.

"Ah, Larry," she says, grabbing me eagerly by the hands, "do you remember all the old nonsense we used to talk in the office, and Joan saying what she'd do with an illegitimate baby, and me saying what I'd do if Jim went off with another woman? And look at us now—three old women!"

No doubt she realizes that she can afford to say things like that to me, for while the music of those voices lingers in my mind she and they will never be old.

A Life of Your Own

JANE HARTY, the pharmacist, lived alone in a little bungalow on the outskirts of the town. She had long ago decided that it was the only way to live a life of her own. In a city like Dublin you could be one of a group without adopting its standards, but girls who took lodgings in the town accepted a discipline stricter than that of home.

"But how do you ever stand it alone in the country, Jane?" one of them would ask. "I'd be terrified."

"To tell you the God's truth, I *am* terrified, girl," Jane would say. "But sure, who'd have me?"

She knew plenty who would have her, but she couldn't live their way, and after her parents' death and her brother's departure for London, she had given up trying. She ran a battered old car and went off on free weekends by herself, without telling anyone where she was going, except the Sullivans. Celia Sullivan had been to school with her and had married the headmaster of the Technical School, an ugly, slow-moving, cynical man whom Celia considered a dull stick but the best she could get. Jane, who did not think Ned dull, realized with irritation that Celia was not quite so clever as she appeared to be.

The bungalow was not very comfortable, and she could afford to have a cleaning woman in only once a week, but it had a garden and a bit of a view, and Jane could have the Sullivans there whenever she pleased and bring the children there when they were

away. Besides, in her native town she was somebody. The poor
people feared and distrusted doctors, and they came to her with their
troubles instead. They knew she didn't mind tramping down dirty
lanes with a prescription or looking at a sick child or fighting with a
drunken husband. She was one of them. Of course, they knew
things about her as well. They had known her from the time she
was a child, and knew she was regarded as a bit of a freak by the
shopkeeping group—all because she wouldn't play the game, and
fell in love with unsuitable men. Unsuitable men seemed to be the
price you had to pay for trying to live a life of your own, but Jane
felt it came cheaper in the long run.

At least she had done so until that night she had come back
from Dublin and felt the panic. She had opened the door, then
stepped back and asked angrily, "Is there somebody there?" There
had been no reply and she had muttered to herself, "You're getting
neurotic, Harty," and gone in. One glance had been enough to show
that it wasn't nerves. Through the open door of the bedroom she
had seen her clothes scattered on the floor. She had searched the two
rooms and the kitchen but had found nothing missing. Yet it had
given her a sick and desolate feeling, like the touch of something
dirty.

Next morning, she went to the police station and made her
complaint to the sergeant, a beefy, boozy man by the name of
Lenihan.

"Ah, it's them kids, Miss Harty," he said gloomily.

"What kids, Joe?"

"That rough gang down by the River Road," he said. "They
didn't take anything?"

"Not that I could see."

"Pity about that," he said moodily. "If only there was anything
taken we could keep an eye out for it. They'd sell anything, even
with your name on it. Young Guard Humphreys lives up your way.
I'll tell him to watch out for any kids going in that direction. In the
meantime, the best thing you could do would be to leave word with
us when you're going away."

That night she went round to the Sullivans' and told her story.

Ned listened in his careful way. Celia, of course, had to tell how her aunt's house was burgled and how she had lost the family jewelry. There was a great dramatist lost in Celia, and at the end of a quarter of an hour it was clear that she had forgotten entirely about Jane's troubles. But Ned hadn't.

"It's no use going to those fellows, Jane," he said in his blunt voice. "When one of them leaves the barrack they can hear his boots at the other side of the town. I'll talk to some of the kids about it. The only way to turn juvenile delinquents into decent citizens is to make policemen of them. God knows, 'twill be a change for some of them."

But neither the police guards nor the Technical School boys were round when the intruder came again. Jane arrived home on Sunday night from Galway, and the first glance was enough to show her that her visitor was no child from the River Road. She felt sick again, but this time anger got the upper hand. She drove back to Humphreys's house, which was on a hill near the main road. Madge Humphreys—a schoolteacher who was determined to read what she called the "clahssics" to her family until their spirit was well broken—answered the door and said her husband was not in, but just at that moment Humphreys spoiled it all by coming out. "Arrah, Madge, a policeman is never off duty," he said amiably as he pulled on his jacket. "I might as well go and see what's up."

When Jane showed him the living room he said softly, "Oh, Christ!" which he certainly would not have said in front of Madge. In the kitchen doorway he halted. "Are these yours?" he asked, nodding at the tea things, and she shook her head, anger giving way to hopelessness. What the hell was the use of trying to live a life of your own? "Better check and see is anything missing from the bedroom," he said, and she preceded him, looking round helplessly. "Try your clothes first," he suggested with a smile, and she began to fold them and put them back. Meanwhile, he sat down and lit a cigarette.

"What's the verdict?" he asked, and she burst into a loud, angry laugh.

"Nothing I can see, only a pair of pants," she said, and then, observing the startled look on his face, realized the significance of what she had just said. "Oh, God!" she added.

"Better make sure of it," he said grimly, and she checked again.

"They're gone all right," she said with a shrug. "Frilly ones— they were a present. I wouldn't wear the blooming things."

"That's bad!" he said and got up and went into the living room.

"You'll have a drink as you're here?" she said.

"Ah, I'd better not," he said with an apologetic smile. "It's Madge. She starts getting nervous when I'm out."

"Well, I'm going to have one," said Jane, knowing well what it was Madge was nervous of—another woman who might talk to him about something besides the "clahssics." But Humphreys, as she had realized long before, was not a fool like his wife.

"Tell me, was any fellow annoying you?" he asked.

"Only the fellow on the telephone," she said. "You must have heard about him."

"Oh, was he after you, too?" Humphreys asked. "That's a gentleman I'd like to lay my hands on sometime. What did you do?"

"What can you do?" she asked angrily. "The first time, I was so appalled I listened to him. It's not natural, of course. I suppose it's like being hypnotized. Afterward, you start to get sick. I never knew people could be like that."

"And what happened the second time?"

"Oh, I did what Ned Sullivan told me. He's left me alone since then."

"What did Ned Sullivan tell you to do?"

"To say he was a very sick man and that he should get treatment at once." She gave a mournful grin. "You know the tone—Dr. Harty, the well-known nerve specialist, giving a free opinion and wondering all the time when she was going to start screaming."

"I wouldn't blame you a bit," Humphreys said unsmilingly. "I'd probably do the same myself. Was he angry?"

"Leaping!" she said with girlish intensity.

"I wish I had Mr. Sullivan's brains," he said despondently. "Does he think it's the same man?"

"I never asked him."

"You should. I don't think it is somehow. You probably never met the telephone boy. This could be someone you know well."

He left the question hanging in the air, and she was sorry about the "clahssics." Why was it that Irish women regarded their husbands as such fools?

"I haven't a notion who it could be, Jack," she said, using his Christian name for the first time.

"Someone who comes into the shop for small things you'd expect his mother or sister to get for him?" he asked, closing one eye.

"I can't think of a blooming soul," she said earnestly. "Anybody that isn't normal, I mean."

"They all look normal enough to begin with," he said grimly. "They won't look so normal in five years' time. You might save someone's life if you could remember. If you do, let me know. . . . Damn it, the bloody house is probably full of fingerprints!" he added gloomily. "For all the use they'd be to us now!"

As he was leaving he played with the lock and said, "I think I'd get a new lock for the door, Jane. And get a spare key and leave it at the barrack. I could hide here some evening you're away and see if he'd come. . . . Anyway, call at the barrack tomorrow and talk to the superintendent. Not that he'll know any more than I do, but he might give *me* a free hand."

She did as he had advised and understood at once what he meant. The superintendent was a bright young idiot who was obviously much happier with papers than with people—papers did not answer him back!

"We could all be killed in our beds, and 'twould only make an interesting statistic for him!" she said at the Sullivans'.

"Ah, you're in no danger like that," Ned said in his gloomy drawl. "That fellow won't come near the place as long as you're there. He's too shy, girl! You'll find there's a loving Irish mother in the background who takes him to Confession herself every Saturday night and writes out his sins for him, the way he won't forget them.

He may get dangerous, but it won't be for a long time yet, and it won't be over you. That's the sort of fellow you have to think of, Jane."

"For God's sake, I'd have to think of half the town," she said lightly, but he didn't even smile.

"I know, but this is something different," he said. "Lord God!" he added, growing bitter himself. "It's unknown the lives people in towns like this have to lead."

It was after that that she began to crack. One night she stopped the car outside the gate and blew the horn to warn off the intruder, and only after she had done it did she realize what it meant. Now she had almost a horror of meeting him. And once more she returned from a weekend and saw that he had been there. He must have come before darkness fell because he had even taken down two of her books. In the bedroom there was the same childish disorder of clothes, and written in lipstick over her bed were the words "I love you."

Somehow those three words that she seemed always to be saying to herself were what broke her down. She stood alone in the room and wept and shook her head. Then, because there seemed to be nothing else to do, she rang the police station and Humphreys answered.

"All right, all right, Jane," he said quickly, comfortingly. "Don't touch anything. I'll try to get along, but if I can't someone else will go. And don't worry! You'll be all right."

"And would you ask whoever is coming to tell Ned Sullivan?" she asked.

"Of course," he said. "I'll see to that."

It sounded as though he understood, but she didn't understand herself why it was that she wanted to see Ned. She was disappointed when Lenihan came and started to inspect the locks and the window catches. Ned came a few minutes later, looking tired.

"I'm sorry I dragged you out," she said.

"Why?" he asked with his sardonic grin. "Would you sooner I heard it in school tomorrow?"

"This is how he got in all right," Lenihan said sagaciously, indicating a window catch. "You should get that seen to, Miss Harty. Blast him anyway!" he added admiringly. "He doesn't miss much."

"'Tis nice to know how he got in," said Ned. "It would be more practical if we knew how to keep him out."

"Oh, we'll get him yet, Mr. Sullivan," Lenihan said excitedly. "He'll come too often, the way they all do. But if I was you, Miss Harty, I wouldn't worry my head about him."

"That's an interesting idea, anyway," Ned said with smoldering rage.

"But why would she, Mr. Sullivan?" Lenihan asked dramatically. "Sure, after all, what is he, only a poor harmless sexual maniac? The country is full of them."

"Joe, I'm not sure but you're right," said Ned, and still Lenihan did not catch the tone.

"So long, of course, as he wouldn't take anything valuable," he added, to indicate that things might go too far.

"I have nothing valuable," said Jane.

"Not a damned thing. Only your peace of mind," Ned added savagely, and she knew that he understood.

When Lenihan had gone, Ned sighed.

"It's no use relying on fellows like that," he said flatly. "They have no notion of who this man is. Either that, or they know and they're not telling. It could be somebody they don't want a fuss made about. But they're right about the danger. He won't injure you. God help us, in his own way he's telling the truth. He loves you. They don't see the real danger you're in."

"What danger is there, only that, Ned?" she asked.

"That fellow could drive you as mad as himself," Ned said sourly. "It would be like living with a ghost. It gives me the horrors, not to mind you. I'm going to have a drink if there's one there."

"Do you really think they know?" she asked as she got him the bottle.

"They may," he admitted. "They're not such fools as they look."

This is probably someone you saw being made a joke of or ignored in some place, and you made a fuss of him. Or you stopped and gave him a lift—the first time in the poor devil's life that a woman treated him as a human being, and it went to his head." He glanced inquiringly at her, but her face was blank, and he knew that she would never remember, because it was something she did naturally and would have no memory of. "Oh, how the hell do I know, girl?" he asked in exasperation. "But it's time you started to make plans for getting out."

"Out where?"

"I suppose you realize that you can't stay here?"

"But where else am I to go, Ned?"

"Somewhere they won't notice when you give somebody a lift," he said. "For God's sake, Jane, don't you realize you have them all frightened. Lenihan is frightened of you; Humphreys's wife is frightened of you. You probably scared the wits out of the superintendent as well. I'll hear about it all in due course in Slattery's Bar. 'The Hartys were always odd.' Sex is a game, Jane," he added wearily. "You have to play a three to beat a two, but you play your ace every time—if you have an ace. You simply can't afford to live naturally in a place like this."

"That's a nice comforting thought," she replied angrily. "Don't you think you'd better go home to Celia quick? She'll be wondering what happened to you."

"She won't," he said with a smile. "Celia isn't as simple as you think, either. She said I was to spend the night on your sofa or bring you home."

Anger was Jane's first response: It was as though Celia were condescending to her. And then she saw the bitter smile on Ned's face and realized that he was warning her against guessing wrong again. Even for her sake he was not going to criticize his wife to her.

"Tell Celia I'm thankful and I'd go back if I could," she said with a touch of formality. "I can't do it, Ned," she added with a smile. "If I gave in now I'd never sleep here alone again."

"And you intend to go on sleeping here alone?" he asked.

"But where else can I go, Ned?"

"Go to Dublin, go to London, go to hell out of this!" he cried. "And you know I'm not saying that for my own sake. What do you think this bloody town is going to be like without you?"

It was as though the tears that had been banked up in her had been waiting for him to speak. He took her in his arms and patted her awkwardly, like a schoolboy. "I know, Jane, I know," he said, as though he were consoling a child, and she knew that he *did* know, and that it would always be this way with her, falling in love with the wrong man or the man she could not have, exactly as though the shopkeepers were right and she did it coldly and deliberately, trying to hurt herself worse.

"You'd better go home, Ned," she said appealingly, and he understood that too. It was better for him to go; otherwise it would mean more remorse and guilt. At the door she waved gaily to him and tried to smile, and then went back and poured herself another drink. The only thing now was to get drunk quick. But before she took the drink she opened the living-room window and stood, looking out at the country road, the bogs and fields, now vague shapes in the darkness. She was sure there was somebody at the end of the garden, looking up at her hopelessly. She knew it could be nobody but the poor simpleton, crushing a pair of her pants in his hands and muttering the words that were forever in her own mind —I love you. She rested her hands on the windowsill and leaned out.

"Are you there?" she called softly.

There was no reply, only the whisper that always ran over the dark uplands at night; and she raised her voice. She tried to speak calmly and confidently.

"Come in, can't you?" she said. "There's nobody here. The guards are gone. I'm all alone. You're perfectly safe."

For some reason she was convinced that he was there, listening to what she said but paralyzed by the gap between dream and reality, trapped in the snare of his own crazy character, even more than she was in hers. And yet, all she had wanted was to come to terms with him, to lure him out of himself and make him realize that there was a world of warmth and friendship where he could be at home. Then she slammed the window down and gave way to an agony of hopelessness. When people had mocked and criticized her she had been afraid, but not as she was afraid now, because now she had to deal with a loneliness deeper than her own.

She knew too that Ned was right and that she no longer had a place of refuge from the outside world. She would never be able to live alone again; never again would she have a life of her own.

•❧ The Corkerys

MAY MACMAHON was a good-looking girl, the only child of Jack MacMahon, the accountant, and his wife, Margaret. They lived in Cork, on Summerhill, the steep street that led from the flat of the city to the heights of Montenotte. She had always lived the life of a girl of good family, with piano lessons, dancing class, and crushes on her school friends' brothers. Only occasionally did she wonder what it was all about, and then she invariably forgot to ask her father, who would certainly know. Her father knew everything, or almost everything. He was a tall, shy, good-looking man who seemed to have been expecting martyrdom from his earliest years and drinking Irish whiskey to endure it. May's mother was small and pretty and very opinionated, though her opinions varied, and anyway did not last long. Her father's opinions never varied, and lasted forever.

When May became friendly with the Corkery family, it turned out that he had always had strong opinions about them as well. Mr. Corkery, a mild, inarticulate solicitor, whom May remembered going for lonely walks for the good of his health, had died and left his family with very limited means, but his widow had good connections and managed to provide an education (mostly free) for all six children. Of the boys, the eldest, Tim, was now a Dominican, and Joe, who came next in line, was also going in for the priesthood. The Church was in the family's blood, because Mrs. Corkery's brother was the Dean and her sister was Mother Superior of the convent of an enclosed order outside the city. Mrs. Corkery's nickname among the children was "Reverend Mother," and they accused her of imitating her sister, but Mrs. Corkery only sniffed and said if everybody became priests and nuns there would soon be no Church left. Mrs. Corkery seemed to believe quite seriously that the needs of the Church were the only possible excuse for sex.

From knowing the Corkerys May began to realize at last what life was about. It was no longer necessary to ask her father. Anyway he wouldn't know. He and her mother were nice but commonplace. Everything they said and did was dull and predictable, and even when they went to Mass on Sunday they did so only because everyone else did it. The Corkerys were rarely dull and never predictable. Though their whole life seemed to center on the Church, they were not in the least pietistic. The Dean fought with Mrs. Corkery; Father Tim fought with Joe; the sisters fought with their brothers, who, they said, were getting all the attention, and fought one another when their brothers were not available. Tessie, the eldest girl, known as "The Limb of the Devil," or just "The Limb," was keeping company with a young stockbroker who told her a lot of dirty stories, which she repeated with great gusto to her brothers, particularly to Father Tim. This, however, was for family reasons, because they all agreed that Tim was inclined to put on airs.

And then The Limb astonished everybody by entering the convent where her aunt was Mother Superior. May attended the reception in the little convent chapel, which struck her to the heart by its combination of poverty and gentility. She felt that the ceremony might have been tolerable in a great cathedral with a choir and thundering organ, but not in that converted drawing room, where the nuns knelt along the side walls and squeaked like mourners. The Limb was laid out on the altar and first covered with roses as though she were dead; then an old nun clipped her long black hair with a shears. It fell and lay at her head as though it too had died. May drew a quick breath and glanced at Joe, who was kneeling beside her. Though he had his hand over his face, she knew from the way his shoulders moved that he was crying. Then she cried, too.

For a full week the ceremony gave her the horrors every time she remembered it, and she felt she should have nothing more to do with such an extraordinary family. All the same, a week with her parents was enough to make her realize the attraction of the Corkerys even more than before.

"Did it scare you, May?" Rosie, the second girl, asked with a wicked grin. "Cripes, it put the fear of God into me. I'm not having any of that *de profundis* stuff; I'm joining a decent missionary order." This was the first May had heard of Rosie's vocation. Inside a year, she, too, was in a convent, but in Rome, and "having a gas time," as she casually reported home.

They really were an extraordinary family, and the Dean was as queer as any of them. The Sunday following the ceremony May was at dinner there, and he put his hand firmly on her shoulder as though he were about to yank off her dress, and gave her a crooked smile that would have convinced any reasonable observer that he was a sex maniac, and yet May knew that almost every waking moment his thoughts were concentrated on outwitting the Bishop, who seemed to be the greatest enemy of the Church since Nero. The Bishop was a Dominican, and the Dean felt that a monk's place was in the cloister.

"The man is a bully!" he said, with an astonishment and grief that would have moved any audience but his own family.

"Oh, now, Mick!" said Mrs. Corkery placidly. She was accustomed to hearing the Bishop denounced.

"I'm sorry, Josephine," the Dean said with a formal regret that rang equally untrue. "The man is a bully. An infernal bully, what's more. I'm not criticizing you or the order, Tim," he said, looking at his nephew over his spectacles, "but monks simply have no place in ecclesiastical affairs. Let them stick to their prayers is what I say."

"And a queer way the world would be only for them," Joe said. Joe was going for the secular priesthood himself, but he didn't like to see his overwhelming uncle get away with too much.

"Their influence on Church history has been disastrous!" the Dean bellowed, reaching for his cigarette case. "Always, or almost always, disastrous. That man thinks he knows everything."

"Maybe he does," said Joe.

"Maybe," said the Dean, like an old bull who cannot ignore a dart from any quarter. "But as well as that, he interferes in everything, and always publicly, always with the greatest possible amount of scandal. 'I don't like the model of that church'; 'Take away that statue'; 'That painting is irreverent.' Begob, Joe, I don't think even you know as much as that. I declare to God, Josephine, I believe if anyone suggested it to him that man would start inspecting the cut of the schoolgirls' panties." And when everyone roared with laughter, the Dean raised his head sternly and said, "I mean it."

Peter, the youngest boy, never got involved in these family arguments about the Bishop, the orders, or the future of the Church. He was the odd man out. He was apprenticed in his father's old firm and would grow up to be owner or partner. In every Irish family there is a boy like Peter whose task it is to take on the family responsibilities. It was merely an accident that he was the youngest. What counted was that he was his mother's favorite. Even before he had a mind to make up, he knew it was not for him to become too involved, because someone would have to look after his mother in her old age. He might marry, but it would have to be a wife who suited her. He was the ugliest of the children, though with a monkey ugliness that was almost as attractive as Father Tim's film-star looks and Joe's ascetic masculine fire. He was slow, watchful, and good-humored, with high cheekbones that grew tiny bushes of hair, and he had a lazy malice that could often be as effective as the uproarious indignation of his brothers and sisters.

May, who saw the part he had been cast for, wondered whether she couldn't woo Mrs. Corkery as well as another girl.

After Rosie there was Joe, who was ordained the following year, and then Sheela did what seemed—in that family, at least—the conventional thing and went into the same convent as Tessie.

It was an extraordinary family, and May was never quite able to understand the fascination it had for her. Partly, of course—and this she felt rather than understood—it was the attraction of the large family for the only child, the sheer relief of never having to wonder what you were going to play next. But beside this there was an attraction rather like that of a large theatrical family—the feeling that everything was related to a larger imaginative world. In a sense, the Corkerys always seemed to be playing.

She knew that her own being in love with Peter was part of her love affair with the family as a whole, the longing to be connected with them, and the teasing she got about Peter from his brothers and sisters suggested that they, too, recognized it and were willing to accept her as one of themselves. But she also saw that her chance of ever marrying Peter was extremely slight, because Peter was not attracted by her. When he could have been out walking with her he was out walking with his friend Mick MacDonald, and when the pair of them came in while she was in the house, Peter behaved to her as though she were nothing more than a welcome stranger. He was always polite, always deferential—unlike Tim and Joe, who treated her as though she were an extra sister, to be slapped on the bottom or pushed out of the way as the mood struck them.

May was a serious girl; she had read books on modern psychology, and she knew that the very quality that made Peter settle for a life in the world made him unsuitable as a husband. It was strange how right the books were about that. He was dominated by his mother, and he could flirt with her as he never flirted with May. Clearly, no other woman would ever entirely replace his mother in his heart. In fact (May was too serious a girl not to give things their proper names), Peter was the very type of the homosexual—the latent homosexual, as she learned to call it.

Other boys *wanted* to go out with her, and she resented Peter's unfailing courtesy, though in more philosophic spells she realized that he probably couldn't help it, and that when he showed his almost boyish hero worship of Mick MacDonald before her it was not his fault but Nature's. All the same, she thought it very un-called-for on the part of Nature, because it left her no particular interest in a world in which the only eligible young man was a queer. After a year or two of this, her thoughts turned more and more to the quiet convent where the Corkery girls contentedly carried on their simple lives of meditation and prayer. Once or twice she dropped a dark hint that she was thinking of becoming a nun herself, but each time it led to a scene with her father.

"You're a fool, girl!" he said harshly, getting up to pour himself an extra drink. May knew he didn't altogether resent being provoked, because it made him feel entitled to drink more.

"Now, Jack, you must not say things like that," her mother said anxiously.

"Of course I have to say it. Look at her! At her age! And she doesn't even have a boy!"

"But if there isn't a boy who interests her!"

"There are plenty of boys who'd interest her if only she behaved like a natural girl," he said gloomily. "What do you think a boy wants to do with a girl? Say the Rosary? She hasn't behaved naturally ever since she got friendly with that family—what's their name?"

"Corkery," Mrs. MacMahon said, having failed to perceive that not remembering the Corkerys' name was the one way the poor man had of getting back at them.

"Whatever their name is, they've turned her into an idiot. That's no great surprise. They never had any brains to distribute, themselves."

"But still, Jack, you will admit they've got on very well."

"They've got on very well!" he echoed scornfully. "In the Church! Except that young fellow, the solicitor's clerk, and I suppose he hadn't brains enough even for the Church. They should have put him in the friars."

"But after all, their uncle is the Dean."

"Wonderful Dean, too," grumbled Jack MacMahon. "He drove me out of twelve-o'clock Mass, so as not to listen to his drivel. He can hardly speak decent English, not to mind preaching a sermon. 'A bunch of baloney!'" he quoted angrily. "If we had a proper bishop, instead of the one we have, he'd make that fellow speak correctly in the pulpit at least."

"But it's only so that his congregation will understand him, Jack."

"Oh, his congregation understands him only too well. Himself and his tall hat and his puffed-up airs! Common, that's what he is, and that's what all the family are, on both sides. If your daughter wants to be a nun, you and the Corkerys can arrange it between you. But not one penny of my money goes into their pockets, believe me!"

May was sorry to upset him, but for herself she did not mind his loathing of the whole Corkery family. She knew that it was only because he was fond of her and dreaded being left without her in his old age. He had spoiled her so long as she was not of an age to answer him back, and she guessed he was looking forward to spoiling his grandchildren even worse because he would not live long enough to hear them answer him back. But this, she realized, was what the Corkerys had done for her—made all that side of life seem unimportant.

She had a long talk with Mother Agatha, Mrs. Corkery's sister, about her vocation, which confirmed her in her resolution. Mother Agatha was very unlike her sister, who was loud-voiced and humorous. The Mother Superior was pale, thin, cool, and with the slightest trace of an ironic wit that might have passed unnoticed by a stupider girl. But May noticed it, and realized that she was being observed very closely indeed.

She and her mother did the shopping for the trousseau, but the bills and parcels were kept carefully out of her father's sight. Drunk or sober, he refused to discuss the matter at all. "It would only upset him just now, poor man," her mother said philosophically. He was drinking heavily, and when he was in liquor he quarreled a lot with her mother about little things. With May he avoided quarrels, or even arguments, and it struck her that he was training himself for a life in which he would no longer have her to quarrel with. On the day of the reception he did not drink at all, which pleased her, and

was icily polite to everybody, but when, later, she appeared behind
the parlor grille, all in white, and the sun caught her, she saw his
face in the darkness of the parlor, with all the life drained out of it,
and suddenly he turned and left without a word. It was only then
that a real feeling of guilt sprang up in her at the thought of the
miserable old age that awaited him—a man like him, who loved
young creatures who could not answer him back, and who would
explain to them unweariedly about the sun and moon and geogra-
phy and figures. She had answered him back in a way that left him
with nothing to look forward to.

All the same, there was something very comforting about the life of
an enclosed order. It had been organized a long, long time before, by
people who knew more about the intrusions of the outside world
than May did. The panics that had seized her about her ability to
sustain the life diminished and finally ceased. The round of duties,
services, and mortifications was exactly what she had needed, and
little by little she felt the last traces of worldliness slip from her—
even the very human worry about the old age of her father and
mother. The convent was poor, and not altogether from choice.
Everything in the house was mean and clean and cheerful, and May
grew to love the old drawing room that had been turned into a
chapel, where she knelt, in her own place, through the black winter
mornings when at home she would still be tucked up comfortably in
bed. She liked the rough feeling of her clothes and the cold of the
floor through her sandals, though mostly she liked the proximity of
Tessie and Sheela.

There were times when, reading the lives of the saints, she
wished she had lived in more heroic times, and she secretly invented
minor mortifications for herself to make sure she could endure
them. It was not until she had been in the convent for close on a
year that she noticed that the minor mortifications were liable to be
followed by major depressions. Though she was a clever woman, she
did not try to analyze this. She merely lay awake at night and

realized that the nuns she lived with—even Tessie and Sheela—were not the stuff of saints and martyrs but ordinary women who behaved in religion very much as they would have behaved in marriage, and who followed the rule in the spirit in which her father went to Mass on Sundays. There was nothing whatever to be said against them, and any man who had got one of them for a wife would probably have considered himself fortunate, but all the same, there was something about them that was not quite grown-up. It was very peculiar and caused her great concern. The things that had really frightened her about the order when she was in the world— the loneliness, the austerity, the ruthless discipline—now seemed to her meaningless and harmless. After that she saw with horror that the great days of the Church were over, and that they were merely a lot of perfectly commonplace women play-acting austerity and meditation.

"But my dear child," Mother Agatha said when May wept out her story to her, "of course we're only children. Of course we're only play-acting. How else does a child learn obedience and discipline?"

And when May talked to her about what the order had been in earlier days, that vague, ironic note crept into Mother Superior's voice, as though she had heard it all many times before. "I know, Sister," she said, with a nod. "Believe me, I do know that the order was stricter in earlier times. But you must remember that it was not founded in a semi-arctic climate like ours, so there was less chance of the sisters' dying of double pneumonia. I have talked to half the plumbers in town, but it seems that central heating is not understood here. . . . Everything is relative. I'm sure we suffer just as much in our very comfortable sandals as the early sisters suffered in their bare feet, and probably at times rather more, but at any rate we are not here for the sole purpose of suffering mortification, whatever pleasures it may hold for us."

Every word Mother Agatha said made perfect sense to May while she was saying it, and May knew she was being ungrateful and hysterical, but when the interview was over and the sound of her sobs had died away, she was left with the impression that Mother Agatha was only another commonplace woman, with a cool manner and a sarcastic tongue, who was also acting the part of a nun. She was alone in a world of bad actors and actresses, and the Catholicism she had known and believed in was dead.

A few weeks later she was taken to a private nursing home. "Just for a short rest, Sister," as Mother Agatha said. "It's a very pleasant place, and you will find a lot of other religious there who need a rest as well."

There followed an endless but timeless phase of weeping and confusion, when all May's ordinary life was broken up and strange men burst into her room and examined her and asked questions she did not understand and replied to questions of hers in a way that showed they had not understood them either. Nobody seemed to realize that she was the last Catholic in the world; nobody understood her tears about it. Above all, nobody seemed to be able to hear the gramophone record that played continuously in her head, and that stopped only when they gave her an injection.

Then, one spring day, she went into the garden for a walk and a young nurse saw her back to her room. Far ahead of them, at the other end of a long, white corridor, she saw an old man with his back to her, and remembered that she had seen his face many times before and had perceived, without paying attention to, his long, gloomy, ironic face. She knew she must have remembered him, because now she could see nothing but his back, and suddenly the words "Who is that queer old man?" broke through the sound of the gramophone record, surprising her as much as they seemed to surprise the young nurse.

"Oh, him!" the nurse said, with a smile. "Don't you know him? He's here for years."

"But why, Nurse?"

"Oh, he doesn't think he's a priest, and he is one really, that's the trouble."

"But how extraordinary!"

"Isn't it?" the nurse said, biting her lower lip in a smile. "Cripes, you'd think 'twas something you wouldn't forget. He's nice, really, though," she added gravely, as though she felt she had been criticizing him.

When they reached May's room, the young nurse grinned again, in a guilty way, and May noticed that she was extravagantly pretty, with small, gleaming front teeth.

"You're getting all right, anyway," she said.

"Oh, really?" May said vaguely, because she knew she was not getting all right. "Why do you think that, Nurse?"

"Oh, you get to spot things," the nurse said with a shrug, and left May uncomforted, because she didn't know if she really did get well how she could face the convent and the other nuns again. All of them, she felt, would be laughing at her. Instead of worrying about the nuns, she went into a mournful daydream about the old priest who did not think he was a priest, and next day, when her father called, she said intensely, "Daddy, there's a priest in here who doesn't believe he's a priest—isn't that extraordinary?" She did not hear the tone of her own voice or know how reasonable it sounded, and so she was surprised when her father looked away and started fumbling mechanically in his jacket pocket for a cigarette.

"Well, you don't have to think you're a nun either," he said, with an unsteady voice. "Your mother has your own room ready for you when you come home."

"Oh, but Daddy, I have to go back to the convent."

"Oh, no you don't. No more convents for you, young lady! That's fixed up already with Mother Superior. It was all a mistake from the beginning. You're coming straight home to your mother and me."

Then May knew she was really going to get well, and she wanted to go home with him at once, not to go back up the stairs behind the big iron door where there was always an attendant on duty. She knew that going back home meant defeat, humiliation, and despair, but she no longer cared even about that. She just wanted to take up her life again at the point where it had gone wrong, when she had first met the Corkerys.

Her father brought her home and acted as though he had rescued her from a dragon's den. Each evening, when he came home from work, he sat with her, sipping at his drink and talking quietly and comfortably. She felt he was making great efforts to assure that she felt protected and relaxed. Most of the time she did, but there were spells when she wanted her mother to put her back in the nursing home.

"Oh, I couldn't do that," her mother said characteristically. "It would upset your poor father too much."

But she did discuss it with the doctor—a young man, thin and rather unhealthy-looking, who looked as though he, too, was living on his nerves—and he argued with May about it.

"But what am I to do, Doctor, when I feel like this?" she asked plaintively.

"Go out and get jarred," he said briskly.

"Get what, Doctor?" she asked feebly.

"Jarred," he repeated without embarrassment. "Stoned. Polluted. Drunk. I don't mean alone, of course. You need a young fellow along with you."

"Oh, not that again, Doctor!" she said, and for some reason her voice came out exactly like Mother Agatha's—which was not how she intended it to sound.

"And some sort of a job," he went on remorselessly. "There isn't a damn thing wrong with you except that you think you're a failure. You're not, of course, but as a result of thinking you are you've scratched the surface of your mind all over, and when you sit here like this, looking out at the rain, you keep rubbing it so that it doesn't heal. Booze, love-making, and hard work—they keep your hands away from the sore surface, and then it heals of its own accord."

She did her best, but it didn't seem to heal as easily as all that. Her father got her a job in the office of a friend, and she listened, in fascination, to the chatter of the other secretaries. She even went out in the evening with a couple of them and listened to their common little love stories. She knew if she had to wait until she talked like that about fellows in order to be well, her case was hopeless. Instead, she got drunk and told them how she had been for years in love with a homosexual, and, as she told it, the story became so hopeless and dreadful that she sobbed over it herself. After that she went home and wept for hours, because she knew that she had been telling lies, and betrayed the only people in the world whom she had really cared for.

Her father made a point of never referring at all to the Corkerys, the convent, or the nursing home. She knew that for him this represented a real triumph of character, because he loathed the Corkerys more than ever for what he believed they had done to her. But even he could not very well ignore the latest development in the saga. It seemed that Mrs. Corkery herself had decided to become a nun. She announced placidly to everyone that she had done her duty by her family, who were now all comfortably settled, and that she felt free to do what she had always wanted to do anyhow. She discussed it with the Dean, who practically excommunicated her on the spot. He said the family would never live down the scandal, and Mrs. Corkery told him it wasn't the scandal that worried him at all but the loss of the one house where he could get a decent meal. If he had a spark of manliness, she said, he would get rid of his housekeeper, who couldn't cook, was a miserable sloven, and ordered him about as if he were a schoolboy. The Dean said she would have to get permission in writing from every one of her children, and Mrs. Corkery replied calmly that there was no difficulty whatever about that.

May's father didn't really want to crow, but he could not resist pointing out that he had always said the Corkerys had a slate loose.

"I don't see anything very queer about it," May said stubbornly.

"A woman with six children entering a convent at her age!" her father said, not even troubling to grow angry with her. "Even the Dean realizes it's mad."

"It *is* a little bit extreme, all right," her mother said, with a frown, but May knew she was thinking of her.

May had the feeling that Mrs. Corkery would make a very good nun if for no other reason than to put her brother and Mother Agatha in their place. And of course, there were other reasons. As a girl she had wanted to be a nun, but for family reasons it was impossible, so she had become a good wife and mother, instead. Now, after thirty years of pinching and scraping, her family had grown away from her and she could return to her early dream. There was nothing unbalanced about that, May thought bitterly. *She* was the one who had proved unbalanced.

For a while it plunged her back into gloomy moods, and they were made worse by the scraps of gossip that people passed on to her, not knowing how they hurt. Mrs. Corkery had collected her six letters of freedom and taken them herself to the Bishop, who had immediately given in. "Spite!" the Dean pronounced gloomily. "Nothing but spite—all because I don't support his mad dream of turning a modern city into a medieval monastery."

On the day of Mrs. Corkery's reception, May did not leave the house at all. It rained, and she sat by the sitting-room window, looking across the city to where the hills were almost invisible. She was living Mrs. Corkery's day through—the last day in the human world of an old woman who had assumed the burden she herself had been too weak to accept. She could see it all as though she were back in that mean, bright little chapel, with the old woman lying out on the altar, covered with roses like a corpse, and an old nun shearing off her thin gray locks. It was all so intolerably vivid that May kept bursting into sudden fits of tears and whimpering like a child.

One evening a few weeks later, she came out of the office in the rain and saw Peter Corkery at the other side of the street. She obeyed her first instinct and bowed her head so as not to look at him. Her heart sank as he crossed the road to accost her.

"Aren't you a great stranger, May?" he asked, with his cheerful grin.

"We're very busy in the office these days, Peter," she replied, with false brightness.

"It was only the other night Joe was talking about you. You know Joe is up in the seminary now?"

"No. What's he doing?"

"Teaching. He finds it a great relief after the mountains. And, of course, you know about the mother." This was it!

"I heard about it. I suppose ye're all delighted?"

"*I* wasn't very delighted," he said, and his lips twisted in pain. "'Twas the most awful day I ever spent. When they cut off her hair—"

"You don't have to remind me."

"I disgraced myself, May. I had to run out of the chapel. And here I had two nuns after me, trying to steer me to the lavatory. Why do nuns always think a man is looking for a lavatory?"

"I wouldn't know. I wasn't a very good one."

"There are different opinions about that," he said gently, but he only hurt her more.

"And I suppose you'll be next?"

"How next?"

"I was sure you had a vocation, too."

"I don't know," he said thoughtfully. "I never really asked myself. I suppose, in a way, it depends on you."

"And what have I to say to it?" she asked in a ladylike tone, though her heart suddenly began to pant.

"Only whether you're going to marry me or not. Now I have the house to myself and only Mrs. Maher looking after me. You remember Mrs. Maher?"

"And you think I'd make a cheap substitute for Mrs. Maher, I suppose?" she asked, and suddenly all the pent-up anger and frustration of years seemed to explode inside her. She realized that it was entirely because of him that she had become a nun, because of him she had been locked up in a nursing home and lived the life of an emotional cripple. "Don't you think that's an extraordinary sort of proposal—if it's intended to be a proposal."

"Why the hell should I be any good at proposing? How many girls do you think I've proposed to?"

"Not many, since they didn't teach you better manners. And it would never occur to yourself to say you loved me. Do you?" she almost shouted. "Do you love me?"

"Sure, of course I do," he said, almost in astonishment. "I wouldn't be asking you to marry me otherwise. But all the same—"

"All the same, all the same, you have reservations!" And suddenly language that would have appalled her to hear a few months before broke from her, before she burst into uncontrollable tears and went running homeward through the rain. "God damn you to Hell, Peter Corkery! I wasted my life on you, and now in the heel of the hunt all you can say to me is 'All the same.' You'd better go back to your damn pansy pals, and say it to them."

She was hysterical by the time she reached Summerhill. Her father's behavior was completely characteristic. He was the born martyr and this was only another of the ordeals for which he had been preparing himself all his life. He got up and poured himself a drink.

"Well, there is one thing I'd better tell you now, daughter," he said quietly but firmly. "That man will never enter this house in my lifetime."

"Oh, nonsense, Jack MacMahon!" his wife said in a rage, and she went and poured herself a drink, a thing she did under her husband's eye only when she was prepared to fling it at him. "You haven't a scrap of sense. Don't you see now that the boy's mother only entered the convent because she knew he'd never feel free while she was in the world?"

"Oh, Mother!" May cried, startled out of her hysterics.

"Well, am I right?" her mother said, drawing herself up.

"Oh, you're right, you're right," May said, beginning to sob again. "Only I was such a fool it never occurred to me. Of course, she was doing it for me."

"And for her son," said her mother. "And if he's anything like his mother, I'll be very proud to claim him for a son-in-law."

She looked at her husband, but saw that she had made her effect and could now enjoy her drink in peace. "Of course, in some ways it's going to be very embarrassing," she went on peaceably. "We can't very well say 'Mr. Peter Corkery, son of Sister Rosina of the Little Flower' or whatever the dear lady's name is. In fact, it's very difficult to see how we're going to get it into the press at all. However, as I always say, if the worst comes to the worst, there's a lot to be said for a quiet wedding. . . . I do hope you were nice to him, May?" she asked.

It was only then that May remembered that she hadn't been in the least nice and, in fact, had used language that would have horrified her mother. Not that it would make much difference. She and Peter had traveled so far together, and by such extraordinary ways.

A Story by Maupassant

PEOPLE WHO HAVE NOT grown up in a provincial town won't know what I mean when I say what Terry Coughlan meant to me. People who have won't need to know.

As kids we lived a few doors from each other on the same terrace, and his sister, Tess, was a friend of my sister, Nan. There was a time when I was rather keen on Tess myself. She was a small plump gay little thing, with rosy cheeks like apples, and she played the piano very well. In those days I sang a bit, though I hadn't much of a voice. When I sang Mozart, Beethoven, or even Wagner Terry would listen with brooding approval. When I sang commonplace stuff Terry would make a face and walk out. He was a good-looking lad with a big brow and curly black hair, a long, pale face, and a pair of intense dark eyes. He was always well-spoken and smart in his appearance. There was nothing sloppy about him.

When he could not learn something by night he got up at five in the morning to do it, and whatever he took up, he mastered. Even as a boy he was always looking forward to the day when he'd have money enough to travel, and he taught himself French and German in the time it took me to find out I could not learn Irish. He was cross with me for wanting to learn it; according to him it had "no cultural significance," but he was crosser still with me because I couldn't learn it. "The first thing you should learn to do is to work," he would say gloomily. "What's going to become of you if you don't?" He had read somewhere that when Keats was depressed, he had a wash and brushup. Keats was his God. Poetry was never much in my line, except Shelley, and Terry didn't think much of him.

We argued about it on our evening walks. Maybe you don't remember the sort of arguments you had when you were young. Lots of people prefer not to remember, but I like thinking of them. A man is never more himself than when he talks nonsense about God, eternity, prostitution, and the necessity for having mistresses. I argued with Terry that the day of poetry was over, and that the big boys of modern literature were the fiction writers—the ones we'd heard of in Cork at that time, I mean—the Russians and Maupassant.

"The Russians are all right," he said to me once. "Maupassant can forget."

"But why, Terry?" I asked.

"Because whatever you say about the Russians, they're noble," he said. "Noble" was a great word of his at the time: Shakespeare was "noble," Turgenev was "noble," Beethoven was "noble." "They are a religious people, like the Greeks, or the English of Shakespeare's time. But Maupassant is slick and coarse and commonplace. Are his stories literature?"

"Ah, to hell with literature!" I said. "It's life."

"Life in this country?"

"Life in his own country, then."

"But how do you know?" Terry asked, stopping and staring at me. "Humanity is the same here as anywhere else. If he's not true of the life we know, he's not true of any sort of life."

Then he got the job in the monks' school and I got the job in Carmody's and we began to drift apart. There was no quarrel. It was just that I liked company and Terry didn't. I got in with a wild group—Marshall and Redmond and Donnelan, the solicitor—and we sat up until morning, drinking and settling the future of humanity. Terry came with us once but he didn't talk, and when Donnelan began to hold forth on Shaw and the Life Force I could see his face getting dark. You know Donnelan's line—"But what I mean—what I want to say—Jasus, will somebody let me talk? I have something important to say." We all knew that Donnelan was a bit of a joke, but when I said good night to Terry in the hall he turned on me with an angry look.

"Do those friends of yours do anything but talk?" he asked.

"Never mind, Terry," I said. "The Revolution is coming."

"Not if they have anything to say to it," Terry said and walked away from me. I stood there for a while feeling sorry for myself, as you do when you know that the end of a friendship is in sight. It didn't make me happier when I went back to the room and Donnelan looked at me as if he didn't believe his eyes.

"Magner," he asked, "am I dreaming or was there someone with you?"

Suddenly, for no particular reason, I lost my temper.

"Yes, Donnelan," I said. "But somebody I wouldn't expect you to recognize."

That, I suppose, was the last flash of the old love, and after that it was bogged down in argument. Donnelan said that Terry lacked flexibility—flexibility!

Occasionally I met Tess with her little shopping basket and her round rosy cheeks, and she would say reproachfully, "Ah, Ted, aren't you becoming a great stranger? What did we do to you at all?" And a couple of times I dropped around to sing a song and borrow a book, and Terry told me about his work as a teacher. He was a bit disillusioned with his job, and you wouldn't wonder. Some of the monks kept a mackintosh and muffler handy so that they could drop out to the pictures after dark with some doll. And then there was a thundering row when Terry discovered that a couple of his brightest boys were being sent up for public examinations under the names of notorious ignoramuses, so as to bolster up the record. When Brother Dunphy, the headmaster, argued with Terry that it was only a simple act of charity, Terry replied sourly that it seemed to him more like a criminal offense. After that he got the reputation of being impossible and was not consulted when Patrick Dempsey, the boy he really liked, was put up for examination as Mike MacNamara, the County Councillor's son—Mike the Moke, as Terry called him.

Now, Donnelan is a gasbag, and, speaking charitably, a bit of a fool, but there were certain things he learned in his Barrack Street slum. One night he said to me, "Ted, does that fellow Coughlan drink?"

"Drink?" I said, laughing outright at him. "Himself and a sparrow would have about the same consumption of liquor." Nothing ever embarrassed Donnelan, who had the hide of a rhinoceros.

"Well, you might be right," he said reasonably, "but, begor, I never saw a sparrow that couldn't hold it."

I thought myself that Donnelan was dreaming, but next time I met Tess I sounded her. "How's that brother of yours keeping?" I asked.

"Ah, fine, Ted, why?" she asked, as though she was really surprised.

"Oh, nothing," I said. "Somebody was telling me that he wasn't looking well."

"Ah, he's that way this long time, Ted," she replied, "and 'tis nothing only the want of sleep. He studies too hard at night, and then he goes wandering all over the country, trying to work off the excitement. Sure, I'm always at him!"

That satisfied me. I knew Tess couldn't tell me a lie. But then, one moonlight night about six months later, three or four of us were standing outside the hotel—the night porter had kicked us out in the middle of an argument, and we were finishing it there. Two was striking from Shandon when I saw Terry coming up the pavement toward us. I never knew whether he recognized me or not, but all at once he crossed the street, and even I could see that the man was drunk.

"Tell me," said Donnelan, peering across at him, "is that a sparrow I see at this hour of night?" All at once he spun round on his heels, splitting his sides with laughing. "Magner's sparrow!" he said. "Magner's sparrow!" I hope in comparing Donnelan with a rhinoceros I haven't done injustice to either party.

I saw then what was happening. Terry was drinking all right, but he was drinking unknown to his mother and sister. You might almost say he was drinking unknown to himself. Other people could be drunkards but not he. So he sat at home reading, or pretending to read, until late at night, and then slunk off to some low pub on the quays where he hoped people wouldn't recognize him, and came home only when he knew his family was in bed.

For a long time I debated with myself about whether I shouldn't talk to him. If I made up my mind to do it once, I did it twenty times. But when I ran into him in town, striding slowly along, and saw the dark, handsome face with the slightly ironic smile, I lost courage. His mind was as keen as ever—it may even have been a shade too keen. He was becoming slightly irritable and arrogant. The manners were as careful and the voice was as pleasant as ever—a little too much so. The way he raised his hat high in the air to some woman who passed and whipped the big handkerchief from his breast pocket reminded me of an old actor going down in the world. The farther down he went the worse the acting got. He wouldn't join me for a drink; no, he had this job that simply must be finished tonight. How could I say to him, "Terry, for God's sake, give up trying to pretend you have work to do. I know you're an impostor and you're drinking yourself to death." You couldn't talk like that to a man of his kind. People like him are all of a piece; they have to stand or fall by something inside themselves.

He was forty when his mother died, and by that time it looked as though he'd have Tess on his hands for life as well. I went back to the house with him after the funeral. He was cruelly broken up. I discovered that he had spent his first few weeks abroad that summer and he was full of it. He had stayed in Paris and visited the cathedrals round, and they had made a deep impression on him. He had never seen real architecture before. I had a vague hope that it might have jolted him out of the rut he had been getting into, but I was wrong. It was worse he was getting.

Then, a couple of years later, I was at home one evening,

finishing up some work, when a knock came to the door. I opened it myself and saw old Pa Hourigan, the policeman, outside. Pa had a schoolgirl complexion and a white mustache, china-blue eyes, and a sour elderly mouth, like a baby who has learned the facts of life too soon. It surprised me because we never did more than pass the time of day.

"May I speak to you for a moment, Mr. Magner?" he asked modestly. "'Tis on a rather private matter."

"You can be sure, Sergeant," I said, joking him. "I'm not a bit afraid. 'Tis years since I played ball on the public street. Have a drink."

"I never touch it, going on night duty," he said, coming into the front room. "I hope you will pardon my calling, but you know I am not a man to interfere in anyone else's private affairs."

By this time he had me puzzled and a bit anxious. I knew him for an exceptionally retiring man, and he was clearly upset.

"Ah, of course you're not," I said. "No one would accuse you of it. Sit down and tell me what the trouble is."

"Aren't you a friend of Mr. Coughlan, the teacher?" he asked.

"I am," I said.

"Mr. Magner," he said, exploding on me, "can you do nothing with the man?"

I looked at him for a moment and had a premonition of disaster.

"Is it as bad as that?" I asked.

"It cannot go on, Mr. Magner," he said, shaking his head. "It cannot go on. I saved him before. Not because he was anything to me, because I hardly knew the man. Not even because of his poor decent sister, though I pity her with my whole heart and soul. It was for the respect I have for education. And you know that, Mr. Magner," he added earnestly, meaning (which was true enough) that I owed it to him that I had never paid a fine for drinking during prohibited hours.

"We all know it, Sergeant," I said. "And I assure you, we appreciate it."

"No one knows, Mr. Magner," he went on, "what sacrifices Mrs.

Hourigan and myself made to put that boy of ours through college, and I would not give it to say to him that an educated man could sink so low. But there are others at the barracks who don't think the way I do. I name no names, Mr. Magner, but there are those who would be glad to see an educated man humiliated."

"What is it, Sergeant?" I asked. "Drink?"

"Mr. Magner," he said indignantly, "when did I ever interfere with an educated man for drinking? I know when a man has a lot on his mind he cannot always do without stimulants."

"You don't mean drugs?" I asked. The idea had crossed my mind once or twice.

"No, Mr. Magner, I do not," he said, quivering with indignation. "I mean those low, loose, abandoned women that I would have whipped and transported."

If he had told me that Terry had turned into a common thief I couldn't have been more astonished and horrified. Horrified is the word.

"You don't mind my saying that I find that very hard to believe, Sergeant?" I asked.

"Mr. Magner," he said with great dignity, "in my calling a man does not use words lightly."

"I know Terry Coughlan since we were boys together, and I never as much as heard an unseemly word from him," I said.

"Then all I can say, Mr. Magner, is that I'm glad, very glad, that you've never seen him as I have, in a condition I would not compare to the beasts." There were real tears in the old man's eyes. "I spoke to him myself about it. At four o'clock this morning I separated him from two of those vile creatures that I knew well were robbing him. I pleaded with him as if he was my own brother. 'Mr. Coughlan,' I said, 'what will your soul do at the Judgment?' And Mr. Magner, in decent society I would not repeat the disgusting reply he made me."

"*Corruptio optimi pessima,*" I said to myself.

"That is Latin, Mr. Magner," the old policeman said with real pleasure.

"And it means 'Lilies that fester smell far worse than weeds,'

Sergeant," I said. "I don't know if I can do anything. I suppose I'll have to try. If he goes on like this he'll destroy himself, body and soul."

"Do what you can for his soul, Mr. Magner," whispered the old man, making for the door. "As for his body, I wouldn't like to answer." At the door he turned with a mad stare in his blue eyes. "I would not like to answer," he repeated, shaking his gray pate again.

It gave me a nasty turn. Pa Hourigan was happy. He had done his duty, but mine still remained to be done. I sat for an hour, thinking about it, and the more I thought, the more hopeless it seemed. Then I put on my hat and went out.

Terry lived at that time in a nice little house on College Road; a little red-brick villa with a bow window. He answered the door himself, a slow, brooding, black-haired man with a long pale face. He didn't let on to be either surprised or pleased.

"Come in," he said with a crooked smile. "You're a great stranger, aren't you?"

"You're a bit of a stranger yourself, Terry," I said jokingly. Then Tess came out, drying her hands in her apron. Her little cheeks were as rosy as ever but the gloss was gone. I had the feeling that now there was nothing much she didn't know about her brother. Even the nervous smile suggested that she knew what I had come for—of course, old Hourigan must have brought him home.

"Ah, Ted, 'tis a cure for sore eyes to see you," she said. "You'll have a cup? You will, to be sure."

"You'll have a drink," Terry said.

"Do you know, I think I will, Terry," I said, seeing a nice natural opening for the sort of talk I had in mind.

"Ah, you may as well have both," said Tess, and a few minutes later she brought in the tea and cake. It was like old times until she left us, and then it wasn't. Terry poured out the whiskey for me and the tea for himself, though his hand was shaking so badly that he could scarcely lift his cup. It was not all pretense; he didn't want to give me an opening, that was all. There was a fine print over his head—I think it was a Constable of Salisbury Cathedral. He talked about the monastery school, the usual clever, bitter contemptuous stuff about monks, inspectors and pupils. The whole thing was too carefully staged, the lifting of the cup and the wiping of the mustache, but it hypnotized me. There was something there you couldn't do violence to. I finished my drink and got up to go.

"What hurry is on you?" he asked irritably.

I mumbled something about its getting late.

"Nonsense!" he said. "You're not a boy any longer."

Was he just showing off his strength of will or hoping to put off the evil hour when he would go slinking down the quays again?

"Ah, they'll be expecting me," I said, and then, as I used to do when we were younger, I turned to the bookcase. "I see you have a lot of Maupassant at last," I said.

"I bought them last time I was in Paris," he said, standing beside me and looking at the books as though he were seeing them for the first time.

"A deathbed repentance?" I asked lightly, but he ignored me.

"I met another great admirer of his there," he said sourly. "A lady you should meet some time."

"I'd love to if I ever get there," I said.

"Her address is the Rue de Grenelle," he said, and then with a wild burst of mockery, "the left-hand pavement."

At last his guard was down, and it was Maupassant's name that had done it. And still I couldn't say anything. An angry flush mounted his pale dark face and made it sinister in its violence.

"I suppose you didn't know I indulged in that hideous vice?" he snarled.

"I heard something," I said. "I'm sorry, Terry."

The angry flush died out of his face and the old brooding look came back.

"A funny thing about those books," he said. "This woman I was speaking about, I thought she was bringing me to a hotel. I suppose I was a bit muddled with drink, but after dark, one of these places is much like another. 'This isn't a hotel,' I said when we got upstairs. 'No,' she said, 'it's my room.'"

As he told it, I could see that he was living it all over again, something he could tell nobody but myself.

"There was a screen in the corner. I suppose it's the result of reading too much romantic fiction, but I thought there might be somebody hidden behind it. There was. You'd never guess what?"

"No."

"A baby," he said, his eyes boring through me. "A child of maybe eighteen months. I wouldn't know. While I was looking, she changed him. He didn't wake."

"What was it?" I asked, searching for the message that he obviously thought the incident contained. "A dodge?"

"No," he said almost grudgingly. "A country girl in trouble, trying to support her child, that's all. We went to bed and she fell asleep. I couldn't. It's many years now since I've been able to sleep like that. So I put on the light and began to read one of these books that I carried round in my pocket. The light woke her and she wanted to see what I had. 'Oh, Maupassant,' she said. 'He's a great writer.' 'Is he?' I said. I thought she might be repeating something she'd picked up from one of her customers. She wasn't. She began to talk about *Boule de Suif*. It reminded me of the arguments we used to have in our young days." Suddenly he gave me a curious boyish smile. "You remember, when we used to walk up the river together."

"Oh, I remember," I said with a sigh.

"We were terrible young idiots, the pair of us," he said sadly. "Then she began to talk about *The Tellier Household*. I said it had poetry. 'Oh, if it's poetry you want, you don't go to Maupassant. You go to Vigny, you go to Musset, and Maupassant is life, and life isn't poetry. It's only when you see what life can do to you that you realize what a great writer Maupassant is.' . . . Wasn't that an extraordinary thing to happen?" he asked fiercely, and again the angry color mounted his cheeks.

"Extraordinary," I said, wondering if Terry himself knew how extraordinary it was. But it was exactly as if he were reading the thoughts as they crossed my mind.

"A prostitute from some French village; a drunken old waster from an Irish provincial town, lying awake in the dawn in Paris, discussing Maupassant. And the baby, of course. Maupassant would have made a lot of the baby."

"I declare to God, I think if I'd been in your shoes, I'd have brought them back with me," I said. I knew when I said it that I was talking nonsense, but it was a sort of release for all the bitterness inside me.

"What?" he asked, mocking me. "A prostitute and her baby? My dear Mr. Magner, you're becoming positively romantic in your old age."

"A man like you should have a wife and children," I said.

"Ah, but that's a different story," he said malevolently. "Maupassant would never have ended a story like that."

And he looked at me almost triumphantly with those mad, dark eyes. I knew how Maupassant would have ended that story all right. Maupassant, as the girl said, was life, and life was pretty nearly through with Terry Coughlan.

A Great Man

ONCE WHEN I WAS VISITING a famous London hospital, I met the matron, Miss Fitzgerald, a small, good-looking woman of fifty. She was Irish, and we discussed acquaintances in common until I mentioned Dermot O'Malley, and then I realized that somehow or other I had said the wrong thing. The matron frowned and went away. A few minutes later she returned, smiling, and asked me to lunch in a way that, for some reason, reminded me of a girl asking a young fellow for the first time to her home. "You know, Dr. O'Malley was a great friend of my father," she said abruptly and then frowned again.

"Begor, I was," said O'Malley when I reported this to him later. "And I'll tell you a story about it, what's more." O'Malley is tall and gentle, and has a wife who is a pain in the neck, though he treats her with a consideration that I can only describe as angelic. "It was when I was a young doctor in Dublin, and my old professor, Dwyer, advised me to apply for a job in the hospital in Dooras. Now, you never heard of Dooras, but we all knew about it then, because that was in the days of Margaret's father, old Jim Fitzgerald, and he was known, all right.

"I met him a couple of nights later in a hotel in Kildare Street. He had come up to Dublin to attend a meeting of doctors. He was a man with piercing eyes and a long, hard face—more the face of a soldier than a doctor. The funny thing was his voice, which was rather high and piping and didn't seem to go at all with his manner.

" 'Dooras is no place for a young man who likes entertainment,' he said.

" 'Ah, I'm a country boy myself,' said I, 'so that wouldn't worry me. And of course, I know the hospital has a great reputation.'

" 'So I understand,' he said grimly. 'You see, O'Malley, I don't believe in all this centralization that's going on. I know it's all for the sake of equipment, and equipment is a good thing, too, but it's taking medicine away from where it belongs. One of these days, when their centralization breaks down, they'll find they haven't hospitals, doctors, or anything else.'

"By the time I'd left him, I'd as good as accepted the job, and it wasn't the job that interested me so much as the man. It could be that, my own father having been a bit of a waster, I'm attracted to men of strong character, and Fitzgerald was a fanatic. I liked that about him.

"Now, Dwyer had warned me that I'd find Dooras queer, and Dwyer knew the Dublin hospitals weren't up to much, but Dooras was dotty. It was an old hospital for infectious diseases that must have dated from about the time of the Famine, and Fitzgerald had got a small local committee to take it over. The first couple of days in it gave me the horrors, and it was weeks before I even began to see what Fitzgerald meant by it all. Then I did begin to see that in spite of all the drawbacks, it worked in a way bigger hospitals didn't work, and it was happy in a way that bigger hospitals are never happy. Everybody knew everybody else, and everybody was madly curious about everybody else, and if anybody ever gave a party, it wasn't something devised by the staff to entertain the patients; it was more likely to be the patients entertaining the staff.

"Partly this was because Margaret Fitzgerald, the woman you met in London, was the head nurse. I don't know what she's like now, and from all I can hear, she's a bit of a Tartar, but in those days she was a pretty little thing with an air of being more efficient than anybody ever was. Whenever you spoke to Margaret, she practically sprang to attention and clicked her heels, and if you were misguided enough to ask her for anything she hadn't handy, she gave you a demonstration of greyhound racing. And, of course, as you can see from the job she has now, she was a damn great nurse.

"But mainly the place worked because of Fitzgerald and his colleagues, the local doctors. Apart from him, none of them struck me as very brilliant, though he himself had a real respect for an old doctor called Pat Duane, a small, round, red-faced man with an old-fashioned choker collar and a wonderful soupy bedside manner. Pat looked as though some kind soul had let him to mature in a sherry cask till all the crude alcohol was drawn out of him. But they were all conscientious; they all listened to advice, even from me— and God knows I hadn't much to offer—and they all deferred in the most extraordinary way to Fitzgerald. Dwyer had described him to me as a remarkable man, and I was beginning to understand the full force of that, because I knew Irish small towns the way only a country boy knows them, and if those men weren't at one another's throats, fighting for every five-bob fee that could be picked up, it was due to his influence. I asked a doctor called MacCarthy about it one night he invited me in for a drink. MacCarthy was a tall old poseur with a terrible passion for local history.

" 'Has it occurred to you that Fitzgerald may have given us back our self-respect, young man?' he asked in his pompous way.

" 'Your what?' I asked in genuine surprise. In those days it hadn't occurred to me that a man could at the same time be a show-box and be lacking in self-respect.

" 'Oh, come, O'Malley, come!' he said, sounding like the last Duke of Dooras. 'As a medical man you are more observant than you pretend. I presume you have met Dr. Duane?'

" 'I have. Yes,' said I.

" 'And it didn't occur to you that Dr. Duane was ever a victim of alcohol?' he went on portentously. 'You understand, of course, that I am not criticizing him. It isn't easy for the professional man in Ireland to maintain his standards of behavior. Fitzgerald has a considerable respect for Dr. Duane's judgment—quite justified, I may add, quite justified. But at any rate, in a very short time Pat eased off on the drink, and even began to read the medical journals again. Now Fitzgerald has him in the hollow of his hand. We all like to feel we are of some use to humanity—even the poor general practitioner. . . . But you saw it all for yourself, of course. You are merely trying to pump a poor country doctor.'

"Fitzgerald was not pretentious. He liked me to drop in on him when I had an hour to spare, and I went to his house every week for dinner. He lived in an old, uncomfortable family house a couple of miles out on the bay. Normally he was cold, concentrated, and irritable, but when he had a few drinks in he got melancholy, and this for some reason caused him to be indiscreet and say dirty things about his committee and even about the other doctors. 'The most interesting thing about MacCarthy,' he said to me once, 'is that he's the seventh son of a seventh son, and so he can diagnose a case without seeing the patient at all. It leaves him a lot of spare time for local history.' I suspected he made the same sort of dirty remarks about me, and that secretly the man had no faith in anyone but himself. I told him so, and I think he enjoyed it. Like all shy men he liked to be insulted in a broad masculine way, and one night when I called him a flaming egotist, he grunted like an old dog when you tickle him and said, 'Drink makes you very offensive, O'Malley. Have some more!'

"It wasn't so much that he was an egotist (though he was) as that he had a pernickety sense of responsibility, and whenever he hadn't a case to worry over, he could always find some equivalent of a fatal disease in the hospital—a porter who was too cheeky or a nurse who made too free with the men patients—and he took it all personally and on a very high level of suffering. He would sulk and snap at Margaret for days over some trifle that didn't matter to anyone, and finally reduce her to tears. At the same time, I suppose it was part of the atmosphere of seriousness he had created about the makeshift hospital, and it kept us all on our toes. Medicine was his life, and his gossip was shop. Duane or MacCarthy or some other local doctor would drop in of an evening to discuss a case—which by some process I never was able to fathom had become Fitzgerald's case—and over the drinks he would grow gloomier and gloomier about our ignorance till at last, without a word to any of us, he got up and telephoned some Dublin specialist he knew. It was part of the man's shyness that he only did it when he was partly drunk and could pretend that instead of asking a favor he was conferring one. Several times I watched that scene with amusement. It was all carefully calculated, because if he hadn't had enough to drink he lacked the brass and became apologetic, whereas if he had had one drink too much he could not describe what it was about the case that really worried him. Not that he rated a specialist's knowledge any higher than ours, but it seemed the best he could do, and if that didn't satisfy him, he ordered the specialist down, even when it meant footing the bill himself. It was only then I began to realize the respect that Dublin specialists had for him, because Dwyer, who was a terrified little man and hated to leave home for fear of what might happen him in out-of-the-way places like Cork and Belfast, would only give out a gentle moan about coming to Dooras. No wonder Duane and MacCarthy swore by him, even if for so much of the time they, like myself, thought him a nuisance.

"Margaret was a second edition of himself, though in her the sense of responsibility conflicted with everything feminine in her till it became a joke. She was small. She was pretty, with one of those miniature faces that seem to have been reduced until every coarse line has been refined in them. She moved at twice the normal speed and was forever fussing and bossing and wheedling, till one of the nurses would lose her temper and say, 'Ah, Margaret, will you for God's sake give us time to breathe!' That sort of impertinence would make Margaret scowl, shrug, and go off somewhere else, but her sulks never lasted, as her father's did. The feminine side of her wouldn't sustain them.

"I remember one night when all hell broke loose in the wards, as it usually does in any hospital once a month. Half a dozen patients decided to die all together, and I was called out of bed. Margaret and the other nurse on night duty, Joan Henderson, had brewed themselves a pot of tea in the kitchen, and they were scurrying round with a mug or a bit of seedcake in their hands. I was giving an injection to one of my patients, who should have been ready for discharge. In the next bed was a dying old mountainy man who had nothing in particular wrong with him except old age and a broken heart. I suddenly looked up from what I was doing and saw he had come out of coma and was staring at Margaret, who was standing at the other side of the bed from me, nibbling the bit of cake over which she had been interrupted. She started when she saw him staring at the cake, because she knew what her father would say if ever he heard that she was eating in the wards. Then she gave a broad grin and said in a country accent, 'Johnny, would 'oo like a bit of seedcake?' and held it to his lips. He hesitated and then began to nibble, too, and then his tongue came out and licked round his mouth, and somehow I knew he was saved. 'Tay, Johnny,'' she said mockingly. 'Thot's what 'oo wants now, isn't it?' And that morning as I went through the wards, my own patient was dead but old Johnny was sitting up, ready for another ten years of the world's hardship. That's nursing.

"Margaret lived at such a pitch of nervous energy that every few weeks she fell ill. 'I keep telling that damn girl to take it easy,' her father would say with a scowl at me, but any time there was the least indication that Margaret was taking it easy, he started to air his sufferings with the anguish of an elephant. She was a girl with a real sense of service, and at one time had tried to join a nursing order in Africa, but dropped it because of his hatred of all nursing orders. In itself this was funny, because Margaret was a liberal Catholic who, like St. Teresa, was 'for the Moors, and martyrdom' but never worried her head about human weaknesses and made no more of an illegitimate baby than if she had them herself every Wednesday, while he was an old-fashioned Catholic and full of obscure prejudices. At the same time, he felt that the religious orders were leaving Ireland without nurses—not that he thought so much of nurses!

" 'And I suppose nuns can't be nurses?' Margaret would ask with a contemptuous shrug.

"'How can they?' he would say, in his shrillest voice. 'The business of religion is with the soul, not the body. My business is with the body. When I'm done with it, the nuns can have it—or anyone else, for that matter.'

"'And why not the soul and the body?' Margaret would ask in her pertest tone.

"'Because you can't serve two masters, girl.'

"'Pooh!' Margaret would say with another shrug. 'You can't serve one Siamese twin, either.'

"As often as I went to dinner in that house, there was hardly a meal without an argument. Sometimes it was about no more than the amount of whiskey he drank. Margaret hated drink, and watched every drop he poured in his glass, so that often, just to spite her, he went on to knock himself out. I used to think that she might have known her father was a man who couldn't resist a challenge. She was as censorious as he was, but she had a pertness and awkwardness that a man rarely has, and suddenly, out of the blue, would come some piece of impertinence that plunged him into gloom and made her cringe away to her bedroom, ready for tears. He and I would go into the big front room, overlooking Dooras Bay, and without a glance at the view he would splash enormous tasheens of whiskey into our glasses, just to indicate how little he cared for her, and say in a shrill, complaining voice, 'I ruined that girl, O'Malley. I know I did. If her mother was alive, she wouldn't talk to me that way.'

"Generally, they gave the impression of two people who hated one another with a passionate intensity, but I knew well that he was crazy about her. He always brought her back something from his trips to Dublin or Cork and once when I was with him, he casually wasted my whole afternoon looking for something nice for her. It never occurred to him that I might have anything else to do. But he could also be thoughtful; for once when for a full week he had been so intolerable that I could scarcely bring myself to answer him he grinned and said, 'I know exactly what you think of me, O'Malley. You think I'm an old slave driver.'

" 'Not exactly,' I said, giving him tit for tat. 'Just an old whoor!'

"At this, he gave a great guffaw and handed me a silver cigarette case, which I knew he must have bought for me in town the previous day, and added sneeringly, 'Now, don't you be going round saying your work is quite unappreciated.'

" 'Did I really say that?' I asked, still keeping my end up, even though there was something familiar about the sentiment.

" 'Or if you do, say it over the loudspeaker. Remember, O'Malley, I hear *everything*.' And the worst of it was, he did!

"Then, one night, when my year's engagement was nearly ended, I went to his house for dinner. That night there was no quarreling, and he and I sat on in the front room, drinking and admiring the view. I should have known there was something wrong, because for once he didn't talk shop. He talked about almost everything else, and all the time he was knocking back whiskey in a way I knew I could never keep pace with. When it grew dark, he said with an air of surprise, 'O'Malley, I'm a bit tight. I think we'd better go for a stroll and clear our heads.'

"We strolled up the avenue of rhododendrons to the gate and turned left up the hill. It was a wild, rocky bit of country, stopped dead by the roadway and then cascading merrily down the little fields to the bay. There was still a coppery light in the sky, and the reflection of a bonfire on one of the islands, like a pendulum, in the water. The road fell again, between demesne walls and ruined gateways where the last of the old gentry lived, and I was touched— partly, I suppose, by all the whiskey, but partly by the place itself.

" 'I'll regret this place when I leave it,' I said.

" 'Oh, no, you won't,' he snapped back at me. 'This is no place for young people.'

" 'I fancy it might be a very pleasant memory if you were in the East End of London,' said I.

" 'It might,' said Fitzgerald, 'if you were quite sure you wouldn't have to go back to it. That's what worries me about Margaret.'

"I had never noticed him worrying very much about Margaret —or anyone else, for that matter—so I took it as merely a matter of form.

" 'Margaret seems to do very well in it,' I said.

" 'It's no place for Margaret,' he said sharply. 'People need friends of their own age and ideas old men like myself can't supply. It's largely my fault for letting her come back here at all. I made this place too much of my life, and that's all right for a man, but it's not good enough for a high-spirited girl like that.'

" 'But doesn't Margaret have friends here?' I asked, trying to comfort him.

" 'She has friends enough, but not of her own age,' he said. 'She's too mature for the girls here that are her own age. Not that I ever cared much for her friends from Dublin,' he added shortly. 'They struck me as a lot of show-boxes. I don't like those intellectual Catholics, talking to me about St. Thomas Aquinas. I never read St. Thomas Aquinas, and from all I can hear I haven't missed much. But young people have to make their own mistakes. All the men around here seem to want is some good-natured cow who'll agree to everything they say, and because she argues with them they think she's pert and knowing. Well, she *is* pert, and she *is* knowing—I realize that as well as anybody. But there's more than that to her. They'd have said the same about me, only I proved to them that I knew what I was doing.'

"Suddenly I began to realize what he was saying, and I was frightened out of my wits. I said to myself that it was impossible, that a man like Fitzgerald could never mean a thing like that, but at the same time I felt that he did mean it, and that it had been in his mind from the first night he met me. I muttered something about her having more chances in Dublin.

" 'That's the trouble,' he said. 'She didn't know what she was letting herself in for when she came back here, and no more did I. Now she won't leave, because I'd be here on my own, and I know I wouldn't like it, but still I have my work to do, and for a man that's enough. I like pitting my wits against parish priests and county councillors and nuns. Besides, when you reach my age you realize that you could have worse, and they'll let me have my own way for the time I have left me. But I haven't so long to live, and when I die, they'll have some champion footballer running the place, and Margaret will be taking orders from the nuns. She thinks now that she won't mind, but she won't do it for long. I know the girl. She ought to marry, and then she'd have to go wherever her husband took her.'

" 'But you don't really think the hospital will go to pieces like that?' I asked, pretending to be deeply concerned but really only trying to head Fitzgerald off the subject he seemed to have on his mind. 'I mean, don't you think Duane and MacCarthy will hold it together?'

" 'How can they?' he asked querulously. 'It's not their life, the way it's been mine. I don't mean they won't do their best, but the place will go to pieces just the same. It's a queer feeling, Dermot, when you come to the end of your time and realize that nothing in the world outlasts the man that made it.'

"That sentence was almost snapped at me, out of the side of his mouth, and yet it sounded like a cry of pain—maybe because he'd used my Christian name for the first time. He was not a man to use Christian names. I didn't know what to say.

" 'Of course, I should have had a son to pass on my responsibilities to,' he added wonderingly. 'I'm not any good with girls. I daresay that was why I liked you, the first time we met—because I might have had a son like you.'

"Then I couldn't bear it any longer, and it broke from me. 'And it wasn't all on one side!'

" 'I guessed that. In certain ways we're not so unlike. And that's what I really wanted to say to you before you go. If ever you and Margaret got to care for one another, it would mean a lot to me. She won't have much, but she'll never be a burden on anybody, and if ever she marries, she'll make a good wife.'

"It was the most embarrassing moment of my life—and mind, it wasn't embarrassing just because I was being asked to marry a nice girl I'd never given a thought to. I'm a country boy, and I knew all about 'made' matches by the time I was seventeen, and I never had anything but contempt for the snobs that pretend to despise them. Damn good matches the most of them are, and a thousand times better than the sort you see nowadays that seem to be made up out of novelettes or moving pictures! Still and all, it's different when it comes to your own turn. I suppose it's only at a moment like that you realize you're just as silly as any little servant girl. But it wasn't only that. It was because I was being proposed to by a great man, a fellow I'd looked up to in a way I never looked up to my own father, and I couldn't do the little thing he wanted me to do. I muttered some nonsense about never having been able to think about marriage—as if there ever was a young fellow that hadn't thought about it every night of his life!—and he saw how upset I was and squeezed my arm.

" 'What did I tell you?' he said. 'I knew I was drunk, and if she ever gets to hear what I said to you, she'll cut me in little bits.'

"And that tone of his broke my heart. I don't even know if you'll understand what I mean, but all I felt was grief to think a great man who'd brought life to a place where life never was before would have to ask a favor of me, and me not to be able to grant it. Because all the time I wanted to be cool and suave and say of course I'd marry his daughter, just to show the way I felt about himself, and I was too much of a coward to do it. In one way, it seemed so impossible, and in another it seemed such a small thing.

"Of course, we never resumed the conversation, but that didn't make it any easier, because it wasn't only between myself and him; it was between me and Margaret. The moment I had time to think of it, I knew Fitzgerald was too much a gentleman to have said anything to me without first making sure that she'd have me.

"Well, you know the rest yourself. When he died, things happened exactly the way he'd prophesied; a local footballer got his job, and the nuns took over the nursing, and there isn't a Dublin doctor under fifty that could even tell you where Dooras is. Fitzgerald was right. Nothing in the world outlasts a man. Margaret, of course, has a great reputation, and I'm told on the best authority that there isn't a doctor in St. Dorothy's she hasn't put the fear of God into so I suppose it's just as well that she never got the opportunity to put it into me. Or don't you agree?"

I didn't, of course, as O'Malley well knew. Anyway, he could hardly have done much worse for himself. And I had met Margaret, and I had seen her autocratic airs, but they hadn't disturbed me much. She was just doing it on temperament, rather than technique —a very Irish way, and probably not so unlike her father's. I knew I didn't have to tell O'Malley that. He was a gentleman himself, and his only reason for telling me the story was that already, with the wisdom that comes of age, he had begun to wonder whether he had not missed something in missing Margaret Fitzgerald. I knew that he had.

❧ The School for Wives

THE REAL TROUBLE with love is that people want contradictory things out of it. Like Jimmy Maguire and his wife. Jimmy was a tall thin fellow with an eager face, and in his younger days he used to be something of a Don Juan. There was a little group of them—the Doctor, Con Bishop, and two or three other bachelors—and they were all out for a good time. They used to go shooting and fishing, and one year, I remember, they took a house in Clare. The things that went on! Any excuse for a party, and it didn't much matter to them where the party was to be—Limerick, Galway, or Cork, what was it, after all, but a day's outing? Jimmy was the most reckless of them. They would be returning to Dublin from one outing when he would hear of a party somewhere else, and decide they ought to crash it. The Doctor, who shared a flat with Jimmy, lived in a continual state of alarm at what Jimmy would do next. Jimmy would do anything if the mood struck him, and whatever he did, the Doctor was swept protesting into his orbit.

"But it's all right," Jimmy would say, raising his hand. "The man is an old friend. I've done business with him for years."

"Business?" the Doctor would say. "You don't even know his name."

"Oh, what's a little thing like that between friends?"

And Jimmy would go up to the house of a perfect stranger and brazen it out. You wouldn't think from his rather formal manners that he was so audacious, but he was. And he could get away with things, for he was personable and plausible. Not only would he gain admittance to the party, he would end by becoming the center of it. The secret of Jimmy's success was his fondness for women. He really liked women, and had a quite genuine interest in their affairs, and a woman could never be with him for long without telling him her troubles. Whatever wonderful way he had of easing their minds, women who confessed to him wanted to go on confessing, and that was where the Doctor came in, because he would talk to them over the telephone in that wonderful, vague, syrupy voice of his, sympathizing with them in their inability to find Jimmy, while Jimmy in stockinged feet tiptoed around him, making hideous faces.

All this greatly scandalized the Doctor. But for all his alarm and pretended disapproval he loved it, of course. He had been devoted to his mother, and, as a result, he was still unmarried and likely to remain so. Jimmy was his secret life, his wild oats. He was lonely and sweet-natured and forever thinking and talking of love. You would go to see him, and he would fuss about with the drinks, murmuring in his gentle, worried way about Jimmy and his girls. "And some of them married, my dear fellow," he would whisper, giving you a dark look over his spectacles. "I forget whether you like soda. Personally, I think it gives you indigestion. And he's so pious! Every year of his life off to Lough Derg on the pilgrimage, trailing round the holy stones on his bare feet. And even there—did I put too much water in it—he picks them up. At the same time—here's health, old man—he keeps trying to reform me. I admit my beliefs mightn't be all that orthodox, but I can't help feeling that his aren't completely sincere. Mind you, he's quite charming about it. He says I'm putting the cart before the horse, and that sins against morals are less important than sins against faith. According to him, I'm a Protestant. He says it's all in the importance you attach to the First Commandment, or something. I really can't follow that sort of argument—I mean, this difference between sins against faith and sins against morals. Can you?"

At last, after years of piety and skirt-hunting, Jimmy found the girl he wanted to marry, and he took her by storm. She was called Roisin Mooney, and I must say he showed great taste. She was a really nice girl, the sort you'd swear would be especially reserved as a reward for virtue. She was enraptured with religion, with the sacraments, with prayer, and with every form of emotional religion. Nor did marriage seem to disillusion her. At least twenty times a day that girl must have told herself that she was the luckiest girl in the world to be married to a king of men like Jimmy, and twenty times a day wondered if God would give her the grace to be worthy of him. It is the unworldly type of woman whose mind is fixed on the saints, suffering, and sublimation who really appreciates the miracle of a man in the bed when she wakes in the morning.

She asked him over and over to explain again from the beginning what he had felt when he first met her and how it was he had seen anything in such a plain, stupid, uneducated girl as herself. And Jimmy, who found it difficult to remember even where he had met her and whose approach to all women had been standardized down the years, tried to look portentous and understanding, and said that a legal training was a great aid in seeing through appearances. Roisin shook her head doubtfully. She had known other lawyers, and they had never seen through her. Clearly it couldn't be anything but inspiration, and she worried her own vivid recollections, trying to see portents and miracles in them, but she couldn't, because, as she recognized herself, she wasn't clever.

Jimmy had a raja's life with her. To say that Roisin was a good housekeeper would be an absurdity. She kept house for him as a musician writes a symphony or a saint pursues a meditation—on her knees, in quest of the absolute. When he got home from the office, she knelt at his feet and took off his shoes, while Jimmy made faces to indicate the various inconsiderate ways in which she hurt his feet. When she had got him a drink and asked him for the tenth time if it was all right, she sat on a little stool and looked up adoringly at him while that scoundrel pontificated. And when he came home drunk and climbed into bed, with his bowler hat down over his eyes and his umbrella resting neatly on his left arm, she gently relieved him of both, took off his shoes and socks, opened his collar and tie, and crept into bed beside him, thanking God for the gift of a wonderful husband. She was a real pet.

Those who had known Jimmy in his bachelor days wondered how long exactly it would take him to grow tired of living with a saint and long for the open road again and the wild parties in Galway and Cork. But that was not how it happened at all. Instead, Jimmy began to drop all his old friends, the Doctor among them. He didn't do it blatantly or rudely, because, whatever faults Jimmy may have had, he was a thorough gentleman. But he dropped them just the same. Occasionally the Doctor would run into him in Dame Street, coming from his office, and Jimmy's face would light up, and the pair of them would drop into the Wicklow Bar or Davy Byrne's, while Jimmy sketched the wonderful party he was going to give for his old friends, till that glazed look came in his eye and he had to go home in a cab.

But the Doctor noticed that no matter how glazed Jimmy's eyes got, the invitation never became more precise.

"Jimmy," he said dryly, "I don't want to be offensive or personal in any way, but if you'd put a tenth of the energy into giving that party that you put into talking about it, we might have some chance of attending it before we die."

"Next week definitely, Pat," said Jimmy, drawing himself up with a frown. "Thursday or Friday, depending. I'll ring you."

But the next week came and he didn't ring, and there was no party. The Doctor was hurt. He realized that Jimmy was dropping the old crowd for business acquaintances, clients, and priests. Particularly priests. A man who is trying to exorcise his past can't do better than priests. Now when he got a bit high, Jimmy talked about the Dialogue Mass instead of ankles, or the difference between ourselves and the Greek Orthodox Church. He took Roisin to the pictures, wearing the impeccable bowler hat and carrying the umbrella. Jimmy was on the way up. In no time now he would be solicitor to half a dozen government agencies.

Jimmy's old friends couldn't help being curious about the eager, dark-haired girl he had married, but what they didn't know was that Roisin was even more curious about them. Marriage was still wonderful. She was having a baby, and she lit candles to Jimmy, she was full of Jimmy, but none of the people he brought to the house really knew Jimmy. When Roisin had one drink in—one drink was always enough to loosen her tongue—she had to tell the whole amazing story of Jimmy's courtship. "And do you know how that fellow proposed to me?" she would say. "He made me sit on the side of the road and then took out his handkerchief and *knelt* in front of me as if I was a statue. 'Jimmy Maguire!' says I. 'Get up out of that or you'll ruin you new trousers.' "

But when she looked at their polite, vague, smiling faces, she had the feeling that they only thought her a fool. And in the middle of the night she woke Jimmy to ask him to tell her frankly whether she hadn't ruined his life. Jimmy yawned and said no, she was doing fine.

"But I want to know the truth. I'd sooner know it now when I might be able to do something about it," she would say, as if she were begging the specialist to hold nothing back from her. "I do my best but I know I haven't the brains. I was always the same. I never could do sums. No wonder if they think I'm mad."

And all the time at the back of Roisin's mind was the thought that the person who would really understand her was Josephine Hanrahan. She knew that Jimmy and Josephine Hanrahan had been very thick. She did not know in which way, nor did she very much care, but she was certain that a woman who had been so fond of Jimmy would understand her feelings. This was where the first rift occurred between Jimmy and herself, for Jimmy did not like the idea at all. Not that he showed how troubled he really was. Instead, he pretended to consider the matter judicially.

"Now, Josephine is a delightful woman," he said in a harsh tone, "but she isn't your class. Please don't think I'm being snobbish. There's nothing I dislike more. But we have to face facts, and it wouldn't be in the woman's best interests."

To sacrifice a pleasure in order to spare pain to Josephine appealed immensely to Roisin's idealistic mind, but all the same she couldn't help wondering if it was really necessary. And Jimmy, in his quiet Machiavellian way, fed her another curate, who kept her quiet for a few months, till she started to wonder what sort of man the Doctor was.

"Well, Paddy is a fellow you might find interesting," Jimmy said thoughtfully, filling his pipe. "As a study, that is. But unfortunately the way we're situated we can't very well ask him to the house. You see, Paddy is an atheist."

"An atheist?" Roisin said, brightening up at once. She had never met an atheist. "You never told me that."

"Ah, well, it's not right to say things like that about your friends," Jimmy said loyally. "But he might just make an offensive remark in front of poor Father Joe that would upset him."

Of course it was a slander; the Doctor was incapable of being offensive to anybody, but Roisin didn't know this and had to rest content with the excuse. Then, after racking his brains, Jimmy dug up some old businessman who had painted water colors in his youth and had known everybody; one night when he was drunk Yeats had brought him home. But his conversation with Yeats seemed to have been of much the same kind as his conversation with Roisin. By this time, Little Liam was born, and for quite a while Roisin's attention was diverted from everything else in the world. Except that even then she was slipping out to the optician's wife next door for a cup of tea or a glass of sherry—anything to escape the curates. The optician's wife was a shrewd, interfering woman. She didn't know what Jimmy was up to, but she knew Jimmy was trying to keep his wife to himself, and that was enough for her.

One evening the Doctor was sitting in the lounge of the Wicklow Hotel with Jimmy when Josephine Hanrahan looked in. The Doctor, who was very polite and very fond of her, jumped to his feet and signaled to her.

"Don't bother to get up Paddy," she said. "I'm not staying. If I'm not good enough to drink with a man in his own house, I see no reason for doing it in public."

"Oh, really, Josephine!" Jimmy protested.

"I didn't think you'd do it, Jimmy," she said bitterly. "I really didn't. I thought you were too big a man to drop your old friends."

Jimmy looked owlishly at the Doctor, then at her, and held out his hands. "Do I look like a man who's dropped his old friends?" he asked triumphantly.

"Oh, you're too clever for that, Jimmy," she replied. "You're not obvious. But you won't ask us to your house, and you won't let us meet your wife. Has Paddy been there?"

"No, dear," the Doctor said, trying to make his voice sound smooth. "Are you sure you won't have a drink?"

"Quite, Paddy," she said. But she was not to be shut up. She turned on Jimmy again. "But you'll invite people who never spoke to you a year ago and wouldn't speak to you tomorrow if you hadn't money in your pocket."

Jimmy took his glasses off and wiped his long, pale face as though to reveal the true features below. The character he was trying to assume now was the haggard, patient, overworked family man, and to give him his due he did it well. "My dear girl," he said kindly, wagging his glasses at her, "in my business I have to entertain people I don't much care for." He stopped and picked up the bowler hat. "This is a façade. And you know it."

"Lies, Jimmy Maguire!" she said in a whisper. "I know your faults. I probably know them better than you do yourself. But you're not mean, and you're not calculating and you're not avaricious."

He drew himself up, smiled, and raised the bowler to her. "Thank you, my dear."

"You didn't let me finish," she went on. "I never said you weren't jealous."

"Jealous?" he echoed as though he didn't know what she meant.

"Yes, jealous."

"But of whom, Josephine?" Jimmy said, with an elaboration of astonishment that did not seem genuine.

"Of your wife."

"That shows all you know about Roisin."

"No, that shows all you know about her. You're afraid she'll do what other wives have done—wives well known to you."

The Doctor didn't know where to look. Jimmy didn't like it either. "Really, Josephine," he said, "that's pretty farfetched, even from you."

"You never made a bigger mistake in your life, Jimmy Maguire," she said contemptuously. "And you'll regret it."

"Extraordinary ideas women get into their heads," Jimmy said when she had gone. "I hope that husband isn't giving her more trouble."

The Doctor could see he was disturbed. That evening he did not reach the glazing stage, and they separated at the bus stop by Trinity College. The Doctor went away feeling thoughtful. For he, too, had been to the optician's house and wondered afterward why on earth he had been invited and why the optician's wife had pressed him to come again. He began to feel that he was involved in an intrigue.

The next time he went there, he saw Con Bishop in a corner, and then he knew that he was right. Con was another of the old group. He was an architect, an excitable young man with an Oxford accent. He flirted with the optician's wife as he flirted with everybody. The Doctor was sitting with another medical man, drinking his whiskey, when the door opened and Roisin Maguire came in. Ignoring everyone else, she went straight up to the Doctor and took his hands in hers and dragged him over to the sofa.

"I'm always wanting to talk to you," she exclaimed intensely, gazing into his eyes.

"It's mutual," he said, never having seen a technique like this before—if it was a technique, which he couldn't be sure of. "But I don't see as much of Jimmy as I used to."

"Ah, who does?" she said in a husky voice. "You can't see him for curates. I love my religion—you probably think I don't, but I do —only I can't bear too many priests round the house. Maybe I shouldn't say it to you, but I can't help it."

"Why on earth shouldn't you say it?" asked the Doctor, over-whelmed by her manner.

"I shouldn't—not to an atheist."

The Doctor was on the point of asking who had told her this when their hostess, who felt this was all much too sudden and public, descended on them. Still Roisin did not let go of the Doctor's hands. Instead, she looked over her shoulder at Mrs. Lacey and said, "Ah, Kitty, haven't I waited long enough for a chance to talk to this fellow? Be a sport and bring me an old drink. Anything at all will do. It all has the same effect on me. . . . Aren't I awful?" she asked the Doctor. "I can never tell the difference between one drink and another." But her mind was not on the drink any more than it was on the party. She had a sort of rapt, entranced quality, as though she were a sleepwalker living out a dream. "Tell me, aren't you the one that bailed Jimmy out when he was arrested in Limerick?"

"No," the Doctor said with amusement. "I'm afraid that was Con, the fair-haired chap over there."

"I want to talk to him, too," she said, squeezing the Doctor's hands. "I'm always hearing about ye. And there was a woman in the car with him the same night, wasn't there? He won't tell me who she was. That fellow is the devil. Do you know was it Josephine Hanrahan?"

"No," the Doctor said cautiously, "I don't think it was." He knew quite well who the woman was, but he felt that this was dangerous ground.

"He'll never tell me anything," she said. "But that's a girl I'd love to meet—Josephine, I mean."

"I fancy she'd like to meet you, too," the Doctor said politely.

"Ah, listen, Paddy," she whispered, laying a hand on his knee, "would you ever bring me round to her place some night? You couldn't tell Jimmy, of course. He has some daft notion that she's not class enough."

"Not class enough? Mrs. Hanrahan?"

"Ah, sure, what was my own father only a floorwalker in the Munster Arcade?" she said impatiently. "I'd ask Kitty Lacey here to invite her, only Kitty is so blooming inquisitive. She'd want to know what you had for your dinner. And I can't help blabbing everything to her. I'm that sort, Paddy. I blab. Isn't it terrible? Do you notice the way I'm blabbing now?"

The suggestion that anyone might apply the word "blabbing" to anything so enchanting as Roisin's conversation came to the Doctor as a shock as great as hearing himself described as an atheist and Josephine as a woman of no class. At the same time, he began to see what the dream was that gave Roisin the air of a sleepwalker. It was a dream of Jimmy. She loved the thought that he was a wild, romantic, reckless man, and when she was polishing his shoes, cooking the dinner, or bathing the child, she was sustained by that vision of him.

He was touched by it, and soon after that he took her to Josephine's little house in Rathgar. He felt nervous about doing it, but then, as I have said, the Doctor rather liked being in the position of having to be nervous. Besides, Roisin herself was in such a state that by force of comforting her he put himself at ease. She "blabbed," as she called it, all the way.

"Tell me, Paddy, do you think I'm mad? Sometimes I think myself I'm not in my right mind. What will Jimmy Maguire say if he hears of it? He might kill me. Did it ever strike you that he has a distinct look of Henry VIII? I call him that sometimes. He only laughs at me."

The Doctor laughed himself at the thought of the ascetic-looking Jimmy, who resembled an El Greco saint, being compared with Henry VIII, but now that he realized Roisin had a hankering after that side of him, it struck him that if the matter were not so delicate and if only Jimmy had remained intimate with him, it might do no harm to indicate to him that an occasional touch of the firebrand would go down well at home. But Jimmy was cautiously extinguishing every bit of the firebrand in himself—either because, as Josephine thought, he was jealous, or because he wanted to get on in the world, or possibly even for a third reason, which the Doctor could not at the moment put his finger on. He had ceased to be hurt by Jimmy's defection. He was almost beginning to feel sorry for him.

The visit to Josephine was a success. When she opened the door to them, she smiled in a way that suggested that she would presently burst into tears, but as Roisin rattled on nervously, Josephine relaxed. When Roisin went upstairs for a moment, Josephine turned to the Doctor and said, "That old humbug! He would have all the luck, wouldn't he?"

"Are you sure it's luck, dear?" the Doctor asked doubtfully.

"Why? There's nothing wrong, is there?"

"No. But I thought you said he'd regret it."

"Oh, that!" she said with a shrug. Like all women, she lacked the courage of her intuitions.

Roisin went home after that visit and the fat was in the fire. If she had been coming back from a date with a man, she couldn't have been more terrified. For now that it was all over she realized her own duplicity. What was worse, she had made an appointment for lunch and shopping with Josephine the following week. She knelt before a picture of the Sacred Heart in her bedroom and asked for strength to be able to tell Jimmy. She explained to the Sacred Heart, as she had to the Doctor or would have explained to anyone else, that she couldn't keep a thing to herself. She was, as the Sacred Heart knew, a blabber. And she asked the Sacred Heart not to let Jimmy be too mad with her. Then, having built up a crisis out of it, she told Jimmy in an offhand way that would have made any man mad, even one without a past like Jimmy's.

"Oh, Jimmy, do you know who I ran into today? Josephine Hanrahan." There was no response at all. "God, Jimmy," Roisin rattled on despairingly, "she's a lovely woman. Why didn't you let me meet her before? We went into her place for a minute."

"We?"

"I met her with Paddy, and she asked us in."

Jimmy knocked the ashes out of his pipe and slowly turned on her. He frightened her. His face looked old and sour and caved in. He said, "Does this mean you intend to defy me?"

"Defy you, Jimmy?" she said, her hands pulling nervously at her dress. "Sure, I never defy you. I said I'd have lunch with her. Is there anything wrong with that?"

"That remains to be seen."

"But what could I say, Jimmy? I didn't want to hurt her feelings."

"You could have put her off," he said. "As you'd put off any other unsuitable invitation."

"But I don't see what there was unsuitable about it. I liked the girl, the little I saw of her."

"The little you saw of her, precisely," Jimmy said, holding up his finger in warning. "You don't really know that woman and I do. There are things about her I'd sooner not discuss. Things I'd prefer not to say about an old friend."

"What things, Jimmy?" Roisin asked eagerly.

"I said I'd sooner not discuss them," Jimmy replied severely. But his training as a lawyer probably made him feel that this was unconvincing. Evidence was what was needed. "I don't remember too well, but there was some talk about a girl in Drumcondra that jumped out of a three-story window."

"Is it in Drumcondra?" exclaimed Roisin, who found it difficult to keep up another person's tone. "Sure if I was living there I'd jump out of a window myself."

"Well, maybe it wasn't Drumcondra," he conceded. "Anyway, she was killed. I'm not saying it was ever brought home to Josephine. For all I know, she may be as innocent as yourself. But you do not want to be mixed up with people like that. Particularly while she's knocking around with a fellow like Paddy Baldwin."

"Ah, for goodness sake, you're not going to say there's anything between the pair of them!" cried Roisin. "I don't believe a word of it, Jimmy. I think he's lonely and she just mothers him." Jimmy laughed harshly, and she looked up at him in surprise.

"Paddy is an old friend," he said, "and I have no wish to criticize him. His mother, God rest her, could have told you the truth."

"His mother?" Roisin cried incredulously. "But Josephine says he was crazy about her."

"She died of a broken heart," Jimmy said.

Then he did an extraordinary thing. He went on his knees and joined his hands. You can imagine Jimmy, six foot of him, on his knees. "Roisin," he said, "won't you keep away from that crowd, for my sake? You're too good for them. They'll only corrupt you the way they've corrupted others, all for their own amusement. I know them of old, and I curse the day I had anything to do with them. That's what I wanted when I married you—to get away from it all. And there's another thing," he added, closing his eyes and staring up in agony at her like a blind man asking for a penny. "I didn't want to tell you, but you'd better know before it's too late. My family were all a little unstable mentally. On my father's side, of course. I couldn't bear a mental shock. My uncle was insane when he died. You wouldn't want to drive me to that."

"Your uncle?" Roisin cried. "Which uncle?"

"Willie," he replied humbly. "It was kept a great secret. We didn't want anyone to know."

"I think," Roisin said, speaking with real indignation, "I might have been told before now."

Extraordinary as it was for her to see this great man at her feet, it wasn't him she was thinking of now. It was Little Liam. Liam was a curious child. He always hated to be denied anything, and if you spoke severely to him he screamed with rage. Was it possible that Liam had inherited the family weakness, and had she in her innocence made it worse by frustrating him when she should have comforted him and given in to him? For the first time, she was really angry with Jimmy, and went upstairs to look at the child, and then knelt by his bedside and promised the Sacred Heart that she would never cross him again, whatever he wanted.

. . .

She was a serious girl, and she knew that she could not imperil her marriage by doing something that Jimmy disapproved of, so she rang up Josephine and excused herself because of illness. But she was also a rotten liar. When Josephine, a woman who'd give you the shift off her back, heard that Roisin was ill, she announced that she was coming over to look after the house for her. Then Roisin's heart misgave her, and she asked Josephine over for tea. She felt terrible about it because she knew that she was no good at explaining things if the explanation involved any improbabilities, and she was certain that Josephine would see through it all. She did. Within five minutes she knew that Roisin was acting under Jimmy's orders and went white with rage. It was bad enough that he would not invite her to the house. To make it plain that he did not think her a proper acquaintance for his wife was too much. When he was ill and a bachelor, he simply packed his bag and came to her house and stayed there till he was well. So she told Roisin this, and Roisin shook her head despairingly.

"What can I do?" she asked.

"Whatever you like," said Josephine. "I wouldn't allow my husband to give me orders like that."

Roisin realized unhappily that a partial explanation was not enough. "But it isn't only that, Josephine," she said. "I'm afraid to contradict him. You see, it's in the family. He had an uncle that was queer."

"It's the first I've heard of it," Josephine said.

"Well, to tell you the truth, it's the first I heard of it, too," said Roisin.

"But who told you?" Josephine persisted.

"He did—Jimmy, I mean. He told me it was dangerous for him to be upset."

"And you're quite sure he's not making it up?"

"Would a man say a thing like that about his own family if it wasn't true? Sure, that would be crazy out and out. I'd sooner 'twas true. You don't think it isn't?" she added anxiously.

"I'll make it my business to find out," Josephine said grimly.

"But if that's not true," Roisin wailed, "then I suppose Paddy's mother didn't die of a broken heart, either."

"Paddy's mother?" cried Josephine. "She worshipped the ground he walked on. And with good reason. I don't know what's come over your husband, Roisin. I never knew him to tell lies like that."

"It isn't lying, that's the awful part of it," Roisin said in distress. "Josephine, I've never breathed it to a soul, and I wouldn't say it now only I know it's not true. Actually, I knew all the time it wasn't true. You will understand me, won't you? I'm only telling you to show how crazy he is. That woman in Drumcondra that was supposed to have committed suicide because of you . . ."

At that point, Josephine nearly went crazy herself, and nothing but loyalty to Roisin prevented her from going straight to Jimmy's office, and demanding a signed retraction. Anyway, it made no difference. For if there is one impression a man must never leave upon his wife it is that he is emotional and unstable, because it means that the woman at once begins to feel the whole business of judgment and decision devolves upon her, and a woman who feels that no longer respects her husband. So Roisin continued to meet the gang, and take one drink, which always made her tight, and she developed a violent crush on Con Bishop, whose Oxford accent probably reminded her of Henry VIII. She and Josephine were devoted to one another, though not in the way Roisin would have wished, with Josephine as the confidante of her passion for Jimmy. Rather, she was the confidante of Roisin's doubts of Jimmy, the woman she would rush to whenever there was trouble between them. Jimmy, on the other hand, forever alienated from all his old friends by his slanders, took to going to chapel in the evenings and praying that his wife would not do something it would have taken a convulsion of nature to make her do, and at home he was ordered about as if he were a child.

Androcles and the Army

"POLITICS AND RELIGION!" Healy said when Cloone announced that he was joining the army. "Even a lion tamer you can't trust not to get patriotic on you. The next thing will be the Clown wanting to join the Trappists." He argued, he pleaded, he threatened proceedings for breach of contract, but Cloone retorted with arguments about the state of the country. Threatened by the Germans, threatened by the English, threatened even by the Americans, she needed all her children. Healy's long red nose, that ascended and descended like a helicopter, shuddered and began to mount at the very mention of Ireland.

"Look, Cloone," he said, reasonably, "there's nothing wrong with the bloody country. It's the show I'm thinking of. 'Twill only be the mercy of God if we can keep going at all. And if you leave us there isn't another man in Ireland can do the job, and with a war on, I'm not going to be able to get one in."

"Ah, damn it, I know, I know," Cloone replied in anguish. "I'm not against the show, and I care more for my lions than I do for the show, but if I have to choose between my lions and my country, I have to choose my country. It's as hard on me as it is on you, but war is always like that. Look at the sugar!"

Till the last moment Healy continued to plead. He knew that not only would it be impossible to get another lion tamer, but even if he did, the man would not be as good as Cloone. Healy knew an artist when he saw one and Cloone was an artist. What others could do by fear, he could do by a simple dropping of his voice. Healy couldn't hear the magic in that sudden change of pitch, but he could see the result, for an angry lion would suddenly uncoil his tightened springs of muscle and lie down to be stroked like a cat. Cloone would play with it like a cat, his blue eyes soft with emotion, and mutter as though to himself, "God, Ned, isn't he beautiful?"

"Beautiful my ass!" Healy would think as his red nose began to ascend, but he would keep it to himself.

Anyone seeing Cloone with animals would be bound to think at once of St. Francis of Assisi, but Healy knew that that was all the saint there was in Cloone. He had a devil of a temper, and brooded for months on imaginary insults and injuries. He would begin to mutter about a half a crown that he swore had been unjustly stopped from his pay six months before till Healy, in despair, raised his eyes and hands to Heaven. "Listen, Cloone," he would say, "I told you fifty times that there was nothing stopped. If you don't believe me, I'll give you the bloody half crown to take your puss off me." Then spasms of injured pride would run through Cloone like electric shocks, and he would cry: "It's not the money, Ned! It's not the money! It's the principle." But Healy, who had been in the show business from the time he was five, knew that when artists talked about principle, it was never anything but temperament, and it took a man like him who hated animals but loved human beings to put up with it at all. Cloone knew that too, and knew that Healy had some sort of hold over him. "Cloone tames lions but I tame Cloone," Healy had boasted one night in a pub, and Cloone had agreed with an exasperated giggle. He would do things for Healy he would do for no one else, but even Healy couldn't persuade him to stay on for the emergency. And it wasn't just because the show was only a ghost of itself, stripped by restrictions and regulations. It was pure, unqualified, bloodthirsty patriotism, a thing Healy simply could not understand in a mature man. "If," he added darkly, "you can ever say an artist is mature."

· · ·

It was a wrench for Cloone, because he really loved the few animals that had been left him; he loved Healy, and he loved the wandering life of the circus and the crowds of the small towns and fair greens. He went away with a breaking heart to be shut up in a Nissen hut, dressed in uniform, stood to attention, stood at ease, presented, formed twos with, formed fours with, as if he himself were only a mangy old circus lion, jumping to a cruel tamer's whip. Besides, he was an awkward, excitable man who could never remember his left from his right, and shouldered arms when he should have presented them, and he had to listen to tongue-lashings from a sergeant and not tell the sergeant what he could do with himself. It often reduced him to mutinous tears, and he lay on his cot at night exhausted, thinking of himself as a caged old animal, its spirit broken, dreaming of the jungle. Then he shed more tears because he felt he had never understood wild animals till his own turn came. All the same his desperate sincerity won through. They had to make a corporal of him, and, in the way of other great artists, he was prouder of his two miserable stripes than of all his other gifts. Drinking in a pub with another man, he couldn't help glancing at his sleeve with a smirk of delight.

Then one day he opened a local paper and saw that Doyle's World-Famous Circus was visiting Asragh one evening the following week. Filled with excitement, he went off to ask for a pass. Of course, everyone in the battalion knew his trade, and he had no difficulty in getting the pass. The trouble was that everyone from the officers down wanted a pass as well. They all felt that they had a personal interest in the circus. On the afternoon of the show two lorryloads of troops left the camp for town. In the main street they scattered to the public houses to wait for the circus, but Cloone hurried off joyously to the Fair Green, where Healy was waiting for him. In his temperamental way he threw his arms about Healy and sobbed with pleasure till Healy, in embarrassment, grabbed him by the shoulders and mockingly inspected his uniform, with the green gloves tucked neatly in the shoulder strap and the natty little cane.

"Give it up, John," he said with a grin. "They'll never make a soldier out of you."

"How well they gave me the stripes!" Cloone said defensively, and followed Healy to his caravan.

"Stripes never made a soldier yet," said Healy. "A raw recruit is all you'll ever be." He took down a bottle and poured half a tumbler of neat whiskey for Cloone and another for himself. "And why? Because that's not where you belong at all, John. You belong round here with the rest of the crowd."

"Ah, God, Ned, I know, I know," said Cloone, wriggling miserably on the edge of the bed. "I wake up in the night and think about it. But the Germans have it all planned out. They caught a parachutist with the plans. You have to face it, Ned."

"I do not have to face it," retorted Healy, his delicate nose vibrating at the very thought of it. "You'll never see a shot fired in this country, man. Sure, who the hell would want it? And anyone that did would be welcome to it as far as I'm concerned. I have enough of it."

"I'll give you my word, the moment it's over, I'll belt it back here," said Cloone. "Sometimes I think it'll never be over. Tell me, who have you on the lions?"

"Who do you think?" Healy asked gloomily. "Darcy—the Strong Man." The last words he added not by way of information but as a sneer, for Healy, who had a wretched stomach, had seen the Strong Man screaming his head off with a toothache, and it had left a terrible impression on him.

"Ah, God, Ned," Cloone moaned, shaking his head, "sure Darcy could never handle a lion. Darcy is too rough."

"Darcy is too frightened," Healy added sternly. "Drink that and we'll finish the bottle."

"Is he any good with them?" asked Cloone.

"Ah, he's all right," Healy replied with a frown—he was a fair man. "They don't like him, that's the only thing."

"But how could they, Ned?" Cloone asked feverishly. "Lions could never get on with a Strong Man. Lions are sensitive, like women. What possessed you to give them to Darcy?"

"Who else could I give them to?" Healy asked angrily. "Damn grateful I was to him for taking them off my hands."

It was like old times for Cloone, sitting in the twilight with his friend, and the old hands dropping in to ask how he was. He told them all about the importance of the army and the danger to the country, and they listened politely but with utter incredulity. It was at times like this that you could see Cloone wasn't really one of them.

When Healy went to take the gate, Cloone with a foolish smile nodded in the direction of the big cage and said, "I'll slip round and have a look at Jumbo and Bess." They might have been two old sweethearts, the way he talked of them, thought Healy.

"Oh, plenty of time, John," he said with a toss of his head. "They won't be on for half an hour yet."

The main satisfaction of the evening from Healy's point of view was the number of soldiers who came, officers and all. Healy could not help liking a bit of style, and style was something that was disappearing from the Irish countryside. He was only sorry for the miserable show he had for them, and the two lions that were all he had left him. And then their turn came, and Darcy stood ready, a huge and handsome man with a self-conscious air as though he did not even see the audience.

"Ladies and Gentlemen," the ringmaster explained, "owing to emergency restrictions, Doyle's collection of wild animals—the greatest in the world—has been considerably reduced. But the two lions you are going to see aren't just ordinary animals. No, ladies and gentlemen, these two terrible lions are among the most savage ever captured alive. In the capture of these two lions—especially for Doyle's Circus—no less than eight famous big-game hunters lost their lives, as well as an untold number of simple natives."

Then the big cage was rolled on; Darcy smartly whipped the curtains back; there was a moment of incredulous silence, and then a laugh that grew into a roar. For, inside the cage with his cap off and his tunic open, was Cloone, sprawled on the ground against the bars, embracing Jumbo with one arm and Bess with the other. The two lions had a meditative air, as if they were posing for a photograph. At the tumult in the audience they raised their heads suspiciously, and fresh screams broke out, because Jumbo was seen to be holding Cloone's green gloves in his jaws while Bess sedately held his cane. There was an atmosphere of intense domesticity about the scene that made one feel that instead of a cage there should be a comfortable living room with a good fire burning.

"Mind the lions or the soldier will ate 'em!" roared someone from the back row, and this brought fresh shrieks. As a turn it was superior to anything that had yet been seen, but to the circus hands it seemed like disaster.

"Oh, my God!" muttered the ringmaster. "This is awful! This is terrible entirely! How could a thing like that happen, Darcy?"

"That's Cloone," said Darcy with a puzzled frown.

"Sure I know damn well 'tis Cloone," said the ringmaster severely. "But how the hell did he get in there, and how are we going to get him out? Come out now, John," he called appealingly. "Come on out and let the show go on!"

"In a minute now, in a minute," replied Cloone with a knowing smile. "We'll give ye yeer show when we're ready."

"Ah, come on now, come on!" snapped the ringmaster. "We'll be the laughingstock of Ireland. Darcy, you go in and get him out!"

"Is it me?" Darcy asked indignantly. "How the hell can I go in with him there? They'd ate you, man. Where's my hot bar?"

Two policemen who had been sitting near the front approached with their uniform caps in their hands to indicate that this was merely friendly curiosity on their part and that nothing had yet occurred that required their official attention.

"Now, lads, what's this disturbance about?" asked the Sergeant in a friendly boom. "Come out of that cage now like a good man, and don't be obstructing the traffic."

Then Cloone began to giggle feebly as the humor of it struck him.

"Ye can't get me," he said coyly.

"What's that you said?" asked the Sergeant.

"You're afraid," said Cloone.

"Who's afraid?" asked the Sergeant.

"You are," replied Cloone with an explosion of laughter. "There's nothing to be afraid of. We're all friends here."

The Sergeant looked at him for a moment and then put on his cap. It had something of the effect of a judge's donning of the black cap in a murder trial. The younger policeman with a shy air put on his own.

"Someone will have to get him," the Sergeant announced in an entirely different tone, the one that went with the cap.

"All right, all right," Darcy said irritably. "Wait till I get my hot bar." He grabbed it with a determined air and opened the door of the cage. The two lions rose and growled at him.

"Put down that bar!" Cloone said in an outraged voice as he staggered to his feet. "Put it down, I say!"

"Get out of my way, God blast you!" snarled Darcy. "Haven't I trouble enough without you?"

All in a moment the atmosphere of domesticity had vanished. It was clear that Darcy hated the lions and Cloone, and Cloone and the lions hated Darcy. For a few moments the lions eyed the Strong Man hungrily and growled; then they slunk slowly back to the end of the cage where a separate compartment was opened. Darcy, white in the face, slammed the door behind them, and then the ringmaster and the policemen, followed by Healy, entered the main cage.

"Come on, John," Healy said, taking Cloone by the arm. "Come on now."

"That's no way to treat my animals," Cloone said, pointing at Darcy.

"John," Healy said in a low voice, "remember the uniform!" A remark, as he said afterward, that he'd have to answer for on the Last Day, because he cared as much about the uniform as he did about the state of the country. But he was a man tamer as Cloone was a lion tamer. Each of them made his own sort of soothing, nonsensical noise.

"All right," muttered Cloone, heading off in the direction of the lions. "Let me say goodby to them and I won't trouble ye again."

"Don't let that man open that cage door again or I won't be responsible!" Darcy shouted in a frenzy.

"I'll be responsible, Darcy," Healy said shortly. "Go on, John, and do whatever you want to do, but do it quick—and for God's sake don't let them out on us! Come on outside, boys, and we'll shut the gate."

And there they had to stand outside the cage, powerlessly, watching the performance within. Cloone opened the gate of the inner cage and stood there for a moment, overcome with emotion. The lions seemed to be overcome as well. After a moment Jumbo sadly raised his big head and joined Cloone. Cloone bent and kissed him on the snout. As he did so Bess came up to him and licked his hand. He kissed her as well. Then, before he closed the door behind him, he drew himself up and gave them a military salute. The soldiers in the audience were delighted with this. "Company, present arms!" yelled one of them. As Healy said, "There was never the like of it seen as show business. If you could have put it on as an act, you'd be turning them away."

But for Cloone, it was anything but show business. As he came out of the big cage he strode up to Darcy.

"You big, bloody bully!" he said. "You had to take a red-hot bar to frighten those poor innocent creatures! Like every other bully, you're a coward."

He gave Darcy a punch, and the Strong Man was so astonished that he went down flat on the grass. There were fresh roars from the audience; the soldiers were getting restive. Darcy rose with a dazed expression as the two policemen seized Cloone from behind. To give them their due, they were less afraid of what Cloone would do to Darcy than of what Darcy would do to Cloone. He was one of those sad powerful men whose tragedy is that they can't have a little disagreement in a pub without running the risk of manslaughter. Cloone pulled himself away, leaving his tunic in the policemen's hands, and dashed for the side of the tent. He disappeared under it with the two guards close behind, and a score of soldiers after the guards, to see that their comrade got fair play. As they were pulling off their belts while they ran, two officers got up as well and ran through the main entrance after them to protect the guards. It was all very confusing, and the show was as good as over for the night.

They ran Cloone to earth at last in the kitchen of a cottage down a lane from which there was no escape. By this time he had had the opportunity of considering his behavior, and all the fight had gone out of him. He apologized to the woman of the house for the fright he had given her, and she moaned over him like a Greek chorus, blaming it all on the bad whiskey. He apologized to the guards for the trouble he had given them and begged them to go back to the circus while he surrendered himself at the barrack. He apologized all over again to the two young lieutenants who appeared soon after; by this time he was trembling like an aspen leaf.

"It's my lions!" he said in a broken voice. "I'd never shame the uniform only for them."

At his court-martial he appeared on a charge of "conduct prejudicial to good order and discipline, in that he, Corporal John Cloone, on the eighteenth day of September, of the current year, had allowed himself to be seen in a public place with his tunic in disorder and minus certain articles of equipment: viz. one pair of gloves and one walking stick (regulation)." The charge of assault was dropped at the instance of the President, who suggested to the prosecution that there might have been provocation. The Prosecutor agreed that, considering the prisoner's occupation in civil life, this might be so. But armies are alike the whole world over, and, whatever their disregard for civilian rights, they all have the same old-maidish preoccupation with their own dignity, and Cloone was lucky to get off with nothing worse than the loss of his stripes. Healy asked him what better he could expect from soldiers, people who tried to turn decent artists into people like themselves. As if anybody had ever succeeded in turning a soldier into anything that was the least use to God or man!

But Healy, as Cloone knew, was lacking in idealism.

✣ *Public Opinion*

NOW I KNOW what you're thinking. You're thinking how nice 'twould be to live in a little town. You could have a king's life in a house like this, with a fine garden and a car so that you could slip up to town whenever you felt in need of company. Living in Dublin, next door to the mail boat and writing things for the American papers, you imagine you could live here and write whatever you liked about MacDunphy of the County Council. Mind, I'm not saying you couldn't say a hell of a lot about him! I said a few things myself from time to time. All I mean is that you wouldn't say it for long. This town broke better men. It broke me and, believe me, I'm no chicken.

When I came here first, ten years ago, I felt exactly the way you do, the way everybody does. At that time, and the same is nearly true today, there wasn't a professional man in this town with a housekeeper under sixty, for fear of what people might say about them. In fact, you might still notice that there isn't one of them who is what you might call "happily" married. They went at it in too much of a hurry.

Oh, of course, I wasn't going to make that mistake! When I went to choose a housekeeper I chose a girl called Bridie Casey, a handsome little girl of seventeen from a village up the coast. At the same time I took my precautions. I drove out there one day when she was at home, and I had a look at the cottage and a talk with her mother and a cup of tea, and after that I didn't need anyone to recommend her. I knew that anything Bridie fell short in her mother would not be long in correcting. After that, there was only one inquiry I wanted to make.

"Have you a boy, Bridie?" said I.

"No, Doctor, I have not," said she with an innocent air that didn't take me in a bit. As a doctor you soon get used to innocent airs.

"Well, you'd better hurry up and get one," said I, "or I'm not going to keep you."

With that she laughed as if she thought I was only joking. I was not joking at all. A housekeeper or maid without a fellow of her own is as bad as a hen with an egg.

"It's no laughing matter," I said. "And when you do get a fellow, if you haven't one already, you can tell him I said he could make free with my beer, but if ever I catch you diluting my whiskey I'll sack you on the spot."

Mind, I made no mistake in Bridie or her mother either. She mightn't be any good in the Shelbourne Hotel, but what that girl could cook she cooked well and anything she cleaned looked as if it was clean. What's more, she could size a patient up better than I could myself. Make no mistake about it, as housekeepers or maids Irish girls are usually not worth a damn, but a girl from a good Irish home can turn her hand to anything. Of course, she was so good-looking that people who came to the house used to pass remarks about us, but that was only jealousy. They hadn't the nerve to employ a good-looking girl themselves for fear of what people would say. But I knew that as long as a girl had a man of her own to look after she'd be no bother to me.

No, what broke up my happy home was something different entirely. You mightn't understand it, but in a place like this 'tis the devil entirely to get ready money out of them. They'll give you anything else in the world only money. Here, everything is what they call "friendship." I suppose the shops give them the habit because a regular customer is always supposed to be in debt and if ever the debt is paid off it's war to the knife. Of course they think a solicitor or a doctor should live the same way, and instead of money what you get is presents: poultry, butter, eggs, and meat that a large family could not eat, let alone a single man. Friendship is all very well, but between you and me it's a poor thing for a man to be relying on at the beginning of his career.

I had one patient in particular called Willie Joe Corcoran of Clashanaddig—I buried him last year, poor man, and my mind is easier already—and Willie Joe seemed to think I was always on the verge of starvation. One Sunday I got in from twelve-o'clock Mass and went to the whiskey cupboard to get myself a drink when I noticed the most extraordinary smell. Doctors are sensitive to smells, of course—we have to be—and I couldn't rest easy till I located that one. I searched the room and I searched the hall and I even poked my head upstairs into the bedrooms before I tried the kitchen. Knowing Bridie, I never even associated the smell with her. When I went in, there she was in a clean white uniform, cooking the dinner, and she looked round at me.

"What the hell is that smell, Bridie?" said I.

She folded her arms and leaned against the wall, as good-looking a little girl as you'd find in five counties.

"I told you before," says she in her thin, high voice, "'tis that side of beef Willie Joe Corcoran left on Thursday. It have the whole house ruined on me."

"But didn't I tell you to throw that out?" I said.

"You did," says she as if I was the most unreasonable man in the world, "but you didn't tell me where I was going to throw it."

"What's wrong with the ash can?" said I.

"What's wrong with the ash can?" says she. "There's nothing wrong with it, only the ashmen won't be here till Tuesday."

"Then for God's sake, girl, can't you throw it over the wall into the field?"

"Into the field," says she, pitching her voice up an octave till she sounded like a sparrow in decline. "And what would people say?"

"Begor, I don't know, Bridie," I said, humoring her. "What do *you* think they'd say?"

"They're bad enough to say anything," says she.

I declare to God I had to look at her to see was she serious. There she was, a girl of seventeen with the face of a nun, suggesting things that I could barely imagine.

"Why, Bridie?" I said, treating it as a joke. "You don't think they'd say I was bringing corpses home from the hospital to cut up?"

"They said worse," she said in a squeak, and I saw that she took a very poor view of my powers of imagination. Because you write books, you think you know a few things, but you should listen to the conversation of pious girls in this town.

"About me, Bridie?" said I in astonishment.

"About you and others," said she. And then, by cripes, I lost my temper with her.

"And is it any wonder they would," said I, "with bloody fools like you paying attention to them?"

I have a very wicked temper when I'm roused and for the time being it scared her more than what people might say of her.

"I'll get Kenefick's boy in the morning and let him take it away," said she. "Will I give him a shilling?"

"Put it in the poor box," said I in a rage. "I'll be going out to Doctor MacMahon's for supper and I'll take it away myself. Any damage that's going to be done to anyone's character can be done to mine. It should be able to stand it. And let me tell you, Bridie Casey, if I was the sort to mind what anyone said about me, you wouldn't be where you are this minute."

I was very vicious to her, but of course I was mad. After all, I had to take my drink and eat my dinner with that smell round the house, and Bridie in a panic, hopping about me like a hen with hydrophobia. When I went out to the pantry to get the side of beef, she gave a yelp as if I'd trodden on her foot. "Mother of God!" says she. "Your new suit!" "Never mind my new suit," said I, and I wrapped the beef in a couple of newspapers and heaved it into the back of the car. I declare, it wasn't wishing to me. I had all the windows open, but even then the smell was high, and I went through town like a coursing match with the people on the footpaths lifting their heads like beatles to sniff after me.

I wouldn't have minded that so much only that Sunday is the one day I have. In those days before I was married I nearly always drove out to Jerry MacMahon's for supper and a game of cards. I knew poor Jerry looked forward to it because the wife was very severe with him in the matter of liquor.

I stopped the car on top of the cliffs to throw out the meat, and just as I was looking for a clear drop I saw a long galoot of a countryman coming up the road towards me. He had a long, melancholy sort of face and mad eyes. Whatever it was about his appearance I didn't want him to see what I was up to. You might think it funny in a professional man but that is the way I am.

"Nice evening," says he.

"Grand evening, thank God," says I, and not to give him an excuse for being too curious I said: "That's a powerful view."

"Well," says he sourly, just giving it a glance, "the view is all right but 'tis no good to the people that has to live in it. There is no earning in that view," says he, and then he cocked his head and began to size me up, and I knew I'd made a great mistake, opening my mouth to him at all. "I suppose now you'd be an artist?" says he.

You might notice about me that I'm very sensitive to inquisitiveness. It is a thing I cannot stand. Even to sign my name to a telegram is a thing I never like to do, and I hate a direct question.

"How did you guess?" said I.

"And I suppose," said he, turning to inspect the view again, "if you painted that, you'd find people to buy it?"

"That's what I was hoping," said I.

So he turned to the scenery again, and this time he gave it a studied appraisal as if it was a cow at a fair.

"I daresay for a large view like that you'd nearly get five pounds?" said he.

"You would and more," said I.

"Ten?" said he with his eyes beginning to pop.

"More," said I.

"That beats all," he said, shaking his head in resignation. "Sure, the whole thing isn't worth that. No wonder the country is the way it is. Good luck!"

"Good luck," said I, and I watched him disappear among the rocks over the road. I waited, and then I saw him peering out at me from behind a rock like some wild mountain animal, and I knew if I stayed there till nightfall I wouldn't shake him off. He was beside himself at the thought of a picture that would be worth as much as a cow, and he probably thought if he stayed long enough he might learn the knack and paint the equivalent of a whole herd of them. The man's mind didn't rise above cows. And, whatever the devil ailed me, I could not give him the satisfaction of seeing what I was really up to. You might think it shortsighted of me, but that is the sort I am.

I got into the car and away with me down to Barney Phelan's pub on the edge of the bay. Barney's pub is the best in this part of the world and Barney himself is a bit of a character; a tall excitable man with wild blue eyes and a holy terror to gossip. He kept filling my glass as fast as I could lower it, and three or four times it was on the tip of my tongue to tell him what I was doing; but I knew he'd make a story out of it for the boys that night and sooner or later it would get back to Willie Joe Corcoran. Bad as Willie Joe was, I would not like to hurt his feelings. That is another great weakness of mine. I never like hurting people's feelings.

Of course that was a mistake, for when I walked out of the pub, the first thing I saw was the cliff dweller and two other yokels peering in at the parcel in the back of my car. At that I really began to feel like murder. I cannot stand that sort of unmannerly inquisitiveness.

"Well," I said, giving the cliff dweller a shoulder out of my way, "I hope ye saw something good."

At that moment Barney came out, drying his hands in his apron and showing his two front teeth like a weasel.

"Are them fellows at your car, Doctor?" says he.

"Oho!" said the cliff dweller to his two friends. "So a docthor is what he is now!"

"And what the hell else did you think he was, you fool?" asked Barney.

"A painter is what he was when last we heard of him," said the lunatic.

"And I suppose he was looking for a little job painting the huts ye have up in Beensheen?" asked Barney with a sneer.

"The huts may be humble but the men are true," said the lunatic solemnly.

"Blast you, man," said Barney, squaring up to him, "are you saying I don't know the Doctor since he was in short trousers?"

"No man knows the soul of another," said the cliff dweller, shaking his head again.

"For God's sake, Barney, don't be bothering yourself with that misfortunate clown," said I. " 'Tis my own fault for bringing the likes of him into the world. Of all the useless occupations, that and breaking stones are the worst."

"I would not be talking against breaking stones," said the cliff dweller sourly. "It might not be long till certain people here would be doing the same."

At that I let a holy oath out of me and drove off in the direction of Jerry MacMahon's. When I glanced in the driving mirror I saw Barney standing in the middle of the road with the three yokels around him, waving their hands. It struck me that in spite of my precautions Barney would have a story for the boys that night, and it would not be about Willie Joe. It would be about me. It also struck me that I was behaving in a very uncalled-for way. If I'd been a real murderer trying to get rid of a real corpse I could hardly have behaved more suspiciously. And why? Because I did not want people discussing my business. I don't know what it is about Irish people that makes them afraid of having their business discussed. It is not that it is any worse than other people's business, only we behave as if it was.

I stopped the car at a nice convenient spot by the edge of the bay miles from anywhere. I could have got rid of the beef then and there but something seemed to have broken in me. I walked up and down that road slowly, looking to right and left to make sure no one was watching. Even then I was perfectly safe, but I saw a farmer crossing a field a mile away up the hill and decided to wait till he was out of sight. That was where the ferryboat left me, because, of course, the moment he glanced over his shoulder and saw a strange man with a car stopped on the road he stopped himself with his head cocked like an old setter. Mind, I'm not blaming him! I blame nobody but myself. Up to that day I had never felt a stime of sympathy with my neurotic patients, giving themselves diseases they hadn't got, but there was I, a doctor, giving myself a disease I hadn't got and with no excuse whatever.

By this time the smell was so bad I knew I wouldn't get it out of the upholstery for days. And there was Jerry MacMahon up in Cahirnamona, waiting for me with a bottle of whiskey his wife wouldn't let him touch till I got there, and I couldn't go for fear of the way he'd laugh at me. I looked again and saw that the man who'd been crossing the field had changed his mind. Instead he'd come down to the gate and was leaning over it, lighting his pipe while he admired the view of the bay and the mountains.

That was the last straw. I knew now that even if I got rid of the beef my Sunday would still be ruined. I got in the car and drove straight home. Then I went to the whiskey cupboard and poured myself a drink that seemed to be reasonably proportionate to the extent of my suffering. Just as I sat down to it Bridie walked in without knocking. This is one fault I should have told you about—all the time she was with me I never trained her to knock. I declare to God when I saw her standing in the doorway I jumped. I'd always been very careful of myself and jumping was a new thing to me.

"Did I tell you to knock before you came into a room?" I shouted.

"I forgot," she said, letting on not to notice the state I was in. "You didn't go to Dr. MacMahon's so?"

"I did not," I said.

"And did you throw away the beef?"

"I didn't," I said. Then as I saw her waiting for an explanation I added: "There were too many people around."

"Look at that now!" she said complacently. "I suppose we'll have to bury it in the garden after dark?"

"I suppose so," I said, not realizing how I had handed myself over to the woman, body and bones, holus-bolus.

That evening I took a spade and dug a deep hole in the back garden and Bridie heaved in the side of beef. The remarkable thing is that the whole time we were doing it we talked in whispers and glanced up at the backs of the other houses in the road to see if we were being watched. But the weight off my mind when it was over! I even felt benevolent to Bridie. Then I went over to Jim Donoghue, the dentist's, and told him the whole story over a couple of drinks. We were splitting our sides over it.

When I say we were splitting our sides I do not mean that this is a funny story. It was very far from being funny for me before it was over. You wouldn't believe the scandal there was about Bridie and myself after that. You'd wonder how people could imagine such things, let alone repeat them. That day changed my whole life. . . . Oh, laugh! Laugh! I was laughing out the other side of my mouth before it was through. Up to that I'd never given a rap what anyone thought of me, but from that day forth I was afraid of my own shadow. With all the talk there was about us I even had to get rid of Bridie and, of course, inside of twelve months I was married like the rest of them. . . . By the way, when I mentioned unhappy marriages I wasn't speaking of my own. Mrs. Ryan and myself get on quite well. I only mentioned it to show what might be in store for yourself if ever you were foolish enough to come and live here. A town like this can bend iron. And if you doubt my word, that's only because you don't know what they are saying about you.

The Party

OLD JOHNNY, one of the Gas Company's watchmen, was a man with a real appreciation of his job. Most of the time, of course, it was a cold, comfortless job, with no one to talk to, and he envied his younger friend Tim Coakley, the postman. Postmen had a cushy time of it—always watched and waited for, bringing good news or bad news, often called in to advise, and (according to Tim, at least) occasionally called in for more intimate purposes. Tim, of course, was an excitable man, and he could be imagining a lot of that, though Johnny gave him the benefit of the doubt. At the same time, queer things happened to Johnny now and again that were stranger than anything Tim could tell. As it seemed to Johnny, people got it worse at night; the wild ones grew wilder, the gloomy ones gloomier. Whatever it was in them that had light in it burned more clearly, the way the stars and moon did when the sun went down. It was the darkness that did it. Johnny would be sitting in his hut for hours in the daylight and no one even gave him a second glance, but once darkness fell, people would cross the street to look at his brazier, and even stop to speak to him.

One night, for instance, in the week before Christmas, he was watching in a big Dublin square, with a railed-off park in the middle of it and doctors' and lawyers' houses on all the streets about it. That suited Johnny fine, particularly at that time of year, when there was lots of visiting and entertaining. He liked to be at the center of things, and he always appreciated the touch of elegance: the stone steps leading up to the tall door, with the figures entering and leaving looking small in the lighted doorway, and the slight voices echoing on the great brick sounding board of the square.

One house in particular attracted him. It was all lit up as if for a party, and the curtains were pulled back to reveal the tall handsome rooms with decorated plaster ceilings. A boy with a basket came and rang, and a young man in evening dress leaned out of the window and told the boy to leave the stuff in the basement. As he did so, a girl came and rested her hand on his shoulder, and she was in evening dress, too. Johnny liked that. He liked people with a bit of style. If he had had the good fortune to grow up in a house like that, he would have done the right thing, too. And even though he hadn't, it pleased him to watch the show. Johnny, who came of a generation before trade unions, knew that in many ways it is pleasanter to observe than to participate. He only hoped there would be singing; he was very partial to a bit of music.

But this night a thing happened the like of which had never happened to Johnny before. The door of the house opened and closed, and a man in a big cloth coat like fur came across the road to him. When he came closer, Johnny saw that he was a tall, thin man with graying hair and a pale discontented face.

"Like to go home to bed for a couple of hours?" the man asked in a low voice.

"What's that?" said Johnny, in astonishment.

"I'll stay here and mind your box."

"Oh, you would, would you?" Johnny said, under the impression that the man must have drink taken.

"I'm not joking," said the man shortly.

The grin faded on Johnny's face, and he hoped God would direct him to say the right thing. This could be dangerous. It suggested only one thing—a checkup—though in this season of good will you'd think people would be a bit more charitable, even if a man had slipped away for a few minutes for a drink. But that was the way of bosses everywhere. Even Christmas wasn't sacred to them. Johnny put on an appearance of great sternness. "Oho," he said, "I can't afford to do things like that. There's valuable property here belonging to the Gas Company. I could lose my job over a thing like that."

"You won't lose your job," the man said. "I won't leave here till you come back. If there's any trouble about it, I'll get you another job. I suppose it's money you want."

"I never asked you for anything," Johnny replied indignantly. "And I can't go home at this hour, with no bus to bring me back."

"I suppose there's other places you can go," the man replied. "There's a quid, and I won't expect you till two."

The sight of the money changed Johnny's view of the matter. If a rich man wanted to amuse himself doing Johnny's job for a while —a little weakness of rich men that Johnny had heard of in other connections—and was willing to pay for it, that was all right. Rich men had to have their little jokes. Or, of course, it could be a bet.

"Oh, well," he said, rising and giving himself a shake, "so long as there's no harm in it!" He hadn't seen the man go into the house where they were having the party, so he must live there. "I suppose it's a joke?" he added, looking at the man out of the corner of his eye.

"It's no joke to me," the man said gloomily.

"Oh, I wasn't being inquisitive, of course," Johnny said hastily. "But I see there was to be a party in the house. I thought it might be something to do with that."

"There's your quid," said the man. "You needn't be back till three unless you want to. I won't get much sleep anyway."

Johnny thanked him profusely and left in high good humor. He foresaw that the man would probably be of great use to him sometime. A man who could offer to get you a job just like that was not to be slighted. And besides he had an idea of how he was going to spend the next hour or so, at least, and a very pleasant way it was. He took a bus to Ringsend to the house of Tim Coakley, the postman. Tim, though a good deal younger, was very friendly with him, and he was an expansive man who loved any excuse for a party.

As Johnny expected, Tim, already on his way to bed, welcomed him with his two arms out and a great shout of laughter. He was bald and fat, with a high-pitched voice. Johnny showed Tim and his wife the money and announced that he was treating them to a dozen of stout. Like the decent man he was, Tim didn't want to take the money for the stout from Johnny, but Johnny insisted. "Wait till I tell you, man!" he said triumphantly. "The like of it never happened before in the whole history of the Gas Company."

As Johnny told the story, it took close on half an hour, though this included Mrs. Coakley's departure and return with the dozen of stout. And then the real pleasure began, because the three of them had to discuss what it all meant. Why was the gentleman in the big coat sitting in the cold of the square looking at the lights and listening to the noise of the party in his own home? It was a real joy to Johnny to hear his friend analyze it, for Tim had a powerful intellect, full of novel ideas, and in no time what had begun as a curious incident in a watchman's life was beginning to expand into a romance, a newspaper case. Tim at once ruled out the idea of a joke. What would be the point in a joke like that? A bet was the more likely possibility. It could be that the man had bet someone he could take the watchman's place for the best part of the night without being detected, but in Tim's view there was one fatal flaw in this explanation. Why would the man wear a coat as conspicuous as the one that Johnny had described? There would be big money on a wager like that, and the man would be bound to try and disguise himself better. No, there must be another explanation, and as Tim drank more stout, his imagination played over the theme with greater audacity and logic, till Johnny himself began to feel uncomfortable. He began to perceive that it might be a more serious matter than he had thought.

"We've agreed that it isn't a joke," said Tim, holding up one finger. "We've agreed that it isn't a bet," he added, holding up another finger. "There is only one explanation that covers the whole facts," he said, holding up his open hand. "The man is watching the house."

"Watching his own house?" Johnny asked incredulously.

"Exactly. Why else would he pay you good money to sit in your box? A man like that, that could go to his club and be drinking champagne and playing cards all night in the best of company? Isn't it plain that he's doing it only to have cover?"

"So 'twould seem," said Johnny meekly, like any interlocutor of Socrates.

"Now, the next question is: Who is he watching?" said Tim.

"Just so," said Johnny with a mystified air.

"So we ask ourselves: Who would a man like that be watching?" Tim went on triumphantly.

"Burglars," said Mrs. Coakley.

"Burglars?" her husband asked with quiet scorn. "I suppose they'd walk in the front door?"

"He might be watching the cars, though," Johnny said. "There's a lot of them young hooligans around, breaking into cars. I seen them."

"Ah, Johnny, will you have sense?" Tim asked wearily. "Look, if that was all the man wanted, couldn't he give you a couple of bob to keep an eye on the cars? For the matter of that, couldn't he have a couple of plain-clothesmen round the square? Not at all, man! He's watching somebody, and what I say is, the one he's watching is his own wife."

"His wife?" Johnny exclaimed, aghast. "What would he want to watch his wife for?"

"Because he thinks someone is going to that house tonight that should not be there. Someone that wouldn't come at all unless he knew the husband was out. So what does the husband do? He pretends to go out, but instead of that he hides in a watchman's box across the road and waits for him. What other explanation is there?"

"Now, couldn't it be someone after his daughter?" said Johnny.

"What daughter?" Tim asked, hurt at Johnny's lack of logic. "What would a well-to-do man like that do if his daughter was going with a fellow he considered unsuitable? First, he would give the daughter a clock in the jaw, and then he would say to the maid or butler or whoever he have, 'If a Mr. Murphy comes to this house again looking for Miss Alice, kindly tell him she is not at home.' That's all he'd do, and that would be the end of your man. No, Johnny, the one he's watching is the wife, and I can only hope it won't get you into any trouble."

"You don't think I should tell the bobbies about it?" Johnny asked in alarm.

"What *could* you tell the bobbies, though?" Tim asked. "That there was a man in your box that paid you a quid to let him use it? What proof have you that a crime is going to be committed? None! All this is only suspicion. There's nothing you can do now, only let things take their course till two o'clock, and then I'll go round with you and see what really happened."

"But what could happen?" Johnny asked irritably.

"He sounds to me like a desperate man," Tim said gravely.

"Oh, desperate entirely," agreed his wife, who was swallowing it all like a box of creams.

"You don't mean you think he might do him in?" asked Johnny.

"Him, or the wife, Johnny," said Tim. "Or both. Of course, it's nothing to do with you what he does," he added comfortingly. "Whatever it is, you had neither hand, act, nor part in it. It is only the annoyance of seeing your name in the papers."

"A man should never take advice from anybody," Johnny commented bitterly, opening another bottle of stout. Johnny was not a drinking man, but he was worried. He valued his own blameless character, and he knew there were people bad enough to pretend he ought not to have left his post for a couple of hours, even at Christmastime, when everybody was visiting friends. He was not a scholar like Tim, and nobody had warned him of the desperate steps that rich men took when their wives acted flighty.

"Come on," Tim said, putting on his coat. "I'm coming with you."

"Now, I don't want your name dragged into this," Johnny protested. "You have a family to think of, too."

"I'm coming with you, Johnny," Tim said in a deep voice, laying his hand on Johnny's arm. "We're old friends, and friends stick together. Besides, as a postman, I'm more accustomed to this sort of thing than you are. You're a simple man. You might say the wrong thing. Leave it to me to answer the questions."

Johnny was grateful and said so. He was a simple man, as Tim said, and, walking back through the sleeping town, expecting to see police cordons and dead bodies all over the place, he was relieved to have a levelheaded fellow like Tim along with him. As they approached the square and their steps perceptibly slowed, Tim suggested in a low voice that Johnny should stand at the corner of the square while he himself scouted round to see if everything was all right. Johnny agreed, and stopped at the corner. Everything seemed quiet enough. There were only two cars outside the house. There were lights still burning in it, but though the windows were open, as though to clear the air, there was no sound from within. His brazier still burned bright and even in the darkness under the trees of the park. Johnny wished he had never left it.

He saw Tim cross to the other side of the road and go slowly by the brazier. Then Tim stopped and said something, but Johnny could not catch the words. After a few moments, Tim went on, turned the corner, and came back round the square. It took him close on ten minutes, and when he reached Johnny it was clear that something was wrong.

"What is it?" Johnny asked in agony.

"Nothing, Johnny," Tim said sadly. "But do you know who that man is?"

"Sure I told you I never saw him before," said Johnny.

"I know him," said Tim. "That's Hardy that owns the big stores in George's Street. It's his house. The man must be worth hundreds of thousands."

"But what about his wife, man?" asked Johnny.

"Ah, his wife died ten years ago. He's a most respectable man. I don't know what he's doing here, but it's nothing for you to fret about. I'm glad for everyone's sake. Good night, Johnny."

"Good night, Tim, and thanks, thanks!" cried Johnny, his heart already lighter.

The Gas Company's property and his reputation were both secure. The strange man had not killed his wife or his wife's admirer, because the poor soul, having been dead for ten years, couldn't have an admirer for her husband or anyone else to kill. And now he could sit in peace by his brazier and watch the dawn come up over the decent city of Dublin. The relief was so sharp that he felt himself superior to Tim. It was all very well for postmen to talk about the interesting life they led, but they hadn't the same experiences as watchmen. Watchmen might seem simple to postmen, but they had a wisdom of their own, a wisdom that came of the silence and darkness when a man is left alone with his thoughts, like a sailor aboard ship. Thinking of the poor man sitting like that in the cold under the stars watching a party at his own house, Johnny wondered that he could ever have paid attention to Tim. He approached his brazier smiling.

"Everything nice and quiet for you?" he asked.

"Except for some gasbag that stopped for a chat five minutes ago," the other replied with rancor. Johnny felt rather pleased to hear Tim described as a gasbag.

"I know the very man you mean," he said with a nod. "He's a nice poor fellow but he talks too much. Party all over?"

"Except for one couple," the other man said, rising from his box. "It's no use waiting for them. They'll probably be at it till morning."

"I daresay," said Johnny. "Why wouldn't you go in and have a chat with them yourself? You could do with a drink by this time, I suppose."

"A pot they care whether I could or not," the man said bitterly. "All that would happen is that they'd say 'Delighted to see you, Mr. Hardy' and then wait for me to go to bed."

"Ah, now, I wouldn't say that," said Johnny.

"I'm not asking whether you'd say it or not," said the other savagely. "I know it. Here I am, that paid for the party, sitting out here all night, getting my death of cold, and did my daughter or my son as much as come to the door to look for me? Did they even notice I wasn't there?"

"Oh, no, no," Johnny said politely, talking to him as if he were a ten-year-old in a tantrum—which, in a sense, Johnny felt he was. The man might have hundreds of thousands, as Tim said, but there was no difference in the world between him and a little boy sitting out in the back on a frosty night, deliberately trying to give himself pneumonia because his younger brother had got a penny and he hadn't. It was no use being hard on a man like that. "Children are very selfish, of course, but what you must remember is that fathers are selfish, too."

"Selfish?" the other exclaimed angrily. "Do you know what those two cost me between private schools and colleges? Do you know what that one party tonight cost me? As much as you'd earn in a year!"

"Oh, I know, I know!" said Johnny, holding his hands up in distress. "I used to feel the same myself, after the wife died. I'd look at the son putting grease on his hair in front of the mirror, and I'd say to myself, 'That's my grease and that's my mirror, and he's going out to amuse himself with some little piece from the lanes, not caring whether I'm alive or dead!' And daughters are worse. You'd expect more from a daughter somehow."

"You'd expect what you wouldn't get," the other said gloomily. "There's that girl inside that I gave everything to, and she'd think more of some spotty college boy that never earned a pound in his life. And if I open my mouth, my children look at me as if they didn't know was I a fool or a lunatic."

"They think you're old-fashioned, of course," said Johnny. "I know. But all the same you're not being fair to them. Children can be fond enough of you, only you'd never see it till you didn't care whether they were or not. That was the mistake I made. If I might have got an old woman for myself after the Missis died, I'd have enjoyed myself more and seen it sooner. That's what you should do. You're a well-to-do man. You could knock down a very good time for yourself. Get some lively little piece to spend your money on who'll make a fuss over you, and then you won't begrudge it to them so much."

"Yes," said the other, "to have more of them wishing I was dead so that they could get at the rest of it."

He strode across the street without even a good night, and Johnny saw the flood of light on the high steps and heard the dull thud of the big door behind him.

Sitting by his brazier, waiting for the dawn over the city square, Johnny felt very fortunate, wise, and good. If ever the man listened to what he had said, he might be very good to Johnny: he might get him a proper job as an indoor watchman; he might even give him a little pension to show his appreciation. If only he took the advice— and it might sink in after a time—it would be worth every penny of it to him. Anyway, if only the job continued for another couple of days, the man would be bound to give him a Christmas box. Five bob. Ten bob. Even a quid. It would be nothing to a man like that.

Though a realist by conviction, Johnny, too, had his dreams.

Achilles' Heel

IN ONE THING ONLY is the Catholic Church more vulnerable than any human institution, and that is in the type of woman who preys on celibates—particularly the priest's housekeeper. The priest's housekeeper is one of the supreme examples of Natural Selection, because it has been practically proved that when for any reason she is transferred to a male who is not celibate, she pines away and dies. To say that she is sexless is to say both too much and too little, for, like the Church itself, she accepts chastity for a higher end—in her case, the subjection of some unfortunate man to a degree unparalleled in marriage. Wives, of course, have a similar ambition, but their purposes are mysteriously deflected by love-making, jealousy of other women, and children, and it is well known that many Irish wives go into hysterics of rage at the thought of the power vested in priests' housekeepers. *Their* victims, being celibate, have no children, and are automatically sealed off from other women, who might encourage them to greater independence.

But the most powerful among these are the housekeepers of bishops. Nellie Conneely, the Bishop of Moyle's housekeeper, had been with him since he was a canon, and even in those days he had been referred to by his parishioners as "Nellie and the Canon." "Nellie and the Canon" didn't approve of all-night dances, so all-night dances were stopped. Half the population depended for patronage on "Nellie and the Canon," and presents were encouraged

—food for the Canon and something a little less perishable for Nellie. The townspeople had no doubt as to which was the more important partner. She had even appeared on the altar steps on one occasion and announced that there would be no eight-o'clock Mass because she was keeping the Canon in bed. She was a comparatively young woman for such a responsible position, and even at the time I speak of she was a well-preserved little body, with a fussy, humble, sugary air that concealed a cold intelligence. Her great rival was Canon Lanigan, who was the favorite in the succession of the diocese. In private he sniggered over her and called her La Maintenon, but when he visited the Bishop he was as sugary as herself and paid her flowery compliments on her cooking and even on her detestable bottled coffee. But Nellie, though she giggled and gushed in response, wasn't in the least taken in; she knew Lanigan preferred old French mishmash to her own candid cooking, and she warned the Bishop not to trust him. "God forgive me," she said sadly, "I don't know how it is I can't warm to Canon Lanigan. There is something about him that is not quite sincere. I know, of course, that I'm only a foolish old woman, and you don't have to mind me."

But the Bishop had to mind her and he did. The poor man had one great fear, which was that he was fading away for lack of proper nourishment. He knew what the old-fashioned clerics were like, with their classical scholarship and their enormous appetites, and, comparing his own accomplishments and theirs, he couldn't see for the life of him how he was ever going to reach ninety. After eating a whole chicken for his dinner, he would sit in his study for hours, wondering what the connection was between serious scholarship and proper meals, till Nellie thrust her head in the door.

"You're all right?" she would ask coyly.

"I'm not, Nellie," he would reply with a worried air. "I'm feeling a bit low tonight."

"'Tis that chicken!" she would cry, making a dramatic entrance. "I knew it. I said it to Tim Murphy. There wasn't a pick on it."

"I was wondering about that myself," he would say, fixing her with his anxious blue eyes. "Murphy's chickens don't seem to be the same at all."

"What you want is a nice grilled chop," she would say authoritatively.

"I don't know," he would mutter, measuring his idea of a chop against his idea of night starvation. "There's a lot of eating in a chop."

"Well, you could have cutlets," she would say with a shrug, implying that she didn't think much of cutlets for a bad case like his own.

"Cutlets make a nice snack," he agreed.

"Ah, they do, but they're too dry," she would cry, waving them away in disgust. "What you want is a good plate of nice curly rashers, with lots of fat on them. 'Twas my own fault. I knew there was nothing in that chicken. I should have served them with the chicken, but I declare to you my wits are wandering. I'm getting too old. . . . And a couple of chips. Sure, 'twill be the making of you."

One day, Nellie came in terrible trouble to the Bishop. She had just been visited by one of the local customs officers, Tim Leary. The Bishop's diocese was on the border between Northern and Southern Ireland, and since there was never a time when something that was plentiful on one side wasn't scarce on the other, there was constant smuggling in both directions. The South sent butter, eggs, ham, and whiskey to the North, and the North sent back petrol, tea, and sugar —all without benefit of duty. The customs officials of the two countries worked together in their efforts to prevent it. Nellie seemed to have the greatest difficulty in explaining to the Bishop what Tim Leary wanted of her. You'd have thought she was not bright in the head.

"You said it yourself," she said ingenuously. "This diocese was ever notorious for backbiting, but why do they pick on me? I suppose they want to have their own housekeeper, someone that would do their whispering for them. It is something I never would do, not even for your sake, and I will not do it for them, even if they do say you're too old."

"Who says I'm too old?" the Bishop asked mildly, but his blue eyes had an angry light in them. He knew the people who would say such things, and there were plenty of them.

"Don't, don't ask me to carry stories!" she begged, almost in frenzy. "I won't do it, even to save my life. Let Canon Lanigan and the rest of them say what they like about me."

"Never mind Canon Lanigan," the Bishop said shortly. "What did Leary say about you?"

"But what could he say about me? What have he against me only old *doorsha-dawrsha* he picked up in the low public houses of the town? Oh, 'tisn't that at all, me Lord, but the questions he asked me. They put the heart across me. 'Who was the chief smuggler?'— wasn't that a nice thing for him to ask me?"

"He thought you knew the chief smuggler?" the Bishop asked incredulously.

"He thought I *was* the chief smuggler," she replied with her hand to her heart. "He didn't say it, but I could read it in that mean little mind of his. Whiskey, petrol, tea, and things, my Lord, that I declare to you and to my Maker, if I was to go before Him at this minute of time, I never even knew the names of."

"He must be mad," the Bishop said with a worried air. "Which Learys is he belonged to? The ones from Clooneavullen?" The Bishop had a notion that most of the mysteries of human conduct could be solved by reference to heredity. He said he had never yet met a good man who came from a bad family.

"Aha!" Nellie cried triumphantly. "Didn't I say it myself? That his own father couldn't read or write, and the joke of the country-side for his foolish talk!"

"Never mind his father," the Bishop said sternly. "He had an uncle in the lunatic asylum. All that family were touched. Tell him to come up here to me tomorrow, and I'll give him a bit of my mind."

"You will to be sure, my Lord," she said complacently as she rose. Then at the door she stopped. "But why would you talk to a little whippersnapper like that—a man like you, that has the ear of the government? I suppose someone put him up to it."

The Bishop meditated on that for a moment. He saw Nellie's point about the impropriety of people's going over his head, and recognized that it might be the work of an enemy. Like Nellie, he knew the secrets of power and understood that the most important is never to deal directly with people you look down on.

"Give me my pen!" he said at last in a voice that made Nellie's heart flutter again. When some parish priest had been seen drunk in a public place, the Bishop would say in the same dry voice to his secretary, "Give me my pen till I suspend Father Tom," or when some gang of wild young curates had started a card club in some remote village, "Give me my pen till I scatter them!" It was the voice of ultimate authority, of the Church Militant personified in her own dear, simple man.

In spite of strenuous detective work, Nellie never did get to see the Bishop's letter to his friend in the government, Seumas Butcher, the Irish Minister of Revenue, but, on the other hand, neither did the Bishop ever get to see the Minister's reply. It was one of the features of Nellie's concern for him that she did not like him to know of anything that would upset his health, and she merely removed such letters from the hall. But even she had never seen a letter so likely to upset the Bishop as that from the Minister:

> *Dear Dr. Gallogly:*
> *It was a real pleasure to hear from you again. Mrs. Butcher was only saying a week ago that it was ages since you paid us a visit. I have had careful inquiries made about the matter you mention, and I am very sorry indeed to inform you that the statements of the local Revenue Officer appear to be fully substantiated. Your housekeeper, Miss Ellen Conneely, is the owner of licensed premises at the other side of the*

*Border which have long been known as the headquarters
of a considerable smuggling organization, whose base on
this side appears to be the Episcopal Palace. You will realise
that the Revenue Officers have no desire to take any steps
that could be an embarrassment to you, but you will also
appreciate that this traffic involves a considerable loss of
revenue for both our country and the North of Ireland, and
might in the event of other gangs operating in the neighborhood being tried and convicted, result in serious charges. I
should be deeply grateful for Your Lordship's kind assist-
ance in putting an early end to it.*

Mise le meas,
Seumas O. Buitseir
Aire

Nellie fully understood, when she had read this, the tone with
which the Bishop said "Give me my pen," as a father might say
"Give me my stick." There were certain matters that could only be
dealt with by a pen like a razor, and that evening she sat in her own
room and wrote:

Dear Sir:
*His Lordship, the Most Reverend Dr. Gallogly, Bishop of
Moyle, has handed me your letter of the 3rd inst. and asked
me to reply to it on his behalf. He says it is a tissue of lies
and that he does not want to be bothered any more with it.
I suppose his Lordship would not know what is going on in
his own house? Or is it a rogue and robber you think he is?
I do not know how you can have the face to say such things
to a bishop. All those lies were started by Tim Leary, and as
his Lordship says, what better could you expect of a man
whose uncle died in the Moyle Asylum, a wet and dirty
case? The public house you talk about is only another of the
lies. It does not belong to me at all but to my poor brother
who, after long years of suffering for Ireland in English*

prisons, is now an incurable invalid with varicose veins and six children. How would the likes of him be a smuggler? Tim Leary will be thrown out if he calls here again. It is all lies. Did Tim Leary suffer for Ireland? Has Tim Leary six children? What has happened our Christian principles and what do we pay taxes for? We were better off when we had the English.

Yours sincerely,
Ellen Conneely

There was something about this letter that gave Nellie a real thrill of pride and satisfaction. Like all women of her kind, she had always had the secret desire to speak out boldly with the whole authority of the Church behind her, and now she had done it.

She had also illustrated to perfection the Achilles' heel of Catholicism, because, though Dr. Gallogly would probably have had a heart attack if he had known the contents of her letter, no layman could be quite sure of this, and the Minister and his staff were left with a vague impression that, somehow or other, the Bishop of Moyle was now the ringleader of a smuggling gang. Being all of them good Catholics, they took the charitable view that the Bishop was no longer responsible for his actions and had taken to smuggling the way some old men take to other peculiar pursuits, but all the same it was a nasty situation. Whatever happened, you could not raid the palace for contraband. The very thought of what the newspapers would say about this made the Minister sick. The *Irish Times* would report it in full, with a smug suggestion that Protestant bishops never did things like that; the *Irish Independent* would assert that instructions for the raid had come direct from Moscow through the local Communist cell; while the *Irish Press* would say, without fear of contradiction, that it was another British plot against the good name of Irishmen.

"Jesus, Joe!" the Minister said, with a moan, to his secretary. "Forget it! Forget it, if you can!"

. . .

But the local customs officers could not forget it. Nellie didn't allow them. Scared by Tim Leary and the Minister's letter, she worked openly and feverishly to get rid of all the contraband in her possession, and the professional pride of the customs officers was mortified. Then, one day, a man was caught trying to cross the border into the North with a keg of whiskey under the seat of his car, and he swore by God and the Twelve Apostles that he had no notion how it had got there. But Tim Leary, who knew the man's friendship with Nellie, knew damn well how it had got there, and went to Paddy Clancy's liquor store in Moyle, from which it had originally come. Paddy, a crushed and quivering poor man, had to admit that the keg had been sold to the Bishop.

"Get me the Bishop's account, Paddy," Tim said stiffly, and poor Paddy produced the ledger. It was an ugly moment, because Paddy was a man who made a point of never interfering with any man's business but he knew of old that the Bishop's liquor account was most peculiar. Tim Leary studied it in stupefaction.

"Honor of God!" he said angrily. "Are you trying to tell me that the Bishop drinks all that?"

"Bishops have a lot of entertaining to do, Tim," Paddy said meekly.

"Bishops don't have to have a bloody bonded store to entertain in!" shouted Tim.

"Well, Tim, 'tis a delicate matter," Paddy said, sweating with anxiety. "If a man is to have customers in this country, he cannot afford to ask questions."

"Well, begod, I'm going to ask a few questions," cried Tim, "and I'm going to do it this very morning, what's more. Give me that ledger!"

Then, with the ledger under his arm, he went straight up to the palace. Nellie tried to head him off. First she said the Bishop was out; then she said the Bishop was ill; finally she said that the Bishop had given orders that Tim was not to be admitted.

"You try to stop me, Nellie, and I'll damn soon show you whether I'm going to be admitted or not," said Tim, pushing past her, and at that moment the study door opened and the Bishop came out. It was no coincidence, and at that moment Nellie knew she was lost, for along with the appetite of a child the Bishop had the curiosity of a child, and a beggar's voice at the door would be sufficient for him to get up and leave the door of his study ajar so that he could listen in comfort to the conversation.

"That will do, Nellie," he said, and then came up to Tim with a menacing air—a handsome old man of six foot two, with a baby complexion and fierce blue eyes.

"What do you want?" he asked sternly, but on his own ground Tim could be as infallible as any bishop.

"I'm investigating the smuggling that's going on in this locality, and I want to ask you a few questions, my Lord," he replied grimly.

"So I heard," said the Bishop. "I told the Minister already I couldn't see why you had to do your investigating in my house."

"I'm a public servant, my Lord," Tim said, his voice rising, "and I'm entitled to make my investigations wherever I have to."

"You're a very independent young man," the Bishop said dryly but without rancor. "Tell me, are you John Leary's son from Clooneavullen?"

"I'm nothing of the sort. Who said I was John Leary's son? My father was from Manister."

"For God's sake!" the Bishop said softly. "You're not Jim Leary's boy, by any chance?"

"I am, then," said Tim with a shrug.

"Come on in," the Bishop said, holding out his hand to Tim, while his eyes searched away into the distance beyond the front door. "Your father was headmaster there when I was a canon. I must have seen you when you were a little fellow. Come in, anyway. No son of Jim Leary's is going to leave this house without a drink."

"But I'm on duty, my Lord," said Tim, following him in.

"Aren't we all?" the Bishop asked mildly as he went to the sideboard. "I'm as much a bishop now as I'll ever be." With shaky hands he produced two glasses and a bottle of whiskey. He gave one tiny glass to Tim and took another himself. It was obviously a duty rather than a pleasure. The Bishop did not go in for drinking, because it seemed to ruin his appetite and that was bad enough already.

"Now, tell me what all this is about," he said comfortably.

Tim was beginning to realize that he really liked the man—an old weakness of his, which, combined with his violent temper, made him a bad investigator. He sometimes thought the bad temper and the good nature were only two aspects of the same thing.

"A man was caught trying to cross the Border a few days ago with a keg of your whiskey in his car," he said firmly as he could.

"A keg of my whiskey?" the Bishop repeated with real interest and apparent enjoyment. "But what would I be doing with a keg of whiskey?"

"That's what I came to ask you," replied Tim. "You seem to have bought enough of them in the past year."

"I never bought a keg of whiskey in my whole life, boy," said the Bishop with amusement. "Sure, if I take a drop of punch before I go to bed, that's all the whiskey I ever see. It's bad for a man of my age," he added earnestly. "I haven't the constitution."

"If you'll take one look at your account in Clancy's ledger, you'll see you're supposed to have an iron constitution," said Tim, and as he opened the book, there was a knock and Nellie came in modestly with a bundle of receipted bills in her hand. "Or maybe this is the one with the iron constitution," Tim added fiercely. He still had not forgotten his unmannerly reception.

"You need say no more," she said briskly. "I admit it, whatever little harm I did to anyone. 'Twas only to keep my unfortunate angashore of a brother out of the workhouse. Between drinking and politics, he was never much head to his poor wife, God rest her. Not one penny did I ever make out of it, and not one penny of his Lordship's money ever went astray. I'll go if I have to, but I will not leave this house without a character."

"I'll give you the character," Tim said savagely. "And furthermore I'll see you have a place to go. You can do all the smuggling you like there—if you're able."

"That will do!" the Bishop said sternly. "Go away, Nellie!" he added over his shoulder, in the tone he used when he asked for his pen to suspend Father Tom.

Nellie looked at him for a moment in stupefaction and then burst into a howl of grief and went out, sobbing to herself about "the fifteen good years of my life that I wasted on him and there's his gratitude." The Bishop waited imperturbably till her sobs had subsided in the kitchen before he spoke again.

"How many people know about this?"

"Begod, my Lord, by this time I think you might say 'twas common property," said Tim with a laugh.

The Bishop did not laugh. "I was afraid of that," he said. "What do they think of it?"

"Well, of course, they all have a great regard for you," Tim replied, in some embarrassment.

"I'm sure of that," the Bishop said without a hint of irony. "They have so much regard for me that they don't care if I turn my house into a smuggler's den. They didn't suggest what I might be doing with the Cathedral?"

Tim saw that the Bishop was more cut up than he affected to be.

"Ah, I wouldn't worry about that," he said anxiously.

"I'm not worrying. What will they do to Nellie?"

"Oh, she'll get the jail," said Tim. "As well as a bloody big fine that'll be worse to her."

"A fine? What sort of a fine?"

"That will be calculated on the value of the contraband," said Tim. "But if you ask me quietly, 'twill run well into the thousands."

"Into the thousands?" the Bishop asked in alarm. "But where would either of us get that sort of money, boy?"

"You may be damn full sure she has it," Tim said grimly.

"Nellie?"

"Aye, and more along with it," said Tim.

"For God's sake!" the Bishop exclaimed softly. He had put away his glass, and his long, fine fingers were intertwined. Then he gave a little snort that might have passed for laughter. "And me thinking she was an old fool! Which of us was the fool, I wonder. After this, they'll be saying I'm not able to look after myself. They'll be putting in a coadjutor over me, as sure as you're there!"

"They wouldn't do that?" Tim asked in astonishment. It had never occurred to him before that there might be anybody who could interfere with a bishop.

"Oh, indeed they would," the Bishop said, almost with enjoyment. "And I wouldn't mind that itself if only they'd leave me my housekeeper. The jail won't take much out of her, but 'twill kill me. At my age I'm not going to be able to find another woman to look after me the way she does. Unless they'd let me go to jail along with her."

Tim was an emotional young man, and he could hardly contemplate the personal problems that the Bishop set up in that casual way of his.

"There's nobody in this place would do anything to upset you," he said, growing red. "I'm sure they'll be well satisfied if she paid the fine, without sending her to jail. The only thing is, from my point of view, could you control her?"

"I could do nothing of the kind," the Bishop replied in his blank way. "If I was to give you my oath to control her for the future, would you believe me? You would not. I couldn't control her. You might be able to do it."

"I'd damn soon do it if I had a free hand," Tim said loyally.

"I'd give you all the hand you want," the Bishop said placidly. "I'd give you quarters here if you wanted them. You see, 'tis more in my interest than yours to stop the scandal, before they have me married to her." From the dryness of his tone, the Bishop, an unemotional man, seemed to be suffering. "I wouldn't forget it for you," he added anxiously. "Anyway, I'll have a talk to Butcher, and see if he can't do something for you. Not that that poor fool knows what he's doing, most of the time."

That afternoon, the Bishop sat on by his window and watched as a lorry drove up before his palace and Tim Leary loaded it with commodities the Bishop had thought long gone from the world—chests of tea, bags of sugar, boxes of butter. There seemed to be no end to them. He felt crushed and humbled. Like all bishops, he was addicted to power, but he saw now that a bishop's power, like a bishop's knowledge, was little better than a shadow. He was just a lonely old man who was dependent on women, exactly as when they had changed his napkin and he had crowed and kicked his heels. There was no escape.

Mercifully, Nellie herself didn't put in an appearance as the premises were gone through. That evening, when she opened the door and said meekly, "Dinner is served, my Lord," the Bishop went in to a royal spread—the juiciest of roast beef, with roast potatoes and tender young peas drowned in butter. The Bishop ate stolidly through it, reading the book in front of his plate and never addressing a word to her. He was too bitter. He went to his study and took down the history of the diocese, which had so often consoled him in earlier griefs, but that night there was no consolation in it. It seemed that none of the men who had held the see before him was of the sort to be dominated by an old housekeeper, except for an eighteenth-century bishop who, in order to inherit a legacy, had become a Protestant. The door opened, and Nellie looked shyly in.

"What way are you feeling now?" she whispered.

"Let me alone," he said in a dry voice, without looking at her. "My heart is broken!"

" 'Tisn't your heart at all," she said shamefastly. " 'Tis that beef. 'Twasn't hung long enough, that's all. There isn't a butcher in this town will be bothered to hang beef. Would I get you a couple of scrambled eggs?"

"Go away, I said."

"You're right, my Lord. There's nothing in eggs. Would I fry you a couple of rashers?"

"I don't want anything, woman!" he said, almost shouting at her.

"The dear knows, the rashers aren't worth it," she admitted

with a heavy sigh. "Nothing only old bones, and the hair still sprouting on them. What you want is a nice little juicy bit of Limerick ham with a couple of mashed potatoes and milk sauce with parsley. That'll make a new man of you."

"All right, all right," he said angrily. "But go away and let me alone."

His mouth was already watering, but he knew that there was no ham in Limerick or out of it that could lift his sorrow; that whenever a woman says something will make a new man of you, all she means is that, like the rest of her crooked devices, it will make an old man of you before your time.

Lost Fatherlands

ONE SPRING DAY, Father Felix in the monastery sent word down to Spike Ward, the motor driver, to pick up a gentleman for the four-fifteen train. Spike had no notion of who the gentleman was. All sorts came and went to that lonesome monastery up the mountain: people on pilgrimage, drunks going in for a cure, cures coming out for a drunk, men joining the novitiate, and others leaving it, some of them within twenty-four hours—they just took one good look at the place and bolted. One of the novices stole a suit of overalls left behind by a house painter and vanished across the mountain. As Spike often said, if it was him he wouldn't have waited to steal the overalls.

It lay across the mountainside, a gaunt, Victorian barracks. Spike drove up to the guesthouse, which stood away in by the end of the chapel. Father Felix, the Guestmaster, was waiting on the steps with the passenger—a tall, well-built, middle-aged man with graying hair. Father Felix himself inclined to fat; he wore big, shiny glasses, and his beard cascaded over his chest. Spike and the passenger loaded the trunk and bag, and Spike noticed that they were labeled for Canada. The liner was due at Cobh two days later.

"Goodbye now," Father Felix said, shaking the passenger's hand. "And mind and don't lead Spike into bad ways on me. He's a fellow I have my eye on this long time. When are you coming up to us for good, Spike?" he asked gravely.

"When ye take a few women into the order, Father," Spike replied in his thin drawl. "What this place needs is a woman's hand."

The passenger sat in front with Spike, and they chatted as they drove down the hill, glancing back at the monks working in the fields behind the monastery. You could see them from a long way off, like magpies.

"Was it on a holiday you were?" asked Spike, not meaning to be inquisitive, only to make conversation.

"A long holiday," said the passenger, with a nod and a smile.

"Ah, well, everyone to his taste," Spike said tolerantly. "I suppose a lot depends on what you're used to. I prefer a bit of a change myself, like Father Felix's dipsos."

"He has a few of them up there now," said the passenger, with a quiet amusement that told Spike he wasn't one of them.

"Well, I'm sure I hope the poor souls are enjoying it," said Spike with unction.

"They weren't enjoying it much at three this morning," said the passenger in the same tone. "One of them was calling for his mother. Father Felix was with him for over an hour, trying to calm him."

"Not criticizing the good man, 'tisn't the same thing at all," Spike said joyously.

"Except for the feeding bottle," said the passenger. And then, as though he were slightly ashamed of his own straight-faced humor: "He does a wonderful job on them."

"Well, they seem to have great faith in him," Spike said, without undue credulity. "He gets them from England and all parts —a decent little man."

"And a saintly little man," the passenger said, almost reproachfully.

"I daresay," Spike said, without enthusiasm. "He'd want to be, judging by the specimens I see."

They reached town with about three quarters of an hour to spare, and put the trunk and bag in the stationmaster's office. Old

Mick Hurley, the stationmaster, was inside, and looked at the bags over his glasses. Even on a warm day, in his own office, he wore his braided frock coat and uniform cap.

"This is a gent from the monastery, Mick," said Spike. "He's traveling by the four-fifteen. Would he have time for the pictures?"

But Spike might have known the joke would be lost on Mick, who gave a hasty glance at the clock behind him and looked alarmed. "He'd hardly have time for that," he said. "She's only about twenty-five minutes late."

"You have over an hour to put in," said Spike as they left the office. "You don't want to be sitting round there the whole time. Hanagan's lounge is comfortable enough, if you like a drink."

"Will you have one with me?" asked the passenger.

"I don't know will I have the time," Spike said. "I have another call at four. I'll have one drink with you, anyway."

They went into the bar, which was all done up in chromium, with concealed lighting. Tommy Hanagan, the Yank, was behind the bar himself. He was a tall, fresh-faced, rather handsome man, with fair hair of a dirty color and smoke-blue eyes. His hat was perched far back on his head. Spike often said Tommy Hanagan was the only man he knew who could make a hat speak. He had earned the price of his public house working in Boston and, according to him, had never ceased to regret his return. Tommy looked as though he lived in hopes that someday when he did something as it should be done, it would turn out to be a convenience to somebody. So far, it had earned him nothing but mockery, and sometimes his blue eyes had a slightly bewildered expression, as though he were wondering what he was doing in that place at all.

Spike loved rousing him. All you had to do was give him one poke about America and the man was off, good for an hour's argument. America was the finest God-damned country on the face of the earth, and the people that criticized it didn't know what they were talking about. In America, even the priests were friends:

"Tommy, where the hell am I going to get a hundred dollars?" "I'll get it for you, Father Joe." In Ireland, it was "*Mister* Hanagan, don't you consider five pounds is a bit on the small side?" "And I don't," the Yank would say, pulling up his shirtsleeves. "I'd sooner give a hundred dollars to a friend than fifteen to a bastard like that." The same with the women. Over there, an Irishman would say, "I'll do the washing up, Mary." Here it was "Where's that bloody tea, woman?" And then bawling her out for it! Not, as Spike noticed, that this ever prevented the Yank from bawling out his own wife twenty times a day. And Spike suspected that however he might enjoy rousing the Yank, the Yank enjoyed it more. It probably gave the poor man the illusion of being alive.

"What are you drinking?" the passenger asked in his low voice.

"Whiskey," said Spike. "I have to take whiskey every time I go up to that monastery. It's to restore the circulation."

"Beer for me, please," said the passenger.

"Your circulation is easily damaged, Spike," said Hanagan as he turned to the whiskey bottle.

"If you knew as much about that place as I do, you'd be looking for whiskey, too."

"Who said I don't know about it?" blustered Hanagan. "I know as much about it as you do; maybe more."

"You do," Spike said mockingly. "Yourself and the kids went up there two years ago, picking primroses. I heard about it. Ye brought the flask and had tea up the mountain two miles away. 'Oh, what a lovely place the monks have! Oh, what a wonderful life they have up here!' Damn all you care about the poor unfortunates, getting up at half past one of a winter's morning and waiting till half five for a bit of breakfast."

The Yank sprawled across the counter, pushing his hat back a shade farther. It was set for reasonable discussion. "But what's that only habit?" he asked.

"Habit!"

"What else is it?" the Yank asked appealingly. "I have to get up at half past six every morning, winter and summer, and I have to worry about a wife and kids, and education and doctors for them, and paying income tax, which is more than the monks have to do."

"Give me the income tax every time!" said Spike. "Even the wife!"

"The remarkable thing about this country," said Hanagan, "is that they'll only get up in the morning when no one asks them to. I never asked the monks to get up at half past one. All I ask is that the people in this blooming town will get up at half past eight and open their shops by nine o'clock. And how many of them will do it?"

"And what the hell has that to do with the argument?" asked Spike, not that he thought it had anything to do with it. He knew only too well the Yank's capacity for getting carried away on a tide of his own eloquence.

"Well, what after all does the argument boil down to?" retorted Hanagan. "The argument is that no one in this blooming country is respected for doing what he ought to do—only for doing what no one ever asked him to do."

"Are people to sit down and wait for someone to ask them to love God?" the passenger growled suddenly. Spike noticed that even though he mentioned God, he looked a nasty customer to cross in a discussion.

"I didn't say that," Hanagan replied peaceably. "But do you know this town?"

"No."

"I do," said Hanagan. "I know it since I was a kid. I spent eighteen years out of it, and for all the difference it made to the town, I might have been out of it for a week. It's dead. The people are dead. They're no use to God or man."

"You didn't answer my question."

"You're talking about one sort of responsibility," said Hanagan. "I'm only saying there are other responsibilities. Why can't the people here see that they have a responsibility to the unfortunate women they marry? Why can't they see their responsibility to their own country?"

"What Tommy means is that people shouldn't be making pilgrimages to the monastery at all," said Spike dryly. "He thinks they should be making pilgrimages to him. He lights candles to himself every night—all because he doesn't beat his wife. Good luck to you now, and don't let him make you miss your train with his old guff."

Spike and the passenger shook hands, and after that Spike put him out of his head completely. Meeting strangers like that, every day of the week, he couldn't remember the half of them. But three evenings later he was waiting in the car outside the station, hoping to pick up a fare from the four-fifteen, when Mick Hurley came flopping out to him with his spectacles down his nose.

"What am I going to do with them bags you left on Tuesday, Spike?" he asked.

What was he to do with the bags? Spike looked at him without comprehension. "What bags, Mick?"

"Them bags for Canada."

"Holy God!" exclaimed Spike, getting slowly out of the car. "Do you mean he forgot his bags?"

"Forgot them?" Mick Hurley repeated indignantly. "He never traveled at all, man."

"Holy God!" repeated Spike. "And the liner gone since yesterday! That's a nice state of affairs."

"Why?" asked Mick. "Who was it?"

"A man from the monastery."

"One of Father Felix's drunks?"

"What the hell would a drunk be coming from Canada for?" asked Spike in exasperation.

"You'd never know," said Mick. "Where did you leave him?"

"Over in Tommy Hanagan's bar."

"Then we'd better ask Tommy."

Hanagan came out to them in his shirtsleeves, his cuffs rolled up and his hat well back.

"Tommy," said Spike, "you remember that passenger I left in your place on Tuesday?"

Tommy's eyes narrowed. "The big, gray-haired bloke?" he said. "What about him?"

"Mick Hurley, here, says he never took that train. You wouldn't know what happened him?"

Tommy rested one bare, powerful arm against the jamb of the door, leaned his head against it, and delicately tilted the hat forward over his eyes. "That sounds bad," he said. "You're sure he didn't go off unknown to you?"

"How could he, man?" asked Mick excitedly, feeling that some slight on the railway company was implied. "His bags are still there. No one but locals traveled on that train."

"The man had a lot of money on him," Hanagan said, looking at the ground.

"You're sure of that, Tommy?" Spike asked, in alarm. It was bad enough for a motor driver to be mixed up in a mysterious disappearance without a murder coming into it as well.

"Up to a hundred pounds," Hanagan said, giving a sharp glance up the street. "I saw it when he paid for the drinks. I noticed Linehan, of the Guards, going in to his dinner. We might as well go over and ask him did he hear anything."

They strode briskly in the direction of the policeman's house. Linehan came shuffling out, buttoning up his tunic—a fat, black-haired man who looked like something out of a butcher's shop.

"I didn't hear a word of it," he said, looking from one to another, as though they might be concealing evidence. "We'll ring up a few of the local stations. Some of them might have word of him."

Hanagan went to get his coat. Mick Hurley had to leave them, to look after the four-fifteen, and at last Spike, Hanagan, and Linehan went to the police station, where the others waited while Linehan had long, confidential chats about football and the weather with other policemen for ten miles round. Guards are lonely souls; they cannot trust their nearest and dearest, and can communicate only with one another, like mountaineers with signal fires. Hanagan sat on the table, pretending to read a paper, though every look and gesture betrayed impatience and disgust. Spike just sat, reflecting mournfully on the loss of his good time and money.

"We'll have to find out what his name was," Linehan said, at last. "The best thing we can do is drive up to the monastery and get more particulars."

"The devil fly away with Mick Hurley!" Spike said bitterly. "Wouldn't you think he'd tell us what happened without waiting three days? If he was after losing an express train, he'd wait a week to see would it turn up."

The three of them got into Spike's car, and he drove off up the mountain road, wondering how he was to get his fare out of it and from whom. The monks were holy enough, but they expected you to run a car on holy water, and a policeman thought he was doing you a favor if he was seen in the car with you. The veiled sunlight went out; they ran into thick mist, and before they reached the mountaintop, it had turned to rain. They could see it driving in for miles from the sea. The lights were on in the chapel; there was some service on. Spike noticed the Yank pause under the traceried window and look away down the valley. Within the church, the choir wailed, *"Et exspecto resurrectionem mortuorum. Et vitam venturi saeculi."*

Father Felix came out and beckoned them in from the rain. His face was very grave. "You needn't tell me what you came about, lads," he said.

"You knew he was missing so, Father?" said Linehan.

"We saw him," said the priest.

"Where, Father?" asked Spike.

"Out there," Father Felix said, with a nod.

"On the mountain?"

"I daresay he's there still."

"But what is he doing?"

"Oh, nothing. Nothing only staring. Staring at the monastery and the monks working in the fields. Poor fellow! Poor fellow!"

"But who is it?"

"One of our own men. One of the old monks. He's here these fifteen years."

"Fifteen years!" exclaimed Linehan. "But what came over him after all that time?"

"Some nervous trouble, I suppose," said Father Felix in the tone of a healthy man who has heard of nerves as a well-recognized ailment of quite respectable people. "A sort of mental blackout, I heard them saying. He wouldn't know where he'd be for a few minutes at a time."

"Ah, poor soul! Poor soul!" sighed Linehan, with a similar blankness of expression.

"But what was taking him to Canada?" asked Hanagan.

"Ah, well, we had to send him somewhere he wouldn't be known," explained Father Felix sadly. "He wanted to settle down in his own place in Kilkenny, but, of course, he couldn't."

"Why not?" asked Hanagan.

"Oh, he couldn't, he couldn't," Linehan said, with a sharp intake of breath as he strode to the window. "Not after leaving the monastery. 'Twould cause terrible scandal."

"That's why I hope you can get him away quietly," Father Felix said. "We did everything we could for him. Now the less talk there is, the better."

"In that bleddy mist you might be searching the mountain for a week," sighed Linehan, who had often shot it. "If we knew where to look itself! We'll go up the road and see would any of Sullivan's boys have word of him."

Sullivan's was the nearest farmhouse. The three men got into the car again and drove slowly down under the trees past the monastery. There was an iron railing, which seemed strangely out of place, and then a field, and then the bare mountain again. It was coming on to dark, and it struck Spike that they would find no one that night. He was sorry for that poor devil, and could not get over the casualness of Mick Hurley. A stationmaster! God, wouldn't you think he'd have some sense?

"It isn't Mick Hurley I blame at all," Hanagan said angrily.

"Ah, well, Tommy, you can't be too hard on the poor monks," Linehan said reasonably. "I suppose they were hoping he'd go away and not cause any scandal."

"A poor bloody loony!" snapped the Yank, his emotion bringing out a strong Boston accent. "Gahd, you wouldn't do it to a dawg!"

"How sure you are he was a loony!" Spike said, with a sneer. "He didn't seem so very loony to me."

"But you heard what Father Felix said!" Hanagan cried. "Mental blackouts. That poor devil is somewhere out on that goddam mountain with his memory gone."

"Ah, I'll believe all I hear when I eat all I get," Spike said in the same tone.

It wasn't that he really disbelieved in the blackouts so much as that he had trained himself to take things lightly, and the Yank was getting on his nerves. At that moment he spotted the passenger out of the corner of his eye. The rain seemed to have caught him somewhere on top of a peak, and he was running, looking for shelter, from rock to rock. Without looking round, Spike stopped the car quietly and lit a cigarette.

"Don't turn round now, boys!" he said. "He's just over there on our right."

"What do you think we should do, Spike?" Linehan asked.

"Get out of the car quietly and break up, so that we can come round him from different directions," said Spike.

"Then you'd scare him properly," said Hanagan. "Let me go and talk to him!"

Before they could hinder him, he was out of the car and running up the slope from the road. Spike swore. He knew if the monk took to his heels now, they might never catch him. Hanagan shouted and the monk halted, stared, then walked toward him.

"It looks as if he might come quietly," said Linehan. He and Spike followed Hanagan slowly.

Hanagan stopped on a little hillock, hatless, his hands in his trousers pockets. The monk came up to him. He, too, was hatless; his raincoat was covered with mud; and he wore what looked like a week's growth of beard. He had a sullen, frightened look, like an old dog called to heel after doing something wrong.

"That's a bad evening now," Hanagan said, with an awkward smile, which made him look unexpectedly boyish.

"I hope you're not taking all this trouble for me," the monk said, looking first at Hanagan, then at Spike and the policeman, who stood a little apart from him.

"Ah, what trouble?" Hanagan said, with fictitious lightness. "We were afraid you might be caught in the mist. It's bad enough even for those that know the mountain. You'd want to get those wet things off you quick."

"I suppose so," the monk said, looking down at his drenched clothes as though he were seeing them for the first time. Spike could now believe in the mental blackout, the man looked so stunned, like a sleepwalker.

"We'll stop at the pub and Spike can bring over whatever bags you want," said Hanagan.

The public-house hotel looked uncannily bright after the loneliness of the mountain. Hanagan was at his most obnoxiously efficient. Linehan wanted to take a statement from the monk, but Hanagan stopped him. "Is it a man in that state? How could he give you a statement?" He rushed in and out, his hat on the back of his head, producing hot whiskeys for them all, sending Spike to the station for the bag, and driving his wife and the maid mad seeing that there was hot water and shaving tackle in the bathroom and that a hot meal was prepared.

When the monk came down, shaved and in dry clothes, Hanagan sat opposite him, his legs spread and his hands on his thighs.

"What you'll do," he said, with a commanding air, "is rest here for a couple of days."

"No, thanks," the monk said, shaking his head.

"It won't cost you anything," Hanagan said, with a smile.

"It's not that," said the monk in a low voice. "I'd better get away from this."

"But you can't, man. You'll have to see about getting your tickets changed. We can see to that for you. You might get pneumonia after being out so long."

"I'll have to go on," the monk said stubbornly. "I have to get away."

"You mean you're afraid you might do the same thing again?" Hanagan said in a disappointed tone. "Maybe you're right. Though what anyone wants to go back to that place for beats me."

"What do people want to go back anywhere for?" the monk asked in a dull tone.

Spike thought it was as close as ever he'd seen anyone get to knocking the Yank off his perch. He grew red. Then he rose and went in the direction of the door, suddenly changed his mind, and turned to grasp the monk's left hand in his own two. "I'm a good one to talk," he said in a thick voice. "Eighteen years, and never a day without thinking of this place. You mightn't believe it, but there were nights I cried myself to sleep. And for what, I ask you? What did I expect?"

He had changed suddenly; no longer the bighearted, officious ward boss looking after someone in trouble, he had become humble and almost deferential. When they were leaving, he half opened the front door and halted. "You're sure you won't stay?" he snapped over his shoulder.

"Sure," said the monk, with a nod.

Hanagan waved his left arm, and they went out across the dark square to the station.

Spike and he saw the last of the monk, who waved to them till the train disappeared in the darkness. Hanagan followed it, waving, with a mawkish smile, as though he were seeing off a girl. Spike could see that he was deeply moved, but what it was all about was beyond him. Spike had never stood on the deck of a liner and watched his fatherland drop away behind him. He didn't know the sort of hurt it can leave in a boy's mind, a hurt that doesn't heal even when you try to conjure away the pain by returning. Nor did he realize, as Hanagan did at that moment, that there are other fatherlands, whose loss can hurt even more deeply.

·❧· The Wreath

WHEN FATHER FOGARTY read of the death of his friend Father Devine in a Dublin nursing home, he was stunned. He was a man who did not understand the irremediable.

He took out an old seminary group, put it on the mantelpiece, and spent the evening looking at it. Devine's clever, pale, shrunken face stood out from all the others, not very different from what it had been in his later years except for the absence of pince-nez. He and Fogarty had been boys together in a provincial town where Devine's father was a schoolmaster and Fogarty's mother kept a shop. Even then everybody had known that Devine was marked by nature for the priesthood. He was clever, docile, and beautifully mannered. Fogarty's vocation had come later and was a surprise.

They had been friends over the years, affectionate when together, critical and sarcastic when apart, and had seen nothing of one another for close on a year. Devine had been unlucky. As long as the old Bishop lived he had been fairly well sheltered, but Lanigan, the new one, disliked him. It was partly his own fault; because he could not keep his mouth shut; because he was witty and waspish and said whatever came into his head about his colleagues who had nothing like his gifts. Fogarty remembered the things Devine had said about himself. He affected to believe that Fogarty was a man of many personalities, and asked with mock humility which of them he was now dealing with—Nero, Napoleon, or St. Francis of Assisi.

It all came back, the occasional jaunts together, the plans for holidays abroad which never came to anything; and now the warm and genuine love for Devine which was natural to him welled up, and realizing that never again in this world would he be able to express it, he began to weep. He was as simple as a child in his emotions. He forgot lightly, remembered suddenly and with exaggerated intensity, and blamed himself cruelly and unjustly for his own shortcomings. He would have been astonished to learn that, for all the intrusions of Nero and Napoleon, his understanding had continued to develop through the years, when that of clever men had dried up, and that he was a better and wiser priest at forty than he had been twenty years before.

Because there was no one else to whom he could communicate his sense of loss, he rang up Jackson, a curate who had been Devine's other friend. He did not really like Jackson, who was worldly, cynical, and a bit of a careerist, and had always wondered what it was that Devine saw in him.

"Isn't that terrible news about Devine?" he said, barely keeping the tears out of his voice.

"Yes," drawled Jackson in his usual cautious, fishy tone, as though even on such a subject he were afraid of committing himself. "I suppose it's a happy release for the poor devil."

This was the sort of talk which maddened Fogarty. It sounded as if Jackson were talking of an old family pet who had been sent to the vet's.

"I daresay," he said gruffly. "I was thinking of going to town and coming back with the funeral. You wouldn't come?"

"I don't see how I could, Jerry," Jackson replied in a tone of concern. "It's only a week since I was up last."

"Ah, well, I'll go myself," said Fogarty. "I suppose you don't know what happened him?"

"Oh, you know he was always anemic. He ought to have looked after himself, but he didn't get much chance with that old brute of a parish priest of his. He was fainting all over the shop. The last time, he fainted at Mass."

"You were in touch with him, then?" Fogarty asked in surprise.

"I just saw him for a while last week. He couldn't talk much, of course."

And again the feeling of his own inadequacy descended on Fogarty. He realized that Jackson, who seemed to have as much feeling as a mowing machine, had kept in touch with Devine and gone out of his way to see him at the end, while he, the warm-hearted, devoted, generous friend, had let him slip from sight into eternity and was now wallowing in the sense of his own loss.

"God, I feel thoroughly ashamed of myself, Jim," he said with a new humility. "I never even knew he was sick."

"I'll see about getting off for the funeral," Jackson said. "I think I might manage it."

II

That evening, the two priests set off in Fogarty's car for the city. Jackson brought Fogarty to a very pleasant restaurant for dinner. He was a tall, thin man with a prim, watchful, clerical air, who knew his way round. He spent at least ten minutes over the menu and the wine list, and the headwaiter danced attendance on him as headwaiters do only when there is a big tip in view or they have to deal with an expert.

"I'm having steak," Fogarty said to cut it short.

"Father Fogarty is having steak, Paddy," said Jackson, looking at the headwaiter over his spectacles. "Make it rare. And stout, I suppose?"

"I'll spare you the stout," said Fogarty. "Red wine."

"Mind, Paddy," said Jackson warningly. "Father Fogarty said *red* wine. You're in Ireland now, remember."

Next morning, they went to the mortuary chapel, where the coffin was resting on trestles before the altar. Beside it, to Fogarty's surprise, was a large wreath of red roses. When they rose from their knees, Devine's uncle Ned had come in with his son. Ned was a broad-faced, dark-haired, nervous man, with the anemic complexion of the family.

"I'm sorry for your trouble, Ned," Father Fogarty said.

"I know that, Father," said Ned.

"I don't know if you know Father Jackson. He was a great friend of Father Willie's."

"I heard him speak of him," said Ned. "He talked a lot about both of you. Ye were his great friends. Poor Father Willie!" he added with a sigh. "He had few enough of them."

Just then the parish priest entered and spoke to Ned Devine. He was a tall man with a stern, unlined, wooden face. He stood for a few moments by the coffin, then studied the breastplate and the wreath, looking closely at the tag of the wreath. It was only then that he beckoned the two younger priests aside.

"Tell me," he asked in a professional tone, "what are we going to do about this?"

"About what?" Fogarty asked in surprise.

"This wreath," said Father Martin, giving him a candid glare.

"What's wrong with it?"

" 'Tis against the rubrics."

"For Heaven's sake!" Fogarty said impatiently. "What have the rubrics to do with it?"

"The rubrics have a lot to do with it," Martin said sternly. "And, apart from that, 'tis a bad custom."

"You mean Masses bring in more money?" Fogarty asked with amused insolence.

"I do not mean Masses bring in more money," said Martin, who seemed to reply to every remark verbatim, like a solicitor's letter. "I mean that flowers are a pagan survival." He looked at the two young priests with the same innocent, anxious, wooden air. "And here am I, week in, week out, preaching against flowers, and a blooming big wreath of them in my own church. And on a priest's coffin too, mind you! What am I going to say about that?"

"Who asked you to say anything?" asked Fogarty. "The man wasn't from your diocese."

"Oh, now, that's all very well," said Martin. "And that's not the whole story, and you know it."

"You mean, the wreath is from a woman?" broke in Jackson.

"I do mean the wreath is from a woman."

"A woman?" Fogarty exclaimed in astonishment. "Does it say so?"

"It does not say so. But 'tis red roses."

"And does that mean it's from a woman?"

"What else could it mean?"

"It could mean it's from somebody who didn't study the language of flowers the way you seem to have done," said Fogarty.

"Oh, well," Jackson intervened again with a shrug, "we know nothing about it. You'll have to decide about it yourself. It's nothing to do with us."

"I don't like doing anything when I wasn't acquainted with the man," said Martin, but he made no further attempt to interfere, and one of the undertaker's men took the wreath and placed it on the hearse. Fogarty controlled himself with difficulty. As he banged open the door of the car and started the engine, his face was very flushed. He drove with his head bowed and his brows jutting down like rocks above his eyes. As they cleared the main streets he burst out.

"That's the sort of thing that makes me ashamed of myself! 'Flowers are a pagan survival.' And they take it from him, Jim! They listen to that sort of stuff instead of telling him to shut his ignorant gob."

"Oh, well," Jackson said in his nonchalant, tolerant way, "he was right, of course."

"Right?"

"I mean, on the appearance of the thing. After all, he didn't know Devine."

"All the more reason why he shouldn't have interfered. Do you realize that he'd have thrown out that wreath only for us being there? And for what? His own dirty, mean, suspicious mind!"

"Ah, I wouldn't say that. I wouldn't have let that wreath go on the coffin."

"You wouldn't? Why not?"

"It was from a woman all right."

Jackson lit his pipe and looked over his spectacles at Fogarty.

"Yes, one of Devine's old maids."

"Ever heard of an old maid sending a wreath of red roses?"

"To tell you the God's truth," Fogarty confessed with boyish candor, "it would never have struck me that there was anything wrong with it."

"It would have struck the old maid, though."

Fogarty missed a turning and reversed with a muttered curse.

"You're not serious, Jim?" he said after a few moments.

"Oh, I'm not saying there was anything wrong in it," Jackson replied with a shrug. "Women get ideas like that. You must have noticed that sort of thing yourself."

"These things can happen in very innocent ways," Fogarty said with ingenuous solemnity. Then he began to scowl again, and a blush spread over his handsome craggy face that was neither anger nor shame. Like all those who live greatly in their imaginations, he was always astonished and shocked at the suggestion that reached him from the outside world: he could live with his fantasies only by assuming that they were nothing more. The country began to grow wilder under the broken spring light; the valley of the river dropped away with a ruined abbey on its bank, and a pine-clad hill rose on their right, the first breath of the mountains. "I can't believe it," he said angrily, shaking his head.

"You don't have to believe it," Jackson said, nursing his pipe. "I'd nearly be glad if Martin's suspicions were right. If ever a man needed somebody to care for him, Devine did."

"But not Devine, Jim," Fogarty said obstinately. "You could believe a thing like that if it was me. I could nearly believe it if it was you. But I knew Devine since we were kids, and he wouldn't be capable of it."

"I never knew him like that," Jackson admitted mildly. "In fact, I scarcely knew him at all, really. But I'd have said he was as capable of it as we are. He was a good deal lonelier than we'll ever be."

"God, don't I know it!" Fogarty ground out in self-reproach. "If it was drinking, I could understand it."

"Devine was too fastidious."

"But that's what I say."

"There's a big difference," said Jackson. "A very intelligent woman, for instance, might have appealed to him. You can imagine how he'd appeal to her. After all, you know what he meant to us; the most civilized chap we could meet. Just fancy what a man like that would mean to some woman in a country town; maybe a woman married to some lout of a shopkeeper or a gentleman farmer."

"He didn't tell you about her?" Fogarty asked incredulously, because Jackson spoke with such plausibility that it impressed him as true.

"Oh, no, no, I'm only guessing," Jackson said hastily, and then he blushed too.

III

Fogarty remained silent, aware that Jackson had confessed something about himself, but he could not get the incredible idea of Devine out of his mind. As the country grew wilder and furze bushes and ruined keeps took the place of pastures and old abbeys, he found his eyes attracted more and more to the wreath that swayed lightly with the swaying of the hearse and seemed to concentrate all the light. It seemed an image of the essential mystery of a priest's life.

What, after all, did he know of Devine? Only what his own temperament suggested, and mostly—when he wasn't being St. Francis of Assisi, in Devine's phrase—he had seen himself as the worldly one of the pair, the practical, coarse-grained man who cut corners, and Devine as the saint, racked by his own fastidiousness and asceticism that exploded in his bitter little jests. Now his mind boggled at the agony which could have driven a man like Devine to seek companionship in such a way; yet the measure of his incredulity was that of the conviction which he would soon feel, the new level on which his thought must move.

"God!" he burst out, "don't we lead lonely lives. We probably knew Devine better than anyone else in the world, and there's that damn thing in front of us, and neither of us has a notion what it means."

"Which might be just as well for our own comfort," Jackson said.

"If you're right, I'll take my oath it did very little for Devine's," Fogarty said grimly.

"Oh, I don't know," Jackson said. "Isn't that the one thing we all really want from life?"

"Would you say so?" Fogarty asked in astonishment. He had always thought of Jackson as a cold fish, a go-getter, and suddenly found himself wondering about that too; wondering what it was in him that had appealed so much to Devine. He had the feeling that Jackson, who was, as he modestly recognized, by far the subtler man, was probing him, and for the same reason. Each of them was looking in the other for the quality which had attracted Devine, and which having made him their friend might make them friends also. "I couldn't do it though, Jim," he said somberly. "I went as close to it as I'm ever likely to do. It was the wife of one of the chaps that was with me in the seminary. She seemed to be all the things I ever wanted a woman to be. Then, when I saw what her marriage to the other fellow was like, I realized that she hated him like poison. It might have been me she hated that way. It's only when you see what marriages are like, as we do, that you know how lucky we are in escaping them."

"Lucky?" Jackson repeated with light irony. "Do you really think we're lucky? Have you ever known a seminary that wasn't full of men who thought themselves lucky? They might be drinking themselves to death, but they never once doubted their luck.

Clerical sour grapes. . . . Anyway, you're rather underrating yourself if you think she'd have hated you."

"You think I might have made her a good husband?" Fogarty
asked, flushing with pleasure, for this was what he had always
thought himself when he permitted his imagination to rest on Una
Whitton.

"Probably. You'd have made a good father at any rate."

"God knows you might be right," said Fogarty. "It's easier to do
without a woman than it is to do without kids. My mother was the
same. She was wrapped up in us; she always wanted us to be better
than anyone else, and when we did badly at school or got into
trouble it nearly broke her heart. She said it was the Fogarty blood
breaking out in us—the Fogartys were all horse dealers." His handsome, happy face clouded again with the old feelings of remorse and
guilt, unjustified, like most of his self-reproach. "I'm afraid she died
under the impression that I was a Fogarty after all."

"If the Fogartys are any relation to the Martins, I'd say it was
most unlikely," said Jackson.

"I never really knew till she was dead how much she meant to
me," Fogarty said broodingly. "I insisted on performing the burial
service myself, though Hennessey warned me not to. My God, the
way we gallop through it till it comes home to ourselves! I broke
down and bawled like a kid and Hennessey got up and finished
it."

Jackson shook his head uncomprehendingly. "You feel these
things more than I do. I'm a cold fish."

It struck Fogarty that, though this was precisely what he had
always believed, he would now believe it no longer. "That settled
me," he said. "Up to that, I used to be a bit flighty, but afterwards, I
knew I could never care for another woman as I cared for her."

"Nonsense!" Jackson said lightly. "That's the best proof you
could offer a woman that you'd care for her as much. Love is just
one thing, not a half dozen. If I had my eye on a woman, I'd take
good care to choose one who cared that way for her father. You're
the sort who'd go to hell for a woman if ever you let yourself go. I

couldn't go to hell for anybody. The nearest I ever got to it was with one woman in a town I was in. I didn't realize the state she was getting herself into till I found her outside my door at two o'clock one morning. She wanted me to take her away! You can imagine what happened to her afterwards."

"She went off with someone else?"

"No. Drink. And it was nothing but loneliness. After that, I decided that people of my sort have no business with love."

IV

At the word "love" Fogarty felt his heart contract. It was partly the wreath, brilliant in the sunlight, that had drawn him out of his habitual reserve and linked him with a man of even greater reserve, partly the excitement of returning to the little town where he had grown up. He hated it; he avoided it; it seemed to be the complete expression of all the narrowness and meanness that he tried to banish from his own thoughts; but at the same time, it contained all the violence and longing that had driven him out of it, and when once he drew near it a tumult of emotions rose in him that half strangled him.

"There it is!" he said triumphantly, pointing to a valley where a tapering Franciscan tower rose from a clutter of low Georgian houses and thatched cabins. "They'll be waiting for us at the bridge. That's the way they'll be waiting for me when my turn comes."

"They" were the priests and townspeople who had come out to escort the hearse to the cemetery. Ned Devine steered people to their places. Four men shouldered the coffin over the high-arched bridge past the ruined castle and up the hilly Main Street. Shutters were up on the shop fronts, blinds were drawn, everything was at a standstill except here and there where a curtain was lifted and an old woman, too feeble to make the journey, peered out.

A laneway led off the hilly road, and they came to the abbey; a tower and a few walls with tombstones thickly sown in choir and nave. The hearse was already drawn up and people gathered in a semicircle about it. Ned Devine came hastily up to the car where the two priests were donning their surplices.

"Whisper, Father Jerry," he muttered in a strained, excited voice. "People are talking about that wreath. I wonder would you know who sent it?"

"I know nothing at all about it, Ned," Fogarty replied roughly, and suddenly felt his heart begin to pant violently.

"Come here a minute, Sheela," Ned called, and a tall, pale girl in black, with the stain of tears on her long, bony face, left the little group of mourners and joined them. "You know Father Jerry. This is Father Jackson, Father Willie's other friend. They don't know anything about it."

"Then I'd let them take it back," she said doggedly.

"What would you say, Father?" Ned asked, appealing to Fogarty.

Fogarty suddenly felt his courage desert him. In arguing with Martin, he had felt himself dealing with an equal, but now the intense passions and prejudices of the little town seemed to rise up and oppose him, and he felt himself again an adolescent, rebellious but frightened.

"I can only tell you what I told Father Martin," he blustered.

"Did Father Martin talk about it too?" Ned asked sharply.

"He did."

"There!" Sheela said vindictively. "What did I tell you?"

"Well, the pair of you may be cleverer than I am," Fogarty said. "I can only say what I said before: I'd never have noticed anything wrong with it."

"It was no proper thing to send to a priest's funeral," she hissed with prim fury. "Whoever sent it was no friend of my brother."

"You wouldn't agree with that, Father?" Ned asked anxiously.

"But I tell you, Uncle Ned, if that wreath goes into the graveyard we'll be the laughingstock of the town," she said furiously.

"Whisht, girl, whisht, and let Father Jerry talk!" he snapped angrily.

"Well, Ned, it seems to me to be entirely a matter for your-selves," Fogarty replied. "I can only tell you what I think." He was really scared now; he realized that he was in danger of behaving imprudently in public, and that sooner or later the story would get back to the Bishop and it would be suggested that he knew more than he pretended.

"If you'll excuse my interrupting, Father," Jackson said suavely, giving him a warning glance over his spectacles, "I know it isn't my place to speak—"

"But that's the very thing we want, Father," Ned said passion-ately. "If you say 'tis all right, that's enough for me."

"Oh, well, Mr. Devine, that would be too great a responsibility for me to take," Jackson said with a cautious smile, though his pale face had grown flushed. "You know this town. I don't. I only know what it would mean in my own place. I've told Father Fogarty already that I agree with Miss Devine. I think it was wrong to send it. But," and his mild voice suddenly grew menacing, and he shrugged his shoulders and spread out his hands with a contemp-tuous look, "if you were to send that wreath back from the grave-yard, you'd make yourself something far worse than a laughing-stock. You'd throw mud on a dead man's name that would never be forgotten for you, the longest day you lived. . . . Things may be different here, of course," he added superciliously.

Ned Devine suddenly came to his senses. He clicked his fingers impatiently.

"Of course, of course, of course," he snarled. "That's something we should have thought of ourselves. 'Twould be giving tongues to the stones."

And he took the wreath and carried it behind the coffin to the graveside. That was sufficient to dissipate the growing hysteria which Fogarty felt about him. He touched Jackson's hand lightly.

"Good man, Jim!" he said in a voice that was full of love and tears.

Side by side they stood at the head of the open grave where the other surpliced priests had gathered. Their voices rose in the psalms for the dead. But Fogarty's brooding, curious eyes swept the crowd of faces he had known since childhood, now caricatured by age and pain, and each time they came to rest on the wreath which stood to one side of the grave. Each time it came over him in a flood of emotion that what he and Jackson had saved was something more than a sentimental token. It was the thing which formerly had linked them to Devine and which now linked them with one another; the feeling of their own integrity as men beside their integrity as priests; the thing which gave significance and beauty to their sacrifice.

The Teacher's Mass

FATHER FOGARTY, the curate in Crislough, used to say in his cynical way that his greatest affliction was having to serve the teacher's Mass every morning. He referred, of course, to his own Mass, the curate's Mass, which was said early so that Father Fogarty could say Mass later in Costello. Nobody ever attended it, except occasionally in summer, when there were visitors at the hotel. The schoolteacher, old Considine, served as acolyte. He had been serving the early Mass long before Fogarty came, and the curate thought he would also probably be doing it long after he had left. Every morning, you saw him coming up the village street, a pedantically attired old man with a hollow face and a big mustache that was turning gray. Everything about him was abstract and angular, even to his voice, which was harsh and without modulation, and sometimes when he and Fogarty came out of the sacristy with Considine leading, carrying the book, his pace was so slow that Fogarty wondered what effect it would have if he gave him one good kick in the behind. It was exactly as Fogarty said—as though *he* were serving Considine's Mass, and the effect of it was to turn Fogarty into a more unruly acolyte than ever he had been in the days when he himself was serving the convent Mass.

Whatever was the cause, Considine always roused a bit of the devil in Fogarty, and he knew that Considine had no great affection for him, either. The old man had been headmaster of the Crislough school until his retirement, and all his life he had kept himself apart from the country people, like a parish priest or a policeman. He was not without learning; he had a quite respectable knowledge of local history, and a very good one of the ecclesiastical history of the Early Middle Ages in its local applications, but it was all book learning, and, like his wing collar, utterly unrelated to the life about him. He had all the childish vanity of the man of dissociated scholarship, wrote occasional scurrilous letters to the local paper to correct some error in etymology, and expected everyone on that account to treat him as an oracle. As a schoolmaster he had sneered cruelly at the barefoot urchins he taught, describing them as "illiterate peasants" who believed in the fairies and in spells, and when, twenty years later, some of them came back from Boston or Brooklyn and showed off before the neighbors, with their big American hats and high-powered cars, he still sneered at them. According to him, they went away illiterate and came home illiterate.

"I see young Carmody is home again," he would say to the curate after Mass.

"Is that so?"

"And he has a car like a house," Considine would add, with bitter amusement. "A car with a grin on it. 'Twould do fine to cart home his mother's turf."

"The blessings of God on him," the curate would say cheerfully. "I wish I had a decent car instead of the old yoke I have."

"I daresay it was the fairies," the old teacher would snarl, with an ugly smile that made his hollow, high-cheeked face look like a skull. "It wasn't anything he ever learned here."

"Maybe we're not giving the fairies their due, Mr. Considine," said the curate, with the private conviction that it would be easier to learn from them than from the schoolmaster.

The old man's scornful remarks irritated Fogarty because he liked the wild, barefooted, inarticulate brats from the mountainy farms, and felt that if they showed off a bit when they returned from America with a few dollars in their pockets, they were well entitled to do so. Whoever was entitled to the credit, it was nothing and nobody at home. The truth was he had periods of terrible gloom when he felt he had mistaken his vocation. Or, rather, the vocation was all right, but the conditions under which he exercised it were all wrong, and those conditions, for him, were well represented by the factitious scholarship of old Considine. It was all in the air. Religion sometimes seemed no more to him than his own dotty old house-keeper, who, whatever he said, invested herself with the authority of a bishop and decided who was to see him and about what, and settled matters on her own whenever she got half a chance. Things were so bad with her that whenever the country people wanted to see him, they bribed one of the acolytes to go and ask him to come himself to their cottages. The law was represented by Sergeant Twomey, who raided the mountain pubs half an hour after closing time, in response to the orders of some lunatic superintendent at the other side of the county, while as for culture, there was the library van every couple of months, from which Considine, who acted as librarian, selected a hundred books, mainly for his own amusement. He was partial to books dealing with voyages in the Congo or Tibet ("Tibet is a very interessting country, Father"). The books that were for general circulation he censored to make sure there were no bad words like "navel" in them that might corrupt the ignorant "peasantry." And then he came to Fogarty and told him he had been reading a very "interessting" book about birdwatching in the South Seas, or something like that.

Fogarty's own temptation was toward action and energy, just as his depression was often no more than the expression of his frustra-tion. He was an energetic and emotional man who in other circum-stances would probably have become a successful businessman. Women were less of a temptation to him than the thought of an active instinctual life. All he wanted in the way of a holiday was to get rid of his collar and take a gun or rod or stand behind the bar of a country hotel. He ran the local hurling team for what it was worth, which wasn't much, and strayed down the shore with the boatmen or up the hills with the poachers and poteen-makers, who all trusted him and never tried to conceal any of their harmless misdemeanors from him. Once, for instance, in the late evening, he came unexpectedly on a party of scared poteen-makers on top of a mountain and sat down on the edge of the hollow where they were operating their still. "Never mind me, lads!" he said, lighting a pipe. "I'm not here at all." "Sure we know damn well you're not here, Father," one old man said, and chuckled. "But how the hell can we offer a drink to a bloody ghost?"

These were his own people, the people he loved and admired, and it was principally the feeling that he could do little or nothing for them that plunged him into those suicidal fits of gloom in which he took to the bottle. When he heard of a dance being held in a farmhouse without the permission of the priest or the police, he said, "The blessings of God on them," and when a girl went and got herself with child by one of the islanders, he said, "More power to her elbow!"—though he had to say these things discreetly, for fear they should get back. But the spirit of them got back, and the acolytes would whisper, "Father, would you ever go out to Dan Mike's when you have the time?" or young men and girls would lie in wait for his car on a country road and signal timidly to him, because the country people knew that from him they would either get a regular blasting in a language they understood or the loan of a few pounds to send a girl to hospital in England so that the neighbors wouldn't know.

Fogarty knew that in the teacher's eyes this was another black mark against him, for old Considine could not understand how any educated man could make so little of the cloth as to sit drinking with "illiterate peasants" instead of talking to a fine, well-informed man like himself about the situation in the Far East or the relationship of the Irish dioceses to the old kingdoms of the Early Middle Ages.

Then one evening Fogarty was summoned to the teacher's house on a sick call. It only struck him when he saw it there at the end of the village—a newish, red-brick box of a house, with pebble dash on the front and a steep stairway up from the front door—that it was like the teacher himself. Maisie, the teacher's unmarried daughter, was a small, plump woman with a face that must once have been attractive, for it was still all in curves, with hair about it like Mona Lisa's, though now she had lost all her freshness, and her skin was red and hard and full of wrinkles. She had a sad smile, and Fogarty could not resist a pang of pity for her because he realized that she was probably another victim of Considine's dislike of "illiterates." How could an "illiterate" boy come to a house like that, or how could the teacher's daughter go out walking with him?

She had got the old man to bed, and he lay there with the engaged look of a human being at grips with his destiny. From his narrow window there was a pleasant view of the sea road and a solitary tree by the water's edge. Beyond the bay was the mountain, with a cap on it—the sign of bad weather. Fogarty gave him the last sacraments, and he confessed and received Communion with a devotion that touched Fogarty in spite of himself. He stayed on with the daughter until the doctor arrived, in case any special medicines were needed. They sat in the tiny box of a front room with a bay window and a high mahogany bookcase that filled one whole wall. She wanted to stay and make polite conversation for the priest, though all the time she was consumed with anxiety. When the doctor left, Fogarty left with him, and pressed Maisie's hand and told her to call on him for anything, at any time.

Dr. Mulloy was more offhand. He was a tall, handsome young man of about Fogarty's own age. Outside, standing beside his car, he said to Fogarty, "Ah, he might last a couple of years if he minded himself. They don't, of course. You know the way it is. A wonder that daughter of his never married."

"How could she?" Fogarty asked in a low voice, turning to glance again at the ill-designed, pretentious little suburban house. "He'd think her too grand for any of the boys round this place."

"Why then, indeed, if he pops off on her, she won't be too grand at all," said the doctor. "A wonder an educated man like that wouldn't have more sense. Sure, he can't have anything to leave her?"

"No more than myself, I daresay," said Fogarty, who saw that the doctor only wanted to find out how much they could pay; and he went off to summon one of the boy acolytes to take Considine's place at Mass next morning.

But the next morning when Fogarty reached the sacristy, instead of the boy he had spoken to, old Considine was waiting, with everything neatly arranged in his usual pedantic manner, and a wan old man's smile on his hollow face.

"Mr. Considine!" Fogarty exclaimed indignantly. "What's the meaning of this?"

"Ah, I'm fine this morning, Father," said the old man, with a sort of fictitious, drunken excitement. "I woke up as fresh as a daisy." Then he smiled malevolently and added, "Jimmy Leary thought he was after doing me out of a job, but Dr. Mulloy was too smart for him."

"But you know yourself what Dr. Mulloy said," Fogarty protested indignantly. "I talked to him myself about it. He said you could live for years, but any exertion might make you go off any time."

"And how can man die better?" retorted the teacher, with the triumphant air he wore whenever he managed to produce an apt quotation. "You remember Macaulay, I suppose," he added doubtfully, and then his face took on a morose look. " 'Tisn't that at all," he said. "But 'tis the only thing I have to look forward to. The day wouldn't be the same to me if I had to miss Mass."

Fogarty knew that he was up against an old man's stubbornness and love of habitual things, and that he was wasting his breath advising Considine himself. Instead, he talked to the parish priest, a holy and muddleheaded old man named Whelan. Whelan shook his head mournfully over the situation, but then he was a man who shook his head over everything. He had apparently decided many years ago that any form of action was hateful, and he took to his bed if people became too pressing.

"He's very obstinate, old John, but at the same time, you wouldn't like to cross him," Whelan said.

"If you don't do something about it, you might as well put back the Costello Mass another half an hour," Fogarty said. He was forever trying to induce Whelan to make up his mind. "He's getting slower every day. One of these days he'll drop dead on me at the altar."

"Oh, I'll mention it to him," the parish priest said regretfully. "But I don't know would it be wise to take too strong a line. You have to humor them when they're as old as that. I daresay we'll be the same ourselves, Father."

Fogarty knew he was wasting his breath on Whelan as well. Whelan would no doubt be as good as his word, and talk about the weather to Considine for an hour, and then end by dropping a hint, which might be entirely lost, that the old teacher shouldn't exert himself too much, and that would be all.

A month later, the old teacher had another attack, but this time Fogarty only heard of it from his mad housekeeper, who knew everything that went on in the village.

"But why didn't he send for me?" he asked sharply.

"Ah, I suppose he wasn't bad enough," replied the housekeeper. "Mrs. MacCarthy said he got over it with pills and a sup of whiskey. They say whiskey is the best thing."

"You're sure he didn't send for me?" Fogarty asked. There were times when he half expected the woman, in the exercise of her authority, to refuse the Last Rites to people she didn't approve of.

"Sure, of course he didn't. It was probably nothing."

All the same, Fogarty was not easy in his mind. He knew what it meant to old people to have the priest with them at the end, and he suspected that if Considine made light of his attack, it could only be because he was afraid Fogarty would take it as final proof that he was not fit to serve Mass. He felt vaguely guilty about it. He strode down the village street, saluting the fishermen who were sitting on the sea wall in the dusk. The teacher's cottage was dark when he reached it. The cobbler, a lively little man who lived next door, was standing outside.

"I hear the old Master was sick again, Tom," said the curate.

"Begor, he was, Father," said the cobbler. "I hear Maisie found him crawling to the fire on his hands and knees. Terrible cold they get when they're like that. He's a sturdy old divil, though. You needn't be afraid you'll lose your altar boy for a long time yet."

"I hope not, Tom," said Fogarty, who knew that the cobbler, a knowledgeable man in his own way, thought there was something funny about the old schoolmaster's serving Mass. "And I hope we're all as good when our own time comes."

He went home, too thoughtful to chat with the fishermen. The cobbler's words had given him a sudden glimpse of old Considine's sufferings, and he was filled with the compassion that almost re-volted him at times for sick bodies and suffering minds. He was an emotional man, and he knew it was partly the cause of his own savage gloom, but he could not restrain it.

Next morning, when he went to the sacristy, there was the old teacher, with his fawning smile, the smile of a guilty small boy who has done it again and this time knows he will not escape without punishment.

"You weren't too good last night, John," the curate said, using Considine's Christian name for the first time.

"No, Father Jeremiah," Considine replied, pronouncing the priest's name slowly and pedantically. "I was a bit poorly in the early evening. But those pills of Dr. Mulloy's are a wonder."

"And isn't it a hard thing to say you never sent for me?" Fogarty went on.

Considine blushed furiously, and this time he looked really guilty and scared.

"But I wasn't that bad, Father," he protested with senile intens-ity, his hands beginning to shake and his eyes to sparkle. "I wasn't as frightened yesterday as I was the first time. It's the first time it frightens you. You feel sure you'll never last it out. But after that you get to expect it."

"Will you promise me never to do a thing like that again?" the curate asked earnestly. "Will you give me your word that you'll send for me, any hour of the day or night?"

"Very well, Father," Considine replied sullenly. " 'Tis very good of you. I'll give you my word I'll send for you."

And they both recognized the further, unspoken part of the compact between them. Considine would send for Fogarty, but nothing Fogarty saw or heard was to permit him again to try to deprive the old teacher of his office. Not that he any longer wished to do so. Now that he recognized the passion of will in the old man, Fogarty's profound humanity only made him anxious to second it and enable Considine to do what clearly he wished to do—die in harness. Fogarty had also begun to recognize that it was not mere obstinacy that got the old man out of his bed each morning and brought him shivering and sighing and shuffling up the village street. There was obstinacy there, and plenty of it, but there was something else, which the curate valued more; something he felt the lack of in himself. It wasn't easy to put a name on it. Faith was one name, but it was no more than a name and was used to cover too many excesses of devotion that the young priest found distasteful. This was something else, something that made him ashamed of his own human weakness and encouraged him to fight the depression, which seemed at times as if it would overwhelm him. It was more like the miracle of the Mass itself, metaphor become reality. Now when he thought of his own joke about serving the teacher's Mass, it didn't seem quite so much like a joke.

One morning in April, Fogarty noticed as he entered the sacristy that the old man was looking very ill. As he helped Fogarty, his hands shook piteously. Even his harsh voice had a quaver in it, and his lips were pale. Fogarty looked at him and wondered if he shouldn't say something, but decided against it. He went in, preceded by Considine, and noticed that though the teacher tried to hold himself erect, his walk was little more than a shuffle. He went up to the altar, but found it almost impossible to concentrate on what he was doing. He heard the laboring steps behind him, and as the old man started to raise the heavy book onto the altar, Fogarty paused for a moment and looked under his brows. Considine's face was now white as a sheet, and as he raised the book he sighed. Fogarty wanted to cry out, "For God's sake, man, lie down!" He wanted to hold Considine's head on his knee and whisper into his ear. Yet he realized that to the strange old man behind him this would be no kindness. The only kindness he could do him was to crush down his own weak warmheartedness and continue the sacrifice. Never had he seemed farther away from the reality of the Mass. He heard the laboring steps, the panting breath, behind him, and it seemed as if they had lasted some timeless time before he heard another heavy sigh as Considine managed to kneel.

At last, Fogarty found himself waiting for a response that did not come. He looked round quickly. The old man had fallen silently forward onto the altar steps. His arm was twisted beneath him and his head was turned sideways. His jaw had fallen, and his eyes were sightless.

"John!" Fogarty called, in a voice that rang through the church. "Can you hear me? John!"

There was no reply, and the curate placed him on his back, with one of the altar cushions beneath his head. Fogarty felt under the surplice for his buttons and unloosed them. He felt for the heart. It had stopped; there was no trace of breathing. Through the big window at the west end he saw the churchyard trees and the sea beyond them, bright in the morning light. The whole church seemed terribly still, so that the mere ticking of the clock filled it with its triumphant mocking of the machine of flesh and blood that had fallen silent.

Fogarty went quickly to the sacristy and returned with the Sacred Oils to anoint the teacher. He knew he had only to cross the road for help, to have the old man's body removed and get an acolyte to finish the Mass, but he wanted no help. He felt strangely lightheaded. Instead, when he had done, he returned to the altar and resumed the Mass where he had left off, murmuring the responses to himself. As he did so, he realized that he was acutely aware of every detail, of every sound, he had no feeling that he was lacking in concentration. When he turned to face the body of the church and said *"Dominus vobiscum,"* he saw as if for the first time the prostrate form with its fallen jaw and weary eyes, under the light that came in from the sea through the trees in their first leaf, and murmured *"Et cum spiritu tuo"* for the man whose spirit had flown. Then, when he had said the prayers after Mass beside the body, he took his biretta, donned it, and walked by the body, carrying his chalice, and feeling as he walked that some figure was walking before him, slowly, saying goodbye. In his excited mind echoed the rubric: "Then, having adored and thanked God for everything, he goes away."

The Martyr

THERE'S YOUR MARTYR! Commandant Myles Hartnett, killed by Free State Troops in Asragh Barrack, November 18, 1922. "For the glory of God and the honor of Ireland." Every year they lay a wreath there.

It was really my fault that he was killed. I was in charge of the barrack. A young fellow called Morrissey captured him, and, as he was carrying a gun at the time, that meant one thing only. I didn't like Morrissey; he was one of those conceited young fellows who go through life with a grievance against everybody, and he had a particular grievance against me because I tried to keep some sort of discipline in the infernal place.

I was alone in the office, wondering what all the row was about, when Morrissey, Daly, and a few others pushed him in. I could see they'd knocked him about pretty badly already. He was a tall, powerful man with fair hair, blue, short-sighted eyes (they had smashed his glasses), and that air of a born athlete that I, for one, always like in a man. Even then, he looked as though he could still have made smithereens of them but for the guns.

"And who have we here?" I asked.

"This is the fellow that organized the Duncartan ambush," said Morrissey triumphantly. Now the Duncartan ambush was a bad slip-up on my part. Believing the information I had got, I had just walked my men right into it. In the scrap I had lost the only friend I had in the barrack, MacDunphy.

"Oh, is that so?" I asked. "You're the chap we're indebted to for our welcome there? How nice!"

"I am not," he said contemptuously.

"You are," shouted Morrissey, clenching his fists. "You were the man who used the Lewis gun that killed MacDunphy. You needn't try to get out of it."

"I'm not trying to get out of it," said Hartnett in the same scornful tone. "I'm only telling you you don't know what you're talking about."

"Shut up, you—liar!" shouted Morrissey, and drove his fist into Hartnett's mouth.

Hartnett took out his handkerchief, wiped off the blood, and looked at me. Then he smiled. I knew what the smile meant and he knew I knew.

"Have you quite finished with the prisoner, Captain Morrissey?" I asked.

"But don't you know this was the fellow that killed Harry MacDunphy?" he shouted.

"No," I said, "and as things are shaping I'm hardly likely to find out."

He muttered an obscenity, turned on his heel, and went out, banging the door.

"Were you in the Duncartan ambush?" I asked.

"Ah, not at all," said Hartnett. "I was over in Derreen the day it happened. Not that it makes any difference."

"Not the least," I said. "All right, Jimmie," I said to Daly, a young lieutenant. "Take him downstairs. And tell the sentry that Captain Morrissey isn't to go into his cell without my permission."

It was the same at the court-martial. He was quiet, self-possessed, and almost contemptuous of the men who were supposed to be trying him. He denied nothing and stood on his right as an officer and prisoner of war. He had the education which they lacked (I discovered he was a spoiled priest), and succeeded in making them look like the fools they were. Not that that made the least difference either. The verdict and sentence were a foregone conclusion; so was the sanction unless he had friends in Headquarters.

Then one night about a week later I was working alone in the office when a sentry came in. He was a little Dubliner, one of my own men and one I could trust.

"Mick," he whispered conspiratorially (he always called me "Mick" when we were alone), "that Hartnett fellow would like to talk to you."

"What does he want to talk to me for at this hour?" I asked irritably.

"He said he wanted to speak to yourself," said the sentry. "Morrissey and Daly are out, boozing. I think you ought to have a word with him."

I knew that Hartnett had managed to get round my sentry and that I wouldn't get any peace till I saw him.

"Oh, all right," I said. "Don't bring him up here. I'll come down and see him later."

"Good man!" said the sentry. "I'll leave on the light in his cell."

I finished up and then went down to the cells with my own keys. It wasn't very pleasant at that hour. The cell was small; the high barred window had no glass in it; the only furniture was a mattress and a couple of blankets. Hartnett was standing up in his shirt sleeves and socks. He had got a spare pair of spectacles. He tried to smile, but it didn't come off.

"I'm sorry for disturbing you at this hour," he said in a low voice so as not to be heard in the neighboring cells.

"Well?" I asked. "What is it?"

"Tell me, by the way," he said, cocking his head, "aren't you a friend of Phil Condon's?"

"Very much by the way," I replied. "Was it to talk about Phil Condon that you brought me here?"

"There are times you'd be glad to talk about anything," he said with a touch of bitterness. Then, after a moment, "I thought any friend of Phil's would be a decent man. That's more than you could say for most of your officers."

"What is it?" I asked.

"I suppose I'm going to be shot?" he asked, throwing back his head and looking at me through the big glasses.

"I'm afraid so," I said without much emotion.

"When, do you know?"

"I don't know. If the sentence is confirmed by tomorrow, probably the following morning. Unless you have friends in Headquarters."

"That gang!" he said scornfully. "I haven't, only all the enemies I have." He put his hands in his trousers pockets and took a couple of short steps up the cell beside the mattress. Then he looked at me over the glasses and dropped his voice still farther. "You could stop that, couldn't you?"

I was a bit taken aback by this direct appeal. It wasn't what I had expected.

"I daresay I could," I said lightly, "but I'm not going to."

"Not on any account?" he asked, still looking at me over the glasses, his eyebrows slightly raised.

"Not on any account."

He waited. Then he took two steps toward me and stood, looking at me.

"Not even if I made it worth your while?"

Again I was taken aback. I felt the first time I saw him that we understood one another, and now I was irritated at his low opinion of me. I tried to smile.

"Are you trying to bribe me?" I asked.

"Were you ever in my position?" he asked, cocking his head again.

"No."

"Would you blame me if I was?"

"I'm not short of money thanks," I said. "If you want anything else you can ask the sentry."

"Ah, you know what I mean all right," he said, nodding. "You know well enough 'tisn't money I'm talking of."

"What the hell is it then?" I asked angrily.

"Something that fellow, Morrissey, said upstairs, about the Duncartan ambush," he said, nodding in the direction of the door. "This MacDunphy—was he a great friend of yours?"

"He was," I said. "Can you bring him back to life?"

"Do you know who the chap was that shot him?"

"I have a fairly good idea."

"The man who had the Lewis gun that day?" he said scornfully, raising his voice so that I was certain he could be heard. "You have not."

"All right," I said. "I haven't."

"You'd like to know who he was, wouldn't you?"

"Why?" I asked mockingly. "Are you thinking of turning informer?"

I was sorry the moment I'd said it. It wasn't fair from a man at liberty to one with only his wits between him and the firing squad. His big face grew as red as if I'd slapped it.

"All right," he muttered, "I was asking for that. But you see the way I am! The man is no particular friend of mine, and it's his life or mine."

"That's what you're assuming," I said.

"And aren't I right?" he asked, pushing his big face into mine with a sort of hypnotic look in his eyes.

The trouble was, he was. That's the curse of civil war. No matter what high notions you start with, it always degenerates into a series of personal quarrels, family against family, individual against individual, until at last you hardly mind what side they're on.

"Very well," I said. "You are. Who was it?"

"Micky Morgan—Monkey Morgan from Dirrane."

"And what was Monkey Morgan from Dirrane doing in Duncartan?"

"Ah, he shouldn't have been there at all, man," he said, tapping me on the elbow, and for a moment it was just one officer speaking to another. " 'Tisn't his area. But fellows like that, nobody can control them."

"And where does Monkey Morgan hang out?" I asked.

"Mostly in Mick Tom Ogue's in Beensheen; Mick is a sort of cousin of his mother's."

"This isn't another invitation like the one in Duncartan?" I asked.

"What sort of fool do you take me for?" he asked contemptuously.

"I don't know," I said. "I was just wondering. . . . All right, hang on!"

Then I went out and ordered up two lorries and twenty men. I made sure the sentry was out of the way before I went back to the cell. I had a cap and greatcoat with me.

"Put these on," I said, and Hartnett did.

"They're a good fit," he said, thrusting his hands into the pockets.

"Yes," I said. "They belonged to MacDunphy."

Then we went out to the waiting lorries. Hartnett avoided the headlights; apart from that there was nothing to show that he wasn't just another officer from Dublin on a tour of inspection.

"All right, Colonel," I said in a loud voice to him. "Step in!"

He sat in front between me and the driver. It was a dark night with brilliant stars. We went up through the hills by roads we both knew well, though he knew them far better than I. Once he made me cross an open field to avoid the delay at a blown-up bridge. At last we stopped at the foot of a lane, and the men got out quietly. He pointed out to me where to post sentries so that the house was completely covered, and then he and I led the way up the lane. When we reached the door of the farmhouse he stood on one side and let me do the knocking. We didn't knock long because the door began to give under the rifle butts, and it was hastily opened for us by an old man in his shirt.

"Ye can't do anything to me," he shouted. "I have varicose veins."

We caught Morgan in the bedroom, pulling on his socks. He made a dive for his Peter the Painter, but two of our men got him on the floor before he could use it. He was a slight man with a long, hard, fighting face. We waited while he dressed. Then he pulled himself erect and went out with his chin in the air. He didn't notice the tall man standing by the door with his chin in his chest. I wondered what Hartnett's feelings were just at that moment.

I wondered more a few days later when I glanced out of the office window and saw the prisoners exercising within the barbed wire. Hartnett and Morgan were walking side by side. I stood leaning for a long time on the window, thinking how curious it was.

It was next day or perhaps the day after that that Morrissey slouched into my office in his usual uninhibited manner with a cigarette hanging from one corner of his mouth. He stood with his back to the fire, his hands folded behind him.

"Did you hear anything about this escape?" he asked.

"No," I said without interest. "Has there been one?"

"There's going to be. It's all arranged with the fellows outside. One of our contacts brought in the news."

"And who's planned it?" I asked. "Hartnett?"

"I don't know. I suppose it is. Listen," he added in a squeaky voice, knocking his ashes behind him into the fire, "when is that fellow going to be bumped?"

I was exasperated almost beyond endurance by the fellow's tone. It was both ill-bred and childish. He was like a schoolboy expecting a prize. Hartnett was his prize.

"I'm not sure that he is going to be—bumped," I said. (In fact, I knew perfectly well that he wasn't, but I was taking care that Morrissey didn't know. Nobody must know if Hartnett's life was to be saved from his own men.)

"Well, all I can say is, it's a damn shame," said Morrissey. "Any idea what's behind it?"

"Some people have friends in high places," I said oracularly.

"Looks like it," Morrissey said impudently, and I knew he meant me.

"You might remember," I said, "that there was a time when people like Hartnett were considered quite useful. . . . All right. I'll speak to him myself. Send him up, will you, please?"

Hartnett was led up a few moments later by the sentry. He looked rather more like himself, confident and at the same time watchful.

"Tell me," I asked, "what's all this about an escape?"

"An escape?" he asked wonderingly. "What escape? 'Tis news to me."

"Oh, is it?" I asked. "Are you quite sure you're not the ring-leader?"

He looked at me doubtfully for a moment and then his lip began to curl.

"You're not by any chance looking for an excuse to break your bargain?" he asked almost contemptuously.

"No," I said without taking offense, "I don't have to look for excuses. Your friend, Morrissey, has just been in to know why you haven't been executed. Several others would like to know the same thing. They're not going to be told if I can manage it. So there isn't going to be any escape. Do you understand?"

He thought for a moment, sighed, and nodded.

"I understand," he said hopelessly. "You're right, of course."

He was going out when I stopped him. I couldn't let him go like that. Afterward I was glad I didn't.

"Don't think I'm criticizing you," I said. "It's just that there are certain actions we can't hedge about, that's all."

He nodded again and went out.

Two days later Morgan was executed. I was wakened by the noises outside and then I lay awake listening for the bangs. "That's for you, MacDunphy," I said, but it gave me no satisfaction. I wondered if Hartnett was awake listening to them, too. Two men regretting a bargain. When I got up there was the usual air of gloom and hysteria in the barrack. Morrissey was on the drink from early morning. Shutters had been put up in the town, and I sent round a lorry of men to take them down again. Then I went off to Moorlough for a conference.

While I was there a telephone message came through from Daly to say that two of our men had been shot in the street. I realized the danger at once.

"All right, Jimmie," I said, trying to make my voice sound natural. "Hold everything till I come back."

I didn't even wait to clear up things after the conference but got the driver to go hell for leather through the dusk. It was the darkness I was afraid of, and darkness had fallen when we reached the barrack gate.

"Everything all right, Sergeant?" I asked at the guardroom.

"Everything all right, sir," he said. "You heard that two of our fellows were shot."

"Yes, I heard that. Nothing else?"

"Only one of the prisoners shot, trying to escape."

"I see," I said. "Hartnett, I suppose?"

"That's right, sir," he said in confusion. "Did they tell you?"

"I was expecting something of the sort," I said. "And Captain Morrissey shot him. Where is the body, Sergeant?"

He began to stammer. The damn fools had even been trying to keep the truth from me! I found the body lying in a shed in the yard, abandoned on the straw. I picked it out with my torch. The head had fallen sideways as though he were trying to sleep. He had been shot through the back.

As I was coming in, Morrissey came up to me; he was recovering from his drinking bout and a bit frightened.

"Oh, about that fellow, Hartnett," he began to stammer.

"I know," I said. "You murdered him. Good night."

Afterward he came up and started hammering on my door, demanding an explanation, but I only told him to go to hell. I felt sick of it all. That's what I mean about civil war. Sooner or later it turns into a set of personal relationships. Hartnett and I were like that; accomplices, if you care to put it that way.

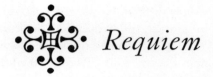 *Requiem*

FATHER FOGARTY, the curate in Crislough, was sitting by the fire one evening when the housekeeper showed in a frail little woman of sixty or sixty-five. She had a long face, with big eyes that looked as though they had wept a great deal, and her smile lit up only the lower half of her face. Father Fogarty was a young man with a warm welcome for the suffering and the old. A man with emotions cut too big for the scale of his existence, he was forever floundering in enthusiasms and disillusionments, wranglings and reconciliations; but he had a heart like a house, and almost before the door closed behind her, he was squeezing the old woman's hand in his own two fat ones.

"You're in trouble," he said in a low voice.

"Wisha, aren't we all, Father?" she replied.

"I'm sorry, I'm sorry," he said. "Is it something I can do for you?"

"Only to say Mass for Timmy, Father."

"I'll do that, to be sure," he said comfortingly. "You're cold. Sit down a minute and warm yourself." Then he laid a big paw on her shoulder and added in a conspiratorial whisper, "Do you take anything? A drop of sherry, maybe?"

"Ah, don't be putting yourself out, Father."

"I'm not putting myself out at all. Or maybe you'd sooner a sup of whiskey. I have some damn good whiskey."

"Wisha, no, Father, I wouldn't, thanks. The whiskey goes to my head."

"It goes to my own," he replied cheerfully. "But the sherry is good, too." He didn't really know whether it was or not, because he rarely drank, but, being a hospitable man, he liked to give his visitors the best. He poured a glass of sherry for her and a small one for himself, and lit one of his favorite cheroots.

The old woman spread her transparent hands to the blaze and sipped at her wine. "Oh, isn't the heat lovely?" she exclaimed with girlish delight, showing her old gums. "And the sherry is lovely, too, Father. Now, I know you're surprised to see me, but I know all about you. They told me to come to you if I was in trouble. And there aren't many priests like that, Father. I was never one to criticize, but I have to say it."

"Ah," he said jovially, throwing himself back in his big leather chair and pulling on his cheroot, "we're like everybody else, Ma'am. A mixed lot."

"I daresay you're right," she said, "but they told me I could talk to you."

"Everyone talks to me," he said without boastfulness. It was true. There was something about him that invited more confidences than a normal man could respect, and Father Fogarty knew he was often indiscreet. "It's not your husband?" he added doubtfully.

"Ah, no, Father," she replied with a wistful smile. "Poor Jim is dead on me these fifteen years. Not, indeed, that I don't miss him just the same," she added thoughtfully. "Sometimes I find myself thinking of him, and he could be in the room with me. No, it's Timmy."

"The son?"

"No, Father. Though he was like a son to me. I never had any of my own. He was Jim's. One of the last things Jim did was to ask me to look after him, and indeed, I did my best. I did my best."

"I'm sure you did, Ma'am," said Father Fogarty, scowling behind his cheroot. He was a man who took death hard, for himself and for others. A stepchild was not the same thing, of course, but he supposed you could get just as attached to one of those. That was the trouble; you could get attached to anything if only you permitted yourself to do so, and he himself was one who had never known how to keep back. "I know how hard it is," he went on, chewing at his cheroot till his left eyebrow descended and seemed to join in the process, and he resembled nothing so much as a film gangster plotting the murder of an innocent victim. "And there's little anyone can say that will console you. All I know from my own experience is that the more loss we feel the more grateful we should be for whatever it was we had to lose. It means we had something worth grieving for. The ones I'm sorry for are the ones that go through life not even knowing what grief is. And you'd be surprised the number of them you'd meet."

"I daresay in one way they're lucky," she said broodingly, looking into the fire.

"They are not lucky, Ma'am, and don't you believe it," he said gruffly. "They miss all the things that make life worth while, without even knowing it. I had a woman in here the other night," he added, pointing his cheroot at the chair she sat in, "sitting where you're sitting now, and she told me when her husband gave the last breath she went on her knees by the bed and thanked God for taking him."

"God help us," the old woman said, clasping her hands. "I hope no one does the same thing over herself someday."

"Thanked God for taking him," Fogarty repeated with his troubled boyish frown. "What sort of mind can a woman like that have?"

"Oh, she's hard, she's hard," agreed the old woman, still looking into the fire.

"Hard as that hearthstone," he said dramatically. "My God, a man she'd lived with the best part of her life, whatever his faults might have been! Wouldn't you think at least she'd have some remorse for the things she'd done to him in all those years?"

"Oh, indeed, 'tis true," she said. "I often blamed myself over poor Jim. Sometimes I think if only I might have been a bit easier on him, he might be here yet."

"Most of us have to go through that sooner or later," he said, feeling that perhaps he had gone too far and reopened old wounds. His own old wounds were never far from breaking open, because often a light or careless word would bring back the memory of his mother and of his diabolical adolescent temperament. "We have to be careful of that, too," he added. "Because it's not the guilty ones who go on brooding but the others—the people who're only partly guilty, or maybe not guilty at all. That can happen, too. I had a man here last week talking about his wife's death, and nothing I could say would persuade him but that he'd wronged her. And I knew for a fact that he was a husband in a million—a saint. It's something we can't afford to indulge. It turns into a sort of cowardice before life. We have to learn to accept our own limitations as human beings— our selfishness and vanity and bad temper."

He spoke with passion, the passion of a man teaching a lesson he has never been able to learn himself. Something in his tone made the old woman look at him, and her face softened into a sweet, toothless old smile.

"Haven't you great wisdom for such a young man!" she exclaimed admiringly.

"Great," he agreed with a jolly laugh. "I'm the biggest idiot of them all."

But she shrugged this off. "Ah, what else were the saints?"

"Look here, Ma'am," he said, rising and standing over her with mock gravity. "Don't you be going round talking about me as a saint or you'll be having me sent to a punishment parish. The poor Bishop has trouble enough on his hands without having to deal with saints. I'll say eight-o'clock Mass on Sunday for your boy. Will that do you?"

"My boy?" she said in surprise. "But Timmy wasn't my son, Father. Sure, I said I had no children."

"No. I took it he was your stepson."

"Is it Jim's?" she exclaimed with a laugh of genuine amusement at his mistake. "Ah, sure, Jim wasn't married before, Father. Don't you see, that's why I had to come to you?"

"I see," he said, though he didn't, and anyhow he felt it was none of his business. The woman, after all, hadn't come to make her confession. "What was his surname so?"

"Ah, Father," she said, still laughing but in a bewildered way, "I'm so distracted that I can't explain myself properly. You have it all mixed up. Sure, I thought I explained it."

"You didn't explain it, Ma'am," he said, repressing his curiosity. "And anyway it's nothing to me who Timmy was. That's a matter between you and your confessor."

"My what?" she cried indignantly. "Ah, Father, you have me distracted completely now. This has nothing to do with confession. Oh, my, what's that Timmy was? If I could only think!"

"Take your time, Ma'am," he said, but he wondered what was coming next.

"A poodle!" she exclaimed. "Now I have it."

"A what?"

"A poodle—a French poodle is what they called him," she said, delighted to remember the proper term. And then her big eyes began to fill with tears. "Oh, Father, I don't know how I'm going to get on without him. He was everything to me. The house isn't the same without him."

"You don't mean you're asking me to say Mass for your *dog*?"

"Oh, I'm not asking you to do it for nothing," she added with dignity, opening her handbag.

"Are you a Catholic at all, Ma'am?" he asked sternly, fixing her with a glowering look that only seemed to amuse her. She tossed her head with a sudden saucy, girlish air.

"Wisha, what else would I be?" she asked gently, and he felt that there was nothing much he could say in reply.

"And do you know what the sacrifice of the Mass is?" he went on.

"Well, as I go every morning of my life, Father, I should have some idea," she replied, and again he had the feeling that she was laughing at him.

"And don't you know that you're asking me to commit sacrilege? Do you even know what sacrilege is?"

"Ah, what sacrilege?" she exclaimed lightly, shrugging it off. She took three five-pound notes from her old handbag. He knew she intended the money as an offering; he knew it was probably all she had in the world, and he found himself torn between blind rage and admiration.

"Here," he said. "Let me get you another drink. And put that blooming money back in your bag or you'll be losing it."

But the very sound of his voice told him that he was losing conviction. The terrible little old woman with her one idea exercised a sort of fascination over him that almost frightened him. He was afraid that is he wasn't careful he would soon find himself agreeing to do what she wanted. He poured her a drink, threw himself back again in his armchair, and at once gave way to his indignation.

"I cannot stand this damn sentimentality!" he shouted, hitting the arm of his chair with his clenched fist. "Every day of my life I have to see good Christians go without food and fire, clothes and medicine, while the rich people taunt them with the sight of their pampered pets. I tell you I can't stand it!"

"Why, then, I'm sure you're right, Father. But I'm not rich, and no poor person was ever sent away from my door with nothing, as long as I had it."

"I'm sure of that, Ma'am," he said humbly, ashamed of his outburst. "I'm sure you're a better Christian than I am, but there are different needs and different duties, and we must not confuse them. There are animal needs and human needs, and human needs and spiritual needs. Your dog has no need of the Mass."

"He was very fond of Mass. Every morning he came with me and lay down outside the chapel door."

"And *why* did you leave him outside the chapel door?" asked Fogarty.

"Why?"

"Yes, why? Wasn't it that you made a distinction between an animal and a spiritual need?"

"It was nothing of the kind," she said hotly. "It was the parish priest that asked me, because some old fools complained. Hah, but I often sneaked him in when they weren't looking, and let me tell you, Father, none of those old craw-thumpers behaved as devotionally as my Timmy. Up with the Gospel and down at the Elevation, without my saying a word to him. And don't tell me that Our Blessed Lord wasn't as pleased with Timmy as with them."

"I'm not telling you anything of the sort," he said, touched and amused. "All I am telling you is that now that your dog is dead, prayers can make no difference to him. Your dog couldn't incur guilt. Your prayers may make a difference to your husband because, like the rest of us, he did incur guilt in this life and may have to atone for it in the next."

"Ah, it's easy seen you didn't know Jim, Father. Poor Jim was innocent as a child. He never did anything wrong only taking the little sup of whiskey when I wouldn't be looking. I know he got a bit cranky when he had a drop in and I wouldn't give him any more, but sure that's a thing you wouldn't give a second thought to. . . . No, Father," she added thoughtfully, looking into the fire again, "I don't mind admitting that the first day or two after he died I wasn't easy in my mind at all. I didn't know what little thing he might have said or done on the side, unknown to me, or what little taste of punishment they might give him. I couldn't rest, thinking of him burning down there in Purgatory, with people he didn't know at all. A shy man, like that, and a man—I won't belie him—that would scream the house down if he as much as got a splinter in his nail. But then I realized that nobody in his right mind could be doing anything to him. Oh, no, Father, that's not why I get Masses said for Jim."

"Then why do you get them said for him?" Fogarty asked, though he knew the answer. His own big heart answered for him when his reason didn't.

"Sure, what other way have I of letting him know I'm thinking about him?" she asked with a childlike smile. "He's always in my mind, morning, noon, and night. And now Timmy is the same."

"And when I tell you that it makes no difference to Timmy—
that Timmy can't know he's in your mind?"

"Ah, well, Father, these things are great mysteries," she replied
comfortably, "and we don't know all about them yet. Oh, I know
there's a difference, and I'm not asking for anything impossible.
Only one small Mass, so that he'll know. But when I talk to people
about it, you'd think I was mad from the way they go on. They tell
me he has no soul, because he never committed sin. How does
anybody know he didn't commit sin? A little child doesn't commit
sin and he has a soul. No, Father," she went on with iron determination, "I know I'm old and I have no one to advise me, and my head
isn't as good as it was, but thank God I still have my wits about me.
Believe me, Father, a dog is no different from a child. When I was
feeling low coming on to Jim's anniversary, Timmy would know it.
He'd know it as if he could read what I was thinking, and he'd
come and put his head on my lap to show how sorry he was. And
when he was sick himself, he'd get into my bed and curl up beside
me, begging me with his eyes to make him better. Yes, indeed, and
when he was dying I felt the same way about him as I felt about
poor Jim—just the way you described it, thinking of all the times I
was hard on him when he didn't deserve it at all. That is the hardest
part of it, Father, when you have to try and forgive yourself."

"I'm sure you have very little to forgive yourself for, Ma'am,"
Fogarty said with a smile. "And God knows, if it was anything I
could do for you I'd do it, but this is something that, as a priest, I
can't do."

"And there's no one else I could go to? You don't think if I
went to the Bishop myself he'd let you do it?"

"I'm quite certain he wouldn't, Ma'am."

"Ah," she said bitterly as she raised herself heavily from her
chair, "if I was younger and smarter with my pen I'd write to the
Pope about it myself." She turned to the door, and Fogarty sprang to
open it for her, but the courtesy was lost on her. She looked at him
with deep mournful eyes that seemed to contain all the loneliness in
the world. "And it's wrong, Father, wrong," she said in a firm voice.

"I'm as good a Catholic as the next, but I'd say it to the Pope himself this minute if he walked into this room. They *have* souls, and people are only deluding themselves about it. Anything that can love has a soul. Show me that bad woman that thanked God her husband was dead and I'll show you someone that maybe hasn't a soul, but don't tell me that my Timmy hadn't one. And I know as I'm standing here that somewhere or other I'll see him again."

"I hope you do, Ma'am," he said, his big voice suddenly growing gentle and timorous. "And whenever you say a prayer for him, don't forget to add one for me."

"I will not indeed, Father," she said quietly. "I know you're a good man, and I'll remember you with the others that were good to me, and one of these days, with God's help, we'll all be together again."

An Act of Charity

THE PARISH PRIEST, Father Maginnis, did not like the second curate, Father Galvin, and Father Fogarty could see why. It was the dislike of the professional for the amateur, no matter how talented, and nobody could have said that Father Galvin had much in the way of talent. Maginnis was a professional to his fingertips. He drove the right car, knew the right people, and could suit his conversation to any company, even that of women. He even varied his accent to make people feel at home. With Deasy, the owner of the garage, he talked about "the caw," but to Lavin, the garage hand, he said "the cyarr," smiling benignly at the homeliness of his touch.

Galvin was thin, pale, irritable, and intense. When he should have kept a straight face he made some stupid joke that stopped the conversation dead; and when he laughed in the proper place at someone else's joke, it was with a slight air of vexation, as though he found it hard to put up with people who made him laugh at all. He worried himself over little embarrassments and what people would think of them, till Fogarty asked bluntly, "What the hell difference does it make what they think?" Then Galvin looked away sadly and said, "I suppose you're right." But Fogarty didn't mind his visits so much except when he had asked other curates in for a drink and a game of cards. Then he took a glass of sherry or something equally harmless and twiddled it awkwardly for half an hour as though it were some sort of patent device for keeping his hands occupied. When one of the curates made a harmless dirty joke, Galvin pretended to be looking at a picture so that he didn't have to comment. Fogarty, who loved giving people nicknames, called him Father Mother's Boy. He called Maginnis the Old Pro, but when that nickname got back, as everything a priest says gets back, it did Fogarty no harm at all. Maginnis was glad he had a curate with so much sense.

He sometimes asked Fogarty to Sunday dinner, but he soon gave up on asking Galvin, and again Fogarty sympathized with him. Maginnis was a professional, even to his dinners. He basted his meat with one sort of wine and his chickens with another, and he liked a guest who could tell the difference. He also liked him to drink two large whiskeys before dinner and to make sensible remarks about the wine; and when he had exhausted the secrets of his kitchen he sat back, smoked his cigar, and told funny stories. They were very good stories, mostly about priests.

"Did I ever tell you the one about Canon Murphy, Father?" he would bellow, his fat face beaming. "Ah, that's damn good. Canon Murphy went on a pilgrimage to Rome, and when he came back he preached a sermon on it. 'So I had a special audience with His Holiness, dearly beloved brethren, and he asked me, "Canon Murphy, where are you now?" "I'm in Dromod, Your Holiness," said I. "What sort of a parish is it, Canon Murphy?" says he. "Ah, 'tis a nice, snug little parish, Your Holiness," says I. "Are they a good class of people?" says he. "Well, they're not bad, Your Holiness," said I. "Are they good-living people?" says he. "Well, they're as good as the next, Your Holiness," says I. "Except when they'd have a drop taken." "Tell me, Canon Murphy," says he, "do they pay their dues?" And like that, I was nearly struck dumb. "There you have me, Your Holiness!" says I. "There you have me!"'"

At heart Fogarty thought Maginnis was a bit of a sham and that most of his stories were fabrications; but he never made the mistake of underestimating him, and he enjoyed the feeling Maginnis gave him of belonging to a group, and that of the best kind—well balanced, humane, and necessary.

At meals in the curates' house, Galvin had a tendency to chatter brightly and aimlessly that irritated Fogarty. He was full of scraps of undigested knowledge, picked up from newspapers and magazines, about new plays and books that he would never either see or read. Fogarty was a moody young man who preferred either to keep silent or engage in long emotional discussions about local scandals that grew murkier and more romantic the more he described them. About such things he was hopelessly indiscreet. "And that fellow notoriously killed his own father," he said once, and Galvin looked at him in distress. "You mean he really killed him?" he asked—as though Fogarty did not really mean everything at the moment he was saying it—and then, to make things worse, added, "It's not something I'd care to repeat—not without evidence, I mean."

"The Romans used eunuchs for civil servants, but we're more enlightened," Fogarty said once to Maginnis. "We prefer the natural ones." Maginnis gave a hearty laugh; it was the sort of remark he liked to repeat. And when Galvin returned after lunching austerely with some maiden ladies and offered half-baked suggestions, Maginnis crushed him, and Fogarty watched with malicious amusement. He knew it was turning into persecution, but he wasn't quite sure which of the two men suffered more.

When he heard the explosion in the middle of the night, he waited for some further noise to interpret it, and then rose and put on the light. The housekeeper was standing outside her bedroom door in a raincoat, her hands joined. She was a widow woman with a history of tragedy behind her, and Fogarty did not like her; for some reason he felt she had the evil eye, and he always addressed her in his most commanding tone.

"What was that, Mary?" he asked.

"I don't know, Father," she said in a whisper. "It sounded as if it was in Father Galvin's room."

Fogarty listened again. There was no sound from Galvin's room, and he knocked and pushed in the door. He closed the door again immediately.

"Get Dr. Carmody quick!" he said brusquely.

"What is it, Father?" she asked. "An accident?"

"Yes, a bad one. And when you're finished, run out and ask Father Maginnis to come in."

"Oh, that old gun!" she moaned softly. "I dreaded it. I'll ring Dr. Carmody." She went hastily down the stairs.

Fogarty followed her and went into the living room to pick up the sacred oils from the cupboard where they were kept. "I don't know, Doctor," he heard Mary moaning. "Father Fogarty said it was an accident." He returned upstairs and lifted the gun from the bed before anointing the dead man. He had just concluded when the door opened and he saw the parish priest come in, wearing a blue flowered dressing gown.

Maginnis went over to the bed and stared down at the figure on it. Then he looked at Fogarty over his glasses, his face almost expressionless. "I was afraid of something like this," he said knowingly. "I knew he was a bit unstable."

"You don't think it could be an accident?" Fogarty asked, though he knew the question sounded ridiculous.

"No," Maginnis said, giving him a downward look through the spectacles. "Do you?"

"But how could he bring himself to do a thing like that?" Fogarty asked incredulously.

"Oh, who knows?" said Maginnis, almost impatiently. "With weak characters it's hard to tell. He doesn't seem to have left any message."

"Not that I can see."

"I'm sorry 'twas Carmody you sent for."

"But he was Galvin's doctor."

"I know, I know, but all the same he's young and a bit immature. I'd have preferred an older man. Make no mistake about it, Father, we have a problem on our hands," he added with sudden resolution. "A very serious problem."

Fogarty did not need to have the problem spelled out for him. The worst thing a priest could do was to commit suicide, since it seemed to deny everything that gave his vocation meaning—Divine Providence and Mercy, forgiveness, Heaven, Hell. That one of God's anointed could come to such a state of despair was something the Church could not admit. It would give too much scandal. It was simply an unacceptable act.

"That's his car now, I fancy," Maginnis said.

Carmody came quickly up the stairs with his bag in his hand and his pink pajamas showing under his tweed jacket. He was a tall, spectacled young man with a long, humorous clown's face, and in ordinary life adopted a manner that went with his face, but Fogarty knew he was both competent and conscientious. He had worked for some years in an English hospital and developed a bluntness of speech that Fogarty found refreshing.

"Christ!" he said as he took in the scene. Then he went over and looked closely at the body. "Poor Peter!" he added. Then he took the shotgun from the bedside table where Fogarty had put it and examined it. "I should have kept a closer eye on him," he said with chagrin. "There isn't much I can do for him now."

"On the contrary, Doctor," Maginnis said. "There was never a time when you could do more for him." Then he gave Fogarty a meaningful glance. "I wonder if you'd mind getting Jack Fitzgerald for me, Father? Talk to himself, and I needn't warn you to be careful what you say."

"Oh, I'll be careful," Fogarty said with gloomy determination. There was something in his nature that always responded to the touch of melodrama, and he knew Maginnis wanted to talk to Carmody alone. He telephoned to Fitzgerald, the undertaker, and then went back upstairs to dress. It was clear he wasn't going to get any more sleep that night.

He heard himself called and returned to Galvin's room. This time he really felt the full shock of it: the big bald parish priest in his dressing gown and the gaunt young doctor with his pajama top open under the jacket. He could see the two men had been arguing.

"Perhaps you'd talk to Dr. Carmody, Father?" Maginnis suggested benignly.

"There's nothing to talk about, Father Fogarty," Carmody said, adopting the formal title he ignored when they were among friends. "I can't sign a certificate saying this was a natural death. You know I can't. It's too unprofessional."

"Professional or not, Dr. Carmody, someone will have to do it," Maginnis said. "I am the priest of this parish. In a manner of speaking I'm a professional man too, you know. And this unfortunate occurrence is something that doesn't concern only me and you. It has consequences that affect the whole parish."

"Your profession doesn't require you to sign your name to a lie, Father," Carmody said angrily. "That's what you want me to do."

"Oh, I wouldn't call that a lie, Dr. Carmody," Maginnis said with dignity. "In considering the nature of a lie we have to take account of its good and bad effects. I can see no possible good effect that might result from a scandal about the death of this poor boy. Not one! In fact, I can see unlimited harm."

"So can I," Fogarty burst out. His voice sounded too loud, too confident, even to his own ears.

"I see," Carmody said sarcastically. "And you think we should keep on denouncing the Swedes and Danes for their suicide statistics, just because they don't fake them the way we do. Ah, for God's sake, man, I'd never be able to respect myself again."

Fogarty saw that Maginnis was right. In some ways Carmody was too immature. "That's all very well, Jim, but Christian charity comes before statistics," he said appealingly. "Forget about the damn statistics, can't you? Father Galvin wasn't only a statistic. He was a human being—somebody we both knew. And what about his family?"

"What about his mother?" Maginnis asked with real pathos. "I gather you have a mother yourself, Dr. Carmody?"

"And you expect me to meet Mrs. Galvin tomorrow and tell her her son was a suicide and can't be buried in consecrated ground?" Fogarty went on emotionally. "Would you like us to do that to your mother if it was your case?"

"A doctor has unpleasant things to do as well, Jerry," said Carmody.

"To tell a mother that her child is dying?" Fogarty asked. "A priest has to do that too, remember. Not to tell her that her child is damned."

But the very word that Fogarty knew had impressed Carmody made the parish priest uncomfortable. "Fortunately, Father, that is in better hands than yours or mine," he said curtly. And at once his manner changed. It was as though he was a little bit tired of them both. "Dr. Carmody," he said, "I think I hear Mr. Fitzgerald. You'd better make up your mind quick. If you're not prepared to sign the death certificate, I'll soon find another doctor who will. That is my simple duty, and I'm going to do it. But as an elderly man who knows a little more about this town than you or Father Fogarty here, I'd advise you not to compel me to bring in another doctor. If word got round that I was forced to do such a thing, it might have very serious effects on your career."

There was no mistaking the threat, and there was something almost admirable about the way it was made. At the same time, it roused the sleeping rebel in Fogarty. Bluff, he thought angrily. Damn bluff! If Carmody walked out on them at that moment, there was very little the parish priest or anyone else could do to him. Of course, any of the other doctors would sign the certificate, but it wouldn't do them any good either. When people really felt the need for a doctor, they didn't necessarily want the doctor the parish priest approved of. But as he looked at Carmody's sullen, resentful face, he realized that Carmody didn't know his own strength in the way that Maginnis knew his. After all, what had he behind him but a few years in a London hospital, while behind Maginnis was that whole vast, historic organization that he was rightly so proud of.

"I can't sign a certificate that death was due to natural causes," Carmody said stubbornly. "Accident, maybe—I don't know. I wasn't here. I'll agree to accident."

"Accident?" Maginnis said contemptuously, and this time he did not even trouble to use Carmody's title. It was as though he were stripping him of any little dignity he had. "Young man, accidents with shotguns do not happen to priests at three o'clock in the morning. Try to talk sense!"

And just as Fogarty realized that the doctor had allowed himself to be crushed, they heard Mary let Fitzgerald in. He came briskly up the stairs. He was a small, spare man, built like a jockey. The parish priest nodded in the direction of the bed and Fitzgerald's brows went up mechanically. He was a man who said little, but he had a face and figure too expressive for his character. It was as though all the opinions he suppressed in life found relief in violent physical movements.

"Naturally, we don't want it talked about, Mr. Fitzgerald," said Maginnis. "Do you think you could handle it yourself?"

The undertaker's eyes popped again, and he glanced swiftly from Maginnis to Carmody and then to Fogarty. He was a great man for efficiency, though; if you had asked him to supply the corpse as well as the coffin, he might have responded automatically, "Male or female?"

"Dr. Carmody will give the certificate, of course?" he asked shrewdly. He hadn't missed much of what was going on.

"It seems I don't have much choice," Carmody replied bitterly.

"Oh, purely as an act of charity, of course," Fitz said hastily. "We all have to do this sort of thing from time to time. The poor relatives have enough to worry them without inquests and things like that. What was the age, Father Maginnis, do you know?" he added, taking out a notebook. A clever little man, thought Fogarty. He had put it all at once upon a normal, businesslike footing.

"Twenty-eight," said Maginnis.

"God help us!" Fitz said perfunctorily, and made a note. After that he took out a rule.

"I'd better get ready and go to see the Bishop myself," Maginnis said. "We'll need his permission, of course, but I haven't much doubt about that. I know he has the reputation for being on the strict side, but I always found him very considerate. I'll send Nora over to help your housekeeper, Father. In the meantime, maybe you'd be good enough to get in touch with the family."

"I'll see to that, Father," Fogarty said. He and Carmody followed Maginnis downstairs. He said goodbye and left, and Fogarty's manner changed abruptly. "Come in and have a drink, Jim," he said.

"I'd rather not, Jerry," Carmody said gloomily.

"Come on! Come on! You need one, man! I need one myself and I can't have it." He shut the door of the living room behind him. "Great God, Jim, who could have suspected it?"

"I suppose I should have," said Carmody. "I got hints enough if only I might have understood them."

"But you couldn't, Jim," Fogarty said excitedly, taking the whiskey from the big cupboard. "Nobody could. Do you think I ever expected it, and I lived closer to him than you did."

The front door opened and they heard the slippers of Nora, Maginnis's housekeeper, in the hall. There was a low mumble of talk outside the door, and then the clank of a bucket as the women went up the stairs. Fitzgerald was coming down at the same time, and Fogarty opened the door a little.

"Well, Jack?"

"Well, Father. I'll do the best I can."

"You wouldn't join us for a—?"

"No, Father. I'll have my hands full for the next couple of hours."

"Good night, Jack. And I'm sorry for the disturbance."

"Ah, 'twas none of your doing. Good night, Father."

The Doctor finished his whiskey in a gulp, and his long, battered face had a bitter smile. "And so this is how it's done!" he said.

"This is how it's done, Jim, and believe me, it's the best way for everybody in the long run," Fogarty replied with real gravity.

But, looking at Carmody's face, he knew the Doctor did not believe it, and he wondered then if he really believed it himself.

When the Doctor had gone, Fogarty got on the telephone to a provincial town fifty miles away. The exchange was closed down, so he had to give his message to the police. In ten minutes or so a guard would set out along the sleeping streets to the house where the Galvins lived. That was one responsibility he was glad to evade.

While he was speaking, he heard the parish priest's car set off and knew he was on his way to the Bishop's palace. Then he shaved, and, about eight, Fitzgerald drove up with the coffin in his van. Silently they carried it between them up the stairs. The body was lying decently composed with a simple bandage about the head. Between them they lifted it into the coffin. Fitzgerald looked questioningly at Fogarty and went on his knees. As he said the brief prayer, Fogarty found his voice unsteady and his eyes full of tears. Fitzgerald gave him a pitying look and then rose and dusted his knees.

"All the same there'll be talk, Father," he said.

"Maybe not as much as there should be, Jack," Fogarty said moodily.

"We'll take him to the chapel, of course?" Fitzgerald went on.

"Everything in order, Jack. Father Maginnis is gone to see the Bishop."

"He couldn't trust the telephone, of course," Fitzgerald said, stroking his unshaven chin. "No fear the Bishop will interfere, though. Father Maginnis is a smart man. You saw him?"

"I saw him."

"No nerves, no hysterics. I saw other people in the same situation. 'Oh, Mr. Fitzgerald, what am I going to do?' His mind on essential things the whole time. He's an object lesson to us all, Father."

"You're right, Jack, he is," Fogarty said despondently.

Suddenly the undertaker's hand shot out and caught him by the upper arm. "Forget about it, boy! Forget about it! What else can you do? Why the hell should you break your heart over it?"

Fogarty still had to meet the family. Later that morning, they drove up to the curates' house. The mother was an actress type and wept a good deal. She wanted somebody to give her a last message, which Fogarty couldn't think up. The sister, a pretty, intense girl, wept a little too, but quietly, with her back turned, while the brother, a young man with a great resemblance to Galvin, said little. Mother and brother accepted without protest the ruling that the coffin was not to be opened, but the sister looked at Fogarty and asked, "You don't think I could see him? Alone? I wouldn't be afraid." When he said the doctor had forbidden it, she turned her back again, and he had an impression that there was a closer link between her and Galvin than between the others and him.

That evening, they brought the body to lie before the altar of the church, and Maginnis received it and said the prayers. The church was crowded, and Fogarty knew with a strange mixture of rejoicing and mortification that the worst was over. Maginnis' master stroke was the new curate, Rowlands, who had arrived within a couple of hours after his own return. He was a tall, thin, ascetic-looking young man, slow-moving and slow-speaking, and Fogarty knew that all eyes were on him.

Everything went with perfect propriety at the Requiem Mass next morning, and after the funeral Fogarty attended the lunch given by Maginnis to the visiting clergy. He almost laughed out loud when he heard Maginnis ask in a low voice, "Father Healy, did I ever tell you the story of Canon Murphy and the Pope?" All that would follow would be the mourning card with the picture of Galvin and the Gothic lettering that said *"Ecce Sacerdos Magnus."* There was no danger of a scandal any longer. Carmody would not talk. Fitzgerald would not talk either. None of the five people involved would. Father Galvin might have spared himself the trouble.

As they returned from the church together, Fogarty tried to talk to the new curate about what had happened, but he soon realized that the whole significance of it had escaped Rowlands, and that Rowlands thought he was only overdramatizing it all. Anybody would think he was overdramatizing it, except Carmody. After his supper he would go to the Doctor's house, and they would talk about it. Only Carmody would really understand what it was they had done between them. No one else would.

What lonely lives we live, he thought unhappily.

The Mass Island

WHEN FATHER JACKSON drove up to the curates' house, it was already drawing on to dusk, the early dusk of late December. The curates' house was a red-brick building on a terrace at one side of the ugly church in Asragh. Father Hamilton seemed to have been waiting for him and opened the front door himself, looking white and strained. He was a tall young man wth a long, melancholy face that you would have taken for weak till you noticed the cut of the jaw.

"Oh, come in, Jim," he said with his mournful smile. " 'Tisn't much of a welcome we have for you, God knows. I suppose you'd like to see poor Jerry before the undertaker comes."

"I might as well," Father Jackson replied briskly. There was nothing melancholy about Jackson, but he affected an air of surprise and shock. " 'Twas very sudden, wasn't it?"

"Well, it was and it wasn't, Jim," Father Hamilton said, closing the front door behind him. "He was going downhill since he got the first heart attack, and he wouldn't look after himself. Sure, you know yourself what he was like."

Jackson knew. Father Fogarty and himself had been friends of a sort, for years. An impractical man, excitable and vehement, Fogarty could have lived for twenty years with his ailment, but instead of that, he allowed himself to become depressed and indifferent. If he couldn't live as he had always lived, he would prefer not to live at all.

They went upstairs and into the bedroom where he was. The character was still plain on the stern, dead face, though, drained of vitality, it had the look of a studio portrait. That bone structure was something you'd have picked out of a thousand faces as Irish, with its odd impression of bluntness and asymmetry, its jutting brows and craggy chin, and the snub nose that looked as though it had probably been broken twenty years before in a public-house row.

When they came downstairs again, Father Hamilton produced half a bottle of whiskey.

"Not for me, thanks," Jackson said hastily. "Unless you have a drop of sherry there?"

"Well, there is some Burgundy," Father Hamilton said. "I don't know is it any good, though."

" 'Twill do me fine," Jackson replied cheerfully, reflecting that Ireland was the country where nobody knew whether Burgundy was good or not. "You're coming with us tomorrow, I suppose?"

"Well, the way it is, Jim," Father Hamilton replied, "I'm afraid neither of us is going. You see, they're burying poor Jerry here."

"They're what?" Jackson asked incredulously.

"Now, I didn't know for sure when I rang you, Jim, but that's what the brother decided, and that's what Father Hanafey decided as well."

"But he told you he wanted to be buried on the Mass Island, didn't he?"

"He told everybody, Jim," Father Hamilton replied with growing excitement and emotion. "That was the sort he was. If he told one, he told five hundred. Only a half an hour ago I had a girl on the telephone from the Island, asking when they could expect us. You see, the old parish priest of the place let Jerry mark out the grave for himself, and they want to know should they open it. But now the old parish priest is dead as well, and, of course, Jerry left nothing in writing."

"Didn't he leave a will, even?" Jackson asked in surprise.

"Well, he did and he didn't, Jim," Father Hamilton said, looking as if he were on the point of tears. "Actually, he did make a will about five or six years ago, and he gave it to Clancy, the other curate, but Clancy went off on the Foreign Mission and God alone knows where he is now. After that, Jerry never bothered his head about it. I mean, you have to admit the man had nothing to leave. Every damn thing he had he gave away—even the old car, after he got the first attack. If there was any loose cash around, I suppose the brother has that."

Jackson sipped his Burgundy, which was even more Australian than he had feared, and wondered at his own irritation. He had been irritated enough before that, with the prospect of two days' motoring in the middle of winter, and a night in a godforsaken pub in the mountains, a hundred and fifty miles away at the other side of Ireland. There, in one of the lakes, was an island where in Cromwell's time, before the causeway and the little oratory were built, Mass was said in secret, and it was here that Father Fogarty had wanted to be buried. It struck Jackson as sheer sentimentality; it wasn't even as if it was Fogarty's native place. Jackson had once allowed Fogarty to lure him there, and had hated every moment of it. It wasn't only the discomfort of the public house, where meals erupted at any hour of the day or night as the spirit took the proprietor, or the rain that kept them confined to the cold dining-and-sitting room that looked out on the gloomy mountainside, with its couple of whitewashed cabins on the shore of the lake. It was the overintimacy of it all, and this was the thing that Father Fogarty apparently loved. He liked to stand in his shirtsleeves behind the bar, taking turns with the proprietor, who was one of his many friends, serving big pints of porter to rough mountainy men, or to sit in their cottages, shaking in all his fat whenever they told broad stories or sang risky folk songs. "God, Jim, isn't it grand?" he would say in his deep voice, and Jackson would look at him over his spectacles with what Fogarty called his "jesuitical look," and say, "Well, I suppose it all depends on what you really like, Jerry." He wasn't even certain that the locals cared for Father Fogarty's intimacy; on the contrary, he had a strong impression that they much preferred their own reserved old parish priest, whom they never saw except twice a year, when he came up the valley to collect his dues. That had made Jackson twice as stiff. And yet now when he found out that the plans that had meant so much inconvenience to him had fallen through, he was as disappointed as though they had been his own.

"Oh, well," he said with a shrug that was intended to conceal his perturbation, "I suppose it doesn't make much difference where they chuck us when our time comes."

"The point is, it mattered to Jerry, Jim," Father Hamilton said with his curious shy obstinacy. "God knows, it's not anything that will ever worry me, but it haunted him, and somehow, you know, I don't feel it's right to flout a dead man's wishes."

"Oh, I know, I know," Jackson said lightly. "I suppose I'd better talk to old Hanafey about it. Knowing I'm a friend of the Bishop's, he might pay more attention to me."

"He might, Jim," Father Hamilton replied sadly, looking away over Jackson's head. "As you say, knowing you're a friend of the Bishop's, he might. But I wouldn't depend too much on it. I talked to him till I was black in the face, and all I got out of him was the law and the rubrics. It's the brother Hanafey is afraid of. You'll see him this evening, and, between ourselves, he's a tough customer. Of course, himself and Jerry never had much to say to one another, and he'd be the last man in the world that Jerry would talk to about his funeral, so now he doesn't want the expense and inconvenience. You wouldn't blame him, of course. I'd probably be the same myself. By the way," Father Hamilton added, lowering his voice, "before he does come, I'd like you to take a look round Jerry's room and see is there any little memento you'd care to have—a photo or a book or anything."

They went into Father Fogarty's sitting room, and Jackson looked at it with a new interest. He knew of old the rather hand-some library—Fogarty had been a man of many enthusiasms, though none of long duration—the picture of the Virgin and Child in Irish country costume over the mantelpiece, which some of his colleagues had thought irreverent, and the couple of fine old prints.

There was a newer picture that Jackson had not seen—a charcoal drawing of the Crucifixion from a fifteenth-century Irish tomb, which was brutal but impressive.

"Good Lord!" Jackson exclaimed with a sudden feeling of loss. "He really had taste, hadn't he?"

"He had, Jim," Father Hamilton said, sticking his long nose into the picture. "This goes to a young couple called Keneally, outside the town, that he was fond of. I think they were very kind to him. Since he had the attack, he was pretty lonely, I'd say."

"Oh, aren't we all, attack or no attack," Jackson said almost irritably.

Father Hanafey, the parish priest of Asragh, was a round, red, cherubic-looking old man with a bald head and big round glasses. His house was on the same terrace as the curates'. He, too, insisted on producing the whiskey Jackson so heartily detested, when the two priests came in to consult him, but Jackson had decided that this time diplomacy required he should show proper appreciation of the dreadful stuff. He felt sure he was going to be very sick next day. He affected great astonishment at the quality of Father Hanafey's whiskey, and first the old parish priest grew shy, like a schoolgirl whose good looks are being praised, then he looked self-satisfied, and finally he became almost emotional. It was a great pleasure, he said, to meet a young priest with a proper understanding of whiskey. Priests no longer seemed to have the same taste, and as far as most of them were concerned, they might as well be drinking poteen. It was only when it was seven years old that Irish began to be interesting, and that was when you had to catch it and store it in sherry casks to draw off what remained of crude alcohol in it, and give it that beautiful roundness that Father Jackson had spotted. But it shouldn't be kept too long, for somewhere along the line the spirit of a whiskey was broken. At ten, or maybe twelve, years old it was just right. But people were losing their palates. He solemnly assured the two priests that of every dozen clerics who came to his house not more than one would realize what he was drinking. Poor Hamilton grew red and began to stutter, but the parish priest's reproofs were not directed at him.

"It isn't you I'm talking about, Father Hamilton, but elderly priests, parish priests, and even canons, that you would think would know better, and I give you my word, I put the two whiskeys side by side in front of them, the shop stuff and my own, and they could not tell the difference."

But though the priest was mollified by Father Jackson's maturity of judgment, he was not prepared to interfere in the arrangements for the funeral of his curate. "It is the wish of the next of kin, Father," he said stubbornly, "and that is something I have no control over. Now that you tell me the same thing as Father Hamilton, I accept it that this was Father Fogarty's wish, and a man's wishes regarding his own interment are always to be respected. I assure you, if I had even one line in Father Fogarty's writing to go on, I would wait for no man's advice. I would take the responsibility on myself. Something on paper, Father, is all I want."

"On the other hand, Father," Jackson said mildly, drawing on his pipe, "if Father Fogarty was the sort to leave written instructions, he'd hardly be the sort to leave such unusual ones. I mean, after all, it isn't even the family burying ground, is it?"

"Well, now, that is true, Father," replied the parish priest, and it was clear that he had been deeply impressed by this rather doubtful logic. "You have a very good point there, and it is one I did not think of myself, and I have given the matter a great deal of thought. You might mention it to his brother. Father Fogarty, God rest him, was *not* a usual type of man. I think you might even go so far as to say that he was a rather *unusual* type of man, and not orderly, as you say—not by any means orderly. I would certainly mention that to the brother and see what he says."

But the brother was not at all impressed by Father Jackson's argument when he turned up at the church in Asragh that evening. He was a good-looking man with a weak and pleasant face and a cold shrewdness in his eyes that had been lacking in his brother's.

"But why, Father?" he asked, turning to Father Hanafey. "I'm a busy man, and I'm being asked to leave my business for a couple of days in the middle of winter, and for what? That is all I ask. What use is it?"

"It is only out of respect for the wishes of the deceased, Mr. Fogarty," said Father Hanafey, who clearly was a little bit afraid of him.

"And where did he express those wishes?" the brother asked. "I'm his only living relative, and it is queer he would not mention a thing like that to me."

"He mentioned it to Father Jackson and Father Hamilton."

"But when, Father?" Mr. Fogarty asked. "You knew Father Jerry, and he was always expressing wishes about something. He was an excitable sort of man, God rest him, and the thing he'd say today might not be the thing he'd say tomorrow. After all, after close on forty years, I think I have the right to say I knew him," he added with a triumphant air that left the two young priests without a leg to stand on.

Over bacon and eggs in the curates' house, Father Hamilton was very despondent. "Well, I suppose we did what we could, Jim," he said.

"I'm not too sure of that," Jackson said with his "jesuitical air," looking at Father Hamilton sidewise over his spectacles. "I'm wondering if we couldn't do something with that family you say he intended the drawing for."

"The Keneallys," said Father Hamilton in a worried voice. "Actually, I saw the wife in the church this evening. You might have noticed her crying."

"Don't you think we should see if they have anything in writing?"

"Well, if they have, it would be about the picture," said Father

Hamilton. "How I know about it is she came to me at the time to ask if I couldn't do something for him. Poor man, he was crying himself that day, according to what she told me."

"Oh dear!" Jackson said politely, but his mind was elsewhere. "I'm not really interested in knowing what would be in a letter like that. It's none of my business. But I would like to make sure that they haven't something in writing. What did Hanafey call it— 'something on paper'?"

"I daresay we should inquire, anyway," said Father Hamilton, and after supper they drove out to the Keneallys', a typical small red-brick villa with a decent garden in front. The family also was eating bacon and eggs, and Jackson shuddered when they asked him to join them. Keneally himself, a tall, gaunt, cadaverous man, poured out more whiskey for them, and again Jackson felt he must make a formal attempt to drink it. At the same time, he thought he saw what attraction the house had for Father Fogarty. Keneally was tough and with no suggestion of lay servility toward the priesthood, and his wife was beautiful and scatterbrained, and talked to herself, the cat, and the children simultaneously. "Rosaleen!" she cried determinedly. "Out! Out I say! I told you if you didn't stop meowing you'd have to go out. . . . Angela Keneally, the stick! . . . You do not want to go to the bathroom, Angela. It's only five minutes since you were there before. I will not let Father Hamilton come up to you at all unless you go to bed at once."

In the children's bedroom, Jackson gave a finger to a stolid-looking infant, who instantly stuffed it into his mouth and began to chew it, apparently under the impression that he would be bound to reach sugar at last.

Later, they sat over their drinks in the sitting room, only interrupted by Angela Keneally, in a fever of curiosity, dropping in every five minutes to ask for a biscuit or a glass of water.

"You see, Father Fogarty left no will," Jackson explained to Keneally. "Consequently, he'll be buried here tomorrow unless something turns up. I suppose he told you where he wanted to be buried?"

"On the Island? Twenty times, if he told us once. I thought he took it too far. Didn't you, Father?"

"And me not to be able to go!" Mrs. Keneally said, beginning to cry. "Isn't it awful, Father?"

"He didn't leave anything in writing with you?" He saw in Keneally's eyes that the letter was really only about the picture, and raised a warning hand. "Mind, if he did, I don't want to know what's in it! In fact, it would be highly improper for anyone to be told before the parish priest and the next of kin were consulted. All I do want to know is whether"—he waited a moment to see that Keneally was following him—"he did leave any written instructions, of any kind, with you."

Mrs. Keneally, drying her tears, suddenly broke into rapid speech. "Sure, that was the day poor Father Jerry was so down in himself because we were his friends and he had nothing to leave us, and—"

"Shut up, woman!" her husband shouted with a glare at her, and then Jackson saw him purse his lips in quiet amusement. He was a man after Jackson's heart. "As you say, Father, we have a letter from him."

"Addressed to anybody in particular?"

"Yes, to the parish priest, to be delivered after his death."

"Did he use those words?" Jackson asked, touched in spite of himself.

"Those very words."

"God help us!" said Father Hamilton.

"But you had not time to deliver it?"

"I only heard of Father Fogarty's death when I got in. Esther was at the church, of course."

"And you're a bit tired, so you wouldn't want to walk all the way over to the presbytery with it. I take it that, in the normal way, you'd post it."

"But the post would be gone," Keneally said with a secret smile. "So that Father Hanafey wouldn't get it until maybe the day after tomorrow. That's what you were afraid of, Father, isn't it?"

"I see we understand one another, Mr. Keneally," Jackson said politely.

"You wouldn't, of course, wish to say anything that wasn't strictly true," said Keneally, who was clearly enjoying himself enormously, though his wife had not the faintest idea of what was afoot. "So perhaps it would be better if the letter was posted now, and not after you leave the house."

"Fine!" said Jackson, and Keneally nodded and went out. When he returned, a few minutes later, the priests rose to go.

"I'll see you at the Mass tomorrow," Keneally said. "Good luck, now."

Jackson felt they'd probably need it. But when Father Hanafey met them in the hall, with the wet snow falling outside, and they explained about the letter, his mood had clearly changed. Jackson's logic might have worked some sort of spell on him, or perhaps it was just that he felt they were three clergymen opposed to a layman.

"It was very unforeseen of Mr. Keneally not to have brought that letter to me at once," he grumbled, "but I must say I was expecting something of the sort. It would have been very peculiar if Father Fogarty had left no instructions at all for me, and I see that we can't just sit round and wait to find out what they were, since the burial is tomorrow. Under the circumstances, Father, I think we'd be justified in arranging for the funeral according to Father Fogarty's known wishes."

"Thanks be to God," Father Hamilton murmured as he and Father Jackson returned to the curates' house. "I never thought we'd get away with that."

"We haven't got away with it yet," said Jackson. "And even if we do get away with it, the real trouble will be later."

All the arrangements had still to be made. When Mr. Fogarty was informed, he slammed down the receiver without comment. Then a phone call had to be made to a police station twelve miles from the Island, and the police sergeant promised to send a man out on a bicycle to have the grave opened. Then the local parish priest and several old friends had to be informed, and a notice inserted in the nearest daily. As Jackson said wearily, romantic men always left their more worldly friends to carry out their romantic intentions.

The scene at the curates' house next morning after Mass scared even Jackson. While the hearse and the funeral car waited in front of the door, Mr. Fogarty sat, white with anger, and let the priests talk. To Jackson's surprise, Father Hanafey put up a stern fight for Father Fogarty's wishes.

"You have to realize, Mr. Fogarty, that to a priest like your brother the Mass is a very solemn thing indeed, and a place where the poor people had to fly in the Penal Days to hear Mass would be one of particular sanctity."

"Father Hanafey," said Mr. Fogarty in a cold, even tone, "I am a simple businessman, and I have no time for sentiment."

"I would not go so far as to call the veneration for sanctified ground mere sentiment, Mr. Fogarty," the old priest said severely. "At any rate, it is now clear that Father Fogarty left instructions to be delivered to me after his death, and if those instructions are what we think them, I would have a serious responsibility for not having paid attention to them."

"I do not think that letter is anything of the kind, Father Hanafey," said Mr. Fogarty. "That's a matter I'm going to inquire into when I get back, and if it turns out to be a hoax, I am going to take it further."

"Oh, Mr. Fogarty. I'm sure it's not a hoax," said the parish priest, with a shocked air, but Mr. Fogarty was not convinced.

"For everybody's sake, we'll hope not," he said grimly.

The funeral procession set off. Mr. Fogarty sat in the front of the car by the driver, sulking. Jackson and Hamilton sat behind and opened their breviaries. When they stopped at a hotel for lunch, Mr. Fogarty said he was not hungry, and stayed outside in the cold. And when he did get hungry and came into the dining room, the priests drifted into the lounge to wait for him. They both realized that he might prove a dangerous enemy.

Then, as they drove on in the dusk, they saw the mountain country ahead of them in a cold, watery light, a light that seemed to fall dead from the ragged edge of a cloud. The towns and villages they passed through were dirtier and more derelict. They drew up at a crossroads, behind the hearse, and heard someone talking to the driver of the hearse. Then a car fell into line behind them. "Someone joining us," Father Hamilton said, but Mr. Fogarty, lost in his own dream of martyrdom, did not reply. Half a dozen times within the next twenty minutes, the same thing happened, though sometimes the cars were waiting in lanes and byroads with their lights on, and each time Jackson saw a heavily coated figure standing in the roadway shouting to the hearse driver: "Is it Father Fogarty ye have there?" At last they came to a village where the local parish priest's car was waiting outside the church, with a little group about it. Their headlights caught a public house, isolated at the other side of the street, glaring with whitewash, while about it was the vague space of a distant mountainside.

Suddenly Mr. Fogarty spoke. "He seems to have been fairly well known," he said with something approaching politeness.

The road went on, with a noisy stream at the right-hand side of it falling from group to group of rocks. They left it for a byroad, which bent to the right, heading toward the stream, and then began to mount, broken by ledges of naked rock, over which hearse and cars seemed to heave themselves like animals. On the left-hand side of the road was a little whitewashed cottage, all lit up, with a big turf fire burning in the open hearth and an oil lamp with an orange glow on the wall above it. There was a man standing by the door, and as they approached he began to pick his way over the rocks toward them, carrying a lantern. Only then did Jackson notice the other lanterns and flashlights, coming down the mountain or crossing the stream, and realize that they represented people, young men and girls and an occasional sturdy old man, all moving in the direction of the Mass Island. Suddenly it hit him, almost like a blow. He told himself not to be a fool, that this was no more than the desire for novelty one should expect to find in out-of-the-way places, mixed perhaps with vanity. It was all that, of course, and he knew it, but he knew, too, it was something more. He had thought when he was here with Fogarty that those people had not respected Fogarty as they respected him and the local parish priest, but he knew that for him, or even for their own parish priest, they would never turn out in midwinter, across the treacherous mountain bogs and wicked rocks. He and the parish priest would never earn more from the people of the mountains than respect; what they gave to the fat, unclerical young man who had served them with pints in the bar and egged them on to tell their old stories and bullied and ragged and even fought them was something infinitely greater.

The funeral procession stopped in a lane that ran along the edge of a lake. The surface of the lake was rough, and they could hear the splash of the water upon the stones. The two priests got out of the car and began to vest themselves, and then Mr. Fogarty got out, too. He was very nervous and hesitant.

"It's very inconvenient, and all the rest of it," he said, "but I don't want you gentlemen to think that I didn't know you were acting from the best motives."

"That's very kind of you, Mr. Fogarty," Jackson said. "Maybe we made mistakes as well."

"Thank you, Father Jackson," Mr. Fogarty said, and held out his hand. The two priests shook hands with him and he went off, raising his hat.

"Well, that's one trouble over," Father Hamilton said wryly as an old man plunged through the mud toward the car.

"Lights is what we're looking for!" he shouted. "Let ye turn her sidewise and throw the headlights on the causeway the way we'll see what we're doing."

Their driver swore, but he reversed and turned the front of the car till it almost faced the lake. Then he turned on his headlights. Somewhere farther up the road the parish priest's car did the same. One by one, the ranked headlights blazed up, and at every moment the scene before them grew more vivid—the gateway and the stile, and beyond it the causeway that ran toward the little brown stone oratory with its mock Romanesque doorway. As the lights strengthened and steadied, the whole island became like a vast piece of theater scenery cut out against the gloomy wall of the mountain with the tiny whitewashed cottages at its base. Far above, caught in a stray flash of moonlight, Jackson saw the snow on its summit. "I'll be after you," he said to Father Hamilton, and watched him, a little perturbed and looking behind him, join the parish priest by the gate. Jackson resented being seen by them because he was weeping, and he was a man who despised tears—his own and others'. It was like a miracle, and Father Jackson didn't really believe in miracles. Standing back by the fence to let the last of the mourners pass, he saw the coffin, like gold in the brilliant light, and heard the steadying voices of the four huge mountainy men who carried it. He saw it sway above the heads, shawled and bare, glittering between the little stunted holly bushes and hazels.

A Note on the Type

THIS BOOK was set on the Linotype in Granjon, a type named in compliment to Robert Granjon, but neither a copy of a classic face nor an entirely original creation. George W. Jones based his designs for this type upon the type used by Claude Garamond (1510–61) in his beautiful French books, and Granjon more closely resembles Garamond's own than do any of the various modern types that bear his name.

Robert Granjon began his career as type-cutter in 1523. The boldest and most original designer of his time, he was one of the first to practice the trade of type-founder apart from that of printer. Between 1557 and 1562 Granjon printed about twenty books in types designed by himself, following, after the fashion of the day, the cursive handwriting of the time. These types, usually known as "caractères de civilité," he himself called "lettres françaises," as especially appropriate to his own country.

This book was composed, printed, and bound by Kingsport Press, Inc., Kingsport, Tennessee. Typography and binding design by Bonnie Spiegel.